CAMPBELL ARMSTRONG

MAMBO

HarperPaperbacks

A Division of HarperCollins*Publishers*

This is a work of fiction. The characters, incidents, and dia-
logues are products of the author's imagination and are not
to be construed as real. Any resemblance to actual events
or persons, living or dead, is entirely coincidental.

HarperPaperbacks   *A Division of* HarperCollins*Publishers*
                    10 East 53rd Street, New York, N.Y. 10022

A hardcover edition of this book was published in 1990 by
Harper & Row, Publishers, Inc.

Cover illustration by Steve Gardner

First HarperPaperbacks printing: April 1991

Printed in the United States of America

HarperPaperbacks and colophon are trademarks of
HarperCollins*Publishers*

10 9 8 7 6 5 4 3 2 1

PRAISE FOR
CAMPBELL ARMSTRONG
AND MAMBO

* * *

"Armstrong . . . has written a fast-moving page-turner . . ."

—Publishers Weekly

* * *

"Heaps of sex, violence, and gunfire. Entertaining reading."

—Booklist

* * *

"A satisfying and intensely readable potboiler."

—Washington Post

* * *

"Very good indeed . . . (Armstrong) unerringly maintains the pace of this gripping thriller."

—Chicago Tribune

* * *

"Complex and thoroughly enjoyable."

—Atlanta Journal and Constitution

continued . . .

PRAISE FOR THE AUTHOR'S
MAZURKA

*   *   *

"Almost unbearable suspense."
>—*Orlando Sentinel*

*   *   *

"A marvelously intricate plot . . . the twists and turns will keep readers rapt."
>—*Publishers Weekly*

*   *   *

"Combines well-examined characters with the detail of a well-done police procedural."
>—*St. Louis Dispatch*

*   *   *

"A fast-paced and highly complicated plot that leaves the reader in suspense until its fiery conclusion."
>—*UPI*

*   *   *

"Fast, furious, and well-written."
>—*James B. Patterson, author of*
>*BLACK MARKET*

PREVIOUS NOVELS
and **JIG**

* * *

"An irresistible page-turner."
—***Booklist***

* * *

"A fast-paced, accomplished novel."
—***Library Journal***

* * *

"Starts off with a bang . . . explodes in the reader's face."
—***The New York Times***

* * *

"A tightly crafted thriller . . . the pages whiz by like tracer bullets."
—***Boston Herald***

* * *

"Wonderfully written and completely thrilling."
—***Susan Isaacs, author of MAGIC HOUR***

Also by Campbell Armstrong

Jig
Mazurka
Brainfire
Asterisk Destiny

This book is dedicated to Thomas Congdon, for his continuing support, encouragement, and friendship.

I would like to thank for their help Lieutenant Nelson Oramas of the Miami Police; Sergeant Bob Hoelscher of the Metro Dade Police; Richards Brams; Ed Breslin and Nick Sayers for their considerable editorial counsel; Dr. Dov Levine; Major R.B. Claybourn (USMCR); Richard and Arthur Pine; Erl and Ann Wilkie for the tour of the auld place; and Eddie Bell for his faith at the right moment.

UNITED STATES
Miami
CUBA
MEXICO
HONDURAS
Cabo Gracias
a Dios

1

On a cold October night two vans and three cars moved in slow procession down a narrow street of terraced houses. The street, already poorly-lit, was darker in those places where Victorian railway bridges straddled it.

Frank Pagan, who rode in a blue Ford Escort directly behind the leading van, had the uneasy feeling that this neighborhood, perched on the farthest edge of Shepherd's Bush, was about to fade into nothing. The houses would give way to vacant sites, half acres of rubble with perhaps here and there some forlorn allotments on which stood broken-down greenhouses. It was not a picturesque part of town, but its drab anonymity and sparse traffic made it as good a choice as any for a safe route.

It was all theory as far as Pagan was concerned. He knew from his own experience what every policeman knew: there was no such thing as complete security.

What you had at best was an illusion of safety. You created diversions, surrounded yourself with some heavy protection, and kept your fingers crossed that good fortune, a fickle administrator of human affairs, would be on your side. Tense, he gazed at the small houses, the television lights thrown upon curtains, the half-moon over the rooftops dimmed by pollution, and he had the thought that in a few years this decrepit neighborhood, like so many formerly dreary London districts, might even be on the rise, resuscitated by real estate developers, the terraced houses refurbished and sold to young professionals who did one thing or another in the City or at the nearby BBC.

For the present, though, it was a labyrinth of slum and shadow, exactly the kind of place through which to transport the monster who sat alongside Pagan in the back of the car and whose name was Gunther Ruhr.

Pagan glanced at Ruhr for a second. He was uncomfortable being this close to the man, uneasy at the touch of Ruhr's leg against his own. Ruhr had one of those faces that suggest flesh long buried in damp earth, a maggot's pallor earned the hard way, hours killed hiding in cellars or somebody's attic. You might imagine that if you cut Ruhr's skin something as viscous as transmission fluid would seep from the veins. Certainly not blood, Pagan thought. Whatever connected Ruhr, with his enormous capacity for brutality, to the rest of the human race, wasn't immediately apparent to Pagan.

The German press, with its unbridled sense of melodrama, had been the first to call Gunther Ruhr *Die Klaüe*, the Claw, a reference to the peculiar prosthetic device Ruhr had been wearing on his right hand at the time of his capture and which had immediately been confiscated from him. Ruhr's right hand was missing both middle fingers. The other two fingers, the first and the last, appeared abnormally distant from each other and unable to move more than a quarter of an inch in any direction and then only stiffly. The deformity, exaggerated by the perfect curve of the thumb, was compelling in its way. Like a morbid man enticed against his better judgment by a freak show, Pagan found himself drawn reluctantly back to it time and again.

Some said Gunther Ruhr had accidentally blown his hand up with one of his own home-made explosive devices back in the days when he was still learning his trade, others that the deformity was a birth-defect. Like everything else connected to Ruhr's life, neither story had any supporting evidence. Ruhr was a mythical monster, created in part by the screaming excesses of the European tabloids, but also by his own pathological need for secrecy and mystery. Without these qualities, nobody could ever have become so successful a terrorist as Gunther Ruhr had done. Nobody, saddled with such a recognizable disfigurement, could have carried out so many atrocities unhindered for so long unless his life and habits were so deeply hidden they couldn't be quarried even by the best specialists in terrorism, who had tracked him for fourteen fruitless years.

The explosion of a Pan Am airliner over Athens in 1975, the mining of a crowded cruise ship in the Mediterranean in 1978, the bombing of a bus carrying teenage soccer players from Spain along the Adriatic Coast in 1980, the destruction of a resort hotel on the shore of the Sea of Japan in the summer of 1984—the list of atrocities which Ruhr had supposedly masterminded was long and bloody. The hotel had been destroyed on behalf of a group of anti-American Japanese extremists; the Spanish boys were said to have died at the command of a violent Basque coalition; the cruise ship had been mined because its passenger list consisted mainly of Jews and Ruhr's employer was rumored to have been a Libyan fanatic. What Ruhr did was done, plain and simple, for money. He had no other master, no political position. His services went to the highest bidders at those secret places where Ruhr's kind of labors were auctioned.

And now Frank Pagan, through one of those small accidents that sometimes brighten a cop's life, had him under arrest and was transporting him through the back streets of London and on to Luton, where he was to be flown to the maximum security prison of Parkhurst on the Isle of Wight. *Under arrest,* Pagan thought, and scanned the street again, seeing TV pictures blink in rooms or the door of a corner pub swing open and shut.

Under arrest was one thing. Getting Ruhr—with all his connections in the violent half-world of international terrorism—to his destination might be something else.

Pagan stared at the two men in the front of the car. The driver was a career policeman called John Torjussen from Special Branch, his companion a thick-necked Metropolitan cop who had once been a prominent amateur wrestler known as Masher. Ron Hardcastle was the man's real name and he spoke with that peculiar Newcastle accent called Geordie, which was almost impenetrable to Pagan. There was something menacingly comforting in Hardcastle's presence.

Pagan looked at the van ahead, which contained four officers from Special Branch and an assortment of rifles and communications equipment. Turning, he glanced next at the two cars behind, then the van at the very back—each vehicle was manned and armed and alert. Menacingly comforting, Pagan thought again. All of it. Everything designed to keep Gunther the Beast safe and secure until he could be firmly caged on the Isle of Wight.

And yet. Frank Pagan felt a strange streak of cold on the back of his neck, and the palms of his hands, normally dry and cool, had become damp. He shut his eyes a moment, conscious of the odd way Ruhr breathed—there was a faint rattle at the back of the man's throat as if something thick had become lodged there. The noise, like everything else about Ruhr, irritated Pagan.

The puzzles of Gunther Ruhr, Pagan thought, and looked briefly at the German. Why had he come to England? What was he doing in Cambridge, of all places? Planning a doctoral thesis on atrocities? Giving tutorials on bloodletting? Ruhr had been interrogated for three days after his capture but he had a nice way with his inquisitors: he simply ignored them. When he condescended to speak, he contradicted himself three or four times in the space of half an hour and yet somehow managed to make each version of his story equally plausible. What Gunther Ruhr did was to surround himself with fresh fictions, recreating himself time and again. Even if there were a real core to the man nobody could ever gain access to it, perhaps not even Ruhr himself.

The Claw, Pagan thought with disdain. He hated the way such nicknames took up residence in the public imagination. After a while they exerted a fascination that often had nothing to do with the acts of the villains themselves. Jack the Ripper was still good for a shudder, but how many people brought to mind the images of disembowelled girls, intestines in tidy piles, hearts cut out, everything bloody and just so? How many really pictured the true nightmare? The tabloids had a way of taking a scumbag like Ruhr and elevating him to a celebrity whose name alone doubled circulation for a time. And somewhere in the course of the international publicity circus the real nature of Ruhr's deeds would be lost and a patina of myth drawn over the man, as if he were some wildly appealing combination of Ripper and legendary terrorist, somebody who made pulses beat a little quicker. It was the wrong side of fame, Pagan thought with some resentment. Ruhr deserved another fate altogether: total oblivion.

In the front seat, Ron Hardcastle lit a cigarette and the air in the car became congested.

Ruhr spoke for the first time since they'd taken him from his cell at Wormwood Scrubs. "You will have a decoy column, of course?" he asked. He had impeccable English, a fact that irked Pagan, who wanted Ruhr's English to be broken and clumsy and laughable.

Pagan didn't answer the question. Ruhr blinked his very pale eyelids and said, "Personally, in your position, I would have a second column somewhere close at hand. Perhaps even a third, although I would put that one on the motorway, I think, and have it travel at high speed. Then my friends—assuming I have any—would be very confused. Where is Gunther? Where can he possibly be?" The German was silent for a second. "Of course, deception's a highly personal thing," and here he smiled, as if he were making some polite little joke for Pagan's benefit. But there was a supercilious quality in the look that caused Pagan to bunch his hands tightly in the pockets of his overcoat and turn his face back toward the street. Ruhr was partly correct. A decoy convoy was travelling in the vicinity of Paddington and Marylebone, but there was no third parade.

"Your voice gets on my bloody nerves, Ruhr," Pagan said, then immediately regretted this unseemly display of hostility because it gave Gunther Ruhr obvious satisfaction, which took the form of a smile as crooked as his bad hand.

There was a miserable silence inside the car, broken only by the hiss of the radio and the message *Nine-twenty, all clear. Proceeding due east on Elm Avenue.* Ah, the dear banality of Elm Avenue, with its dim shabbiness, a small brokendown corner of what had once been another England. Now heroin and crack replaced tea and crumpets of an afternoon.

Pagan opened the window a half inch, releasing some of Hardcastle's smoke. The small houses were misshapen by moon and shadow. The occasional pub or fish and chip shop looked unnaturally bright.

"You are so very tense," Ruhr said in a soothing voice. He might have been a physician calming a nervous patient. "Surely you don't expect somebody is going to rescue me, do you?"

Pagan said nothing. It was best not to be drawn, to stay aloof. There were levels to which you could descend, places where all you ever encountered was your own worst self, and Frank Pagan had no desire to slip that far down. His temper had a sometimes abrasive edge and he was getting a little too old to keep cutting himself on it. Do the bloody job, get this scum to Luton, go home. But just don't let it get personal. You hate a man like Gunther Ruhr, and you loathe the forced intimacy of this small car, and breathing the same damned air is repulsive—but what did feelings, those expendable luxuries, have to do with it?

"Such people would have to be mad," Ruhr said. "Or very clever and daring."

Pagan shut the window. Ron Hardcastle turned in his seat and glared angrily at the German. "Just say the word, Frank, and I'll do this bastard for you. Be a right fooking pleasure."

There was a generous quality in Masher Hardcastle's offer of violence, and Pagan didn't doubt that big Ron would enjoy inflicting physical damage on Ruhr. Despite some temptation, it was a sorry equation all the same. Pagan couldn't see matching Ruhr's taste for violence with that of Ron Hardcastle, law enforcement officer and former wrestler. There was increased tension in the car now, as if it had found its way in from the darkened street like a thin vapor. It had a name, Pagan thought: impotence. You might want to unleash the snarling dog inside Hardcastle, you might even want a piece of Gunther Ruhr for yourself, but the laws *Die Klaüe* flouted so viciously afforded him some protection from brutality.

Pagan put a weary smile on his face and looked at the German. It was an amusing consolation to think of the circumstances of Ruhr's apprehension in Cambridge, how the elusive terrorist, whose newspaper reviews had called him 'the man without a shadow' and 'the phantom beyond human needs and desires', had been captured in a bedroom in a lodging-house near St. Andrews Road. The memory was a perfect diversion from stress.

"I've got you, Gunther," Pagan said quietly now. "And that's what it comes down to in the end. *I've got you,* and all because you couldn't keep your pecker in your trousers." He waited for Ruhr's expression to change to one of discomfort, perhaps even wrath, but Ruhr was too good at this game to give up control of that awful white face. He merely looked at Pagan with a raised eyebrow.

"Was she worth it, Gunther?" Pagan asked. "Was she worth the risk? Or can you only get it when you pay for it? Too bad she didn't want to go the rest of the way with you—you wouldn't be here now if she'd kept her mouth shut, would you? You wouldn't be here if she'd been a fucking sicko like you."

If these were low blows, if they were supposed to vent some of Pagan's annoyance, they certainly weren't causing the German any pain. Ruhr, whose hands were cuffed in his lap, laughed and said, "I never have to pay for anything, Pagan."

"Until now," Pagan said. Christ, he was feeling vindictive and petty.

"Die Reise ist nicht au Ende bis zur Anhuntf." Gunther Ruhr spoke quietly. Pagan, whose grasp of the German language was poor, recognized only a couple of words. He had no way of knowing that Ruhr's phrase fully meant *the journey is never over until the arrival,* nor did he intend to ask for a translation. He wasn't going to give Ruhr even the simplest kind of satisfaction.

There was a pub on a corner, a place called The Lord Nelson. A voice came over the car radio. *Proceeding west along Mulberry Avenue. All clear.* Pagan looked at the pub, then saw some modern blocks of flats rising beyond, where thin lawns and stunted trees grew under pale lamps, many of which had been vandalized and cast no light. It wasn't a good place. It looked wrong and it smelled wrong and the extended reaches of darkness bothered him. He sat forward in his seat, anxiously studying the unlit areas and thinking how vandalism was a way of life in a neighborhood like this. Public phones, shop windows, anything that was both motionless and fragile was a target for a kid with a stone in his hand and nothing in his mind save breakage. But then the high-rise buildings receded and there were more streets of 1930s terraced houses and the voice on the radio was saying *Proceeding due east along Acacia Avenue* and Pagan felt the quick little tide of unease ebb inside him. If there was going to be an attempt made to rescue Ruhr, the dark places back there would have been eminently suitable. Acacia Avenue, narrow and comparatively well-lit, was benign by contrast.

He sat back again, observing the parked cars along the curb, and hearing the sound of what he took at first to be a light aircraft. But it was louder than that, and close, a throbbing that had its source two or three hundred feet above the rooftops. Ron Hardcastle turned his big red face around to look at Pagan questioningly.

"What the bloody hell's that?" he asked.

Pagan tried to see through his window, but his angle was bad. Then the voice came over the radio again: *There's a helicopter above at approximately one hundred and fifty feet and descending rapidly.*

The sound of the low-flying chopper became thunderous now, deafening, vibrating with such intensity that the car shook as if it were travelling over ruts. Pagan leaned forward and shouted into the radio. "What the hell does it want?"

The pilot won't identify himself. I've asked for ID three times and he doesn't bloody answer, Frank.

Pagan had briefly entertained the hope that the chopper might belong to Scotland Yard, something the Commissioner had finally decided to add to the convoy at the last moment. Now he was worried. He looked at Ruhr, who shrugged and said, "I know nothing about it."

It was a statement Pagan didn't have time to question, because suddenly the darkness was transformed. What had been nothing but slight menace and an unidentifiable anxiety before was suddenly changed. Pagan saw the leading van, fifteen feet ahead, catch fire as flares were dropped on it from the sky. The shape of the helicopter was visible for a second, but in an unreal way, like an after-image on a retina. The Ford Escort braked just as an enormous column of unruly flame roared out of the van, and streaked up and died in a vast series of starry sparks.

And then everything was ablaze in the most spectacular way. All the cars parked along the curb exploded and burned as if they'd been timed to ignite simultaneously. Acacia Avenue was illuminated by flames as bright as daylight. Pagan opened his door, his first shocked instinct that of rushing toward the burning van in front of him because he thought he heard somebody scream inside the wreck, but the heat thrust him back at once. *Dear Christ*, it was a force of nature, seeming to melt his skin and weld it against his bones. He couldn't move any closer, nor did he hear the screaming again. Who could survive that inferno? Those four poor bastards would have been charred almost at once. The rear van and the other two sedans, also fire-bombed by the helicopter—which had wheeled away, whirring up toward the moon and disappearing—were alight too, their occupants scrambling out into the street, shadowy figures desperately trying to avoid the flames surrounding them. Confusion and chaos and smells sickeningly intermingled—burning rubber, smoldering upholstery, kindled shrubbery, scorched flesh. Gunshots too, as policemen fired upward in the general path of the chopper.

Pagan did the only thing he could think of. He grabbed Ruhr by the shoulders and dragged him out of the Escort because no matter what, no matter the extent of the calamity, it was still his job to secure the German. The Ford, stalled and engulfed by smoke, wasn't going anywhere. The only possibility of movement now was on foot.

Pagan pushed Ruhr forward in the direction of the sidewalk, seeking a space between burning cars, feeling his eyes smart and his nostrils fill with smoke. Nothing could be breathed here without searing the tissue of your lungs and throat. Conscious of Hardcastle at his back, and Torjussen moving just ahead, Pagan shoved Ruhr again, because the German was lagging, as if, like some demented bug, he wanted to linger close to the brightness of the flames.

"Fooking move, bastard," Ron Hardcastle said, and made one hand into a thick fist, which he smacked directly into Ruhr's spine. Ruhr gasped and his legs buckled as Pagan hauled him through the dense smoke to the sidewalk. This whole damned place reminded Pagan of old photographs of wartime London just after a heart-breaking air assault. People were screaming and hurrying out of their houses now, windows shattering, doors kicked open, a landscape of flame and bitter smoke and red-hot metal, total ruin made all the more appalling by the way it had bloomed so violently out of a commonplace night on a commonplace street.

Ruhr must have known, Pagan thought. He must have been waiting for this moment. He must have expected a rescue effort. In his own heart, Pagan had half-expected it too. He just hadn't anticipated anything on this destructive scale. But who could have foreseen this? who could have looked into the old crystal-ball and come up with this fiery scenario? Pagan recalled raising the subject of air surveillance at one of the many meetings concerning the transportation of Ruhr, meetings complicated by the noisy extradition demands and political requirements of Spain and Greece and the United States, but the notion had been overruled as being too ostentatious, too obvious, by a committee of well-meaning men, who thought the secret route to be travelled by Ruhr was perfectly safe, something that could never be penetrated. And wasn't stealth more appropriate than the high visibility of a police helicopter rattling the slates of suburban rooftops? These were men who lived in a dream world. They weren't out here on the streets now. Besides, there was never a way to cover every possible occurrence. You could plan until your jaw dropped off, but in the end a man had to be moved, and from the moment Gunther Ruhr had ridden out of Wormwood Scrubs the risk had grown. Whoever wanted Ruhr free wanted him with an extravagant sense of destruction Pagan had encountered only once or twice in his lifetime. An ambitious deed, deadly and painful and tragic, but it wasn't over yet.

Pagan shoved the terrorist quickly along the sidewalk, seeking safe passage through the furnace that devoured cars on one side, hedgerows on the other. The blast of heat was solid and crippling. He had the notion of getting to the next intersection, a place beyond the flames, and then commandeering somebody's house, calling in reinforcements and new vehicles. It was vague, more of an instinct than a plan, but he had to get Ruhr off the streets quickly. The perpetrators of this elaborate attack weren't about to go home empty-handed.

Hardcastle had his gun out now, and so did Torjussen, who was a step ahead of Pagan and Ruhr—a party of four locked in a fiercely hot dance amid the crackling of wood and the *whooshing* made by fuel tanks exploding. Smoke, thicker than any fog, blinded Pagan and scorched his face.

He saw the assault squad only briefly when a wintry breeze scoured the street and cleared the air.

Five, six men, he couldn't be sure how many. They wore ski or ice-hockey masks—it was another detail of which he would never be certain. They were dressed in camouflage and carried automatic rifles. Pagan was conscious of Gunther Ruhr throwing himself face down on the concrete and then Ron Hardcastle firing his gun in the direction of the squad, but smoke billowed in again, obscuring everything. There was more gunfire, much of it random and wild.

Ron Hardcastle fell and Torjussen disappeared somewhere and Pagan reached down to grab Ruhr and drag him back along the sidewalk, thinking there might yet be some safe corner of the world in which to hide his prisoner. Away from here, away from all this destruction, a small, safe place.

But the weather conspired against the plan. The wind came a second time. It whined over the houses and blew the length of the burning street and cleared the smoke. With his gun in his hand, Pagan faced the squad over a distance that might have been no more than a hundred feet.

Gunther Ruhr, who lay on the sidewalk, smiled up at Pagan in an odd way. Pagan raised his weapon, a Bernardelli, but he was cut down by gunfire before he could get off more than two shots in the direction of the group.

He'd known pain before. But he'd never felt anything quite like this, so crucifying and raw. It had no specific location in his body. It consumed all of him.

He had a blinding moment when he registered the fact that his legs no longer existed and his heart had been yanked out of his chest; and another when he understood that this kind of pain was a black reservoir of very hot tar in which he could only go down and down, round and round, drowning under a black surface.

2

Magdalena Torrente crossed Calle Ocho, the main street of Little Havana. She looked up once at the sky, which was clouding toward darkness and heavy with the possibility of warm October rain, then she headed west. She passed Eduardo's furniture store, a bright island of art deco sofas and lamps, an expensive anomaly in this neighborhood of *farmacias* and little cafes selling *cafe cubano* in paper cups. She ignored the approving comments and whistles of men who stood outside the cafes and took time out from their constant preoccupation—how to assassinate that *barbudo hijo de puta*, Fidel Castro—to register and appreciate the beautiful, mature woman passing quickly in the humid twilight.

She made her way through traffic at an intersection where the air smelled of coffee and fried foods, and then turned right, entering a narrow street darker than Calle Ocho. Here windows were boarded and barred and small houses had the appearance of undergoing a siege; in this city of easy death and abundant drugs and murderous addicts who thought burglary every doper's birthright, it was a very real impression. She'd parked her car several blocks away at the Malaga Restaurant, thinking it best to move on foot in case her licence plate was noticed and remembered by one of the spies Fernando Garrido was always lecturing her about. Now, given the hazards of the district, she wondered if she'd made the right decision. The car would have been some kind of protection. Without it she felt vulnerable, despite the gun she carried in the pocket of her leather jacket.

From an open upstairs window a man shouted down at her *Hey, hey bebe,* and then laughed in a fractured drunken way—*ka ha ka ha,* a sound that dissolved in a cough like a baby's rattle. Latin music, fast, tropical, overheated, played from a radio in an open doorway where several shadowy figures, lost in the ether of drugs, stared out at her. She hurried now, pausing only when she reached the Casa del Media Noche, a restaurant that specialized in Cuban food. It was said to serve the best langosta enchiladas in all Miami. Through the window she could see a crowd of diners, waiters bustling back and forth, busboys hurrying with carafes of ice water. Festive Cuban music was playing loudly on a jukebox.

Magdalena Torrente stepped into the alley that ran behind the restaurant. She knocked on the back door, which was opened by a tall man of about seventy. He wore a panama hat and a crisp white suit of the kind called a *dril ciel,* made from an Irish linen so special that only one mill in the Republic of Ireland still supplied it. Fernando Garrido took her hand and kissed it, a brushing of lips on flesh, a simple courtesy in a world

grown weary of good manners and civilized behavior.
Then he led her toward a boxlike room without windows, where cans of tomatoes and bags of beans formed
pyramids in the middle of the floor.

"There's no place for you to sit, Magdalena," Garrido said. He spoke Cuban Spanish, with its generous
vowel sounds.

"It doesn't matter," she said.

He shrugged, and she thought there was some
small despair in the gesture, that of a man disappointed
by the directions of his life. Once, in another world,
Fernando Garrido had been the mayor of Santiago, the
second largest city in Cuba. He'd had political ambitions. He'd dreamed vibrant dreams of replacing the sequence of malignant dictatorships, those dreadful reefs
on which Cuba had foundered and rotted, with democracy and social justice. And then his notions had been
overtaken by Castro's revolution, which he'd supported at first in a wary manner, more out of relief at
the end of the dictatorship of Batista than any great
faith in the stated ideals of Fidel, whom he'd never
trusted and personally didn't like.

In July 1960, one year after the Revolution—
which had accomplished nothing except to trade one
set of gangsters for another—Fernando Garrido had
been arrested by Castro's security forces. He was
charged with the sort of 'crime' so common in Communist societies, undefined and unfounded, absurd and
yet sinister. It was a 'crime' devised by dull Marxist
imaginations and framed in such a vague way that it
could never be grasped by its 'perpetrator'. This kind
of nebulous offense was often called 'counterrevolutionary', a term that had any meaning the regime attached to it. So far as Garrido could tell, his only misde-
meanor was to have been a politician during the reign

of the dictator Batista. Guilt by association—and for that he'd been imprisoned for seven long years on the Isle of Pines, severely beaten, given electric shocks, then released and expelled from the country without explanation! The experience had left him with a tremor in his hands, a recurring nightmare of violence, and a hatred of Castro that was acute and constant, like shrapnel in his heart.

Garrido moved to the center of the room, where a light-bulb, crusted with dead moths, hung from an old cord. He looked to Magdalena Torrente like a plantation owner in an old sepia picture, benign yet strict, generous but careful with his kindness. He took off his hat. His hair, dyed an incongruous brown and brilliantined, an old man's vanity, glistened under the light like a waxy skullcap. He had lived for almost thirty years in exile and the weight of that expulsion showed on his face. Once a prominent politician, now he was merely the owner of a successful restaurant. But his dreams, which would not lie still and let him savor in peace the fruits of his thriving business, were still powerful. He wanted the one thing all exiles crave and few achieve—a triumphant return to the motherland, a vindication.

"This neighborhood," he said. He appeared to lose his train of thought a moment. "It gets worse every day. Drugs. Violence. I remember when it was a good place to have a business. Now it gets too dangerous."

Magdalena didn't want to listen to Garrido's regular complaints about how the massive influx of Cubans from Mariel in 1980 had altered the fabric of life in Miami for the worse. She already knew how Castro had shipped out all his undesirables, his criminals and addicts, his deranged and schizophrenic, and unloaded them upon an angry Florida. She already knew how drugs and murder had poisoned the Cuban community. She wanted to pick up what she'd come for and leave, but something about Fernando Garrido always made her linger. She knew what it was: he was a link to her father, the last one left to her. The thought made her feel lonely for a moment.

Garrido lit a small cigar and blew a stream of smoke up at the light-bulb. "Did anyone follow you here?"

It was his regular question. She shook her head. Her long black hair was thick and fibrous. "Nobody followed me."

"You're a beautiful woman and very noticeable, Magdalena. You can never be sure. Castro's agents infiltrate very well. They're good at anything underhand. Never underestimate them."

She said she didn't. She told him firmly that she didn't take chances. He smoked quietly, surveying her face, watching her with an intensity that made her uncomfortable. She knew from his expression what he was going to say, and she was anxious to avoid the long, flowery comparisons with her dead mother. Garrido would reminisce about the old life in Cuba when they'd all been very young, himself and Humberto Torrente and the lovely Oliva, oh, they'd been a great threesome, an inseparable trio going everywhere together, *aieee*, beaches and restaurants and nightclubs. Garrido's Latin sentimentality, his ornate phrases, irritated Magdalena because the past wasn't what mattered to her any more. Then Garrido would always say the same thing half-jokingly: *Your mother's only fault was she married the wrong man in Humberto. Honorable as Humberto was, Oliva should have listened more closely to my entreaties*. And he'd smile and kiss Magdalena's brow, and sometimes there would be tears in his dark brown eyes.

She looked at her watch. She had hours before she was due at the airport but she wanted to give an impression of haste. There was laughter from the restaurant; the music grew louder.

"You're anxious to leave," he said.

She nodded her head, glanced again at her watch. The small room was stifling. She watched him walk in the direction of some bare metal shelves where two pistols lay side by side. He removed a section of shelf in a very deliberate way, then set it on the floor.

"My secret place," he said.

The wall had a concealed panel built into it. Garrido slid it aside, reached into the black space and took out a briefcase. "Before I give you this, I must ask a question you may find unpardonable," he said. "Do you really trust him? After all, our association with him goes back four years. One might be pardoned for expecting results very soon."

A tiny night moth fluttered against Magdalena's lips and she brushed it gently aside. "The question's perfectly understandable, Fernando, and the answer's simple. I trust him." How could she not? she wondered. If you loved, you had to trust: one was a basic corollary of the other. A fact of life. "Besides, something this intricate takes time."

Garrido tapped his fingernails on his front dentures, a *click click click* that indicated thought. "Do I detect something else? Something a little more than trust? If so, I caution you to go carefully."

"I'm always careful." She raised a hand to her hair. His insight surprised her. Was she that obvious? Did she wear her feelings like a necklace? She was a little embarrassed. She'd always imagined she knew how to conceal herself from the world. But Fernando had been familiar with her since childhood; he'd become accustomed to reading her expressions. Defensively she said, "I don't mean to be rude, but my private life isn't really any of your business, Fernando."

"You're right, of course. I shouldn't try to counsel you. If you trust him, that's good enough for me." Garrido stepped closer to her. He pressed the handle of the case into the palm of her hand. Even though there was nobody else present in the room, the gesture was surreptitious. It was force of habit. Garrido had spent years living in fear of Castro's spies in Miami, years raising funds for nocturnal raids and acts of sabotage inside Cuba, blowing up power stations and electric pylons, dynamiting naval installations and airfields, or spraying beach-front tourist resorts with guns fired from sea-going craft. He'd participated personally in many of these maneuvers until his nerve had gone. It was a game for the young and valiant.

Garrido inclined his face in a rather formal way, pressing his lips upon her cheek, an avuncular kiss. She smelled mint and tobacco and something else, something alcoholic, on his breath. She held the briefcase casually, as if it contained nothing of any importance. Then she stepped toward the door, but Garrido caught her by the wrist. His skin was damp.

"We have enemies," he said quietly.

"I know."

"Even among our friends. Remember that."

Garrido dropped his hand and backed away from her, smiling for the first time now. His dentures, the color of his suit, gleamed. "But I don't need to tell you anything, do I? You're not a child any more. I have to keep reminding myself you're not Humberto's little girl."

Humberto's little girl. Garrido had a good heart, a heart as big as Cuba itself, but he could never overcome his old-fashioned patronizing manner. Wouldn't he ever grasp the fact that she was thirty-nine years old, for God's sake? That she was dedicated to the same cause as himself and had an important voice in it? That the role she played in the political schemes of the exile community here in Miami was just as important as his own?

"I haven't fit that description for a very long time, Fernando."

Garrido was very apologetic. "The trouble with growing old is that you don't want things to change. You want everybody to stay the same age because it means you don't grow old yourself. It's a nice folly. Forgive me for it."

Magdalena reached the door. Well-mannered as ever, Garrido opened it for her. In the dark hallway a massive figure emerged from the shadows. Carlos, a taciturn giant from Las Tunas Province, Garrido's watchdog. He wore a shoulder holster beneath his dark jacket. He moved slowly and quietly, his musculature evident under his clothes; a powerful man, sleek and silent. Magdalena thought there was something a little spooky about Carlos. He had the look of a man who has been involved in more than a few premature deaths.

"Where did you park, Magdalena?" Garrido asked.

"At the Malaga Restaurant."

"Carlos will escort you there."

She was about to say she had a gun, she didn't need protection, but she didn't utter a word. Carlos would follow her anyway. Garrido wasn't going to allow anybody to carry that briefcase through the streets of Little Havana without an armed escort.

She smiled her best smile, which dazzled Garrido, then she raised a hand as she left. Garrido, seemingly frozen in the doorway of the small square room, stood without moving for a long time. He listened to the silences that followed Magdalena's departure. Then he took a cigar from the pocket of his vest and lit it.

Garrido, once known in politics as *El Ganador*, the winner, closed his eyes. He sucked smoke into the back of his throat and remembered how it had felt to be that man of victory. The man who controlled Santiago de Cuba in the early 1950s, the young reformer—ah, the golden naivety of those years—who wanted to change a festering system. All that sweet energy, that devotion to his calling. How remote it all seemed to him suddenly, and Cuba so very far away; and yet, as if affected by some untreatable malaria of the heart, he could still shiver when he thought of going back to his homeland.

He shut the door of the room. He thought about Magdalena out there in the darkness, the long trip in front of her. Jesus! The way she trusted! He hadn't trusted anything in that uncluttered way for years! Nor would he do so now. Especially now. He would do precisely what had to be done, what should have been done a long time ago; and Magdalena might never need to know.

He listened to the music that played on the juke-box and prayed Magdalena would take the same kind of care with her heart that she would with the contents of the case.

Magdalena Torrente drove her gray BMW from Calle Ocho to the Rickenbacker Causeway and then Key Biscayne. Here, on the shores of Biscayne Bay, were opulent houses protected by elaborate security systems and regular patrols which echoed the same state of siege that existed in the poorer neighborhoods of Miami. It was as if the siege had simply risen several notches on the social scale, and the differences between Key Biscayne and areas like Little Havana were finally only cosmetic.

At eight-thirty she parked in the driveway of the house she'd inherited from Humberto Torrente. Surrounded by lush palm and bougainvillaea and rubber trees, it was located some yards inland from the shore, where a motor-boat was tied to a wooden slip. Magdalena unlocked the front door, went inside, crossed the tiled entranceway, passed under a large skylight filled with stars. Across the living-room an enormous bay window framed dark water. There was an unobstructed view of Miami, lights and neon, approaching aircraft, traffic on the silvery Causeway: a glittering city trapped under a canopy of humidity.

She climbed the stairs. Her bedroom was plain. She had no taste for the bright shades, such as gold drapes and red rugs, you often found in Hispanic homes; nor were there any of the customary religious artifacts, the gory Christs, the saints with their cartoon placidity, the prim Virgins, the whole panoply of blood and pain, chastity and redemption.

The only decoration in the bedroom was a black and white picture depicting Humberto Torrente in the uniform of a Colonel in the Cuban Air Force, taken in 1956 at some social function at the Havana Yacht Club. At his side stood his wife Oliva, dark-haired and exquisite, in a white cocktail dress. They looked prosperous, healthy, in love, and yet there seemed to be a glaze across their smiles, a sadness half-hidden, as if they knew that within six years of the snapshot both of them would be dead.

Magdalena gazed at the photograph for a time. 1956: she'd been five years old then. She was ten when her parents died their separate deaths. For her whole adolescence she was fated to a life of guardians, some of them nuns in boarding-schools, others widowed aunts in Miami Beach. She'd spent her fifteenth year in Garrido's custody at his big house in Coral Gables. Time and again he had explained his view of Cuban history, one of endless struggle, endless betrayal. He insisted that Humberto's death captured in miniature the tragedy of Cuba. Hadn't Humberto struggled for liberty with all his passion? And hadn't he been betrayed in the end?

Magdalena didn't buy all the way into Garrido's melodrama. Where Cuban politics were concerned, she tried to temper her passion with a certain objectivity. But it was the passion, inherited from Humberto, which had led her restlessly during her twenties and early thirties from one exiled group to another—to those with arsenals stashed in the Everglades and others who had bomb factories in South Miami and others still with safe houses in the Keys where semi-automatic weapons were converted to the real thing. She'd enjoyed the feel of guns in her hands and the idea of belonging to a secret army—the elaborate security precautions and the passwords and the intensity of the young men who trained with the kind of total concentration that made them good soldiers though poor lovers. She'd made love to many of them, and couldn't differentiate one from another now, those quick, silent boys, all of whom put the death of Castro above complete enjoyment of life. It was as if they were destined to live every day of their lives with a shadow of their own making across the face of the sun. So long as Fidel lived, there would always be this eclipse.

After ten years of association with one exile movement or another, Magdalena Torrente's experience of direct anti-Castro action had consisted of an effort to dynamite crates of Soviet weapons in the heavily-guarded Havana harbor (there were no weapons, only boxes of agricultural machinery; intelligence had been wrong), and the delivery of explosives to underground members in Pinar del Rio. She had flown the twin-engine Piper herself, a skill she'd learned from exiled pilots, while her three companions dropped the supplies by parachute to men and women waiting in darkened tobacco fields below.

Both sorties into Cuba had been thrilling, both heavy with the clammy menace of capture and death. Both had brought Magdalena closer to an understanding of what the cause meant. It was no mere abstraction, no games played in bomb factories, no simple rhetoric of freedom. It was life and death, and in particular her own life and death, that the cause demanded. And yet these adventures lacked something. She had the feeling of futility that might have dogged a person attacking an elephant with a can of mosquito repellent. One could sting Castro with nocturnal assaults, but they were never fatal.

In her middle thirties she'd realized that to be a soldier was not enough in itself. You had to be closer to the center, to the place where strategic decisions were made. You had to be near the power. To fire weapons in the Everglades or assemble guns in the Keys (from where, frustratingly, you could practically smell Havana on the wind) was useful; but useful wasn't enough. The ability to fire a gun or fly surreptitiously into Cuba were not going to keep a dream alive. So she had entered the political world of Fernando Garrido and his cronies. It was a tiresome group at times, one that squabbled endlessly in the Cuban way, but influential and rich and committed without question to the destruction of Fidel.

Magdalena had won a reputation in these political

circles as an energetic voice, somebody to be listened to, someone whose role was less illusory, and perhaps more practical, than knowing the parts of an M-16 rifle. Here, too, she came to realize she had deeper ambitions than to scurry in and out of Cuba under cover of the dark. And so she attended committee meetings, and she whispered in the ears of powerful figures in the exile community, and she listened to the pulses that beat in the darkness and smelled the breezes that blew through Miami and tracked their direction—and she detected in herself an immeasurable impatience. She wanted things to change in Cuba quickly. Not tomorrow. Not the next day. Now.

When Castro finally fell . . .

She touched the photograph of her parents, fingertips on glass, tentative, loving. She remembered her father as a serious man whose rare displays of levity were all the more precious for their scarcity. Somber, hardworking, Humberto Torrente had been dedicated to a patriotic ideal. He'd chosen the wrong way to realize it, that was all. His mistake was to place all his hopes on American military assistance and he'd died for that false expectation in 1961 at the Bay of Pigs, the B-26 he piloted shot down by Castro's artillery over San Blas in Cuba. What Humberto failed to realize was that outside forces alone could never have unseated Castro at that time. The Americans, led by a vacillating Kennedy, had chickened out at the Bay of Pigs, withholding air support and naval artillery, leaving Cuban freedom fighters stranded on beaches. No, outside assaults could be useful up to a point, but the successful overthrow of Castro could come only from within Cuba, from men who hated the whole suffocating regime and who had the means and the courage to replace it with a free society.

Magdalena's mother, Oliva, hadn't been interested in Humberto's goals. Her own world was limited, constructed as it was around husband, home and child. The way Magdalena had turned out would have shocked her. What good was a woman who hadn't borne children? who didn't know how to cook? who didn't have a man to keep house for? What good was this kind of woman?

Shortly before Christmas 1961, Oliva Torrente, unhinged by her husband's death, swallowed an overdose of barbiturates. As if to emphasize how little she cared for a world without Humberto, she'd elected the sin of suicide over the burden of living a widow's life.

Magdalena considered the past an irrelevant encumbrance. Only the future mattered, only the task ahead. Memories were indulgences. She turned away from the photograph. She took the gun from her pocket, removed the leather jacket, locked the weapon in her bedside table. She put Garrido's briefcase on the bed, opened a closet, removed a full-length suede coat. She placed the chocolate-colored coat beside the case, then opened the case. The money was tightly bundled. There were stacks of hundred dollar bills. Under these were other stacks in one thousand dollar denominations.

The total was close to a million dollars, collected throughout the Cuban community from donations made by respectable doctors and lawyers and bank officials, cash skimmed from the *bolito* games and jai-alai betting and gathered quietly in Cuban bars, illicit money from drug dealers whose astronomical profits had endowed them with an indiscriminating sense of charity. It came from all manner of sources, and was amassed, as it had been for the last four years, in the Casa del Media Noche by Fernando Garrido, head of the group that called itself the Committee for the Restoration of Democracy in Cuba, an organization whose wealthy members preferred anonymity to public notoriety.

In a sense the cash was dream money, the money of ancient pains and grievances, dollars thrown up by the need for vengeance against a system that had broken families and plundered property, capital dampened by the blood of those who'd already been martyred in a cause growing old and impatient. The cash was destined for Cuba, there to be used by the democratic underground movement for its operating expenses, which included illegal radio transmitters, pamphlets and newspapers. It bought food and guns for those obliged to hide in the mountains. It clothed and fed the children of these fugitives. It also purchased explosives used in acts of internal sabotage. Counter-revolution was an expensive business.

Magdalena undid the buttons of the coat. The lining, specially prepared for her by a seamstress in Hialeah, was divided into a series of pockets, each of which would hold a large number of bank-notes. It was skillful tailoring. There was no way a casual observer could tell the coat contained anything other than the body of the person who wore it; a smuggler's garment, designed for one purpose only.

Magdalena transferred notes from the briefcase to the lining of the suede coat. It took her twenty minutes to empty the case. She tried the coat on: weighty but tolerable. She looked at herself in a mirror. She didn't appear in any way different, no artificial plumpness, no unseemly bulges. She would be nothing more than a beautiful black-haired woman travelling alone on a long flight. Her looks—the way her thick hair fell mysteriously on her shoulders and how the lean line of her jaw emphasized a delightful mouth, the eyes that were knowingly dark and secretive, like those of a torch-singer—would draw attention as they always did. But the coat wouldn't cause anybody a second glance, which was all that mattered.

From the closet she removed a small suitcase she'd packed that morning. She went down the stairs, turned off the lights. Outside, the night was weighted with moisture. Over the Rickenbacker Causeway silver lightning flashed, then thunder crackled as if the sky were a vast radio receiver picking up static. Magdalena stepped inside her car, backed it out of the driveway.

Across the street, Carlos sat in a black Pontiac parked under a twisted rubber tree. When she drove past she gave him a thumbs up sign, then for amusement tried to lose him in traffic, but Carlos, with his watchful black eyes and unsmiling features, was an expert at bird-dogging. Slipping coolly through traffic, he managed to stay directly behind her all the way to Miami International Airport.

Norfolk, England

It was dawn, and cold, when the girl rode the chestnut mare to the top of the rise. The ground was hard with frost and the horse's hoofs thumped solidly. The animal's breath hung on the chill air, tiny clouds turned red by the first touch of sunlight. The girl rode with all the confidence of someone who has been mounting horses since early childhood. This particular mare was a special favorite, a big mellow horse that loved to be ridden.

The girl reined the animal at the top of the rise and

looked out across the countryside. This corner of England, some seventy-five miles from London, was almost exclusively flat, fields stretching toward a horizon that seemed very far away. Here and there isolated antique villages of the kind so adored by tourists interrupted the monotony of the furrows; occasionally a marsh or pond seeped up through meadowland and created a watery diversion. The girl, whose name was Stephanie Brough, had lived all her fourteen years in this vicinity. The nearest cities were Norwich to the north and Ipswich to the south, and in between, as she sometimes phrased it, was *sheer bloody boring contemptible nothing.*

She dismounted in a stand of thin birch trees. The rise sloped down to bare fields that would become muddy as soon as the frost melted. She liked all this— riding in the early dawn, avoiding the *awful* breakfasts with her parents and that twit of a brother Tim (who sometimes flicked pellets of soggy Corn Flakes at her when he thought nobody was looking; *Timmy Twit*, she thought. Everybody expected *him* to go up to *Oxford* in two years! He couldn't find his way to the bloody *loo* without a map! And her parents doted on him in such a sickening way: *Tim's so smart, oooh, fawn and scrape*). She liked the huge secrecy, the feeling that the world belonged only to her at this time of morning before school.

A casual onlooker would have seen a slim, pretty girl, trim in her blue jeans and white cotton sweater, her small breasts barely evident, her yellow hair cut very close to her scalp in a fashion that was almost boy-like. But nobody was watching Stephanie Brough, not at this hour of the morning.

She gazed down the slope. She had a clear view of the place she'd come to see. About three hundred yards from where she stood was the white-washed farmhouse that belonged to a family called Yardley. Old Man Yardley had died last year, and his sons, delighted they didn't have to work the land for the nasty old tyrant, had upped and left for London. (Such smart buggers, she thought.) Ever since then the place had been empty. Steffie had supposed it would always remain that way—who'd want to rent or buy that old dump with the black fields surrounding it? It was isolated and run-down and the willow trees that drooped around it made it look creepy.

Yesterday, though, to her great surprise, something was different. During her morning ride she'd seen a dark-blue Range Rover outside the house. Intrigued by the possibility of some new happening in a part of the world where fresh occurrences were rare, she'd come back to see if the vehicle was still there, or perhaps even catch sight of the new occupant. In this rustic environment information was a prize, something to be seized then passed along to the next person, like a great favor. *Oh, by the way, there's some new people at the old Yardley place. You didn't know?*

The vehicle was parked where it had been the day before. But the house still looked disappointingly empty, the windows dark and bare. A crow was scratching around in the soil. Leaves, fallen from the willows, had become piled against the east wall of the property. It was all rather desolate. Steffie enjoyed little mysteries, and in her mind the dead appearance of the old house was exactly that—something to be solved. Why was there a Range Rover and no sign of life? Why was there no smoke from the chimney, no dog in the yard? Everybody had dogs around here.

She wanted a closer look. She left the mare chewing on a clump of grass, then moved down the incline a little way. She stopped after a few yards, uneasy at the idea of trespassing on other people's property. Divided between her natural curiosity and her sense of intrusion, she wasn't sure if she should go any further. But really, what harm could it possibly do to pop down there and just sniff around? If anybody discovered her she'd just tell them she lived on her father's horse-breeding farm three miles away, and then introduce herself as the next door neighbor practically.

She was halfway down when she heard the noise—a penetrating *crack*. Her first startled reaction was that a jet from an air-base nearby had shattered the sound barrier, a common occurrence round here. But then she realized the noise was closer than that and more focussed: it had come from the house. The raven, cawing harshly, rose in the clear air.

If it hadn't been a supersonic plane—

She suddenly realized what had caused the sound. She turned back up the rise, moving quickly, her heartbeat rapid. The noise had faded but she could still hear it perfectly inside her head. *Crack.* Just like that. When she reached the top of the slope she glanced one last time down at the house.

The building was as lifeless as it had been before, the windows opaque in the chill dawn.

But somebody had to be inside. Somebody had to have fired the gun. Guns did not go off by themselves. Unless there were spirits, and Steffie was too sophisticated to believe in anything like that.

She rode the mare hard between the birches, intrigued more than ever, and afraid in a way that was quite new to her and strangely interesting.

Crack.

She'd come back tomorrow. She couldn't leave the mystery alone.

3

When his wife Roxanne had been killed seven years ago by an IRA bomb detonated in a London street, Frank Pagan had lived for some time in a world of incomprehensible pain, a bleak place where his will to live was smothered. It was the sort of pain that lingered in bewildering ways long after the event. A resemblance on a street, a phrase from a certain song, the creak of a floor in his apartment—these things stirred the ghost, and the pain returned, always swift, never less than savage. He'd come to accept that this emptiness was a lifelong thing. He'd combatted it to some extent, but there was always the residue. Sometimes he'd caught himself waiting for the approach of Roxanne Pagan's memory. The anticipation of pain, a gentle masochism.

That was one kind of hurt.

In this white hospital room, whose translucence suggested an hallucination, he was beginning to understand another form of pain altogether. When he raised his face hot threads tightened malignantly in his chest. When he had to get out of bed and go to the toilet— he defiantly refused to take the wheelchair, which was transportation for the damned only—he walked like a man negotiating a field of broken glass. Any sudden motion sent a violent response up through his bandaged chest. At times his heart seemed charged with electricity, as if copper wires were conducting a brisk current through it.

He really hadn't needed to be reminded so forcibly of his own mortality. What also shook him was the sense of violation, his body breached by a force that might have destroyed him. This notion was shocking: he'd been shot at before, but never hit, and perhaps he'd come to think it was one of those things that happened to other people, never to oneself.

It didn't matter that his Pakistani physician Ghose, a sweet chain-smoking man with fidgety hands, kept telling him he was *wery wery* lucky. After all, six policemen had died during the carnage four days ago in Shepherd's Bush. Another inch to the left, Ghose had reminded him, another short inch, and the total would have been seven. *Imagine it, Mister Pagan—the tiny distance of infinity.* The idea of six dead policemen, four inside the leading van, one in the third car, and poor Ron Hardcastle from a devastating head wound, took something away from any contemplation of his own luck. Even the knowledge that two of the assailants had also been killed didn't quite cut the gloom.

On the morning after Pagan's admission to the hospital, Ghose had held up x-rays in his smoky orange fingers, pointing enthusiastically to the pathway of the bullet, which had gone straight through the right lung. *Absolutely no functional disturbance*, Ghose had said.

*No fractured ribs. No debris. Very little crushed tis-
sue. A wonderfully clean exit. I'm utterly delighted.
I rarely see such symmetry. You must thank God for
the insignificant yaw of the bullet.*

Yaw: now there was a nice little word. Pagan had
wondered why, if it was such a terrific wound, aestheti-
cally so pleasing to Ghose and with a low yaw factor
into the bargain, he was in such terrible *pain* those first
three days.

Initially he'd been injected with morphine. A
thoracostomy tube had been inserted in his chest to re-
inflate the lung, and then attached to a chest-draining
unit. The wound had been closed on the third day.
He'd been given anti-tetanus therapy and antibiotics,
and Ghose prescribed Pethidine, so that this fourth day
was the most comfortable Pagan had spent. But comfort
in the circumstances was merely relative: he was more
glazed by drugs than truly soothed. Just when he
thought the pain had subsided it would come back and
lance him, causing him to gasp and his eyes to water.

And then, Christ, there were the dreams. In most
of them he was back on that terrible street again, surrounded by searing flames, hearing the same explosions. Sometimes he rushed toward the burning van
and tried to get the door open to release the trapped
men, but he never quite made it. Infuriating dreams,
frustrating and tragic. He always scorched his hands in
these nightmares. At other times he dreamed of Gunther Ruhr, hearing over and over the drily-uttered German phrase Ruhr had used in the car. *Die Reise ist
nicht au Ende bis zur Anhuntf*—endlessly repeated,
echoing. He reached out in anger to silence Ruhr, but
invariably the German had vaporized, courtesy of that
special chemistry of dreams, and Pagan would wake
sweating, filled with a sense of desperation.

What he really needed was to be discharged from this place. He couldn't do anything from a hospital bed. He couldn't bring the outside world into this boring room of tubes and charts and starched bedsheets. He couldn't begin to get at Ruhr, who had disappeared without the courtesy of a clue. He'd asked Ghose only that morning to release him. With that inscrutable look all doctors must learn in medical school, the physician said he'd consider it.

Restless, Pagan turned his face to the window, where a rare October sun shone on the dusty glass. A tree, gloriously lit by autumn, pressed against the window-pane and tantalized. There was a high breeze outside, the kind of spirited wind that dries laundry. All this contributed to his impatience. All this made him doubly determined to find a way out of here before it was night again and nurses came to dispense sleeping-pills with the persistence of drug-dealers. *Now, Frank, you really must swallow this, do you the world of good.* Or *Come on, Frank, be a good boy.* He didn't *want* to be a good anything. He wanted to be cantankerous, an irascible pain in the arse to doctors and nurses alike. He wanted out: he wanted Gunther Ruhr.

When the door of his private room opened he saw Martin Burr step inside. Burr, the Commissioner of Scotland Yard, carried a bottle of that British panacea called Lucozade and a small bag of fruit, both of which he set down on the bedside table. Haggard from insomnia, he'd been coming twice a day ever since Pagan had been rushed here by ambulance. The Commissioner propped his walnut cane against the bed and sat down, smiling at Pagan, who noticed how a streak of sunlight struck the dark-green plastic patch over Burr's blinded right eye.

"How are we today, Frank?"

"We're a long way from wonderful," Pagan replied. "We would like to get the hell out of here."

Burr reached for his cane and tapped it on the floor, sighing as he did so. "You're always in such a damned hurry, Frank. Accept the fact you've been wounded, and even if you're released from this place you need time to convalesce. You still look awful." Burr looked round. "Rather nice place. Room to yourself. TV. Magazines to read. Enjoy the privacy, Frank. Think of it as an enforced vacation."

"With respect, what I need is to get back on the job."

Burr's smile was small and strained, barely concealing the stress of a man who had just spent the worst four days of his life. There had been endless news conferences, and questions raised in the House of Commons about events in Shepherd's Bush. A commission of inquiry was being set up, which meant that a bunch of professors and civil servants would be asking all kinds of bloody questions. And the press, good God, the press had squeezed the tragedy for everything it was worth and more. The breakdown of law and order. The incompetence of British security forces. The supremacy of the 'super-terrorist'. On and on without end. A mob was howling for blood, preferably Martin Burr's. And the Home Secretary had commanded Burr to attend a private interview, which could only mean that the Commissioner's job security was somewhat in doubt. These were not good times. The temper of the country was bad; the citizens were horrified when policemen were killed.

Burr said, "What would it accomplish if you returned to work? You'd wear yourself out within a day, Frank. You'd be back in this bed in no time flat."

"I don't think so. Basically I think I'm in good shape."

"Notwithstanding a hole clean through your chest. Think of the shock to your system."

"I can't just lie here."

"Afraid you have to," Burr said. "Anyway, everything that can be done is being done."

"And Ruhr's back in custody?"

"Cheap shot, Frank."

Burr leaned toward the bed. He laid both hands over his face and massaged his flesh in a tired way. When he spoke there were hollows of fatigue in his voice. "Let me bring you up to date. Our explosions people say the parked cars that exploded along Acacia Avenue were detonated by a timing-device and the explosives used were of Czech origin."

"Brilliant work," Pagan remarked drily.

Martin Burr gave Pagan a dark look. "I realize you have very little patience for the kind of systematic work technicians have to do, Frank. Nevertheless, it has to be done."

Pagan shut his eyes. There was a tickle in his nostrils. A sneeze was building up. If it succeeded, it would send uncontrollable bolts of pain through his chest. He struggled to overcome it, reaching for a Kleenex just in case.

Burr continued. "Twenty-six cars were detonated simultaneously. Nobody we interviewed in the vicinity saw anybody plant the explosives in the first place. The whole thing was done with an extraordinary degree of stealth."

Pagan opened his eyes. The sneeze had faded. He lowered the Kleenex and looked at Martin Burr. "I think we can take stealth for granted," he said. *That tone*—it was close to petulant sarcasm. He'd have to be careful not to push it. Alienation of Martin Burr wasn't a good thing.

Burr fingered his plastic eye patch, which he did when he was annoyed. "I understand your impatience, Frank. I also understand that a gunshot wound affects a man's perceptions. However, I didn't come here to listen to your cutting little asides. I've got enough on my plate as it is."

Whenever he was irritated, Burr resorted to a patronizing tone that Pagan disliked. Chided, Pagan stared at the window, the gorgeous sunlight, and resolved he'd leave this place today no matter how the considerations of Doctor Ghose turned out. He'd swallow some Pethidine and walk out of this bloody hospital under his own steam. By mid-afternoon he'd be back in his office overlooking Golden Square in Soho, where his anti-terrorist section was located. Lord of his own domain again.

"Now where was I?" Martin Burr said. "Ah, yes. I was coming to the two terrorists killed in the assault."

Pagan felt his interest quicken. "Is there anything new?"

"We haven't been able to identify one of the men. The other, however, was an Australian citizen by the name of Ralph Masters."

"It doesn't ring any bells," Pagan said.

Burr sat back in his chair. "Born Adelaide 1940. Served in the Australian Army in 1960. Nothing for a long time. Then he turns up again in Biafra, nowadays Nigeria, in 1967. He was in the Congo in 1968. After that, he makes an appearance in Nicaragua in the mid 1970s."

"The mercenary circuit."

"Indeed."

"Is there anything more recent on him?"

Burr shook his head. "So far as we know, he'd been sitting quietly in Sydney. He installed telephones for a living."

"That must have bored him senseless. Some people can't settle after they've tasted war. Is there a record of him entering this country?"

Burr shook his head. "We don't know when he came in, nor how he got here. We don't know who employed him."

"The same people who employed Gunther Ruhr. Who else?" Pagan plucked a purple grape from the bunch Burr had brought. He popped it in his mouth and bit into the soft skin.

"Whoever they are." The Commissioner was morosely silent. Pagan had never seen him quite so dejected. He felt an enormous sympathy for Burr, who took the death of the policemen hard. Recent events had obviously been a heartbreak for him, visiting the widows, the fatherless kids, mouthing platitudes that amounted in the end to nothing. The Commissioner, a candid man who had no glib political skills, was not above genuine tears.

"I keep thinking about how our security was breached, Frank. I come back time and again to that. That aspect of the whole thing depresses me. It's not only the dead officers, although God knows that would be monstrous enough in itself."

"Too many people knew the route," Pagan said. "And somebody blabbered."

"The itinerary was decided at the highest level. The Home Office was involved. It was decided by all parties that instead of an ostentatious escort we would transport Ruhr quietly by a highly secret route. An awful mistake, as it turned out."

A secret was hard to keep in a world of committees, Pagan thought.

Burr made circles in the tiled floor with the tip of his cane. "I seem to remember you were the only one who raised the subject of air cover, Frank. I wish the rest of us had paid more attention."

Pagan shrugged. None of the Commissioner's wishes could alter the past. Both men were quiet for a long time before Burr went on, "I'd like to think that if somebody gabbed out of turn then it was from sheer carelessness rather than outright treachery. I don't like the idea of a mole."

"But it's a distinct possibility," Pagan said.

Burr got up from the chair and walked to the window. He was a big man, wide-shouldered and heavy around the center. He looked out into the sunlight and blinked. "Ten people knew the route, including ourselves."

"I don't think you can stop at ten, Commissioner. If you include secretaries and assistants, who have an odd knack of getting wind of everything, the number's probably closer to thirty, thirty-five. And out of that lot somebody—by accident or design—had a connection to Ruhr's friends."

Pagan paused. His mouth was very dry. He sipped some water before going on. "The trouble is, it's difficult to run a really thorough investigation of some thirty individuals, especially if it has to be done quickly. And since Ruhr's obviously up to something in this country—otherwise the big rescue makes no sense—time's a factor. He's not over here to sit around twiddling his thumbs for weeks, is he? He's an expensive commodity. Somebody paid for him to be here. That same somebody spent a lot of money on the rescue. I suspect we're looking at a matter of days before

Ruhr does whatever he's here to do. Perhaps less."
Pagan hadn't spoken more than a couple of short sentences since his wound and now he was hoarse. There was an ache in his chest, a brass screw turning.

Burr stared at him. "If you're saying that our real priority is to find Ruhr and put the security breach on the back burner, I wholeheartedly agree. Easier said than done, alas. Half the police force of England is looking for him right now, Frank. We've had reports of the bugger in Torquay and Wolverhampton and York and all the way up to Scotland. In terms of false sightings, Gunther Ruhr rivals unidentified flying objects."

Pagan had a mild Pethidine rush, a weird little sense of distance from himself. At times he floated beyond everything, spaced-out, drifting, a cosmonaut in his own private galaxy. It was a pleasant sort of feeling. It was easy to see how people became addicted to Pethidine. It relegated terrorists and dead policemen and gunshot wounds to another world, one connected to reality only tenuously.

Pagan shut his eyes and tried very hard to concentrate. "Ruhr specializes in destruction. The question is, what is he here to destroy? And why was he in Cambridge? What's so interesting about the place?"

"Not a great deal, Frank." Martin Burr, an Oxford man with no high regard for the rival university, helped himself to a small glass of Lucozade. He drank, made a face, wondered about the masochism of whole generations of English that had sought good health in the oversweet liquid.

"What about the countryside around Cambridge? Aren't there a couple of military bases?" Pagan asked.

"There's a NATO installation about forty miles away in Norfolk. Also a number of RAF bases within a hundred mile radius of Cambridge, plus a couple of army camps. We've been doing a spot of map-reading."

"I thought the NATO base was going out of business."

Martin Burr nodded. "To a large extent. The terms of the American-Soviet disarmament treaty call for mid-range ballistic missiles to be removed from bases, shipped back to the United States and then destroyed—with Russian observers on hand to ensure fair play. There's a laughable contradiction in terms. I've yet to hear of a Bolshevik who understood fair play."

Pagan rarely paid attention to the Commissioner's bias against Communism. It was a facet of Burr's personality: a form of phobia, and really quite harmless.

"Any one of those places is a candidate for Ruhr," Pagan said.

"They've all beefed up security heavily in the last few days for that very reason. They wouldn't be easy targets for our German friend."

"Is there anything else that might attract him to the area?"

"I've been thinking about that too. Ruhr's target could be a person rather than a place. Or a group of people. In which case, where the devil do we begin? At least three international conferences are coming up in the next week or so in Cambridge. The city's going to be filled with all kinds of experts. Environmentalists, meteorologists, chemists—and that's only in Cambridge. What if Ruhr's target lies in Northampton? Or Bury St. Edmunds? What then?"

Pagan considered the Commissioner's remarks for a moment. Ruhr had become endowed with almost supernatural powers: he was everywhere, and capable of anything. "Here's another possibility to make things a little more complicated: Ruhr was just passing through

Cambridge on the way to someplace else—London, Birmingham—and he stopped to have some fun, if you can call it that.''

Pagan remembered the girl who had been with Ruhr at the time of his capture. A skinny little thing, anaemic, small-breasted. Her name was Penny Ford and she lived in a one-room flat where she'd taken Ruhr after a casual encounter in a pub. When Pagan had interviewed her she'd said that she wasn't in the habit of inviting strange fellows home, you understand, but Ruhr had been, well, bloody persistent and anyhow he didn't have a place to stay, and she was only human after all. And her rent was almost due into the bargain and she was a bit short of the readies. She'd imagined a straight screw, Pagan thought. Uncomplicated sex, a quick exchange of money, end of the matter. Ruhr had other notions.

Penny Ford hadn't been able to tell Pagan why Ruhr was in Cambridge or how he had travelled there or where he was living. She knew nothing about him. She was informative only when it came to his sexual demands. Pagan remembered the girl's quiet voice. *We had sex, and I thought that was the end of it . . . I went inside the lavatory and when I came back he was sitting up on the edge of the bed and looking at me . . . well, in a funny kind of way . . . And he was making this dry whistling sort of noise, you know, tuneless like, but weird, like he wants to whistle only he doesn't know how . . . He asks me to come over. Which I did, because I thought he wanted another go. He asks me to sit on his knee. Which I also did.*

And then?

He has this terrible disfigured hand, of course. That made me sympathetic to him at first. I see him take something out of his jacket, which is hanging on the back of a chair. It's a metal contraption with a leather strap, strangest thing I ever saw. And ugly as sin.

Ugly as sin, Pagan thought. What had so spooked Penny Ford was an unusual artifact consisting of a strap and two long steel protuberances, both sharpened at the end. At first glance the contraption had no apparent function, until you realized—as Penny Ford did—that it was a kind of prosthetic device Ruhr fastened over his deformed hand. The two sharp metal columns, each about six inches long, took the place of the missing fingers.

He wants me to spread my legs so he can stick that bloody thing inside me, honest to God . . . Can you imagine what that sharp steel would have done to me? I mean, sex is one thing, but that was evil . . .

Evil: Pagan remembered thinking it was an impressive word. Penny understandably resisted Ruhr's request and the German had become threatening, catching her by the hair and trying to force her to obey him. She'd struggled and screamed. Ruhr might have been able to silence the girl and slip away easily, but by sheer chance two plainclothes detectives were already inside the house questioning a first-floor tenant about a recent burglary. They responded to the screams immediately, imagining at worst a domestic dispute. They hadn't expected to corner the world's most wanted terrorist with his trousers hanging round his knees and his underwear at half-mast. Pagan had found this image very entertaining before. In the shadow of recent events it didn't seem remotely amusing now. Ruhr was sick and vicious. Worse, he was also at liberty, and Frank Pagan was not.

Pagan sat upright. "Christ, I want out of here."

Martin Burr shook his head. "There are persons in

the morgue with more color than you. Accept your fate and be still."

"I need some fresh air, that's all."

Burr smiled. "Even if you were able to leave, you don't have anything here to wear. When they brought you in, your suit was totally ruined."

"Ruined?"

"Bloodstained and torn."

The suit, made specially for him by a tailor with basement premises in Soho, had cost Frank Pagan a month's salary. In normal circumstances he would have lamented the wreckage of a fashionable beige linen suit, but not now. "I'll leave in a bloody bedsheet if I have to."

"Frank Pagan wandering the West End in a bedsheet. The mind is boggled."

"All I do is lie here and feel useless. Sometimes Ghose teaches me new words. I just learned 'hemothorax', and that's the highlight of the whole day." Pagan looked at Martin Burr with disarming intensity. "I need to be in on this one. You know that."

Martin Burr ignored Pagan's plea and took a pocket watch from his waistcoat. He flipped the silver lid open. "I must be running along, Frank. Busy busy. Things to do. I'll see if I can come back again tonight. Can't promise."

"And I stay right here?"

"Exactly."

Pagan watched Martin Burr go toward the door. "Is that an order, Commissioner?"

Martin Burr sailed out of the room, neither answering Pagan's question nor acknowledging it, even though he must have heard it. Was it some sly tactic on the Commissioner's part? Was he telling Pagan to take total responsibility if he discharged himself? Pagan listened to the click of Burr's cane as it faded down the tiled corridor. Then he lay very still for a time before he smiled and reached for the telephone at the side of the bed.

4

Glasgow

Two men sat in the glass-walled conservatory of the Copthorne Hotel overlooking that heart of Victorian Glasgow called George Square, a large open space dominated by statues and the massive edifice of the City Chambers. On this rainy afternoon in October the Chambers, built in the Italian Renaissance style, looked vaguely unreal and uninhabited, as if the civil servants who were its usual occupants had fled in a scandalous hurry. The whole rain-washed square gave the same empty impression despite the occasional pedestrian hurrying under an umbrella.

The older of the two men, a small white-haired figure called Enrico Caporelli, gazed pensively through the wet glass. Every five minutes or so he could see his black limousine pass in front of the conservatory while the driver killed time circling the area. Caporelli, five feet tall and sixty years of age, swung his dainty little feet in their expensive Milanese shoes a half-inch off the floor.

Everything about the Italian was tiny, except, it was said, his cunning and his sexual organ. He'd been legendary for his dalliances with showgirls in his old Havana days. Whenever he thought of the floor-shows at the Tropicana or the Nacional—before the *barbudos* had come down from the hills and fucked everything and everybody on Cuba—he remembered them with fondness and loss. He rubbed his hands, which were smooth as vellum, and said, "I've always enjoyed the statues here. Things were built to last back then. They were expected to be *doorable.*"

The younger man nodded, although the statues in the square didn't appeal to him. They lacked flair. Passion, uncommon in damp presbyterian climates, was missing.

Caporelli gazed at Queen Victoria a moment, then turned his face away from the drenched stone likeness of the monarch. He changed the subject suddenly. "Nobody on God's earth is worth such a price."

"Normally I would agree with you. But not in this case. Believe me." The younger man, Rafael Rosabal, was tall and muscular, handsome in a manner that was particularly Latin. He had the kind of face, symmetrical and perhaps a little too perfect, that at first beguiles most women, then later begins to trouble them in some indefinable way.

Rosabal was cold in this climate. He'd been cold ever since he'd left Havana ten days ago. Despite the heavy woollen overcoat he'd purchased in Moscow, he was still uncomfortable. He wondered why Caporelli always chose unlikely cities for their meetings. Saint-Etienne, Leeds, now Glasgow. Presumably Caporelli had business interests in these places.

"If he's as smart as I'm always being told, how come he got himself in this godawful mess in the first place?" Caporelli posed questions with an authority that came from years of giving orders and having them obeyed. He had the often haughty dignity of a cardinal accustomed to having his ring kissed.

Rosabal shrugged. "He has tastes, peculiarities. Sometimes he gives in to them."

"I don't want to know." Caporelli raised a hand. He had no interest in the sexual foibles of other people. "A man that allows his tastes to overcome his head— I don't like that kind of man."

"I saw him yesterday. He's in a safe place. I assure you the problem is under control."

Caporelli spoke gravely, his voice without cadence, his accent an odd hybrid of Calabria and Long Island. "At great expense, I gave you the financial backing you said you would need for the operation. My generosity resulted in tragedy. Who likes dead policemen and hysterical newspaper headlines? I'm too old for anger, my friend. It's a drain. I only have so much energy. I want to spend it contemplating pleasant things."

Rosabal plucked a cube of sugar out of the bowl and placed it on his tongue, an old habit. He was amused by the way Caporelli talked about his 'generosity', as if everything had been an act of charity, a personal donation from Enrico's private account, and there was going to be nothing in this for the Italian but a sense of well-being. San Enrico. All heart. The patron saint of terror.

"We got him back," Rosabal said. "That's the important thing, Enrico."

"We should never have been placed in such a position to begin with. Having to bail out a man who's supposed to be doing a job for us—tsssss, that's not how to do business."

Rosabal silently cursed Gunther Ruhr's proclivity for strange sex. It was the only cavalier aspect of Ruhr's life, which was otherwise as rigidly dedicated to terror as a monk's to prayer. "Nobody else can deliver. That's the important thing to remember."

All this violence made Caporelli touchy. He liked the idea that he was too civilized for violence. After all, didn't he own some of the world's finest paintings? Hadn't he invested in great sculptures and financed operas and symphonies and ballet companies? A number of cities in North America and Europe were unknowingly indebted to Caporelli for their cultural lives.

So it was no source of joy for him to be associated, even remotely, with men who were little better than animals, scum like this German that had to be rescued four days ago in London. A goddam bloodbath, he thought. Who needed it? Even if this kraut was the only man in the goddam known universe capable of doing the job, who needed the heartache?

When Rosabal had requested many thousands of dollars to rescue the German, Caporelli, turning the same blind eye he'd turned all his life whenever profit was threatened, had managed to convince himself that the cash was for a vast amount of grease, *la mordida,* bribes for prison officials, guards, cops. In his wildest fantasies he couldn't have come up with what the British newspapers were calling The Shepherd's Bush Massacre. He had developed a form of immunity to the realities of violence and an awesome capacity to distance himself from any personal culpability. Like many men whose hearts are basically vicious, Enrico Caporelli had discovered the ultimate hiding-place: denial.

He said quietly, "I don't like the idea of new widows. I hate it when women cry. I'm suckered by tears. Orphaned children eat my heart out."

Hipocrita, Rosabal thought. A few orphans, a few widows, what did these really matter to the Italian? Caporelli sometimes strutted the stage of his life as if it were a melodrama. Rosabal said, "I'm not delighted either. But it couldn't be avoided. The alternative was to dump Ruhr."

"What I also don't like is this manhunt I read about. Every cop in the country is looking for Ruhr. He's too hot."

"Nobody is going to find him."

"Still. My gut tells me we should look elsewhere, get somebody else."

The Cuban said, "From now on, no more accidents, Enrico. No more mistakes. Smooth," and he planed the surface of the table with his palm for emphasis. "You have my word."

Rafael Rosabal glanced at a nearby table where two middle-aged women drank tea. They had the furrowed brows and glazed eyes of habitual eavesdroppers and they bothered the Cuban, who regularly experienced the sensation that he was being watched or followed. In the Soviet Union recently he knew he'd been observed by the KGB, which was standard practice. Here, in Britain, there might be surveillance from the internal security arm of intelligence. He hadn't seen anyone suspicious, but that didn't mean he *wasn't* being watched. He leaned across the table, closer to Caporelli, whose fussy caution annoyed him. Rosabal understood that the stakes were too high for Enrico to abandon Ruhr at this stage. Caporelli would go with the German in the end, but first there had to be this song and dance.

"We have to trust each other, Enrico," Rosabal said. "I need to know that when I return to Cuba you won't change the way things have been set up. I need that assurance. If you drop Ruhr now, you abandon everything. That's the bottom line. Keep this in mind—we want the same thing. We have the same goals."

The same goals, Caporelli thought. The rich, gravy-filled pie that was Cuba. He said, "I asked for this meeting because I wanted to find out what safeguards you could give me. But my cup of confidence isn't exactly overflowing, Rafael."

Rosabal plucked another sugar cube from the bowl. "What would you have me do? Put Ruhr in a straitjacket until the time comes? He isn't going to be a problem. He's on his best behavior. I give my word. I stand or fall by that. If my word isn't good enough for you . . . You want to drop the plan, tell me now. The first stage is only two days away."

Caporelli pinched the bridge of his nose. What were two days when you weighed it against the thirty years that had passed since the barbarians had taken control of the island and given everybody the shaft with their so-called Revolution? Two days: if the first stage went without flaw then he and his associates would see things through to the end.

He looked at Rosabal and what he perceived in the young Cuban's face was bottomless determination and in those dark eyes an intensity of fierce ambition such as he hadn't seen in a long time. He liked these qualities. He liked this young man's conviction. In a world where trust was a debased currency, he trusted Rafael Rosabal, even if he had the feeling that the Cuban sometimes wasn't sure how to walk the fine line between restraint and impatience. A flaw of youth, that was all. A little too much fire in the belly.

"How is the Vedado these days?" he asked. The

Vedado was his favorite part of Havana, where the large hotels and enormous private residences had been built. He'd always thought of it as his own sector of the city, his personal domain, and he'd ridden the streets with a proprietorial attitude. He'd been an intimate of former President Batista, who'd conferred honorary Cuban citizenship upon him. He still had a photograph of the ceremony. Government ministers had owed him favors.

He'd owned a magnificent baroque house near the University—cobbled courtyard with bronze statues, mango and pomegranate trees growing against the walls, the smell of the ocean through the open windows of the huge master bedroom. The bathroom had been built out of the finest Italian marble with gold faucets, in the shape of gargoyles, created by the kind of proud craftsmen who no longer existed in Castro's shabby socialist paradise. He'd heard that his beautiful house, confiscated in 1959 on behalf of the bullshit Revolution, was now occupied by a department of MINAZ, the Ministry of the Sugar Industry, or one of those other godawful bureaucracies the *fidelistas* were so fond of creating.

Incompetent bastards, he thought. Goddam Caribbean Communists—they couldn't run a one-car funeral without a wreck.

He wanted that house again. He wanted it back so badly he ached. He lusted after it with an intensity that was beyond simple greed. It was *his* house; he had always imagined dying in it one day. He could hear the sound of his heels echo in the tiled entranceway and the laughter of girls in the upstairs room. Tall women, huge breasts, invariably blond, that was how he'd always liked them. Back then, he'd been blessed with amazing stamina and a lot of lead in his pencil.

But it was more than just the house.

"The Vedado could use a coat of paint," Rosabal said. "Like everything else on Cuba."

Enrico Caporelli rose from his chair and took a pair of leather gloves out of the pocket of his black overcoat.

"Then we must see if we can give it one, Rafael," he said. "Fresh paint is one of my favorite smells."

The rainclouds over Glasgow grew darker and heavier as the limousine left the city and approached the coastal road to Ardrossan and then south to Ayr. On the Firth of Clyde, the stretch of water that eventually became the Irish Sea, the rain turned to mist, drawing a lacy invisibility over the Island of Arran and the imposing mountain called Goat Fell. Once, in a dramatic way, the peak pierced the mist like a fabulous horned creature, but was gone again before Caporelli was sure he'd seen it.

He dozed in the back of the big car, waking every so often to look out at the rainy green countryside or some small town floating past. At Ballantrae, fifty miles from Glasgow, the car turned away from the coast and headed inland on a forlorn road that was rutted and pocked. This narrow strip passed between tall hedgerows. Here and there, where the hedges parted, overgrown meadows sloped toward a distant stand of thick, misty trees. How could any place be this green? The darker the green, the more secretive the landscape. Caporelli had the sensation he was travelling into a kingdom of rainy silences. A secure kingdom, certainly; he saw at least two men with shotguns stalking the spaces between trees.

The house came finally in view, a large sandstone edifice built in the early part of the twentieth century, although its style echoed much earlier times. Circular towers suggested fortresses of the late 1500s. Darkened by rain, the house had shed some of its red stone warmth, and looked uninviting. The limousine entered the driveway and came to a stop at the ornate front door, which was immediately opened by Freddie Kinnaird, whose florid face appeared to float through the rain like a balloon escaped from a child's hand.

Caporelli waited until the chauffeur, a taciturn man called Rod, had opened the door for him before he got out. Then, ducking under an umbrella Rod held, he stepped toward the house where Freddie Kinnaird shook his hand vigorously. "Welcome to Kinnaird's folly."

They were improbable associates, the beefy red-faced Englishman with hair the color of sand and the tiny white Italian. Kinnaird placed a hand on Caporelli's elbow and steered him inside the enormous flag-stoned hall of the house where a fire burned in the baronial fireplace. Caporelli spread his palms before the flames, thinking he didn't much care for the size of this room or the stuffed animal heads that hung high on the walls—elks, boars, deer. They had the glassy, haunted look of all animals slain before their time.

"Why did you buy this place, Freddie? Did you need something small and intimate?"

Freddie Kinnaird poured two small sherries from a decanter and smiled a generous white-toothed smile. "It has some obvious benefits. One hundred and twenty acres of thick green countryside, spot of nice fishing, no inquisitive neighbors, which makes security inexpensive. I picked the whole thing up for a song a few years ago. Upkeep's high, but it makes a splendid change from the hurly-burly of dear old London."

Caporelli took one of the glasses and clinked it lightly against Kinnaird's. There was the standard Society toast, the simple *To the success of friendship.* No matter the language—English, Italian, German or, more recently, Japanese—the form never varied. Freddie Kinnaird tossed a log on the fire and it blazed at once, sending sparks up into the chimney.

"The others are upstairs." Kinnaird raised his face and looked up at the mahogany gallery. Constructed halfway between floor and ceiling, it ran the length of the wall. "The Americans arrived half an hour ago."

"Good," Caporelli said.

"What did Rosabal say?" Kinnaird set down his empty glass.

"He gave me assurances. I accepted. I like this Rosabal. He's so desperate to deliver I can smell it on him. There's no scent so strong as the musk of sheer goddam ambition. And I trust him. After all, he provided us with the locations of Cuban military defense units and their strength and only an ambitious man, a man who knows what he wants, would go to that kind of trouble. For him it's a simple equation. If he keeps Ruhr under control, he stands a chance of getting his hands on the political machinery of Cuba and all the benefits and patronage that go with the job. President Rosabal. He's in love with the sound of that title. As for us, if the first act doesn't play, we withdraw. We take our losses, check out alternatives."

"Not a notion I relish. The mere idea of starting all over again overwhelms me."

The Italian smiled. "I don't think we'll have to."

Kinnaird picked up his empty glass and studied it, looking like a professor of archaeology surprised by some odd find. "Before we go up, Enrico, you should be prepared for some opposition to Ruhr."

Caporelli dismissed the threat. "Tssss. I think I can

convince them to wait and see. Where do you stand, Freddie?''

''With you,'' Kinnaird said. ''But the holocaust in Shepherd's Bush has left me with a very bad taste in my mouth. Nobody expected that, least of all me.''

''You can do one of two things with a bad taste,'' Caporelli said. ''Swallow it. Or spit it out. What you can't do is gargle it, Freddie.''

''What have you done with yours?'' Kinnaird asked.

''I swallowed the sonofabitch.''

They climbed upstairs to the gallery, and moved through a warren of rooms, most of them unfurnished and only half-decorated. Ladders and rolls of wallpaper and paint-cans were scattered everywhere. Plaster had been stripped, revealing lathe underneath. Kinnaird made excuses for the state of things. Local workmen were slow, and supplies sometimes had to be ordered from Glasgow or London. There was more than a touch of *manana* in this part of the world. Caporelli followed his host, noticing how the high ceilings were lost in shadow. Long windows were rattled by rainsqualls. Outside, trees shuddered in the bleak wet wind.

Finally Kinnaird led the way inside a room that resembled a corporate boardroom. Men sat at a large oval table and the air, thick with tobacco smoke, hung over their heads like ectoplasm. Velvet curtains had been drawn across the windows and little fringed lamps were lit, imparting an atmosphere of genteel clubiness. A liquor cabinet provided a variety of expensive Scotches and vintage brandy. What made this gathering different from any board-meeting was the fact that the table was bare. No papers, no notepads, no folders, no pens. The men here didn't take notes. They were forbidden by their own statutes to create reminders or memoranda of these gatherings.

Enrico Caporelli moved to the empty chair at the top of the table, his place as Director. He sat down, looked round. There was uncertainty here, but Caporelli knew he could play his colleagues like an orchestra. In the past he'd steered them, by sheer force of personality and some theatrical ability, into decisions they'd been reluctant to make.

Apart from himself, there were six dark-suited men around the table; of this number, only the Americans presented any kind of real obstacle. The German, Rudolf Kluger, a somber, bespectacled man with the smooth discretionary air of a banker from Frankfurt, usually agreed with Caporelli. The French representative, M. J-P Chapotin, who was a handsome silverhaired man in his late fifties, generally came into line after some initial Gallic posturing. Freddie Kinnaird, by his own admission, was a foregone conclusion. The thin, unsmiling Japanese member, Kenzaburo Magiwara, who had the appearance of a man who carries important secrets in his skull, frequently agreed with the majority because he believed there was strength through unity. Otherwise why had the Society of Friends endured? Caporelli reflected on how the Japanese had only recently been admitted, a gesture in the direction of changing times.

And then the Americans! Who could predict the reactions of Sheridan Perry and his companion, the gaunt man known as Hurt? They had that quiet arrogance found in some Americans. It was the understated yet persistent superiority of people who think they have invented the twentieth-century and franchised it to the rest of the world.

Sheridan Perry, flabby in his middle age like some

fifty-year-old cherub, and Harry Hurt, lean as only a compulsive jogger can look—how could they appear so dissimilar and yet both emit a quality Caporelli found slightly sinister? They were an ambitious pair with the ease and confidence of men who come from a reality in which ambition is to be encouraged and pursued. It was no dirty little word, it was a way of life.

Hurt was an athlete who had graduated from Princeton and then spent many years in the military, rising to the elevated rank of Lieutenant-General. Later, he'd been an advisor in such outposts as Nicaragua and El Salvador. He sometimes seemed to be issuing orders to invisible subordinates, men of limited mental capacity, when he talked. Perry, whose jowls overhung the collar of his shirt, came from old midwestern money, railroads and banks and farmlands. He had been educated at Harvard Business School but there was still the vague suggestion of the provincial about him. True sophistication was just beyond him, something that lay over the next ridge. He reminded Caporelli of a man who knew how to talk and how to choose his suits and shirts but in the final analysis some small detail always betrayed him, perhaps his cologne, perhaps his mouthwash.

Caporelli observed the two Americans a moment. He had himself spent many profitable years in the United States and still maintained homes on Long Island and in Florida. He had a great fondness for Americans despite his aversion to their rather unshakable conviction in the correctness of their own moral vision. In this sense, Hurt and Perry were typical. But this narrowness of perception, this self-righteousness, also made the two Americans good capitalists. Unfortunately, though, they tended to think of the Society as something they deserved to own.

Now Caporelli cleared his throat and ran quickly through some items of business that in other circumstances would have been considered important. The manipulation of South African diamond prices, the request of a deposed Asian dictator to launder enormous sums of stolen money, the opportunity to purchase a controlling interest in a score of troubled American savings and loans banks, the question of funding a weakening military junta in a South American republic notorious for political turbulence. These were the usual affairs with which the Society concerned itself during its long and sometimes argumentative semi-annual meetings.

Today Caporelli dispensed with all this quickly. He knew there was only one real item on the agenda and the members were impatient to get to it. He spoke in the kind of voice he reserved for wakes. He summarized the situation, moving nimbly over recent 'unhappy events in London' and insisting on the need to look at the larger picture. He reiterated his faith in the plan that had been concocted years before. Why tinker with running clockwork? He admitted Ruhr had brought a volatile element into the situation, but Rafael Rosabal, a trustworthy man, had pledged his word: everything was in place. And the timing was *ah, perfetto*. How long could the Soviets go on funding Castro's private little reality at a time when they were tightening their purse-strings all over the globe? Cuba, already an economic leper, was certain to be disowned by its niggardly Russian masters. An orphaned Cuba, weak, neglected. Who could wish for a better opportunity?

When he saw doubtful expressions on the faces of some members he became eloquent, reminding them of the prize to be won. An island paradise presently run by 'animals', Cuba was a prime piece of Caribbean real estate, a tropical delight, a licence to print money. His delivery was good, his manner confident. As a final gesture in the direction of the Americans, Caporelli spoke of the moral imperative involved in the plan. What could be more right than the end of a corrupt regime?

He sat down. He sipped from a glass of water. Not such a bad performance, he thought.

Sheridan Perry spoke in one of those flat voices in which you could hear two things: the winds of the Great Plains and an underlay of Harvard Yard. He said, "As you point out, Enrico, the elements are present. But how can you be sure Ruhr is under control?"

Enrico Caporelli shrugged. "I can't say with one hundred per cent certainty he's going to be a pussycat, Sheridan. There's never such certainty in anything."

Sheridan Perry had a nice smile and perfect little teeth. "Ruhr screwed up with the hooker in England and God knows he might do it again. Why didn't you let him rot in jail? Why compound the problem by giving the go-ahead to some completely reckless rescue—planned, incidentally, by Rosabal, your man of honor?"

"I exercised my judgment as Director. There were excesses."

Sheridan Perry raised his eyebrows. "Judgment, Enrico? Excesses? The London incident has shocked all of us in this room. The Society can't condone that kind of violence. Matter of interest, how much did your Shepherd's Bush extravaganza cost us?"

Enrico Caporelli mentioned a figure that was slightly more than one hundred thousand pounds. "A drop in the ocean," he added. "Compared with what's at stake."

Harry Hurt talked now in his patient, slightly professorial way. "Money aside, we don't kill defendants of law and order, because it promotes anarchy. The Society has never done that. We stabilize regimes. We don't *undermine* them. Unless they're run by bandits."

"Like Cuba," Sheridan Perry said.

In spite of Perry's hostility, Caporelli had the feeling the Americans would support the plan finally, but they were after something in return. He'd known Perry and Hurt for too many years not to recognize the signs: the air of collusion, the sense that they'd rehearsed their position before the meeting. Caporelli remembered Perry's father from fifteen years ago, a banker with a rough tongue who'd imparted both his position in the Society and his self-righteousness to Sheridan.

"We want your word." Sheridan Perry stared at Caporelli with an evangelical look, very sincere, as if he had salvation to sell. "We want your *solemn* word, Enrico. If Ruhr blows it again, you'll offer your resignation. We want that promise."

So that was it. Caporelli wasn't entirely surprised. Perry lusted after the Director's chair, which he'd missed by only two votes last time.

"I give it gladly," Caporelli said. The Directorship didn't enthrall him. It had some advantages. It gave one a certain freedom to make decisions on one's own. But that same freedom was also a heavy responsibility and he wasn't intrigued by titles these days anyway. All he really wanted was what was owed him—with interest. Accounts had to be balanced before they could be closed, and his Cuban account had gone unsettled for far too long.

Caporelli solicited the other members around the table. A vote was taken: the plan would proceed. If the first stage wasn't completed, the scheme would be aborted. The Director's promise of resignation was noted.

Caporelli, who felt he'd won a tiny victory, looked

at Hurt. "Let's go on to the next item of business—Harry's report on the situation in Central America."

Harry Hurt had jogged all round Kinnaird's estate earlier. Then he'd showered, and meditated for twenty minutes, and now he exuded the glow of sheer good health. He sat at the table like a human lamp. "There are no problems. Everything's primed. Officially, the Hondurans accept the story we're constructing a resort fifty miles from Cabo Gracias a Dios. Unofficially, they know we're doing something else. It's costly to bridge that gap between the official and unofficial perception in Central America. Everybody's schizophrenic down there. We forge ahead, greasing palms as we go. The airstrip's finished. We're rolling."

"How many men are assembled now?" M. Chapotin asked.

"Twelve hundred," Hurt said.

"And what will the total commitment be?" Mr. Magiwara asked.

"Fifteen. But we could go with twelve." Hurt smiled his jogger's angular grin. "In point of fact, we could take the whole goddam Caribbean first thing in the morning and still have time for ham and eggs in Key West. If we wanted."

The room was silent. Caporelli looked at the faces, waiting for further questions or comments. Harry Hurt always spoke with such authority that he left no doors open. When it came to military matters, he was the resident expert. It was known that he had friends in high places in Washington who had assisted, if only indirectly, in the creation of the military force in Honduras.

Caporelli stood up slowly. He declared the meeting adjourned.

He left the room as drinks were being poured and chairs pushed back. The formality of the meeting di-

minished in more relaxed small talk. What Freddie Kinnaird had called 'the holocaust in London' had already
been assimilated by the members and subjugated to the
prospect of profit, as if it were nothing more than a delayed cargo or an adverse stock market or a foreign currency plummeting, just another item of business. The
Society of Friends, whose very name had Quaker reso-
nances of peace and stability, had absorbed many
shocks in its history. It had always survived them.

Freddie Kinnaird, a gracious host, had placed a bedroom at Caporelli's disposal. Perched at the top of a
tower, it was round with slit-like windows. Caporelli
removed his suit and silk underwear and lay down
naked, listening to the relentless rush of wind and rain
on the tower. He closed his eyes.

He remembered Cuba.

He remembered that April morning in 1959 when
the three *barbudos* had come to his house in The Vedado. They wore green fatigues. With their beards they
might have been cloned from a sliver of Fidel's flesh.
They carried revolvers and their boots thudded on the
Italian marble entrance. They'd been drinking, still cel-
ebrating Fidel's success. It was a twilight time, Caporelli
recalled, between hope and fear of disappointment.
Soon the Revolution would deteriorate in mass arrests,
firing-squads, disgusting show-trials, expulsions, Communism. For the moment it was still something to celebrate, if you were a *fidelista*. The *barbudos* were led
by a man who called himself Major Estrada, a fat man
with a black beard and a face pitted with old acne. He
wore green-tinted glasses. Even now, Caporelli could
envisage him with astonishing clarity: the pockmarks,
the flake of spinach or parsley lodged in the beard, the

brown teeth, the black eyes hidden behind cheap green glass.

Major Estrada flashed a crumpled piece of paper under Caporelli's face, a 'document of transfer' so hastily printed the ink was still damp. It was as if the Revolution had rushed to bestow legality on itself. In the name of the Revolution, all Caporelli's property was to be confiscated. This included the house in The Vedado, the Hotel St. Clara located on Aguir Street near the Havana Stock Exchange, the apartment buildings on A Street and First, the large General Motors dealership at the corner of 25th and Hospital. They wanted it all.

Major Estrada took his revolver from his belt and waved it in the air. Caporelli, he said, was little better than a parasite sucking the blood of the poor. Caporelli had been thirty years old at the time, brashly confident that his powerful associates could clarify this misunderstanding quickly. But he'd misread the Revolution. Those of his friends who hadn't left the island had smelled the wind and were busy stashing such money as they could before Castro took it from them.

Caporelli made futile phonecalls while Estrada's two soldiers ransacked the house. They created a destructive passage through the place—broken glass, mirrors, overturned vases, silk drapes hauled from windows, statues riddled with gunfire.

The American girl asleep in the upstairs bedroom, a dancer called Lynette, a passionate young woman Caporelli had stolen from a floor-show, was wakened by the noise of the soldiers. Caporelli remembered hearing her swear at them and then she appeared, wrapped in a peach-colored silk robe, at the top of the stairs.

"What the hell's going on, Enrico?"

"Tell the young woman to shut up and get dressed," Estrada said.

Caporelli shrugged. Either he defied the Major to impress the girl, or he obeyed Estrada and looked feeble in his own house.

The girl said, "Enrico, can't you get rid of these guys?"

Estrada said, "Why don't you do that, Enrico?"

Caporelli turned to look at the Major, who was smiling, enormously pleased with the situation. Then he faced the girl again, whose silk robe shimmered in the sun that streamed through a skylight above her. Angelic, Caporelli thought. How could he disappoint this angel?

He was about to say something when Estrada tried to press the piece of paper into his hand. It was of extreme importance to the Major to serve the document. He was a bailiff of La Revolucion, a process server for the new order, and he took the task seriously.

"You must accept the paper," he said. "As for the girl, tell her to get dressed and leave. She has no future here."

From the top of the stairs the girl put a little whine into her voice and said, "Enrico, what the hell do these characters want? Can't you do something about them? They're tearing your house apart."

Caporelli looked at the paper, refused to accept it. "Stick the document up your ass," he told Estrada.

It was a moment in which Enrico Caporelli was pleased with the sheer beauty of defiance, a heightened moment wherein he had a sense of his own unlimited potential. He perceived himself through the eyes of the girl and he was beautiful and cocksure and eternal.

Major Estrada struck Caporelli across the face with his pistol. The girl screamed, a shrill noise that reverberated across marble surfaces. Nauseated by pain, embarrassed, Caporelli slipped to the marble floor. He couldn't remember now if he'd lost consciousness for thirty seconds or five minutes: there was a dark passage at the end of which was Estrada's hand holding the gun, pushing the barrel between Caporelli's lips.

Caporelli felt the warm gun against the roof of his mouth. He was aware of the smell of booze on the man's breath. Alcohol and revolutionary fervor. The Major was capable of anything. On the landing, the girl was holding the corner of her silk robe to her mouth. She'd believed Caporelli was protected by the powers in Cuba, that he had the kind of clout which made him impregnable. Last night he'd been tireless, a demon lover, coming at her time and again with a remorseless quality that was extraordinary even in her wide experience. Now he was reduced. He looked tiny to her down there in the entranceway, and sad.

"Take the paper," Estrada said, and released the safety catch. It was the most lethal sound Caporelli had ever heard. Nevertheless, he defied the Cuban again. He said *Kiss off,* his tongue dry upon the steel barrel.

"*Payaso,*" Estrada said, and shoved the gun hard. Caporelli made pitiful retching noises. Later, he thought how little dignity there was in the situation. Stark fear diminished you, reduced you to nothing. Everything you imagined yourself to be was peeled away from you, and nothing else mattered but the proximity of the weapon and the fact that your heart was still beating and you were prepared to strike any kind of deal to keep it pumping. The presence of the girl was already forgotten. The idea that she witnessed this shameful incident meant nothing to him just then.

Estrada took a rosary from his tunic and ran the beads through the fingers of one hand. "God have mercy on you," he whispered. "Adios."

And then the little scene, poised so bleakly on the

edge of death, dissolved in laughter as Estrada wrenched the gun out of Caporelli's mouth. The two soldiers, who had reappeared, were also laughing; it was the raucous laughter of drunks enjoying a great joke. Caporelli shut his eyes. His stomach had dropped. His mouth flooded with viscous saliva. He thought he felt a warm trickle of urine against his inner thigh, and he prayed it wouldn't show.

Estrada said, ''Now, Enrico. Take the paper.''

Caporelli reached out without opening his eyes but Estrada, teasing, held the document away from the out-stretched hand. The girl was immobile on the landing.

''Let me hear you beg a little, Enrico, or I stick the gun back in your mouth. Only this time no joke.''

''I beg,'' Caporelli said. Although he couldn't see her, he was conscious of the girl moving now, the hem of her robe brushing the marble staircase.

''For what?''

There was dryness in Caporelli's mouth. ''I beg you. Give me the paper.''

Caporelli's hand closed around the document. Estrada reached down, patted him on the head. Like a dog, a pet that had misbehaved and was now to be banished.

''Big shot, eh? Friend of Batista, eh? You think you own Havana! The Revolution is stronger than you and all your friends, companero. The Revolution will bring you and your friends to their fucking knees! Now you've got ten minutes to get the hell out of here. Pack what you can carry in a small suitcase and go. Cuba doesn't need you. Cuba doesn't need your women.''

Caporelli listened to the sound of the three men strut across the courtyard. He remained on his knees for a long time afterwards, humiliated, ashamed by his failure of nerve. Why hadn't he gone on defying Estrada? Why had he caved in and begged? The answer was devastatingly simple: he'd been to a place he'd never visited before in his young life, the borderline between living and dying. It was a place without sunshine and women, a terrifying place where all your money and power didn't amount to shit. Life was better than death, even if humiliation was the price you paid.

When he stood up he saw the embarrassing trickle of urine on the marble, and he cleaned it with a white linen handkerchief monogrammed with the initials EC. The girl was standing over him.

She said, "Oh Enrico," and then she was silent and he couldn't decide what was in her tone, whether disappointment or horror, embarrassment or sympathy.

Thirty years later, he could still hear the mocking laughter of the men. He could see Estrada's scarred face and the expensive handkerchief stained with piss. He could still feel the pistol against the roof of his mouth and smell the girl's perfume. He trembled with rage when he remembered Estrada's control of the situation, and his own disgrace in the presence of the girl.

He sat up, took his wallet from his jacket. He flipped it open, removed a crumpled sheet of paper. He smoothed it on the bed, his hand trembling the way it always did when he remembered Major Estrada. It was the document of transfer, the *traspaso de propriedad.* He had made up his mind a long time ago that he wasn't going to destroy this forlorn keepsake until he was back in Havana.

He closed his eyes. How could you count what Cuba had cost him? In monetary terms he'd been robbed of three million dollars in 1959, worth about seventy million thirty years later. But he had a melancholy sense of having lost something other than money: Estrada had stripped him of honor. But Estrada wasn't the real culprit. It was Castro, whose shadow fell like that of a great dark vulture across Cuba. It was Castro who had robbed him and it was Castro against whom he would have his revenge.

5

Frank Pagan's unit, officially known as SATO, the Special Anti-Terrorist Operation, occupied two floors of an anonymous building in Golden Square in Soho. The unit had come into existence in 1979 as a specific response to Irish terrorism. In the middle of the 1980s it had been disbanded and integrated into the structure of other Scotland Yard departments. Last year, however, at the direction of Martin Burr, the unit was revived and its charter expanded beyond Irish matters. Pagan, despite internal opposition at Scotland Yard from men who resented the publicity he'd generated in his career, had been named officer in charge. Small minds, Burr had said. Small people. Pagan had a fuck-you attitude to these gnomes who criticized his personal style, his fashionable suits and colored shirts, the American Camaro he drove, the rock and roll he favored.

On this cold evening in October, Pagan sat at the

window of his office and looked down into the darkness of Golden Square. He had secured his release from hospital that same afternoon by the simple if painful expedient of rising from the bed, dressing in the clothes brought to him by his assistant Foxworth, and strolling past the nurse's station. He'd been assailed at once by the matron, a bollard of a woman who ruled the wards with a tyrant's flair. She'd prevented Pagan's exit until Dr. Ghose could be summoned. When the physician arrived, he'd berated Pagan for taking things into his own hands, but he'd seen a strong resolve in the Englishman that was outside his experience. What else could he do but permit Pagan freedom on the condition that he change his bandage once every day, take his painkillers and antibiotics, refrain from any energetic activity, and return within three days for a check-up?

Loaded with gauze and bandages, armed with prescriptions, uttering lavish promises, Pagan stepped out into the late afternoon a free man. The adrenaline rush of liberty hadn't lasted long before he discovered that his freedom wasn't from pain. Inside the taxi on the way to Golden Square he doubled over, clutching his chest and alarming Foxie, who didn't know what to do. Pagan swallowed a painkiller and the fit passed shortly thereafter, but it drained him, leaving him paler than before.

Now, sitting at the window of his office, he poured himself a small shot of Auchentoshan, a Lowland malt whisky of unsurpassed smoothness he'd begun to drink lately. Combined with Pethidine, it banished all misery. It encased the brain in a velvet envelope.

"How do you feel?" Foxworth asked. He sat on the opposite side of Pagan's desk. He was a tall man, the same height as Frank Pagan. His bright red hair was cut short, but it still resembled an unmanageable bush.

"I feel like something a dog might throw up. But I thank my lucky yaw I'm still alive," Pagan replied.

"I understand a good yaw's priceless," Foxie remarked. He'd been Pagan's assistant during SATO's first incarnation. Pagan had recently rescued him from the Forgery squad to bring him back into the fold. Foxie had been horrified by the shooting in Shepherd's Bush. Pagan's wounding in particular was too close to home, too unnerving. A darkness had coursed through the whole unit at the news. On the first floor the computers had gone unmanned while operators hovered near the coffee machine to await developments. Upstairs, detectives moped behind their partitions, afraid to answer phones for fear there might be a tragic bulletin from the hospital concerning Pagan.

Now that Pagan had come back work was in progress again, but Foxie thought his return premature. Frank was pallid, and the diet of malt whisky and dope wasn't likely to be beneficial, no matter how strong his constitution might be. It was vintage Pagan. He couldn't keep away. Gunther Ruhr was preying on him, burning a hole in his brain.

Foxie studied his superior a moment. There was a new gauntness about Frank's features. He looked like a bleached-out holograph of himself, as if he were on the edge of fading away entirely. There was the usual flinty light of determination in Pagan's gray eyes but it seemed faintly manic to Foxworth.

Pagan stood up. His shadow fell across the massive pop-art silk-screen of Buddy Holly that dominated the wall behind him, a splash of extraordinary color in a room that was otherwise whitewalled and merely functional. "Let's start with this dead Australian," he said.

"I'm a little ahead of you, Frank," Foxworth said. He reached for Pagan's in-tray and retrieved a telex that had come from Sydney only that morning. "It's not exciting."

Pagan stared at the report. It said only that the man killed in Shepherd's Bush was one Ralph Masters, age 50, a former sergeant in the Australian Army. There was a brief mention of the man's mercenary activities, but no criminal record. He lived alone, no known relatives. "A bloody bore," Pagan remarked. "Is that the best they can send us? Excuse me if I nod off."

"I'll follow it up by telephone later," Foxie said.

Pagan looked across the Square. It was eight-thirty and the streets were quiet and a faint mist adhered to the lamps. By altering his angle slightly he could see taxicabs cruise along Beak Street. In the other direction he could see the harsh, frosted lights of Piccadilly.

"I'll need the usual list."

"It's already here," Foxie said, patting the in-tray. "Updated this very morning."

"You're fast, Foxie."

"Greased lightning. That's me."

Pagan stared at the lengthy computer print-out Foxworth passed to him. Prepared by the Home Office and available to a variety of law enforcement agencies, it was a list of people who had entered the United Kingdom recently, and whose names appeared on the Home Office data base under the category 'questionable'. This included visitors involved in political activity in their homelands, alleged radicals, Communists, businessmen employed in dubious concerns (for example, suspected of having narcotics connections), anti-monarchists, and assorted others. The list showed a high preponderance of Libyans, Irishmen, Iranians, Palestinians and Colombians. None of those named had been denied entry into the country. They weren't considered 'undesirable' enough for that measure. The 'undesirables' belonged on another catalog altogether and were usually detained, interviewed, then deported before they had more than a couple of lungfuls of British air.

"Have you run these names through our own computers?" Pagan asked. The length of the print-out depressed him. There must have been more than four hundred individuals. Was all the world's riff-raff cheerfully entering this green land?

"It's being done even as we speak," Foxie said.

"You're really on top of things here, aren't you? I should have stayed in hospital."

"Which would have shown remarkable judgment, Frank."

Pagan squeezed out a small smile and sat down. He went into a slump for a moment. Where the hell did you start? Where did you go to find Ruhr? It struck him as an overwhelming task. Looking for a terrorist in hiding was going to be the kind of thing where luck, that grinning bitch, would play a significant role. Or sheer doggedness. Pagan much preferred flair, the sudden insight, the flash of *knowing*, to all the humdrum police procedures of knocking on doors and slogging the streets and interviewing people who thought they were about to be arrested for old parking fines.

"Are you sure you're all right?" Foxie asked.

"Do me a favor, Foxie. Stop looking at me as if I'm going to collapse in a coma."

"Sorry."

"I'm not about to keel over. Understand?" Pagan rattled the print-out, just a little annoyed by the concerned look on Foxworth's face. Was he destined to be scrutinized at every turn by his fellow officers looking for signs of infirmity? "Where was I?"

"The list, Frank."

"Right. The list. The trouble is, the people who

rescued Ruhr aren't likely to show up on any damned list. The Australian didn't. Why should we expect any of the others to be cooperative enough to make an appearance? It's just not on. I don't think we can expect any leads to Gunther from the print-out. Besides, the people who rescued Ruhr might be home-grown talent, Foxie, and they wouldn't be on this index. The only import might have been the Aussie."

"Could be."

"What the hell, it's procedure, and we'll follow it, but I'm not getting my hopes up." Pagan put the print-out aside, sipped his drink. He set the empty glass down. "Another thing, Foxie. I don't want any information leaving this office unless it's cleared by me personally. If there's a leak, I don't want it being traced back here. I want a scrambler on my line to the Commissioner's office."

"Noted," Foxworth said.

"Do you have reports on the search for Ruhr? Is there any pattern?"

Foxie shook his head. "The usual hysteria, Frank. The good people of the land peer from behind lace curtains and think, Ah-hah, Gunther the Beast is lurking in the shrubbery. The mass imagination. Wonderful thing."

Pagan sighed. "Where does that leave us, Foxie?"

"There's the rub. Where indeed?"

Pagan gazed through the window again. He was thinking of the terrorist groups and their sympathizers in the darkness of this great city, loose clans of rightists, leftists, Leninists, Marxists, Marxist-Leninists, white supremacists, radicals who plotted to overthrow the monarchy (a notion with which Pagan sometimes had a modicum of sympathy), Libyans who sat in Mayfair and paid vast sums of money for explosives and weapons, Palestinians in Earl's Court scheming to get their homeland back—they were out there in the dark corners, murmuring, planning, talking to themselves, in an atmosphere of paranoia.

Pagan had had encounters with a great variety of them, from the silly groups that consisted of two or three very lonely people putting doomed home-made bombs together in garden sheds to groups like the Libyans, some of whom lived in bullet-proof apartments in the West End and controlled banks and had access to funds beyond reckoning. He knew their worlds. He knew that if there was to be any useful information about Ruhr and his associates it would be out there among the sympathizers and the financiers and fellow-travellers. It could be anything, an item of gossip, a whispered rumor, the kind of information that never percolated up from street level to official channels. And he wasn't going to get it sitting in Golden Square.

"I think I need a ride in the fresh air, Foxie. Will you get us a car?"

"A car?" Foxie thought that an early night would be the best thing for Pagan, but didn't say so.

"Car. Four wheels, chassis, internal combustion device—you remember."

Foxie smiled, picked up the telephone. The car was a Rover and Foxworth drove, following directions given to him by Pagan, who constantly consulted a small red notebook. This, Foxie realized, was Chairman Frank's famous Red Book, in which were said to be inscribed the names and addresses of all Pagan's connections in the terrorist network. It was Foxie's first sight of the legendary book.

They went first to an apartment belonging to Syrians in Dover Street, Mayfair, then to a Libyan house in Kensington, disturbing people who watched TV or prepared evening meals. At the Kensington house a party was going on, black tuxedos, ladies in cocktail dresses, delicate little sausages on toothpicks. Pagan didn't care that his timing was terrible. He was, Foxie noticed, in full flight and for the moment at least like the Pagan of old. No formalities, no niceties of etiquette, were going to get in his way. He helped himself to coffee, swallowed a sausage, and looked around as if the dinner party wasn't taking place at all. There was a lot of surly conversation, the kind that originates in suspicion and outright resentment. *We don't know Gunther Ruhr. We don't know anything about him or his friends. We are innocent of any illegal activities, Mr. Pagan—kindly leave us in peace or speak to our lawyers.* They all had lawyers nowadays, Pagan thought. They all had smooth-faced men in pricey pinstripes who manipulated legal niceties for hefty fees. Lawyers appalled Pagan. They had the moral awareness of toadstools and the untrammelled greed of very small spoiled children.

Next, a basement flat in Chelsea occupied by a group of very intense men who called themselves The Iranian Revolutionary Front aka TIRF. Acronyms were like test-tubes in which radicals appeared to spawn. If you didn't have a decent acronym you didn't have an image, and without an image no new recruits. TIRF opposed both the new Ayatollah *and* American imperialism. Pagan tried to goad them by asking about the ideological confusion in such a position, but they didn't want to be drawn into a dialogue with a reactionary policeman, the representative of a monarchy. They'd suffered under the Shah and to them the Queen of England might have been Pahlevi's wicked sister. The Iranians barely raised their faces from their bowls

of rice, avoiding eye-contact with both Pagan and Foxworth. A surly zero there.

Across the river after that, to a house overlooking
Battersea Park where a bald West German in a velvet
smoking-jacket spoke in a knowledgeable manner
about the terrorist connections between Europe and
Northern Ireland. *Perhaps Ruhr's working for the
Irish, Mr. Pagan*, the German suggested. Why import
Ruhr? Pagan wondered. The Irish had their own gang-
sters.

From Battersea to Wandsworth. In a prim semi-
detached house a lovely young Czech woman, who had
been arrested once for her membership in a gang of terrorists that had made an elaborate attempt to bomb the
Russian Embassy in Bonn, brewed cups of herbal tea
and denounced Gunther Ruhr for 'excessive violence'.
She didn't know where to find him, nor had she any
idea who had rescued him. In pursuit of the quiet life,
she'd lost touch with her former associates. Now she
grew organic vegetables and consulted the *I Ching* and
breast-fed a baby that had begun to cry in an adjoining
room. Like everyone else encountered during this
strange tour of Pagan's London, she knew nothing,
heard nothing. All was blind silence and frustration.
Houses in Camberwell and Whitechapel, inhabited by
Lebanese and Palestinians respectively, brought similar
results. Absolutely no information about Gunther
Ruhr or his employers or his rescuers made the underground circuit. Final.

On the way back to Golden Square Pagan said, "A
waste of bloody time."

"At least you put the word out," Foxie said.

"A fat lot of good, Foxie. Whoever employs Ruhr
works in complete secrecy. And the rescue operation

might have been carried out by phantoms. Nobody knows a damn thing."

Pagan and Foxworth rode in the elevator, an ancient iron coffin that clanged and rocked up to the second floor. Inside his office Pagan had another small taste of Auchentoshan and settled down behind his desk. He was out of breath. He'd gone beyond mere fatigue. He was in another world where you couldn't quite trust the evidence of the senses. It was like jet-lag magnified, almost as if you saw the world reflected in bevelled mirrors. He stared at the darkened window, listening to the faint whirring of the three computers on the floor below. It was just after midnight, and the silence of the streets accentuated the noise of the electronics, which were sinister to Pagan because he had no affinity with them.

I got up from my deathbed for you, Ruhr, he thought. I got up and I walked. You could at least provide me with a hint. You could at least tell me how much time I have left before you do something monstrous. The time factor! It was unsettling to be adrift on a planet whose only clock belonged to Gunther Ruhr.

Foxworth came into the office with a computer print-out. "This is what you wanted. Our computers analyzed all four hundred and seventeen names on the Home Office list, all people who arrived in the United Kingdom in the last month. Out of that lot, there are twenty-nine on whom we have active files of our own."

Pagan scanned the sheets with blurred eyes. Twenty-nine match-ups. That was practically a crowd. He had only eight investigators at his disposal. It wasn't possible to conduct twenty-nine investigations simultaneously. Even if he managed it somehow, by borrowing men from other departments, how could he be sure he wasn't wasting manpower and time? Since it was almost a certainty that neither Ruhr nor his associates had entered the UK legally, the names on the list would yield nothing. Twenty-nine!

"I think I'll stretch out on the sofa," he said. "Get some of the weight off my feet."

Foxworth frowned. "Wouldn't you be better off going home, Frank? Happy to drive you."

Pagan shook his head.

Determined bastard, Foxie thought. Frank had to have the constitution of a Clydesdale.

Pagan walked very slowly to the couch in the corner of the office. It was an old horsehair piece, overstuffed and creaky and cratered. Even though he lay down with great care, a shaft of pain pierced him and he moaned slightly. *Shit.* When you thought you had it silenced for the night, back it came just to remind you you're no longer master of your own system.

"I'd like a map," Pagan said. "A decent one that covers the whole Cambridge area."

"I have one in my own office."

"Bring it in here and pin it above my desk, will you?"

"Right away." Briskly, eager to please, even to pamper him, Foxie stepped out.

Flat on his back, Pagan raised the computer printout above his eyes and squinted at the list of names. Beneath each name was nationality, followed by the reasons why the person had been entered in SATO's computers in the first place. There was a Dutchman called Vanderberg known for his skill in building custom rifles, an American who had some questionable connections in the Lebanon, an Italian journalist notorious for his radical left-wing sympathies and his 'exclusive' interviews—florid and sycophantic—with fugitive terrorists. If Pagan couldn't find the time and manpower to run a check on the people who had access to the allegedly secret route used on the night of the Shepherd's Bush disaster, how could he justify the investigation of these twenty-nine, not one of whom suggested a plausible bridge to Gunther Ruhr?

And yet. How could he know for sure? Thoroughness was a bloody dictator. If you were Frank Pagan, you were imprisoned by your own exactitude. Everyone on the list would have to be contacted, interviewed even if only briefly, or watched. The likely outcome was that all twenty-nine would be eliminated from having any association with Gunther Ruhr. End of the matter. Heigh-ho. The joys of police work. The enviable glamour.

He was about to set the print-out aside, and ponder the matter of delegating the inquiries to cops purloined from some other department, when he noticed a name at the foot of the second page.

It blinded him at first. He thought he'd hallucinated it, a set of letters created by the morphine-like effect of Pethidine. He shut his eyes, hearing Foxie come inside the room, hearing Foxie say something about a map, noises off-stage, off-center, as if Foxworth had stepped toward the outer limits of the world and could barely be heard. Pagan opened his eyes. It was still there. Unchanged.

Dear Christ, how many years had passed?

Pagan turned his face toward Foxworth, who was standing on a chair and thumbtacking the map to the wall.

"Foxie," Pagan said.

Foxworth stepped down from the chair and moved across the room to the sofa. He thought Frank looked very odd all at once, as if more than pain troubled him.

"What's the matter? Is something wrong?" he asked.

Pagan pointed to the name on the sheet. Foxie looked closely. It meant nothing to him.

"I'd like to know where this person can be found, Foxie."

"It may take a little time."

"Do it."

There was an uncharacteristic note in Pagan's voice, the grumpy irritability of somebody confronted by a puzzle he couldn't understand, one he thought he'd solved a long time ago.

Foxie wrote the name down.

From the window of her hotel room Magdalena Torrente saw the expanse of darkness that was Hyde Park. Black and whispering, it created a shadow at the heart of London. It was a long time since Magdalena had been in England. It would be pleasant to come one day as a tourist, spend some time, see sights. This trip, like the last one, was going to be brief.

The last time here: she didn't want to think about that.

She shut the window, looked at her watch. It was two AM. She moved across the room, pushed the bathroom door open, saw her own reflection in the fluorescent glare of the tiled toilet, dark circles under her eyes and colorless lips. She considered makeup, but he didn't like her in cosmetics. A real woman, he sometimes said, doesn't need to paint herself into falsehood.

She lay on the bed. The elevator rumbled in the shaft along the corridor. It stopped, the doors slid open. Magdalena closed her eyes and listened carefully. The thick carpet in the hallway muffled the movement of anyone passing. *Do you trust him?* She wondered why

Garrido's objectionable question came back to her now. Old men knew how to ask tiresome questions. Old men with ambitions, like Garrido, could be especially taxing. Running out of time, they needed answers in a hurry. All their questions were blunt ones. *Do you trust him?*

She heard the key turn in the lock. She pretended to sleep. It was part of a lover's game. He would kiss her awake from a sleep he knew wasn't genuine. He came inside the room very quietly and crossed the floor and she felt the mattress yield as he sat down beside her. He raised her hands to his lips. She felt her pulses jump and her heartbeat rage. He did this to her without fail. The touch of his flesh made her fall apart, a sweet disintegration that was like nothing else she'd ever felt. She lost herself along the way, imploded, turned to fragments. Sometimes she couldn't remember her own name. Love's amnesia. She had no patience when it came to him. She took his hand and guided it between her legs. Her short skirt—he liked them short—slipped up her thighs. She wore nothing under the skirt. His hand went directly to the core of her and she gasped because she felt as if he'd penetrated some secret she'd been keeping from the rest of the world. He knew her in the most intimate ways, the deepest ways. She spread her legs, astounded by her own wetness. His finger went inside her and she moaned, biting on her lip because she knew she'd scream if she didn't keep her mouth closed. She turned slightly, reaching out for him. He was hard and ready and beautiful. Her lover. Her love. She said his name once, twice, lingering over syllables until they became meaninglessly joyful, less like sounds than delicate tastes in her mouth.

He tugged the skirt from her hips, slid the blouse from her shoulders. He kissed her breasts, her throat, her mouth, and each time his lips touched her skin she felt a delightful giddiness. She was in flight and soaring. She closed the palm of her hand around his cock and stroked it softly, drawing it closer to her own body as she did so. Sheer impatience made her bold and aggressive. She spread her legs as widely as she could and led him inside her, then she locked her heels on his spine, rocking him, hard then harder, as if she were trying to trap something that couldn't quite be caught, an essence, an elusive moment.

Hard, harder still, she held on to him, and the dance grew quicker and simpler and more forcefully intimate until nothing separated her from him. There was only love and this insane freefalling bliss. She bit his shoulder and clawed his back, arching her hips, lifting herself up to intensify the connection, and then she came and kept coming until she was quite drained and he'd gone limp inside her. They collapsed together in silence, both breathless, both very still, paralyzed.

When finally she got up from the bed her thighs felt weak, her legs distant. She walked to the window and gazed out over the park. A match was struck, a cigarette lit. The room filled with the acrid smell of tobacco. She turned, seeing his face in the pale red glow of his cigarette. She moved back toward the bed. It was always this way; she immediately wanted him again, as if the first encounter had been nothing more than preamble, a surface scratched. There were other levels to reach, other satisfactions to be had. He drew on his cigarette and the reddish glow illuminated his bare chest.

"Your goodies are on the bedside table," she said.

She saw him smile. It was a good smile, lively and attractive, open and genuine. She loved his face. If she were blinded she would have known the face by touch alone, its familiar topography. She shivered because the intimacy of all this overwhelmed her. At times, her careless sense of love frightened her. Only if you consider futures, she thought. The trick is to live in the moment. That way you can't think of fate. Fate is what happens tomorrow.

"You're too thoughtful," he said.

"How can anybody be too thoughtful? I like doing things for you. I think about you all the time. I can't get you out of my head. I try, you know. I wake up and I tell myself—I must have a day, one lousy day, when I don't think about him. And it never happens."

He was quiet for a long time. He stubbed out his cigarette. Then he said, "Do you think it's any different for me?"

"I hope you suffer the way I do." She tried to make this sound light-hearted but it came out with more gravity than she'd intended. She sat on the bed and took his hand, pressing the palm over a breast. "I want us to be together. Always together. I hate the way we're kept apart."

"It's a matter of time."

"Patience isn't one of my virtues. I have to practice it. Every time we meet I panic when I think of how little time we have together. I want it to be different."

"Soon. Everything will be fine soon." The welcome certitude in his voice filled her with hope. Things would work out in the end because they had to. She had the same uncomplicated belief in the triumph of love some people have in the prophetic qualities of the stars. Other men paled by comparison now. She thought of how he dominated her imagination. In the few times when she considered this love clearly, she saw it as some form of addiction, as demanding as any narcotic.

"Did you have any problems?" he asked.

"With the money?" She shook her head. "I sailed straight through. I knew I would. I have this look I sometimes do—haughty and regal. Nobody meddles with it. Especially customs officials." She gestured toward the closet. "It's all there. I put it in a briefcase. Exactly the way you like it."

"You do everything the way I like," he said.

She laughed. She had a laugh that was a little too deep to be ladylike. "I want to please you," she said.

He stroked her breast almost absent-mindedly. He had moments like this when an essential part of him disappeared. She was frightened by these times. They undermined her, riddled her already frail sense of security. She went to the bathroom, filled a glass with water, returned to the bed.

"Garrido isn't sure about you," she said.

"At times Garrido's an old woman."

"He's still sharp. He's intuitive. He knows what I feel for you, but I'm not sure he approves."

"Garrido worries me, Magdalena. His age—"

"You can't go back on your promise," she said. "Garrido and everyone else on the Committee expect some kind of positions of authority. They think of themselves as the provisional government in exile. It's been that way for years. He sees himself as the Minister of the Interior or something just as elevated. It's the only thing he lives for. He's a hero in the community. You can't even *think* of excluding him."

He sighed, patted the back of her hand. "It's going to be all right. I'll keep my word."

The atmosphere in the room had changed slightly. There was a vague darkness all at once, almost a gloom. She knew what it was. She'd opened the door and allowed Garrido to come inside, Garrido and all the politics of *el exilio*. This bedroom was sacrosanct, a place for lovers only, not for politics, and dreams, and plots.

She wanted to dispel the melancholy. Lightness, something trivial. She reached to the bedside table and picked up the small silver bowl containing cubes, each nicely wrapped with the name of the hotel written on them. She undid one, held it out, popped it in the man's mouth. It was another game they played together, another tiny familiarity.

She laid the tip of her finger between his lips. Then she kissed him. The small crystals of sugar that adhered to his tongue made the kiss wildly sweet.

"I love you," she said. She whispered his name several times. She'd been taught as a child that when you said a word often enough you understood its true meaning, its innermost reality. So she repeated her lover's name, searching for an intimacy inside an intimacy, a revelation, the blinding insight that she was loved as much as she loved. She wanted the ultimate security.

He made her sit on the edge of the bed, then he gently parted her legs. She watched him, with anticipation and delight, as he kneeled on the floor, his mouth level with her knees. She continued to observe his face as it disappeared into the shadows between her thighs and then she trembled, throwing back her head and closing her eyes, her hands made into slack fists, her mouth open.

A voice that was not her own said *I love you, Rafael. I love you.*

New York

It was ten PM local time and drizzling lightly all across

the Eastern seaboard when Kenzaburo Magiwara arrived at Kennedy Airport. He passed nimbly through customs and immigration where his passport, densely stamped, much-used, caused the immigration officer to make a mild joke about how Mr. Magiwara should have a season ticket to America. Magiwara never smiled. It was not just that occidental humor eluded him, which was true; it was more the fact that the mask of his face had not been built for easy merriment. To most Europeans Magiwara bore a strong resemblance to a younger version of the late Emperor Hirohito. Small saddles of flesh sagged under his eyes and his mouth was arrogant. He emitted a sense of power, although its precise source was hard to locate. Did it come from the sharp little eyes and the impression they'd seen every hand of poker ever played? Was it from the disdainful mouth, about which there was some slight secretive quality? Or was it something more simple—like the assured way the man moved, as if he knew doors were going to be opened for him before he reached them, as if he understood that flunkies were going to attend to his baggage and transportation and that all the insignificant details of his life were taken care of by others?

A chauffeured limousine was waiting just outside the Pan Am terminal. It transported Magiwara in the direction of Manhattan. He sat in the back, feeling a little sleepy, looking forward to his arrival at the apartment he owned on Central Park South. It had been a good trip, at least in the sense that the Society of Friends had seen fit to continue on its present course.

Magiwara was the first Japanese ever to have been invited to join the Society, which connected him to a world wherein enormous profits could be made and fortunes increased beyond dreams. It was a form of freemasonry, although he had no prejudices in that direction.

Quite the contrary, secret societies had existed in Japan for centuries and Magiwara had been associated with a few of them in his time—business groups, fraternities of a political nature, religious organizations.

But the Society of Friends was different. It had no secret handshakes, no secret languages, no rituals of indoctrination, no masonic trappings. The Society, although profoundly secretive and jealous of its own anonymity, had gone beyond those forms of play-acting. It promised more than fabulous wealth, it pledged a share in power, in shaping the destinies of countries like Cuba, sinking under the miserable weight of Communist mismanagement. The Society assured personal contact with history. It rendered senseless the notion that men were powerless before destiny. Some men, such as the members of the Society, could make an amazing difference. That they could make incalculable fortunes at the same time was not unattractive.

Magiwara gazed through his glasses into the drizzly streets. He believed he had a great deal to contribute to the Society, some of whose members bore him a residual resentment for his race. Caporelli, for example, had always seemed vaguely indifferent to him, and the two Americans, whom he didn't trust, treated him with the condescension of men who have eaten sushi once and, finding it deplorable, have condemned all of Japanese culture as being crude.

Magiwara knew he'd overcome these obstacles in time. He'd never yet been defeated by a hurdle placed in his way. At the age of fifty-eight he had amassed a personal fortune of seventy-three million dollars. Membership in the Society of Friends would increase that sum a hundredfold. The legality of the Society's business didn't perplex him. He knew there were gray areas, underexplored by routine capitalists, in which creative men might construct profitable enterprises. Such as Cuba, he thought.

He had studied the Society's history, at least the little that had been made available to him in the archives, stored in a bank-vault in the Italian town of Bari. These documents provided a broad outline of the Society's development, from the late nineteenth century when it had come into existence as a banking adjunct to the Mafia, laundering Sicilian money, investing it discreetly and legally, managing it as it grew. Then through the 1920s and 30s when the Society, reorganizing and naming itself for the first time The Society of Friends, a title whose ironic religious resonance escaped Magiwara, had seen the urgent need to move away from the violent excesses and the adverse publicity generated by men like Capone. The Society, far more secretive than the Mafia—which had become a public corporation, a soap opera, its innermost workings exposed for all and sundry to relish—now existed quite apart from the organization that had spawned it. Few contemporary Mafiosi even knew of the Society's existence. If they'd heard of it at all it was only as ancient history, an obscure group that had gone out of existence before the Second World War, having 'lost' considerable sums of the Mafia's money in 'regrettable market trading'. In fact, the missing money had been embezzled cleanly away by officers of the Society and now the Society owned banks and investment houses that had once belonged to the great financial barons of the West, managed funds, manipulated massive amounts of the currencies that flowed between the stock exchanges of different countries. It influenced prices on the world's markets, funded anti-Communist movements in Central America, Asia, and Africa. It never avoided its fiscal responsibilities. Its various fronts—banks, financial houses, shipping companies—all paid taxes in the countries where they were located. Whenever difficulties arose, whenever there was a tax dispute, these disagreements were always somehow settled very quietly, man to man, banker to revenue officer, and the Society of Friends was never mentioned. It moved unobtrusively and swiftly like a great shark seeking the shadowy places where it might be glimpsed but never identified. Sinewy, elegant, contemptuous of weakness, indifferent to ethics, it was firmly entrenched in the structure of world capitalism. And Kenzaburo Magiwara was a part of this great organization.

He looked out of the limousine. Almost home. He laid his hands on his thighs, drummed his delicate fingers. There was a skeletal delicacy about his whole body, as if his skin were no more than one thin membranous layer stretched tightly across bone. The delicacy was more apparent than real. Magiwara was hard and acquisitive and ambitious. Apart from accumulating a personal fortune, he also owned two United States congressmen, a British Member of Parliament, a Christian Democrat in Italy, two members of the Austrian *Bundesrat*, and assorted police chiefs in European and Asian cities—all useful acquisitions.

The big car slowed to a halt at a traffic signal. The rainy street was quiet, practically empty save for a small car, a black Dodge Colt that slowed alongside the limousine. Magiwara paid it no attention.

The light changed from red to green. The limousine didn't move. Magiwara leaned forward and tapped the smoked-glass partition separating him from the driver. There was no response. He pressed the button that rolled the partition down.

It was the strangest thing. The driver wasn't behind the wheel. Magiwara raised himself up, peered into the driving compartment, thinking that his driver had suffered something—a heart attack, say—and slithered to the floor. But he wasn't anywhere in the vehicle.

Puzzled, not panicked, Magiwara frowned. He was aware of the Dodge Colt alongside, which also hadn't moved. A side window opened in the small car. Magiwara anticipated a face, but none appeared.

The rolled-down window revealed only a darkness in which something metallic glinted. It took him only a moment to recognize the object. It was blunt, terrible, archaic, and he was seized by a sense of unreality, of some awful mistake being perpetrated here.

The blast of the sawed-off shotgun rocked the limousine. It crashed through the glass and all Magiwara heard just before it blew his face away was the piercing sound of shaved air and eternity.

6

Gunther Ruhr listened to the tiresome sound of a ping-pong ball clicking on the surface of a table. He rose from the narrow iron bed and went to the doorway of the living-room, on the far side of which two men were casually playing table tennis. Everything here irritated Ruhr, not just the racket of the ball but also this isolated house surrounded by mud and broken chicken coops and the bitter smell of dry rot that filled his nostrils night after night. A chill rain fell predictably every afternoon, but mainly what depressed him was the company he was obliged to keep.

There were four men in all. They had taken part in Ruhr's rescue from the English police, and he admired their reckless courage—but on a simple social level they tended to talk in single syllables, or when speech failed them, as it often did, they grunted. When you'd been stuck for days in a run-down farmhouse with no fellowship save the noise of the rain on the window and nothing to read but a mildewed Baedeker's 1913 *Handbook for Paris* (the only volume he'd found in the whole house), you needed some kind of diversion, which Baedeker couldn't supply: *In the Rue St. Martin, opposite St. Nicolas-de-Champs, is one of the chief entrances to the vast network of Sewers which undermine Paris . . .*

The two preening Argentineans, Flavell and Zapino, were dark-faced characters who spent a great deal of time running combs through their slick black hair. Now and again they'd congratulate themselves for the successful rescue of Ruhr, as if they were men at a school reunion remembering old pranks. When there was nothing to interest them on the old black and white TV, they dismantled weapons and cleaned them. They looked like contented lovers at such times. Yesterday morning Flavell had accidentally discharged a pistol, firing it into the ceiling and causing great consternation.

The other pair, the ping-pong players, were the Americans, one a cadaverous man called Trevaskis (the most articulate of the four; no great compliment), the other a pale white giant known, rather ordinarily, as Rick. The Americans kept to themselves, conversing in a form of English that Ruhr found hard to follow. Street patois, slang, mangled words. Trevaskis, who was all bone, and whose eyes shone with a missionary fervor, looked across the room at Gunther Ruhr.

There was contempt in the look. It was an expression Ruhr inspired in other people, one he'd seen all his life. People tended to step away from him, as if they intuited some terrible quality in him, a thing both lifeless and contagious. When they were too stubborn to move, they gazed just as Trevaskis was doing now, trying to stare down the demon. It amused the German.

He sometimes thought of himself as a prism in which other people might glimpse a blackly intimidating aspect of the human condition.

Trevaskis, something of a joker, said, "Sleep well, Mr. Claw?"

The giant Rick, dressed in white t-shirt and blue jeans, smiled. He smiled at everything Trevaskis said. The two Argentineans put their combs away and turned to look. Ruhr remained in the doorway, folding his arms across his chest. The Claw. He neither liked nor disliked his nickname. It had been created by the press, merchants who traded in revulsion.

The same press had bestowed the status of legend on him, and he was pleased by that. He kept clippings under the floorboards of the tiny attic apartment he secretly maintained in the Schwabing area of Munich. These invariably referred to his lack of moral values and his coldness toward human suffering. He was called barbarous, a monster. He sometimes leafed through the cuttings and felt removed from these descriptions. They missed the point. It wasn't so much his *lack* of certain qualities. It was more the fact that he considered ordinary human virtues undesirable. Everybody wanted love and affection: therefore they were commonplace and debased. Everybody deplored needless violence: therefore it was acceptable. Ruhr's logic was based on perversity. What other men might strive for, Ruhr wanted to destroy. What some men might exalt, Ruhr ridiculed. The sea of his feelings ran contrary to any common tide. Even his physical deformity, which he liked because he thought it mirrored the inner Ruhr, separated him from other people. He was alone in the world. He'd never felt any other way.

Ruhr stepped into the living-room. He raised the perfect hand to his face, stroked the firm jaw. An intriguing aspect of the recent misadventure in Cambridge was that suddenly, after years of anonymity, he had recognizable features! He was a public figure whose photograph had been printed in newspapers all over the world! His face was almost as well-known as that of any movie star, which was not an altogether unpleasant novelty. He liked it the way any actor, formerly obliged to perform as a masked character, might enjoy recognition after years of doing his best work in the shadows.

He caught the ping-pong ball in midair and closed his left hand around it. "We have work to do. Tomorrow is the day."

The four men were silent. They watched Ruhr closely. They were more than his rescuers, more than the soldiers in his command, they were also his guards, instructed by the Cuban to keep him from harm, to limit his movements and make sure he didn't repeat the disastrous business in Cambridge. Ruhr had nothing but disdain for the men who bought his services. He had no sense of being an employee. Instead he considered himself the master of those who hired him. Nor did he ever trust the men who paid him, because they were usually slaves of one ideology or another, lackeys to this obsession or that. They seldom had themselves under control; consequently, they were unable to control anything around them.

The Cuban, for example: Ruhr no more trusted him than he believed in God. You could see all the Cuban's wretched ambition in his eyes, in every word he spoke, every gesture he made. He'd come here two days ago, breathing fire, warning Ruhr not to screw things up, trying to hide the fact he was afraid because his aspirations were menaced, and Ruhr had played the obedient little dog with a theatrical contrition the

Cuban, wrapped up in his own aims, apparently missed. Yessir, yessir. I'll be good, sir.

What the Cuban did not know was that Gunther Ruhr always took precautions for his own safety; documents, papers, numbers of bank accounts, copies of cashier's checks, diaries describing assignments and naming names—these were in sealed boxes in the possession of a certain Herr Wilhelm Schiller, a lawyer in Hamburg, who had instructions to open them only in the event of Ruhr's death or disappearance. Ruhr believed in protecting himself.

Now the four men were watching over him, sentries circling the cage of an unpredictable madman. Ruhr was thrilled by the idea of creating tension in other people.

"Get the map," he said.

The Argentineans produced a detailed Ordnance Survey map. Ruhr spread it on the table. He had an amazing memory, a mind that seized the essential details of anything and stored them for instant recall at any future date. He had studied this map once and he didn't need to look at it again for his own sake. He was rehearsing the others.

He pointed to a minor road that ran between woodlands. There was a windmill to the east, a canal in the west. A mile past the windmill was the crucial fork in the road. A thin pathway ran in one direction toward a dairy farm; the other tine, smooth and concrete, sliced through more woodland, lovely and dense and unfenced, affording marvellous opportunities for concealment and surprise. Here and there on the map were villages and hamlets. The only village of interest, Ruhr said, was the one known as St. Giles. Six miles beyond St. Giles it was the airfield of the East Anglia Flying Club. This was the most crucial location in the whole operation. If Ruhr and his men were somehow prevented from reaching the airfield, they would separate. If they were not already dead, Ruhr added, and smiled in his usual thin way, the expression of a man whose sense of humor, misunderstood by all, had doomed him to a life of smiling alone.

The Argentineans asked questions about time. They both wore very expensive watches and they believed that these instruments had to be 'seenchronized'. Ruhr told them that time was his own business, something he kept to himself for security reasons. The South Americans understood and became silent.

Ruhr folded the map. He went inside the kitchen. Eggshells, bacon rinds, twisted pieces of cellophane, matches, cigarette butts, open jars of meat paste—trash everywhere. Ruhr filled a glass with water, drank slowly. He didn't like the chaos in this room. He preferred a world of clean angles and well-defined spaces. But it wasn't always possible to live in such a perfect universe. All too often there were intrusions, such as this kitchen and its dirty disorder.

Or the girl in Cambridge . . .

He remembered her unsunned thighs and the way she'd shivered when she'd taken her jeans off and how she'd drawn a thin curtain across the window, trying to look provocative but succeeding only in appearing pathetic. And then the expression on her face when the steel gleamed on his hand—she'd screamed, and after that came the chaos and ignominy of capture.

He remembered the policeman called Pagan who asked all kinds of questions. Ruhr made up stories, weaving them off the top of his head. Like any good storyteller, he believed in his fictions. He was a salesman with a line in time-share condominiums, an absent-minded Egyptologist on a backpacking vacation, an urbane professor of Swiss Literature (a part-time occupation, you understand, he'd said to an unsmiling Pagan)—identities, some of them amusing to him, flooded Ruhr as fast as he could assume them.

Pagan refused to be entertained by the ever-changing cast of characters. He'd been demanding. Frustrated, he'd thump his fist on the table in the interview room. At other moments he tried to disguise his irritation by falling silent and looking directly into Ruhr's eyes. The Englishman had determined gray eyes, but Ruhr had met their challenge without flinching. And now the English cop was wounded, or so the TV news had said. Lying in a hospital bed, Ruhr thought, frustrated and angry and desperate. A man like that could be extremely dangerous if he were out on the streets. A man like that wasn't likely to be confined too long to a hospital.

But he had the measure of Pagan; he was confident of that. Pagan was dogged, but clearly not inspired. In a contest between himself and the Englishman, his own superiority would triumph every time. Pagan had intuitions, of course, but they would be dull compared to Ruhr's own. Ruhr could slip in and out of other souls; Frank Pagan, at best, could only hope to read—by means of emotional braille—other people's behavior and through this slight empathy predict their future actions. Guesswork! Ruhr had no affinity with anything so unreliable. He put his credence only in certainty, and the supreme certainty was his faith in himself.

Ruhr raised his glass to his lips. The memory of the girl was still strong. She hadn't been beautiful, perhaps not even pretty, but Ruhr didn't care about ordinary beauty. Her paleness, her fragility, glass to be shattered—that was what had attracted him. But then he'd become blinded by his need to put the deformed hand inside her and twist it upward into her womb, and hear flesh come away, that soft whimpering sound of skin and sinew torn and muscle cut. Usually the girls fainted. Sometimes they bled to death. At such times it seemed to Ruhr that he wasn't entirely involved in these acts, that he stood outside himself, hypnotized by his own need to dominate and hurt, entranced by the simplicity, the purity, of power. There was another factor too, and that was his curiosity about the female anatomy, the way it worked, the intricate arrangement of womb and tubes, a fascination that had begun when he'd first seen a medical text at the age of eight and glimpsed, in a rose-colored sectional diagram, the soft pink secrets of the female interior, and its essential vulnerability. The sight of it aroused a perplexing hunger inside the young boy Ruhr had been, and he'd never forgotten those detailed sketches. For a time he had toyed with the notion of becoming a doctor, perhaps a gynaecologist, but the idea had lost its intrigue, vanquished by Ruhr's preference for destruction over restoration.

Now what troubled him was to have been caught in Cambridge so stupidly! Was it slackness? Was he too old at thirty-seven to be as cautious, as vigilant, as he'd always been? Why hadn't he clamped a hand round the girl's mouth and silenced her? Was he becoming simply blasé, arrogant to the point of indifference? Or had it come down to something more elemental: the idea of creating a contest for himself, his own brilliance matched against another mind, a protagonist—Frank Pagan, for example? Was Pagan even worthy of that consideration?

Trevaskis came into the kitchen. "It's cold, Ruhr. The guys want permission to light a fire."

"No fire," Ruhr said. He disliked Trevaskis. The

other men were acquiescent, but Trevaskis had an independent streak that was going to prove troublesome in the end. The American would have to be watched over. "What would happen if somebody saw smoke from the chimney? Perhaps you would rather go up on the roof and wave a big red flag?"

Trevaskis shrugged. Ruhr's sarcasm didn't go down big with him. A silver St. Christopher around his neck shimmered. "This place isn't exactly a day at the beach, Ruhr."

"As long as I'm in charge, my friend, there will be no fire. When you remember how much you're being paid, Trevaskis, you'll find that discomfort has a way of becoming tolerable."

Trevaskis fingered his medallion. He had never worked with Ruhr before. He thought the German unstable, like an unpinned hand-grenade in a closed fist. The business with the metal claw—what sort of sick shit was that? And then the goddam rescue, which had cost the lives of the Australian and the other guy, the little Swede called Anderssen—all that stoked Trevaskis's general resentment. He wasn't going to get into a fight with Ruhr, though. When this job was finished, there was going to be a quarter of a million dollars in hard cash, and you didn't blow off that kind of bonanza. You didn't let Ruhr do anything to fuck it up either. The Cuban guy had quietly promised Trevaskis there would be a big bonus if Ruhr behaved himself.

"You're the boss," Trevaskis said. *The fucking fuhrer,* he thought.

Ruhr drained his glass and set it down in the sink. He let his left hand touch the pistol tucked into the waistband of his corduroy pants. "Keep that fact in mind, Trevaskis."

"It's like tattooed right here," and Trevaskis

tapped his head. *Asshole.* He shivered in an exaggerated way, blowing on his hands as he shuffled toward the door of the kitchen.

"One other matter," Ruhr said. "This room needs to be cleaned. If the men are complaining of cold, a little hard work might quickly warm them up."

"Great idea," Trevaskis remarked.

"You're so agreeable I feel I can delegate the task to you with every confidence."

Trevaskis smiled oddly. "Spick and span. Shipshape. Every surface like a mirror. Count on it."

Ruhr said, "You know what cleanliness is next to."

"I've heard."

Ruhr raised his deformed hand suddenly and laid the palm on Trevaskis's shoulder. He watched with some delight the American flinch, then try to conceal his gesture of revulsion behind a stupid little grin.

"Godliness," Ruhr said. "If you believe in God."

Trevaskis didn't move.

"I have no such belief," Ruhr went on. "This hand, for example. Would a caring God allow a child to be born with a deformity like this? Why would any God wish to punish an innocent child? What sin could I possibly have committed in my mother's womb to deserve to be born a freak?"

Trevaskis said nothing. Ruhr's touch offended him. But how could he back away without admitting a surrender of some kind?

"I lie," Ruhr said. "I wasn't born this way at all, Trevaskis. I was born with five fingers. Perfectly natural. When I was twelve I took my mother's kitchen-knife and I hacked off the two middle fingers. I remember a rather boring juvenile desire to understand pain. So I experimented on the only subject available—myself."

Trevaskis moved an inch or so, getting out from under the hand. But Ruhr was quick. He brought his palm up to Trevaskis's cheek and laid it there. It was an odd gesture that might have been affectionate in some other circumstances, but here it was sinister. Ruhr's clammy flesh had a strange smell to it, like decay. Trevaskis stood motionless. He wanted to smack Ruhr's hand away. This close to the German you could practically hear him ticking.

Ruhr said, "I was a child wonder, Trevaskis. A marvel. At the age of eight I had read Kant. I found the Categorical Imperative less of a directive than the urge to discover what lay under a girl's skirt, which I did at ten." Here Ruhr laughed in a dry, quiet way.

"By the time I was eleven, I knew how to make gunpowder. First the intellectual pursuits, then the sexual, finally the destructive. I learned one thing with great certainty: the effect of a bomb is more immediate than all Kant's philosophy. The only way to kill a man with Kant is to strike him over the head with the Complete Works in German."

There were elements of truth in Ruhr's brief narrative. He'd read Kant at eight, as he claimed, and he had indeed learned to make gunpowder at eleven. But these strands had become so interwoven with myth that they were hard to separate: he no longer knew if he'd been born deformed or caused it to happen. He no longer cared either way. The reality of his past was often mundane, so he altered it. Self-mutilation was much more intriguing than some genetic error.

Ruhr had been born in Munich, the child of itinerant fundamentalists who were members of a proselytizing American sect with headquarters in Baton Rouge, hard-core scriptural believers who thought Galileo and Darwin brothers of Satan. Ruhr's parents, both rather distant persons who considered their very bright child something of an unexpected encumbrance, moved around Europe with such frequency that a three-week lease on a cheap apartment was deemed stability. It became clear to Gunther Ruhr that he was needless baggage to his parents—gaunt people with bright, spacey eyes and a disarmingly naive zest for accosting strangers on street corners and shoving fundamentalist pamphlets into their hands. They despised the child, and he in turn was embarrassed by them and what seemed to him the sham of their religious beliefs: God was a mass of philosophical contradictions, so why bother with Him? Life was simpler without a deity.

Somewhere along the way, Ruhr's parents managed to leave him behind. Either they simply forgot him in their religious obsession or were too troubled by his outspoken cleverness, and his inclination toward atheism, to want his company. He was boarded out at a variety of schools where his natural brightness overwhelmed all around him. Abstract subjects were grasped in moments and committed forever to a memory that was a well-tooled trap. Other students bored him, wasted his time. He befriended nobody. At the age of sixteen he qualified for a place at the University of Hamburg, which he entered during a time of social unrest when student activists were erecting barricades in streets. Attracted by destruction, thrilled by streets made foggy from tear-gas and the daily battles against the police, Ruhr came to life as he'd never before. He discovered in himself a knack for subterfuge, an affinity for the cellars where people made up revolutions and schemed to bring society down. He was a natural.

At the age of seventeen, he took part in his first bank robbery, led by a student radical shot and killed in the course of the theft. Ruhr took the fallen leader's place without asking or being asked. For the next two years he and his gang robbed banks throughout Europe. During this time Ruhr developed all manner of alliances that would later form the foundation of his terrorist network.

In 1974, he was contacted in Rome by a representative from a certain Middle Eastern nation who needed some 'demolition' work done—the bombing of an airplane, to be specific. Ruhr, amazed that he was being offered such a large sum of money to undertake a task he might have done for nothing save expenses, accepted the assignment.

It was his first *real* act of mercenary terrorism. By contrast, bank robberies were trifles, small local jobs with no international significance. The airplane, with crew and one hundred and eighteen passengers, exploded on the ground at Tel Aviv. Ruhr remembered the fascinating newspaper pictures, the TV shots. It was at this time he began to make a scrapbook of his deeds. The press, interested in Ruhr's terrorist activities for some time, uncovered his role in the tragedy and began to delve into what little was known of his history. With that strange fascination newspapermen always reserve for people of high intelligence gone somehow 'wrong', journalists turned Ruhr into that archetype of brilliance and violence combined, the 'mad genius', 'the sick boy wonder'. It was at this time too he first wore the strange stainless steel prosthetic device and discovered that his taste for destruction, that unfathomable need, went beyond the bombing of airplanes.

Now Ruhr smiled at Trevaskis, then let the hand fall back to his side. "You hated me touching you, didn't you?"

Trevaskis's mouth was dry. "It didn't faze me, Ruhr."

Ruhr said, "You're a bad liar. Nobody likes me to touch them. I can feel their revulsion. This interesting appendage"—and here he turned the hand over and over—"creates abhorrence in other people, which they try either to disguise as sympathy, or ignore. Such fools. I see through people, Trevaskis. I read the fine print on their hearts."

Trevaskis moved toward the kitchen door. He wanted to get away from Ruhr. Sometimes you looked into another man's eyes and what you saw there was unknowable. It was like dark mysterious water when you had no sounding instrument to probe the depths. Ruhr, whether truthful or lying, gave Trevaskis the impression of an unpleasant illusion done with mirrors.

"Now clean this horrible place," Ruhr said.

The giant Rick appeared just then, bending his head a little to clear the top of the door. He had watery brown eyes and a mouth too small for his enormous white face. He gave the impression of great physical strength without a mind to direct it.

"There's somebody out front," he said. His voice was a whisper.

"Who?" Ruhr asked.

"I didn't get a real good look. I saw somebody step across the front yard and go behind the vehicle."

"One? More than one?" Ruhr asked.

"Only saw one," Rick replied.

Ruhr moved quickly out of the kitchen. He went from the living-room to his bedroom, the window of which looked directly out into the yard. He parted the damp yellow blind an eighth of an inch: all he saw was the Range Rover in the heavy, slanting rain. And yet he had a feeling of a scene recently disturbed, a stillness through which some trespasser has moved. He couldn't say why, simply an old instinct. He took the pistol from his waistband, returned to the living-room. When he moved with stealth and speed he was impressive, graceful, a man whose quiet elegance had been honed by more than fifteen years of surreptitious acts.

The Argentineans had automatic rifles clutched in their arms. Trevaskis and Rick carried handguns.

"Flavell, Zapino, stay at the windows, but don't show yourself," Ruhr said. "Trevaskis, you and Rick cover me from the kitchen."

"You're going out there?" Trevaskis asked.

Ruhr didn't answer. He was already moving to the kitchen. There was a side door that opened on to the place where the rundown chicken hatches were located.

"Wait," Trevaskis said. "Let somebody else go outside. You oughta stay here."

Ruhr heard nothing. When he was involved in action he closed his senses down to anything extraneous. Action was everything, singleminded, demanding all one's concentration. He opened the kitchen door softly. The cold mid-afternoon rain stung his face. He loved the sensation. Trevaskis stood behind, whispering his useless objections.

"You shouldn't go out there. Stay in here, for Chrissakes."

Ruhr stared across the mud. Raindrops rattled the old coops. He took a step outside. He was insubstantial now, merging with the elements, a kind of transformation that Trevaskis could only admire from the kitchen doorway. This was no ordinary man sneaking through the rain with a gun: Ruhr melted into the grayness of the weather, as if the rain created a funnel of camouflage around him.

Ruhr reached the corner of the house. He looked at the Range Rover. The muddy yard was empty. He stood motionless against the wall of the house. Water ran from his thin hair over the lids of his eyes. Then he heard the sound, something that lay under the incessant squabble of the rain, a wet noise but different, a squelching pressure on soft mud.

And there she was.

A child, a girl dressed in school uniform, short black skirt and maroon blazer and long maroon scarf trailing over her shoulder. She was running, breaking free from the cover of the Rover, but the black mud fettered her movements and disturbed her balance. She was heading toward the slope that rose up behind the farmhouse, arms stretched on either side for equilibrium, a dancer in the slime. Ruhr went after her, enjoying the certainty of catching her. He moved with long strides, strong ones, cutting down the distance between himself and the girl at will. Her beret flew off. Her short blond hair quickly became soaked with rain.

Ruhr grabbed her around the waist before she was even half way up the slope. He swung her round to face him and she blinked from all the rainwater in her eyes. Through her soaked blouse could be seen the small white brassiere she wore. She tried to tear herself away, but Ruhr, laughing, moved behind her and locked one arm tightly under her chin, forcing her tiny face back.

"Why were you spying?"

"Shit, you're hurting me."

Ruhr applied more pressure. "What were you doing sneaking around my house?"

"Nothing . . . cross my heart . . . let me go!"

Ruhr released her and she rubbed her neck at the place where he'd bruised her.

"I can hardly breathe," she said.

"You'll be all right."

"I live a few miles away, I wanted to say hello, introduce myself, but you're obviously not friendly—"

Ruhr said, "If you're so innocent, why did you run?"

She shook her wet hair. "Scared."

"Scared? Of what?"

"The gun in your hand," the girl said. She walked a few steps, reached down to pick up her beret, turned it round between her fingers. Ruhr watched the short skirt rise upon her young thigh. The expanse of flesh between the knee-length stockings and the hem of the risen skirt was all the more provocative for its innocence. She was slim, and pretty in the awkward fashion of the young. Insecure about her own looks, uncertain about her place in the world, she projected a fragile sexuality that had never been touched nor aroused nor explored.

Ruhr put the gun in his waistband.

"I'll leave," the girl said. "I won't bother you again, I swear it."

"Tell me your name first."

"Steffie."

"What a very ugly name," Ruhr said.

"Stephanie then."

"That's better." It occurred to Ruhr that he could let this girl walk away. By tomorrow morning he'd be gone from this place anyhow. What did it matter? He looked down at the house; he thought he saw the shadows of the two South Americans in the windows.

"Well," the girl said, and there was a flutter of fear in her voice. "I suppose I'd better leave."

Ruhr watched her face. There was renewed anxiety in her eyes and her mouth had become very tense. And of course he knew why.

"I can't let you go."

She backed away. "I didn't see anything. I swear I didn't."

He stepped toward her. She slipped as she moved backward. She lay in the mud, the skirt above her waist, white underwear showing, her legs raised and bent at the knees. He stood over her.

"You know who I am, don't you?"

She shook her head, tried to rise, slipped again. "Please," she said. "I won't say anything. Not to a living soul. I promise."

"You saw my picture in the newspapers. You saw this," and he raised his right hand.

Tears rolled over her cheeks. "I only want to go home."

"We all want that, Steffie."

He reached for her arm, hauled her to her feet, led her down the slope to the house. She wouldn't stop crying; he hit her once, rather softly, across the side of her face. After that she sobbed in silence, as if something inside her had begun to break. He pushed her into the house, slammed the door shut.

"What the fuck is this?" Trevaskis asked.

"A little gem," Ruhr said. "Isn't it surprising what a man can find in an otherwise dreary English landscape?"

At the summit of the slope, under bare, sodden trees, the girl's horse whinnied, a sound obliterated by wind and rain.

Nobody in the farmhouse heard.

London

Martin Burr dreaded visits to the Home Secretary's office. It was a vast oak-panelled room hung with faded oil-paintings of politicians past. Under the scrutiny of the portraits the Commissioner felt like a defendant in the dock of history, judged by the stern faces of an awesome jury—the first Earl of Chatham, Gladstone, Lord Acton, Sir Robert Peel. Their faces glowered disapprovingly into the room as if abruptly summoned from a long, well-deserved sleep. Martin Burr looked round the room for a sign of something less imposing, less official, and found it parked in a dim corner—a small, bedraggled canary in a brass cage. The little bird shivered miserably.

Burr turned when the door opened and the Home Secretary came in. "Sorry to have kept you waiting, Martin." He tossed some folders down on his enormous desk, then rummaged in a drawer and brought out an eye-dropper filled with clear liquid. He went to the bird cage and pushed the dropper through the bars, letting fluid drip into the canary's food dish. "Bird's got some kind of flu. This stuff's supposed to help it. It's touch and go, I fear. We live in hope." The Home Secretary gently rattled the cage and whispered to the canary. "Don't we, Charlie? Don't we live in hope?"

He walked back to his desk, sat down. "Now then. This bloody Ruhr business. Where are we exactly?"

Burr, who half-expected to be axed, gazed at the window. The afternoon sky over the Thames was low and leaden. "Not as far along as I would have liked, Secretary," he said. "The search continues. Sea ports are being watched. Air terminals. Railways. All public transportation. Ruhr's picture is plastered everywhere. Frank Pagan's office is examining all known terrorist connections."

"Pagan? Shouldn't he be in hospital or something?"

"He's a stubborn bastard," Burr said. That damned Pagan. "He discharged himself yesterday."

The Home Secretary turned his face toward the window and appeared to consider this information. Then he turned back to the Commissioner. "What news of the leak, Martin?"

Martin Burr imagined he saw Sir Robert Peel frown. He glanced up at the portrait of the man who had founded the London police force in 1829. Then he looked elsewhere. "I've imposed unusually strict limits on the number of people who have access to the paperwork generated by the Ruhr investigation. Memoranda and confidential reports on the affair no longer circulate in the usual way. Pagan has tightened his own departmental security—restricted access to computer data, telephone scrambling devices, that sort of thing. When we communicate with each other in the future, we do so directly, either face to face, or on a safe line. No third parties."

"But you haven't sniffed out the culprit?"

"No, but that isn't our top priority, Secretary. After all, the damage caused by the leak is already done. We're concentrating exclusively on Ruhr. When we catch him, then I can turn my attention to our internal shortcomings."

The Home Secretary was silent for a time. "Sound approach, Martin," he said finally.

This unexpected vote of confidence startled Burr. He poked his walnut cane into the weave of the Secretary's Persian rug. He had come here expecting his own execution or, at best, a severe reprimand. The Home Secretary wasn't famed for a kind heart. A compliment from him had been known to make otherwise somber men light-headed for weeks. Perhaps the Secretary's mild approval was merely a way to soften the inevitable blow. Burr braced himself.

"Do we have *any* idea why this German is here?" the Secretary asked.

Martin Burr shook his head. "There's a list of possibilities that grows longer by the moment."

"Possibilities or guesses, Martin?"

"Guesses," Burr said.

The Secretary was quiet for a time. "When six policemen die, when we have an atrocity of that magnitude, it's common to look immediately for an individual to take the total blame. The obvious choice, Martin, would be you. Commissioner of Scotland Yard, the man in charge of Ruhr's transport, the responsible commanding officer, etcetera etcetera. The great masses, who have quite a taste for the blood of fallible officials, would not be unhappy with a public hanging."

Burr sighed and nodded his head. A public hanging: he saw himself turned out of office, a long retirement at his house in the Sussex countryside. He saw himself stooped and ancient, pottering around in a garden whose fruits and flowers didn't remotely interest him but were merely things one grew on the way to the grave.

"What damn good is a scapegoat?" the Home Secretary asked. "Your record is distinguished, Martin. And I stand squarely behind you. I will say so in public at any time."

Surprised, Burr brightened at once. "I appreciate that."

"I am one of your staunchest supporters, Martin. And I am certain the Commission of Inquiry will exonerate you in due course."

Burr felt a surge of gratitude that rose to his head like blood. He wasn't sure what to say. He saw the

Home Secretary reach across the desk and extend his hand, which Burr shook. It was a vigorous grip between two men who have sworn to uphold the laws of a nation.

"Go back to work with a clear mind, Martin," the Home Secretary said. "I don't want you to be hindered by criticism. I don't want the Commission of Inquiry to distress you in any way. Remember this. You have an ally in me."

"I'm very grateful, Secretary."

"No need. If you were an incompetent buffoon I would have you out of office in two shakes of a lamb's tail. But you're not. Your record speaks for itself."

Burr rose from his chair. A weight had been removed from him and he felt quite spry all at once. Even the portraits appeared less uncompromising, as if Burr had passed some kind of test and his examiners were, for the moment at least, pleased with him.

The canary cheeped bravely. The Home Secretary walked to the cage and looked inside. "Bird's first sound in days. Perhaps it's a good omen." He drew a fingernail over the bars, making a dull harp-like noise. "Keep me posted daily, Martin. That's all I ask. When anything comes up, I will expect to hear from you."

"Of course, Sir Frederick."

The Home Secretary smiled. It was the easy expression of a man who, though born into wealth, prides himself on having the common touch. For this reason he was never called Sir Frederick in the newspapers. It was always the more colloquial Sir Freddie.

He walked Martin Burr to the door.

"Good luck, Commissioner."

"We'll need it," Burr said.

Still smiling, clapping Martin Burr on the back, Sir Freddie Kinnaird closed the door.

7

By mid-afternoon on his first full day of freedom, Frank
Pagan had coaxed extra help from a variety of departments. Men had been called in to do extra shifts or
work their day off. A few had been summoned from the
twilight world of semi-retirement and sent out into the
streets, grumbling yet grudgingly pleased to be useful.
Officers travelled to a score of different places, Ealing
and Wembley, Poole and Ramsgate, anywhere the
names of those on the computer list had been located.
It was a thankless undertaking, but what alternatives
were there? Ignore the twenty-nine names? No. Pagan
wanted to cover as many bases as he could. Later, there
might be the consolation that he'd done everything
possible and hadn't skimped. He had three officers
checking private airfields in the Home Counties for any
evidence of the helicopter used in Shepherd's Bush; another bloody long shot.

By four o'clock, Pagan had also sent two men to

Cambridge to analyze potential targets in the area with the Chief Constable. Another five had been ordered to meet the security officers of military bases throughout East Anglia, from Colchester in the south to Hunstanton in the north, an area some eighty miles wide and sixty miles long. Bounded by The Wash and the North Sea, it was a region of waterways, leafy lanes, ancient churches. Villages, some of them surprisingly remote, still had timbered houses. Across this flat green landscape, Air Force jets screamed out of bases and left fading trails in the sky.

In Golden Square two officers were employed fulltime taking phonecalls from people who claimed to have seen Ruhr. These came from every corner of England; The Claw had been observed by a lonely old man in Hull, a young drunk in Plymouth, a very proper lady in Sevenoaks, an octogenarian in Radlett. He had also been spotted on Westminster Bridge, and in a restaurant on the Grand Parade in Eastbourne by a short-sighted French waiter who'd never forgotten the humiliation imposed on France by the Germans at the Maginot Line. Ruhr, it seemed, was as common as hedgerow, and his movements just as tangled.

Even though officers were scurrying all over the place, and business was being conducted briskly, Pagan was still beset by a sense of having overlooked something very simple, except he wasn't sure what. It was a flavor in his mouth he couldn't name, a word he couldn't get off the tip of his tongue. He wanted to think that it was simply his impatience with dull routine, and a general frustration at the failure of sudden insight—the bright spark of the imagination which reveals the truth in one swift flash. Too many Pethidine, too little sleep on the hideous office sofa. He had the feeling that his brain, knocked off-center, was dealing with the German only in a peripheral way. And the deficiency of his muse had really nothing to do with insomnia or pain. Face it, Frank, he told himself in that stern inner voice he kept for self-honesty: you've been bollixed by the last name on the bloody list.

The twenty-ninth name. As he looked down into the darkening afternoon in Golden Square, he was uneasy.

He wished he could set the past aside, lock it inside a box labelled oblivion. But it was a sneaky intruder, and it came upon you with the quietness of a shadow. He thought that perhaps Foxworth hadn't been able to track the person down, and maybe that would be a relief, but all the particles of his curiosity were wildly activated. Sometimes the urge to visit your own history was overwhelming and so you walked old neighborhoods regardless. The reckless heart, Pagan thought. It went where it wanted to go, striding to its own timetable, and there was nothing you could do but follow, even if the journey took you into the red light district of your memories.

Foxworth entered the office, whistling slyly. "Has anybody mentioned your resemblance to Quasimodo?" he asked.

Pagan shook his head. "I must be missing something."

"It's how you carry yourself, Frank," Foxie said. "Like Charlie Laughton. All you need is a fair-sized hump."

"I can't think of any other way to be comfortable." Pagan had placed all his weight on the left side of his body. His right arm hung rather uselessly, and the right shoulder was raised a little. It wasn't a pretty sight, but it was an improvement on total discomfort.

"I'll get you a bell for Christmas."

"I'd settle for Gunther Ruhr."

Foxworth stopped whistling. He took out his note-book, flipped the pages. He tore out a sheet, slid it across the desk to Pagan. "I found the individual you wanted. Wasn't easy, actually. She checked into a hotel in Victoria two days ago, then promptly settled the bill and moved without explanation in the middle of the night. Arrived in a second hotel in Knightsbridge the day before yesterday. Did the same damn thing all over again. Paid the bill, arrivederci, upped and moved to the address you now have. Strange behavior. One might say suspicious."

"One might." Pagan looked at the piece of paper, then tucked it in his pocket.

"You'll need a driver," Foxie said, thinking that what Frank really needed was a nurse and three weeks in a quiet room with an ocean view.

"And that might as well be you, Foxie."

"I was hoping you'd ask."

Pagan was silent and nervous in the car as Fox-worth drove along Piccadilly and up through the clogged streets of Mayfair. Late afternoon yielded to evening. Feeble sunlight pierced the slate-colored sky, laying a dirty amber streak across Berkeley Square. Park Lane loomed ahead, and Hyde Park beyond, where evening had already settled among the trees. Pagan folded his hands in his lap. His mouth was very dry. This visit wasn't the most practical thing he'd ever done. He could have assigned somebody else, even Foxie, to make this call. But how could he have resisted and let the chance slip past and then have to kick himself in regret?

The monolithic hotels of Park Lane were ahead

now, great slabs of glass and concrete that overlooked Hyde Park. Foxie parked the Rover outside one of the hotels and followed Pagan through the glass doors. Pagan inquired at the desk for the room number he wanted, then shuffled over the thick-piled carpet to the elevators.

"You go the rest of the way alone. Correct?" Foxworth asked.

"Correct," Pagan said. Sometimes Foxie's face was like a kid's; he wasn't very accomplished in the craft of concealment. He had been very curious about Pagan's odd reaction last night, and he was even more curious today, and now he was to be denied direct access to the secret. Bloody Frank! he thought. Furtive bastard!

"Sit in the bar or something," Pagan said. "I don't expect to be very long."

"I'm disappointed, Frank."

"Those are the breaks, Foxie." Pagan stepped inside the elevator, pressed a button for the twelfth floor. When he got out in a corridor that was deserted and weirdly quiet, he had the urge to return to the lobby and leave. Empty hallways in hotels unnerved him.

How long had it been? Twelve years? Thirteen? If it had lain dormant that length of time, why disturb it now? It had turned first to dross, and then the years had refined it further, and now there was surely nothing left but dust. *Dust, my arse!* If that was all, why would you be here?

He moved along the corridor. He found room 1209 and knocked on the door. After a few moments it opened about half an inch. The gap was filled with darkness and Pagan could make out only the eyes at first, but that was all he needed to see. They were unmistakable, blacker than he'd remembered; sad and reflective and deep and lovely, they drew him down into them even as they'd done twelve, thirteen years ago. Down and down; all those years ago there had been bliss at the end of this fall. He smiled uncertainly. He was tense, knotted.

"Frank?" The voice was the same too. Perhaps a half-tone deeper, a little throatier. It was a voice made for risqué jokes and laughter in a bar just before closing time.

A ghost touched him. He had the overpowering desire to put his hand out and feel her—no innocent contact between his fingers and her cheek, nothing smacking of mere fondness, but a truly intimate touch, his fingers on her nipples, her belly, between her legs. This was how she'd always affected him, and time apparently hadn't altered that. It was fascinating to find an old passion lodged in the blood still. Remembered love was the most tantalizing of all, flavored with things that might have been, small regrets, unfulfilled desires, sorrows.

"Frank Pagan. I can't believe it."

"Can I come in?" he asked.

A beat of hesitation. Then she said, "Could I stop you if I wanted to?"

He shook his head. There was a time, he thought, when I would have done anything for you. Rational, irrational, good, bad—these terms lost all meaning when love had you dazzled. He took a few steps forward. Curtains were drawn, a TV playing, no volume. A smell of cigarette smoke and perfume lay in the air. This was something new; she hadn't smoked in the past.

She wore a green silk robe belted not at the waist but lower, slinking around the hips. She wore clothes like few other women. She gave them a personality entirely her own, smart, a little sluttish, conspiratorial in a way, because she wanted you and only you to know what soft secrets lay under the garments. She always looked as if she were about to disrobe, as if clothes fettered her natural urge to go naked, which gave her an edge of unpredictability. And Pagan, twenty-eight years of age at the time of his passion for this woman, had thrived on this brink even as it had threatened him. He'd known bottomless jealousy and terrifying insecurity; when you loved Magdalena you lived with fear of loss, but you lived gloriously just the same. She made all your nerve-endings taut and your blood never stopped singing strange and unfamiliar tunes. Siren, whore, lover, friend—she'd bewildered the young Pagan with her permutations.

"How did you know I was in London?" she asked.

"Your name's on a list. Everything's on a computer these days," he said.

"A list? You make it sound very grim. I take it this isn't a social call?" She sat on the unmade double bed and glanced past him across the room. The door to the toilet was shut. A band of light glowed in the space between floor and door.

"Not entirely," Pagan said. He wanted to go closer to her, but he stood some five or six feet from the bed, conscious of how his sharp remembrance of old intimacies made him feel awkward.

She pushed a hand through her marvelously thick hair. "How long has it been?"

"Thirteen years, give or take."

"Sweet Jesus. I was a child back then."

"You were twenty-six."

"And naive."

"We were both naive."

"Yeah, but didn't we have a time?" She smiled,

reached for the bedside lamp, switched it on. He saw now, in the light that flooded her features, small lines beneath the eyes and around the corners of the mouth. But these minor incisions of time took nothing away from her. Quite the contrary, they gave her more depth and softened the beauty that had once been too perfect. She had the kind of looks that turned heads so quickly one could almost hear the separation of vertebrae.

Thirteen years ago Pagan's world had been transformed by this woman. Before his marriage to Roxanne he'd played the field, but his encounter with Magdalena Torrente had reduced that field to a dried-out pasture, consisting as it did of pallid girls whose notion of passion was as thrilling as taffeta. Cups of tea in bed, biscuit crumbs, damp little flats and whining gas-fires. Magdalena Torrente, a creature from another world, had come in like a tropical storm, cutting through Pagan's Anglo-Saxon cool with her ardor. And he'd lost control.

"I've thought about you often," Pagan said, and wondered at the banal language of reunions. Reunions and grief had that in common: a thin lexicon.

"Likewise," she said.

"You look wonderful."

"My hair's a mess. No makeup."

"When did you ever need it?"

"You've still got that silver tongue, Pagan."

Pagan's ribcage had begun to hurt. He had to sit down.

"You look sick," she said.

He told her briefly about Ruhr, and the shooting. He sat in an armchair, swallowed a painkiller.

"How bad is it?"

"It comes and goes. Mostly it comes."

"Poor Frank," she said.

He liked the sympathy in her voice. For a moment he wished she'd get up and cross the space that divided them and perhaps hold him, baby him, soothe him. And then he was glad she didn't touch him because when it came to Magdalena he'd never quite been able to get enough of her. She resisted complete possession. Her passions were real and intense, her heart sincere, but he always felt that she kept something in reserve, something unreachable despite all the intimacy between them.

"I behaved badly in those days, didn't I?" he said.

"I don't remember that, Frank."

"I couldn't take you at face value. I never quite knew how to behave around you. I wanted to own you."

"But I played you like a guitar," she said quietly. "I manipulated you. I was a self-centered monster."

"I was just as bad. I remember we were in a restaurant, a place in Soho. I thought you were flirting with the maître d' and I couldn't stand it."

"You didn't talk to me all night long," she said. "You sat in a huff. As I recall, I slid my foot into your crotch under the table, and you pretended nothing was happening."

Pagan smiled at the memory. Water under the bridge, he thought. But it wasn't swift-running; it passed under him sluggishly, giving him time to look down at reflections. "I'd never felt that kind of jealousy before. I couldn't think straight."

"I felt very powerful, Frank. Control over a hotshot young cop! What an ego trip." She stood up, smoothing the front of her green silk robe with the palms of her fine hands. She could perform the most simple maneuver and change it; the striking of a match could be transmuted into an erotic gesture, the application of eye-shadow as bewitching as a high-class strip show. She was theater, and Pagan had been her willing audience.

"How long are you here for?" he asked.

"I leave tomorrow."

Pagan wondered why Magdalena was still in her robe at this hour of the day, but he wouldn't ask. "Do you have time for dinner?"

"There's something I can't cancel. I would if I could."

"How about tomorrow?"

"I can't, Frank. Sorry."

"Why do I still feel a very old jealousy?"

"Because you're crazy. Because you're a romantic."

"I'm not sure that's how I like to be defined."

"You'll always be a romantic, Frank. You'll always occupy a special place in my memory."

Something sounded sad to Pagan, as if he existed in Magdalena's mind only as a fossil, relegated to the museum where former lovers lay mummified. There was no question so far as he was concerned—he had once loved this woman in a way he'd never quite loved again, a tempestuous affair, probably self-destructive, but dramatic and more turbulently physical than anything else he'd ever experienced. She took him to his limits then pushed him beyond them, forcing him to soar through the barriers of his reserve and aloofness.

"Thirteen years." She shook her head, as if the passage of time bewildered her. "I don't think I'm over the surprise of seeing you yet. And the suspicion."

"Suspicion?"

"You're not here just to reminisce. You said it wasn't exactly a social call."

Pagan was silent. He wondered if he'd hoped for

something that the situation couldn't possibly yield, perhaps a brief rekindling of old sensations, a liaison even; but this was pure bloody fantasy. People moved on. They built other lives. They had other loves.

"The computer kicked out your name," he said. Jesus, he didn't want to talk about *this*.

"Does that mean I'm up shit creek?" She put a hand over her open mouth; mock horror.

"It depends on why you're in London. The last time you were trying to buy weapons."

She laughed. "Don't remind me. I was naive then."

"Naive enough to look for guns on the black market anyway. And get yourself arrested."

"You were the nicest arresting officer I could have hoped for."

"Are you still involved in the same cause? Still trying to buy guns?"

"Hey, look at me, Frank. I'm thirty-nine and mellow. Guns in the hands of some Cuban extremists isn't the answer. I changed direction."

Pagan stared at the TV a moment. A man was mutely reading the evening news. "What direction are you pointed in now, Magdalena?"

"We still want Castro out. That never changes. But I know it isn't going to happen unless it comes from inside Cuba, and with only a minimal amount of force. I don't know if you've been paying attention, Frank, but there are people in Cuba who believe in bringing democracy to the island. I'm a sympathizer."

"How is this supposed to be achieved?" Pagan asked.

"What do you think?"

"A coup?"

She didn't answer.

"Bloodless?" Pagan asked.

"I can't see into the future."

"How could it be accomplished without *some* bloodshed? And what exactly is a 'minimal amount' of force? How do you actually measure that?"

Magdalena Torrente said nothing.

"But you believe this coup is a possibility?" Pagan asked.

She didn't answer directly. "The democratic underground in Cuba keeps growing. People are sick of deprivation. Communism has a big personnel problem. For every good man it attracts, it enlists a hundred bullies and fuck-ups who don't know Karl Marx from Harpo. Whenever there's a new problem, which is ten times every day, they think rationing's the answer. No shoes? No baby food? No drinking water? No fish to eat? Tough shit, those are all just mere inconveniences en route to the perfection of the state, which is coming. Maybe in a couple of centuries, but it's coming. Meantime, we're sorry we have to grind your face in the dirt."

Pagan remembered taking Magdalena Torrente into custody after she'd been arrested in 1977 in a gun dealer's flat on Baker Street. He'd been part of a team watching that place for weeks, listening to tapped phone conversations, waiting for the precise moment to swoop on the dealer, a Belgian whose cover was that of a dealer in nineteenth-century Flemish art. When the raid happened Magdalena was in the middle of bargaining over the price of one hundred FN rifles intended for a group of anti-Castro rebels in the Escambray region of Cuba. The guns would be channelled through Miami to Cuba by a Florida group who had run afoul of the FBI and therefore had to buy weapons abroad. So Magdalena had been despatched to London with a huge sum of cash.

When she'd been arrested the money was confiscated. The judge, who thought Communism akin to rabies or a rattlesnake's bite and believed democracy the British Empire's one true gift to the planet, had lectured her in the fashion of a stern uncle but he'd refused to imprison or deport her. She had been 'misguided by her own youthful zeal for liberty', a nice judicial phrase, a kindness. Obviously, the good justice had been mildly infatuated with the beautiful young Cuban-American who stood in the dock before him.

After her acquittal, Frank Pagan defied protocol and good sense by spending ten days and nights with her. He'd known it wasn't a bright career move to fraternize with your prisoner, even if she'd been discharged. But that was how she affected him. She made him blind to consequences.

"What brings you here this time, Magdalena?"

"I'm a tourist."

"A very fussy one when it comes to hotels, I gather."

She stared at him. She was capable of making her eyes seem like two hard stones, which stripped her face of all expression. She had masks that could be terrifying. "You've been spying."

"No. You move so often we had trouble tracking you down."

"I'm a hard woman to please. A hotel has to be comfortable."

"Look at it from a police point of view. Maybe you're up to something and you want to make it difficult to be followed. You take the precaution of moving around."

"You can shove that one, Frank. I didn't like the

first two hotels. There's nothing sinister in that. I don't know what you're fishing for. I was in Paris before London. Before that Rome. You know how superficial we Americans can be. Six hours in Barcelona and we've seen everything. Now it's London's turn. Three antique stores, Harrods, the changing of the guards, and I'm out of here.''

Pagan experienced one of those drugged moments in which the strip of electricity under the bathroom door seemed to vibrate. He rubbed his eyes, looked away.

''Do you have any more questions, Frank? Or are we through?''

There, he thought. A sliver of ice in her voice; a little frost. He said, ''Look, I already told you your name had to be checked, that's all. You haven't been singled out especially. There's a whole slew of names.''

''It's got something to do with this character Ruhr?''

''Yes.''

''You don't imagine for a moment that I'd ever be connected to anybody like that?''

''Of course not.''

''But you just had to see me.''

''I had to see you. Did you come here alone?''

''Sure. I often travel on my own. I'm reaching that stage—set in my ways. I like solitude.''

Something troubled him here. An element was wrong, a balance disturbed. Somehow he was having difficulty imagining Magdalena, gregarious Magdalena, travelling alone.

That isn't quite it either, Frank.

He said, ''Sometimes I wonder what would have happened if you hadn't gone back home thirteen years ago.''

"Do you think we ever really stood a chance, Frank? Do you think we'd still be together?"

"Tough question." He remembered trips along the river to Richmond, strolling in Kew Gardens, walking hand-in-hand around The Serpentine. Bistros in Chelsea, antique shops on the Fulham Road, Petticoat Lane. He'd taken her to a cricket match at the Oval and she'd fallen asleep. Tourists and lovers in starry, brilliant London.

"And totally unanswerable," she said. "You're a British cop. I'm a Cuban democrat exiled in Florida. It's a big divide."

Pagan looked round the room. He didn't want to leave. Screw divides, he thought. Why didn't she ask him to stay a little longer?

He realized with a quiet little shock that he knew the answer to that question, that he'd known it for some minutes now, but hadn't wanted to admit it to himself. The light under the bathroom door shimmered like mercury, then seemed to expand. *Of course!* Bright light in a closed room. The mystery of Magdalena's new-found love of her own companionship. The strange uneasiness he'd felt. It tumbled into place like so many coins slowly falling.

She was looking at her wristwatch on the bedside table; a surreptitious glance. "It was good to see you again, Frank. But I'm already late for my appointment. I'm sorry we don't have more time. I hope you get your man."

He finally gave way to an impulse, pulled her toward him, perhaps just a little too sharply, and kissed her. He surprised himself, but she didn't resist, she offered her open mouth and the tip of her tongue, and when he placed a hand inside her robe she didn't immediately push him away. For a few seconds he forgot

Ruhr, and the wound, and the way the world trespassed. He remembered what it was like to be inside
this woman, that collision of flesh, and how her breasts
tasted between his lips. The memory had all the odd
luminosity of an hallucination and the poignancy of a
dead love.

"Go," she said.

He opened the door. "I'm already past tense."

He stepped into the corridor, turning once to look
at her, seeing only one hand raised in farewell as the
door closed on her. One hand. A fragment of Magdalena. It was somehow very fitting.

Downstairs in the lobby he found Foxworth sitting
impatiently under a vast spidery plant. Foxie stood up.

"I want you to go up to the twelfth floor," Pagan
said.

"Oh?"

Pagan grunted and lowered himself cautiously into
the sofa alongside his assistant. The plant created a dark
green umbrella over his head. "The room number's
twelve oh nine. Keep an eye on it in a casual way. See
if you can look like the house detective."

"May I ask why?"

"I want to find out who's hiding in the bathroom."

"Bathroom? Can you fill me in slowly, Frank?"

Pagan looked in the direction of the elevators.
"Later."

Rafael Rosabal dried his face, then tossed the towel
aside. "I didn't know you had friends in this town."

"It was a long time ago," she said.

"Yeah? *Poor Frank.* I heard." He opened the closet,
removed a shirt, pulled it on. "It sounded like it was
only yesterday."

"You're jealous. How wonderful. You're actually jealous!"

Rosabal said nothing. He clipped his cufflinks neatly in place. Silver and diamond, they gleamed in the lamplight. He was fastidious about his appearance.

She went on, "You heard him. He came here on a routine matter. There's a hunt going on for this German, whatever his name is. Pagan isn't the kind of guy to cut corners. He sees stones, he turns them all over. Compulsive. I just happened to be one of his stones."

"Was he also compulsive as a lover? Did he make love to you all the time? Was he insatiable?"

"I don't remember."

"You obviously still mean something to him. But does he mean anything to you?"

She laughed because she was enjoying this moment. She'd never seen him even remotely jealous before. "We're planning to run away together. We lowered our voices when it came to that part so you wouldn't overhear."

Rosabal took her in his arms and held her. Had he really been jealous? He wasn't sure. He thought about Pagan and Magdalena for a moment—a surprising little fluke, a trinket of fate, amusing the way all such concurrences can be, but it meant nothing in the end. There was no way the English policeman could link Magdalena to him; and even if Pagan made such a connection, what did it matter? How could the Englishman possibly discover any association between Rosabal and Gunther Ruhr?

"Is he likely to catch the German?" he asked.

"I don't give a damn. I don't want to spend our last half hour together wondering about some lunatic on the run. We've got better things to do."

"I was just curious. If he's compulsive, presumably he isn't going to sleep until the man is caught."

"Who cares? What difference does it make to you?" She unclipped his cufflinks, slid her hands up his arms and felt the fine hair stir as if touched by electricity. She undid the buttons of his shirt, then pushed him back across the bed; he was distracted.

"I'm just interested in the kind of man your former lover is," he said. "Natural curiosity. Was he better than me?"

"Forget him. Nobody's better than you."

She lowered her face and kissed the hairs that grew across his chest. Where the hairs faded, his skin was brown and almost satin to the touch; she opened her eyes, studied a small blue vein that travelled crookedly just beneath the surface of flesh. She said, "I adore you. I wish I had words to tell you how much."

Rosabal lay silent, his eyes shut. She felt his fingertips against the back of her neck, small indentations of pressure; he had powerful hands and sometimes he underestimated his own strength. She moved her head and his hands slackened and the pressure diminished.

She opened his fly slowly. She always knew how to arouse him and change his mood. "My sweet darling," she said. *Vida mia.*

He saw her hair fall over his thighs. He shut his eyes and held his breath as if he meant to contain the explosion in this fashion, but he couldn't. He heard the way she moaned joyfully, her hands cupped together under his testicles; he came with a surge that rocked him. She raised her face. A glistening thread of semen lay on her lip and she removed it with a fingertip. She held this frail memento, this filament, toward the light, then it drifted away. There was a profound intimacy she had with Rafael that with any other man would have been unthinkable. Certainly she'd never known it with another lover. It excluded the rest of the world. She found herself doing things she'd never done before, thinking thoughts that would never have entered her mind until now. She looked at him. He was so beautiful at times he made her ache.

They lay together in silence.

Then she said, "I want to leave before you. I don't like waiting behind after you've gone."

"Of course."

She shut her eyes very tightly. At the back of her mind she could already feel the sorrow that always came, like some vindictive wraith, whenever they parted. And there was always the same penetrating doubt, the heartache of wondering if, and when, they would meet again.

"Tell me we're going to win," she said. This was another troublesome matter for her; she needed reassurances here too. Her love for Rosabal, her political beliefs, her desire to play a significant role in changing Cuba—these were bound together so tightly as to be inseparable.

"Do you doubt it?"

"I like to hear you say it, that's all."

He turned his face toward her. "We're going to win. Nothing can stand in our way."

Her face propped against the palm of her hand, she gazed at him. *The ultimate victory.* There were moments in which she could feel it as certainly as she might some fever in her blood—a raging flood of light and warmth. She had one such moment now as she studied her lover's face. Her fears and doubts drifted away like so much steam.

She turned over on her back, looked up at the ceiling. She thought about the role she would play later, in the time after Castro. Rosabal had brought it up a year ago in Mexico City; the only true democracy, he'd said, was one based on elections that were not only free but fair. And with that delightful smile on his face which contained her future, he told her how he had come up with a special job for her, namely Minister of Elections, a post he'd create for her when the time came, a powerful position that would bestow upon her the responsibility of ensuring elections free of corruption and coercion, elections that would be untainted by fraud as they so frequently were in such countries as Panama and Chile. Cuban democracy would be a model for the rest of Latin America.

Besides, what damn good was a rotten democracy? he'd asked. What good was it if votes could be bought with money or threats of violence? People had to cast their ballots without fear. Her job, as Rafael had enthusiastically described it, would be more than merely overseeing the impartial counting of ballots; a whole nation accustomed to one antiquated system for which *nobody had ever voted* had to be re-educated, an enormous task that affected every stratum of society. Immense propaganda would have to be created in schools, factories, farms. Simple democracy; an alien concept for a whole generation of Cubans who had to be wakened, and shaken, and remade! And he had absolutely no doubt that she had the energy for this; she had the zeal, the dedication, there was no question.

The prospect, and Rafael's faith in her, filled her with excitement; he intended to make her the principal architect of free elections in Cuba. In 1961 at the Bay of Pigs scores of men, including her own father, had died in pursuit of that ideal. She shut her eyes. She said, "Do you know what makes me really happy? It's not just the importance of this job—it's the fact *you* understand what it means to me. Even after we're married, you want me to have a life of my own." She opened her eyes, looked at him.

He said, "You have too much to contribute. I wouldn't expect you to give up your independence. I've told you that before. In any case, it's part of your charm." He smiled now. "Presidente Rosabal and his wife Magdalena," he added, as if testing the coupling. "It sounds so very right."

And it was; what could be more natural? she wondered. Rafael and Magdalena. Lovers. Husband and wife. President and Minister. All along the line they fitted smoothly together. Sometimes this realization overwhelmed her. She, who had always looked upon marriage as a relic of a simpler age when women blindly entered into unfair contracts—she wanted to be this man's wife; she *wanted* Rafael as her husband. He had asked her a year ago in Mexico City; her acceptance had been the most tranquil moment of her life. But she had known from the beginning that she'd never be just a decoration at Rosabal's side, never window-dressing. She wanted more. And she was going to get it.

Rafael Rosabal was silent for a long time. Then he pointed his index finger, gunlike, at the ceiling, and made a clicking sound.

"Castro is a dead man," he said in a toneless voice.

"Yes." Magdalena Torrente laid her face upon her lover's chest. "A corpse."

Dover, Delaware

The house, overgrown with weeds and shrubbery, had no ostentation. It was large and anonymous, rather like its owner John Merkandome, who was known in intelligence circles as the Grim Reaper. Located a couple of miles from the Little Creek Wilderness Area, the house commanded some splendid views of Delaware Bay, but it was otherwise plain and unadorned. Merkandome paid very little attention to his surroundings. He enjoyed the indoor pool in which he presently floated, but beyond that he had no time for luxuries.

He breast-stroked to the side of the pool and hauled himself halfway out of the blue water, which dripped from his gray hair into his eyes. He was a lean man with an odd skin condition that caused his flesh to appear marbled. He sat down on a step and blinked as he said, "All our studies came to the same conclusion. Every single hypothesis led to the same result."

"With tragic consequences in London." The other person in the pool was a round-cheeked man called Allen Falk. Falk, who had wavy hair oiled and styled in a way that suggested the mid 1950s, had advised the last two Presidents and the present incumbent on Central American matters. He was an influential counsellor whose love affairs were as public as his professional life was wrapped in mystery. He was said to have parlayed his leverage in the White House into a crucial role in defining CIA policy in Central America.

Nobody really knew the extent of Falk's power. How far it reached was a matter of ongoing rumor. In his social and sexual life he dallied with actresses, lady novelists, and on one occasion a beautiful pop singer who later had a nervous breakdown. Falk's fame was of a curiously American kind. Those things of substance he might have achieved played no part in it; only the margins of his life—his women, his cologne, the make of his sunglasses—were taken into account by the gods who decide the credentials of celebrity.

Merkandome, who was approaching his fifty-seventh year, got out of the pool. He was in good shape for his age, better than Al Falk, who was slightly plump and relied on tailors more than exercise for his appearance. Falk swam in his ungainly way to the side of the pool. The stench of chlorine was heavy in the air.

Merkandome draped a towel round his shoulders. "Those are the accidents we learn to live with, Al," he said in his New England accent. "Tragedies are an occupational hazard. You should know that by now. You should also know that no study can take into account every possible human factor. In this case, a sick German's sexual peccadilloes. Incomplete input, Al, equals incomplete equation."

Falk would personally have preferred another plan of action from the start, but Merkandome was the expert in plausibility studies, not he. It was the Grim Reaper who created models and ran them through computers in his private lab in a grubby building owned by a front called Dome Electronics in Wilmington, Delaware. The CIA knew the building well because Merkandome was a major consultant to the agency even though he was no longer on any official payroll these days. For thirty years he'd worked at Langley, an organization man.

In 1961 he had been involved in planning the operation that turned out to be the fiasco at the Bay of Pigs. For the rest of his life Merkandome lived with the idea that not only had he failed to bring down Castro but he had also provided that sonofabitch with one of his most glorious public relations victories—the chance to gloat over the defeat of American-backed forces.

"I pay bright young graduates from MIT a lot of money to run plausibility studies, Al. They don't leave stones unturned. They're smart fellows. More than that, though, they're *thorough*. And give me thorough over smart every time."

Al Falk climbed up out of the pool, reached for a towel, began to dry himself off. His pectorals sagged, a gloomy fact he noticed in an absent-minded way. "If we hadn't needed the hardware, we wouldn't have needed Ruhr," he remarked. Falk hated conditionals. They cluttered a man's life.

"Sure, but we needed the hardware," Merkandome said. "Every single study came up with that, Al. Without hardware, there's no good pretext to go in and get the job done. We worked it through from hundreds of angles. For example. We considered the phony kidnapping of a Senator's son by Cuban agents. We played with the idea of poisoning the water-supply to the U.S. base at Guantanamo and blaming it on Castro. We went through one scenario after another, Al. Some plausible. Some downright stupid. Most of them far too soft. You don't have to hear them all. What it always came back to was the notion of our own shores being menaced. You threaten a fellow in his own backyard, and he becomes irate. Any action he takes to defend his life and property is justifiable. That was the strongest concept of all. But we didn't figure Ruhr's weakness into our equations. How could we? We didn't know about it."

Allen Falk tossed his towel aside. He looked up at the glass ceiling, beyond which sultry afternoon clouds clung to a weak yellow sun. "Apparently nobody knew," he said.

"See? The human factor," Merkandome remarked.

Fuck the human factor, Falk thought. Why weren't things always cut and dry? Why were they so damned ragged? Falk, even though he was a master of court intrigue and knew how to play the byzantine game of White House politics, nevertheless longed for simplicity at times; a world in which all your plans actually worked—what a terrific place that would be. People always considered Falk a complicated man. They were wrong—he was a simple man in complex circumstances.

Falk got to his feet. He thought of the cops dead in that London suburb, the people injured, the property destroyed. The trouble was that everything had its price. Especially freedom. He had no intention of cancelling the program now, even if he wanted to, and he didn't. Too much was already involved, too much invested. And not just money.

He glanced at the Grim Reaper and said, "The show goes on."

"They said you were a trooper, Al," John Merkandome replied.

London

Shortly before midnight, at a well-preserved eighteenth-century house overlooking the Thames in Chelsea, Jean-Paul Chapotin slipped his key inside the lock, opened the door, stepped into a narrow hallway carpeted in vile red. He placed his briefcase on the three-legged table in the hall, then entered the sitting-room, which might have been decorated by a fop. Eighteenth-century furniture was permissible, to be admired even, but Chapotin loathed the powder-blue walls and ceiling and the curtains the color of a new moon.

He sat on the sofa, which was too narrow for a man of his bulk, but the whole house was too narrow and cramped. He made a telephone call to his wife Gabrielle in Paris. Gabrielle, who would be wearing whatever absurd garment that had been mandated by the queens who ruled haute couture, answered in a voice made dreamy by tranquilizers.

"I have to stay here another day," Chapotin said.

"Then I'll see you tomorrow?"

"Yes yes." Chapotin heard a floorboard creak at the top of the stairs. "Is everything well?"

"Why wouldn't it be?"

Chapotin shrugged. Conversations with his wife had become impossibly dull over the years. What had once been wild adoration had dwindled during the course of their twenty-year marriage to the kind of mutual tolerance that communicates itself best in silence; and when silence failed, there were always domestic trivialities to crowd the minutes. The plumbing in the house near the Bois de Boulogne, the servant problem at the country estate in Provence, the drunken behavior of a certain stable-hand at the stud farm in the Loire Valley.

"Will I pick you up at the airport?" she asked.

"Send a car."

The conversation terminated. He was weary suddenly, and stretched his legs. He yawned. Once again, from the upper part of the house, he heard the creak of a floorboard.

He rose, walked into the hallway, looked up the flight of stairs.

"Melody?" he said.

It was a silly name, he thought. The only thing remotely musical about Melody was her love of the noise made by cash-registers ringing, the song of money, Chapotin's money. But, dear God! The little English debutante was beautiful in a way Chapotin, normally a sensible man of moderate inclinations, found irresistible.

She appeared on the landing, a vague, skinny girl whose large blue eyes, alas empty, dominated her features. She wore an ostrich boa—selected, no doubt, from one of the 'junk' shops in the neighborhood and charged to Chapotin's account—and a 1920s flapper dress with shimmering fringes. She had on very bright pink shoes. Her taste in clothing and interior design was, charitably, eclectic. Her moussed hair was pressed down on her skull and artfully arranged around her ears.

"Ahoy," she said.

Chapotin was always in two minds about his mistress. The accountant in him wanted to dump her; but the libertine couldn't bear to part with this vacuous, sexy girl. She came down the stairs slowly, trailing the boa behind her.

"Kiss kiss." She stood on the bottom step.

Chapotin kissed her. She tasted of baby soap and vermouth and was completely desirable.

"Take me places, Chappie. You never take me anywhere. Fly me to new continents."

"Where would you like to go?" he asked. He could hardly wait to undress her and have her; the lust he experienced was impossible.

"Paree," she said. "Naturellement."

"I have a little problem with that one, cheri."

"Melly's stuck in boooooring old London while Chappie jets all over creation," she said.

"Soon. We'll go to Hawaii."

"Luaus chill me. Grass skirts demoralize me. I'm not thrilled."

"Then where would you like to go?"

Melody shrugged and trailed the boa inside the

sitting-room. Chapotin went after her. Why did he put up with this child? What kink did he have in his character? It came down to something really quite simple. His regular life was so demandingly somber and filled with stress that he'd forgotten how to play and have sheer fun—until Melody, like a creature from some far planet, had crashlanded on his staid, tightly-buttoned little world.

She sat down on the sofa. Her white stockings had a lacy design. She wore very black eye makeup. Chapotin sat beside her. He laid one hand on her wrist.

"I'll take you on a world cruise." When would he ever find the time?

"Ocean waves! I would vomit constantly."

Chapotin wondered how his fellow Society members would react to this girl if they ever met her—which, of course, could never be allowed to happen: the Society did not permit private lives to touch its affairs. Enrico Caporelli, who had a roving eye, might be charmed by the girl's odd sexuality, but the others—especially those prudish Americans and the slightly sinister Magiwara—might sniff with disdain.

Chapotin understood that his devotion to this child would be considered by some a weakness, but he had a romantic's incurable heart and a lust that gripped him like a hot fist.

He put his hand on her knee.

"We'll come to some accommodation," he said.

Melody blinked her long false lashes. "We shall see what we shall see, Chappie. In the meantime, I may order new curtains and new rugs to match."

Chapotin had the gruesome feeling that his mistress would one day come to resemble his wife, that his whole life would be one long barrage of domesticity. Curtains! Plumbing! Carpets! What he needed was the escape route of Melody's sweet young flesh. He lunged toward her but she was as slippery as the material of her dress, and she glided out from under his hands.

"Ah-hah," he said.

"Ah-hah yourself, Jaypee. No foreign junket, no fuckee."

Chapotin lunged again. Melody nimbly stepped aside. He was amused. He liked the hunt.

"You can't catch me," she said, and laughed.

Jean-Paul Chapotin struck out his hand and grabbed the dress, which ripped as soon as she whirled away from him, revealing the extraordinary sight of Melody Logue's pale and lovely inner thigh. A tattooed robin, red-breasted, wings spread, nestled close to her vulva. It was so lifelike it had quite startled Chapotin the first time he'd seen it.

"Leave her royal bloody highness and live with me," she said.

"Leave my wife?"

Yes, he thought. Yes yes yes. To get at that bird he'd do anything, anything at all. Chapotin stretched out one trembling hand but Melody slipped away again.

"Say the word and win the bird!"

Chapotin laughed. This romping eighteen-year-old nincompoop who blessed his life—how could he leave Gabrielle for this? On the other hand, how could he *not?*

He heard the sound of glass breaking, muffled by the thickness of the curtains. Without thinking, Chapotin caught the girl and dragged her to the floor with him. He barely registered the two orbs that rolled across the carpet. He knew what they were, but recognition didn't prompt an instant response. It was a joke, an execrable joke, it wasn't real. The girl clutched him and said *Oooo* just as the grenades exploded.

Chapotin had time only to reflect how strangely quiet the whole thing was, like a noise inside a vacuum. Shrapnel pierced the girl's neck. Her skin-tissue flew through the air into Chapotin's eyes, blinding him. He tried to raise his hands to his face. Severed at the wrists by the hot blast of metal, they were gone.

8

Fife, Scotland

At six-thirteen AM, a transport plane was cleared for takeoff from an air base in Fife on the east coast of Scotland. The plane, a C-130 painted in camouflage, was normally deployed shuttling men and equipment between various NATO bases and the United States. An impressive flying machine over ninety feet long, it was capable of carrying as much as seventy-thousand pounds of cargo. On this rainy morning, the C-130's approved flight plan would take it south into England and across the Channel to Germany, where it was scheduled to pick up sixty paratroopers in Wiesbaden and return them to Alabama. The crew consisted of pilot, co-pilot, navigator and flight engineer.

The takeoff was smooth. The great plane went out over the North Sea into clouds, then turned back inland and began its climb toward Edinburgh. Cantankerous rain slashed at the fuselage and every so often the craft bucked the turbulence like a whale on the tide.

In the cargo area crates of spare parts and tools rattled around and some loose sacking slid back and forth. But something else also moved, unnoticed by the crew on the flight deck, something that had been concealed on board for many hours and waiting, with nervous impatience, for just this occasion.

Directly over the Border Country, that under-populated and lovely tract of land dividing two nations, three armed men stepped inside the flight deck. They carried automatic pistols and wore fatigues. There were no masks because there was no need to conceal their faces. After all, the men intended to leave no witnesses. The leader of the four was a black-haired man in his early forties called Joseph Sweeney. It was Sweeney who pressed his gun directly into the pilot's skull and ordered him to relinquish the controls. One of Sweeney's men took the pilot's seat. The co-pilot was also ordered to give up his position. He complied. Only the flight engineer complained and he was struck across the mouth for his troubles.

Sweeney led the crew back into the cargo area. It wasn't immediately apparent to any crew member what the hijacker intended to do to them. They feared his pistol, but nobody imagined he'd fire inside the aircraft—if he had any sense. At the worst, they expected to be bound and flown wherever the hijackers might have in mind and then traded or bargained over. Certainly none of the crew anticipated that Joseph Sweeney would do what he did.

He ordered the flight engineer, who was bleeding freely from the mouth, to open the paratroop door. There was a momentary hesitation before the engineer responded: they were going to get parachutes, weren't they?

Sweeney waved the gun and the engineer opened the door and cold misty rain blew inside. Understanding of Sweeney's purpose came swiftly to the crew. They were supposed to jump, yes, but without parachutes. If they didn't, Sweeney would shoot them.

The flight engineer was told to go first. When he resisted, Sweeney fired one shot into the man's groin. Still the engineer wouldn't go through the open door and Sweeney was becoming annoyed by two things—the cold rain that had started to soak his clothing, and the man's stubbornness. The other three crew members had a kind of stunned desperation about them; they began to look for ways out of this horrifying predicament—a stray wrench, a hammer, anything they might grab as a weapon. Sweeney read the signs of resistance and didn't like them. He called for one of his fellow hijackers to come out of the cockpit and join him. A strong surly man who looked Arabic came from the flight-deck and struggled with the engineer and finally hurled him out. The falling body made a tunnel through clouds as it dropped from a height of seventeen thousand feet over wet moorlands.

One by one, the other crew members were despatched from the plane. The pilot resisted with the greatest ferocity and Sweeney had to shoot him between the eyes before tossing him out. Sweeney shut the door. He was shivering.

The plane continued south, flying over Newcastle and the River Tyne and then heading for the industrial Midlands, where pollution and weather conspired to create a perfect canopy of impenetrable cloudiness.

London

It was six-twenty AM when Foxworth woke Frank Pagan, who had slept once again on his office sofa. Foxie had brewed strong coffee, which roused Pagan from his Pethidine dreams, which were senseless and inchoate. He woke slowly, reaching for the cup Foxie held before him. Cautiously he moved into an upright position and sipped the hot black liquid. It was good stuff. Foxworth, a well-bred young man with a taste for the finer things, always ground his own Jamaican Blue Mountain beans.

"Nectar," Pagan said, blinking at the very thin yellow light that had begun to stretch across Golden Square like a skin graft that hadn't quite taken. He had some vague recollection of Magdalena in one of his bizarre dreams, but the form was lost to him.

Foxworth produced some gauze and scissors. "Today we have the changing of bandages," he said.

"Let me get this down first." Pagan drained his cup, then he reached for his painkillers on the window ledge. He drew his hand back. "I'll see if I can get by without them for a while. I wouldn't want to end up in some treatment center for dopers. I lean toward compulsive behavior as it is."

Foxworth agreed with that assessment. "Let's get the old bandage off."

"Foxworth Nightingale," Pagan remarked.

"I was a Boy Scout. I had a drawerful of First Aid badges. Now turn to the side, Frank."

Pagan obliged. Foxworth removed the old bandage and dressing and discarded them. With impressive neatness, he snipped a length of new bandage and placed it around Pagan's chest, then fastened it.

"The exit wound looks raw," Foxie said. "The entrance isn't so bad, though. Put this on."

"A clean shirt?"

"I took the liberty of going to your flat. I didn't think you'd mind. I brought you a clean suit and some underwear. Also shoes and socks. I hope everything matches."

The suit was brown linen, the shoes black, the socks gray, the shirt pale blue herringbone. Pagan didn't have the heart to criticize the color scheme. Besides, he was looking for Gunther Ruhr, not dining at Le Caprice. Foxworth, for his part, had had a terrible time going through Pagan's wardrobe, the shirts that suggested bad dreams, parrots and Hawaiian plants and swirls of vivid color, the array of shoes that covered the spectrum from bright canvas espadrilles to shiny black leather, the dozen suits of all kinds, linen and tweed and silk, summer and winter, formal and otherwise, single- and double-breasted.

"You'd make a fine gentleman's gentleman, Foxie."

"I'll keep that in mind."

"Is there more coffee?"

Foxworth opened a thermos flask and refilled Pagan's cup. "A couple of overnight items, Frank. I'll run through them for you. First, the usual sightings of Gunther. Sheffield, Morecambe, Newcastle."

"Now he's travelling north," Pagan said drily. "Soon we'll hear he's in bloody Reykjavik trying to take out Icelandic citizenship."

"He was also seen in Sloane Square and Pimlico and stepping aboard a train at Victoria Station. Also in Brighton, Canterbury and—here's a nice one—Stonehenge, where he was spotted by a couple of druids."

Pagan shook his head. Druids, he thought. Stonehenge drew all kinds of oddballs, like a giant bug light in the middle of Salisbury Plain.

"What other news, Foxie?"

"We've had reports from our men in East Anglia. They say security at military installations is tight. As for the Chief Constable in Cambridge, he's got every available policeman in the county beating the fields with sticks, in a manner of speaking."

Pagan stood up now, walked to the window, saw a few early-morning drones cross the Square in the direction of their offices. He had a sudden sense of dread. All the order he saw beneath him—the streets, the parked cars, this somnolent London square—had a transient quality. A man like Ruhr, if he went unchecked, could demolish a city block with very little trouble.

"Is there any progress from the manhunt?" Pagan asked.

"Drudgery," Foxie said. "Door to door drudgery. Our men keep knocking and they keep asking, but no Gunther."

"The bastard's somewhere," Pagan said.

Foxie picked up a thick manilla folder, opened it, took out a sheet of paper. He said, "By the way, there were two murders last night in Chelsea. It's outside our bailiwick, but I mention it because of the MO. Two grenades tossed through a window. Boom boom and cheerio. The report mentions the fact that the weapons were extremely powerful but home-made."

"Home-made? Irish?"

Foxworth shrugged. "It's very remote. The victims were a French businessman called Chapotin and his bit of fluff, a girl by the name of Melody Logue, who happened to be the niece of Lord somebody or other. I don't see any reason the Irish would want to dispose of the pair. I also considered the idea that it could be the work of Ruhr, but home-made isn't his style. Unless he's changed.''

Pagan made a gesture of impatience. "I'll read the written stuff when I've got time."

"There's one interesting little snippet about Chapotin."

"Which is?"

"From 1957 until 1959, Jean-Paul Chapotin was the Deputy French Ambassador to Cuba."

"Cuba." Pagan considered this item a moment, but it didn't have a place in the framework of his preoccupation with Gunther.

"Cuba brings me to the last item, of course," Foxworth said. "It took some hours and a lot of looking through the Foreign Office's mug-shots, but finally I was able to identify Magdalena Torrente's friend."

"And?" There was impatience in Pagan's voice. He wanted to pretend that Magdalena's roommate meant nothing to him. It was the kind of inquiry one made on the side. A personal tangent, the geometry of an old love, that was all.

Foxie rummaged back inside his folder and brought out a small stack of flimsy sheets; across each were the words For Internal File Only. Foxie smiled in a way that suggested larceny. "It took some persuasion and a bit of the old school tie to get these, Frank. Domestic surveillance division of intelligence. Ever since a Cuban diplomat tried to shoot one of our intelligence chaps on a London street in 1988, surveillance of Cubans on diplomatic or any other kind of business here has increased considerably. The Watchers don't want to let Cubans out of their sight. Besides, all this surveillance irritates Castro, and everybody loves getting old Fidel's goat—''

"The point, Foxie."

"The point, Frank, is a man called Rafael Rosabal."

Norfolk

Stephanie Brough pressed her tongue against the strip of rayon that had been used to gag her. Her arms were tied behind her back with short lengths of rope that cut into her skin, and her ankles were bound so tightly bone was forced against bone. The loose ends of her restraints had been knotted to the frame of the narrow bed on which she lay. There was a window above her. It was dawn and heavy clouds rushed across the sky.

She hadn't slept at all. How could she? Even with her eyes shut she'd been conscious of Ruhr sitting in the corner of the room in an old armchair. He'd been there most of the night, sometimes just gazing at her. You couldn't tell anything from his expression. You couldn't tell what he was thinking or planning. He just looked so chilling.

Oh Steffie, she thought. *Perhaps today they'll release you.* She wondered about her poor mare, which she'd left in the rain. The horse would trot home eventually, she was sure of that. And then Steffie's Dad would go to the police—it was really that simple, wasn't it? He would have gone to the police already, wouldn't he?

She shut her eyes. She heard voices from the kitchen. The skinny man, the American whose name she didn't know, was talking to Ruhr. They were arguing, and she knew it had something to do with her, but she didn't want to listen.

What she remembered was how her father had

talked about Ruhr, and the killing of those poor police-men, and how Ruhr was a monster who deserved to hang. She hadn't paid *close* attention because her father was always saying that so-and-so should be hung, or that hanging was too good for some people. Her father was a bloody dinosaur, but really quite nice.

She'd seen Ruhr's picture in newspapers and on TV. And yesterday, when she'd recognized him, her heart had withered and something had dropped like a boulder into her stomach. When he'd dragged her back to the house she couldn't help thinking of all the terrible things he was said to have done.

Is he going to kill you, Steffie? Are you just another victim?

She turned her face to the wall. If somebody was going to shoot her, she didn't want to have to see the killer come in the room. Think other things! Think music or books or The Lord's Prayer! The argument in the kitchen was still going on. The harsh voices were almost audible as they rose and fell, Ruhr's especially, high-pitched and nasal. She tried to tune it out. A few drops of rain knocked on the window above, and the branch of a dead tree flapped.

What would it be like to be shot through the skull? Probably nothing. No sensation. The end. Panicked, she struggled for a few seconds against her bonds, but it was hopeless. The harder she labored the more painfully the ropes cut. Her eyes watered in sheer frustration.

Ruhr came into the bedroom. He carried a rifle; tucked into his waistband was a handgun. His bad hand was concealed inside a pocket. He approached the bed and smiled, but she couldn't stand to see that smile, which was unreal, like something razored out of his face, a damp slit. He sat down, slid the gag from her lips. She was thankful to him for that at least, but her gratitude lasted only a second.

"Are you hungry?" he asked.

She shook her head. She wouldn't speak. She'd be perfectly quiet, like one of those nuns who have taken vows of silence. It was a small rebellion, but she couldn't think of any other kind of resistance.

"You don't want to speak?" Ruhr asked. He set his rifle down, propping it against the mattress.

Steffie said nothing. Actually, silence was pleasant, like a great estuary of motionless water; she could float and go on floating across its surface. Lilypads and serene swans and reflections of the sky. She stared at Ruhr, remembering how he'd smacked her yesterday, and suddenly the surface of her silence seemed fragile. He could strike her again and make her talk, if he wanted.

"Little girl," Ruhr said. He put his good hand on her stomach, the palm flat. She had a firm belly, no slack, none of the softness that comes with the collapse of time. "Pretty little girl. Your friends tell you, no? They tell you how pretty you are. I imagine you have many boyfriends."

Silence; rain on the window; the branch drumming. She thought, *These are a few of my favorite things.*

Ruhr moved his good hand. He slid it under her blouse—her white blouse, caked with hardened mud, disgusting—and then unhooked her brassiere from the front. She had the thought that if she let him do whatever he wanted then surely he'd set her free. Ruhr tugged the brassiere from her body and turned it over in his hand, smiling as he studied it. Then he lowered his face into the garment and didn't move for a while.

"The smell of a young girl," he said. "There is nothing quite so fresh and lovely."

Steffie felt her stomach rise up into her throat. How could she bear it if he touched her again? He was ugly and white and the very idea of being kissed by him —*he wouldn't stop at kissing! he'd screw her!*—filled her with terror. The nearest she'd come to sex was with Jason Turnberry in the summer just past; not the whole way—he'd fondled her breasts and she'd let him touch her between the legs for a second, but Jason wasn't Gunther Ruhr, Jason was a lovely timid boy, and he stopped when you told him to.

"You are so afraid," he said. "There is really no need, Stephanie. Sometimes when you are afraid it becomes contagious, and the people around you begin to be afraid also, and then they do irrational things out of fear. Be calm, little girl."

Steffie licked her dry lips. What bloody good was silence anyway? It was too meek, too feeble. If she was going to get anywhere, she'd have to speak. Her voice was hoarse when she whispered, "If you let me leave, I swear I'll never say a thing to anybody. I'll make a solemn vow."

Ruhr said, "In my experience, people who make solemn vows are usually the first to make betrayals also."

"I wouldn't do that. I promise."

Ruhr looked at her for a while. He slowly transferred the small brassiere from his good hand to the bad one. "I am sure you believe what you say right at this moment. But my answer is the same. You see"—and he patted her knuckles; his skin was like damp slate— "I have business to conduct and I can't afford to let you go home to your parents. Do you understand that? It would be imprudent of me to release you."

"When will you let me go? When your business is finished?"

Ruhr stood up. He looked down at her. "In about twenty minutes from now, we are going to take a short trip."

"Where?"

Ruhr placed a fingertip to his mouth, a gesture of secrecy.

"But," was all she managed to say before Ruhr replaced the gag.

Outside the house, Trevaskis and Rick loaded the Range Rover with M-16s, tear gas canisters, rocket launchers, grenades, gas masks. The guns, which had been cleaned yet again last night by the Argentineans, were all in excellent condition. Ruhr's inspection of the weapons had been thorough.

Trevaskis, half-listening to the car radio, said, "You ask me, it's fucked, the whole situation."

Rick, as taciturn as he was massive, grunted as he loaded a box of ammunition.

"Some things you don't fuck with," Trevaskis said. "This kid, now. What's the point? I wouldn't have brought her inside the house in the first goddam place. No way. A quick bullet in the skull, kid's dead, you got no extra baggage."

"Right," Rick agreed.

"And if you don't want her blood on your hands, then all you gotta do is tie her up real tight and leave her in the house. Sooner or later somebody's gonna find her." Trevaskis, who didn't much like the idea of violence being done to a child, was quiet for a moment. "He's one sick sonofabitch, lemme tell you. Look into his eyes, man. I seen saner guys in county asylums."

Slicks of rain ran down Trevaskis's face to his neck and slithered over his St. Christopher. "So long as he don't screw up the whole deal, I don't care. I'll tell you one thing for free: I can't stand that bastard. If he crosses me . . ." Trevaskis let his sentence hang unfinished. Then he added, "There's only one goddam reason to bring the chick along."

"What's that?"

"Think about it, Rick."

Ruhr came out of the house just then. The Americans fell silent at once. Ruhr walked round the Range Rover and stood with his arms folded. He stared up at the dawn sky. The clouds and the rainy haze weren't going to be unfavorable factors. He looked at his wristwatch: 6:58.

"I still say we don't take her with us." Trevaskis stared at Ruhr, a hard look that didn't impress the German, who simply made an impatient gesture. "Either we shoot her, or we leave her behind and secure."

"She goes in the back of the vehicle. We've discussed all this. The matter is closed, Trevaskis."

"And then what? What happens to her afterward?"

Ruhr said nothing. Trevaskis wearied him. The American stuck his thumbs in his belt loops and said, "I just heard on the car radio your man Pagan's back on the job, Ruhr. He's outta the hospital and coming after you. How's that grab you, Mr. Claw?"

Ruhr walked some yards from the vehicle. He wasn't even going to dignify Trevaskis's information, thrown at him like some feeble gauntlet, with any kind of comment. Pagan was a policeman and one cop was much like any other; they all had dead imaginations. The best one could hope for from a man such as Pagan was that his injury might have made him a more dangerous adversary, that he was looking less to recapture Ruhr than he was to avenge the death of his comrades.

A cop on a personal mission was always more interesting than one plodding through dull routine.

But he'd deal with the question of Pagan later, because something else had begun to bother him slightly.

There were times when he stood in a landscape or stepped inside a room and he had an instinct, almost a certainty, an animal sense, that something adverse was about to happen. Often this premonitory ability gave him time to take evasive action. But right now whatever troubled him was so vague it was like a faint scent blown on a haphazard breeze.

He looked up the slope of land that rose from the farmhouse, up through mud and wet trees and clumps of nettles. Whatever made him uneasy lay on the rise, he was sure of that much. He covered the butt of his pistol with the palm of his hand and studied the landscape. The trees dripped, the foliage stirred, the mud was covered with puddles that reflected the sky like so many tiny cracked mirrors.

Ruhr thought about the girl. Her parents would have begun last night by calling their daughter's friends. There would have been no panic at first, a mere uneasiness, perhaps a certain irritation after a time. Then they might have gone out on foot to search for her. Rain and mud and the absence of light would halt them, at least until dawn. They would also have called the local police.

But how many men were available in a country constabulary? And the terrain, covered with muddy fields and ditches and a tortuous network of lanes, could not be combed quickly. Even though it was mainly a flat landscape, it was a secretive one, with hollows, and tall grasses, and dense stands of trees. There were hundreds of isolated farmhouses, weekend cottages for Londoners, windmills, abandoned ruins.

Ruhr took a couple of steps toward the slope. He might have done what Trevaskis had recommended. He might have shot the child. He'd already considered the idea. In time, no doubt, he would jettison her. But he remembered the feel of her skin, and the small white brassiere flecked with mud, and he thought about the high cheekbones and the thin oval face and the way her short skirt hardly covered her thighs. He was flooded with a longing both familiar and dangerous. The youthfulness of the child, her silken vulnerability: these were the two elements of an equation whose sum was terror. And what was terror but a means of total control? Besides, when he thought of the girl in Cambridge he had a sense of unfinished business, which he didn't like.

There was another factor in the girl's favor. He imagined a situation in which he might need a hostage, a human shield, a bargaining chip. In his past experience he'd found hostages useful tools. It was astonishing how the forces of law and order would silence their guns when they knew innocent lives might be jeopardized. The terrified face of a hostage was a mirror that reflected the image of an orderly society threatened. Let the hostage be killed and what did you have—the failure of the state to protect its innocents, the dreaded anarchy the forces of law existed to prevent.

Trevaskis might have shot the girl, but therein lay the difference between the American and Ruhr. The former never considered the possibility of finding gold in dross; Ruhr, on the other hand, had a genius for turning the unexpected to his advantage. How else had he survived this long?

Now the wind blew, running through the trees as if a congregation of squirrels had set the branches dancing. Under that rattle there was something else. Not the wind.

Then Ruhr saw.

There, at the crest of the slope, a man pushing a bicycle appeared. He was coming down toward the house; Ruhr at once recognized the man's uniform as that of a police constable. Here, in this rustic corner of England, country policemen still cycled their beat. Ruhr watched the man come down the incline, then he turned slightly, conscious of how Trevaskis and Rick were motionless now, and how the two South Americans stood very still in the open doorway of the house.

The policeman reached the foot of the slope. He was middle-aged and slightly overweight and he wheezed a little.

"Morning," he said.

Ruhr kept his pistol covered.

"Bloody awful day," the policeman added. He made sure his bike was well balanced against the trunk of a tree, then he strolled toward Ruhr. Mud squelched beneath his heavy boots as he moved. About six feet from Gunther Ruhr he stopped.

"I'm looking for a girl that's gone missing," the constable said. "Seems she was out riding and her horse came home without her last night. I was wondering if you'd seen any sign of the child."

A horse; the girl hadn't mentioned an animal. "I'm sorry," Ruhr said.

"Well then," the constable said. "Keep your eyes open, sir, if you don't mind. Always appreciate any information. You new around here?"

Ruhr nodded. He saw it suddenly in the man's face: recognition, disguised behind a large uneasy smile, but recognition just the same. It was unmistakable.

The policeman scratched the side of his face and said, "We all know how young girls are nowadays. Spend nights with their boyfriends. Parents are the last to know, of course." The constable had himself in check now. He had control. He could go through the motions without showing the excitement of discovery. This was the terrorist being hunted all across England—and here he was, right in your own back yard!

"Thanks for your time, sir." The policeman glanced at the house, then walked to his bicycle. "Sorry to have troubled you."

He wheeled the vehicle out from under the tree and when he'd pushed the bike about ten feet, Ruhr called out to him.

"Constable. One moment."

The policeman turned. Ruhr moved toward him. The wind gathered force and shook every tree on the slope and blew a quick flurry of dead leaves through the air.

"Sir?" the policeman asked. A solitary leaf had settled on his shoulder.

Three feet from the constable, Ruhr stopped. In a swift gesture, which looked superficially innocent—a man bending to adjust a sock, a shoelace—he reached beneath the cuff of his pants and into the leather sheath he kept strapped to his shin. The knife was in his hand before the constable could move, and before the weapon registered the policeman was all but dead. He couldn't move quickly enough for Ruhr, who came up with the knife at an oblique angle and drove the blade into the throat. The policeman cried out, clutched the slash in his neck, then slid to his knees as if, astonished by imminent death, he needed to pray. Ruhr stabbed the man a second time, twisting the blade deep in the ribs.

The policeman fell back, knocking his bicycle over and causing the front wheel to rise in the air, where it spun idly. Ruhr wiped the blade with some leaves.

''Fucking impressive,'' Trevaskis said to Rick.

9

Villa Clara Province, Cuba

The house overlooked the ocean and the group of islands known as the Archipelago de Sabana. It was a large white stucco affair constructed around a central courtyard; moonlit water splashed out of a fountain and cascaded over a statue in the shape of a naked girl. The statue was a fine example of social realism, but the Lider Maximo, who stood on a balcony overlooking the fountain, wasn't exactly famous for his appreciation of anything artistic, though he always talked otherwise, since nobody *ever* questioned his judgments. He surrounded himself at times with swarms of words—like a beekeeper of language—phrases heaped on phrases, intricate and often colorful, yet frequently convoluted and downright enigmatic.

He fought with the urge to smoke one of the cigars he'd given up awhile ago. He looked up at the sky. It was a gorgeous Cuban midnight with thin high clouds and the sound of the tide, a night of coolness and clarity. But the Lider Maximo wasn't in any mood to appreciate such things.

Noises rose from the party in the room below. A piano played. Somebody told a joke to polite laughter. Across the courtyard, beneath arched doorways, armed guards stood in shadows. There were always guards wherever the Lider Maximo went. He even had people who tasted his food before he consumed it.

He turned away from the sight of the statue and walked inside the house, intolerant of this social gathering tonight; the chitchat, the men who wanted to shake his hand, the requests whispered in his ear, a favor here, a favor there, everything was a bore. He listened a moment to the piano. He had no ear for music—especially now, when he was this impatient.

Where was the Minister of Finance? What was keeping him?

The Lider Maximo went down the stairs. The piano was silent. In the large living-room all heads turned as he entered. His unsmiling condition had been noticed earlier and the party had adjusted itself. What might have been loud was muted and discreet. Everybody tried to please the Lider Maximo. They stepped around him as if he lived at the center of a large pampa of unbroken eggs. Everybody breathed softly in his presence and smiled just a little too eagerly. Women, some of whom underwent a suppressed hysteria in the man's company, were shrill in their pleasantries. But he was more than a man; he was as much an icon in Cuba as the old plaster Christs and Madonnas one still found concealed all the way from the Golfo de Guanahacabibes in the west to Punta Caleta in the east.

Communist Party officials and military leaders and attractive women filled the room. Some spilled out on to a patio where the remains of a roast pig turned on a spit and charcoals glowed and wine bottles stood in disarray on small tables. The Lider Maximo, stroking his beard, stared through the open door and across the patio.

The car would come from that direction.

He tried to be charming to a handsome silver-haired woman, a Danish journalist, who wanted to know something about political prisoners—but he was surrounded by his attendants and assistants and the usual Colombian novelist with three names who was something of a house pet. The entourage that swirled about him also included a group of Communist functionaries, some of whom had come from Italy and Spain and India, sightseers of Caribbean Communism: *fidelismo.*

He was too tense for this congregation. He stomped outside and waved his followers away. He wanted a moment's solitude, which wasn't such a selfish desire in a life that had not been his own since 1959. For thirty years he'd been public property, as much nationalized as the sugar industry, or the tobacco companies, or the banks. He was very tired and growing old; he knew that the young people of Cuba referred to him as El Viejo, the old one. Where was the stamina of yesterday? where the legendary strength?

In his starched gaberdine fatigues he strutted across the patio. He tore a chunk of flesh from the hot pig and thrust it into his mouth. It had the taste of a highly spiced automobile tire. He spat it out. The piano began to play again, and there was a round of quiet laughter, more of relief than genuine pleasure. He created a black hole wherever he went tonight; his absence from the main room allowed the guests to relax. He sat slumped in a chair and looked absently at a plate of scorched pig skin, leftovers. In an ill temper he pushed the plate aside and it clattered to the tiles, where it broke, scattering the discarded food. Nobody turned to look. When El Jefe broke anything, whether a plate or a law, no voices were raised in criticism.

There wasn't enough food on the island. Every day shortages grew worse. Every day brought some new complaint. Once, the criticism had centered around ideology. People asked him questions about the urgency behind universal literacy when reading material was restricted, or why Cuba had aligned itself with the Soviet bloc. Nowadays, ideology wasn't uppermost in the minds of Cubans; they wanted better food, better consumer goods. They heard U.S. radio broadcasts and saw smuggled movies, videotapes, outlawed magazines, and they felt deprived. Ninety miles away in the USA people had everything. In Cuba stores had empty shelves and useless goods and clothing designed in such centers of haute couture as Varna, Bulgaria, or Brasov, Rumania.

For the first time in many years, the Lider Maximo was afraid.

He'd known fear before. In the Sierra Maestra in the late 1950s when he'd fought the armies of Batista with only a few men. In 1953, when he'd led an unsuccessful assault on the Moncada barracks in Santiago. Yes, he'd known *el temor*, but he'd never been cowardly. What had they always said about him in Cuba? Fidel, he has the largest *timbales* on the whole goddam island! But this was very different, another stratum of fear; it was as if he could hear the ship of this eight-hundred-mile-long island grind to a halt, the engine broken beyond repair, the fuel tanks empty.

Sometimes, too, the fear yielded to an odd panic. He became easily confused, and amnesiac, and caught himself in the midst of a sentence whose end he'd quite forgotten, or in the middle of an action whose purpose was a puzzle. Now and again he felt slight pains in his stomach, too inconsequential to have his physicians treat. On one occasion, a coldness had seized his heart like a gauntlet of frost, a disquieting sensation that had lasted perhaps for ten seconds. It was age, he thought. Eyesight and teeth went, so did the interior plumbing and the central pump. A man was no more than an intricate machine; and all the blueprints to explain his parts and repair them were incomplete because medicine was still a primitive quasi-science.

Perhaps fear was something else age brought in its merciless wake.

He tilted his head to one side, listening to the croaking of frogs in the distance, so many it was practically a roar. He gazed across the patio, seeing how his armed guards had taken up new positions in the shadows. Inside the house the piano was playing something composed by Silvio Rodriguez, considered a 'safe' musician by the regime. The Lider Maximo knew that if he hadn't been present the pianist would have performed Cole Porter or Irving Berlin or some other Yanqui music. The Lider Maximo was deferred to, even revered. But he knew people carped behind his back and ran him down and accused him of bankrupting Cuba.

There was the sound of a car. He stood up, tugged at his beard. He saw headlights approach. At a point in the road where the concrete twisted toward the ocean, the car lights illuminated white surf. Then the motor died, and a door slammed. The Lider Maximo moved quickly across the patio to embrace the new arrival and whisk him away to a quiet upper room where they might talk, free from the noise of the party.

The room was small, containing only a desk and two chairs and piles of unsorted books. A green-shaded lamp provided the only light. The Lider Maximo said, "You're very late."

"There were flight delays," the visitor replied.

The Lider Maximo waved a hand impatiently. "Speak to me. Tell me the outcome."

The visitor said, "It's just as we feared. The well's running dry."

The Lider Maximo tossed his head back and looked up at the ceiling where a large motionless fan threw a cross-like shadow; it was possible to see, through the hairs of his beard, the thick double chin. "They want me out, am I right? They want me to step aside."

"No, Commandante. They expressed no such desire."

The Lider Maximo scoffed. "They wouldn't tell you to your face. The Russians don't operate that way. They smile at you, toast you, and after ten vodkas they hug you. Best of friends. Comrades! Only later do you realize you've been lied to and cheated. Make no mistake, companero, they want me out. I'm too disobedient. Too unruly. They can't always control me the way they would like. If they had a weak man in my position, they might open their purses more generously to Cuba."

The visitor said, "I don't think it has anything to do with you, Commandante. They say they'll no longer invest money in Cuba at the levels we've come to expect. The new Politburo has more on its collective mind than Cuba. They'll continue to buy sugar—"

"Oh, this makes my heart glad." The Lider Maximo's sarcasm was too grim to be amusing. Besides, his sense of humor was always slightly skewed and too heavy-handed to cause much mirth. The charm for which he'd been famous earlier in life had deserted him to a large extent. The world had eroded it.

"—at the present prices. But there will be severe cutbacks in technological help. As many as three hundred advisors will be withdrawn. Joint construction projects already under way, such as the nuclear generating plant at Jurugua, will be halted. No new ones will be started. We can no longer expect—and I quote—favored treatment."

The Lider Maximo was angry. "Favored treatment!" He spluttered. "We've always had a special arrangement with them!"

"The Soviets are economizing worldwide, Commandante. It's really that simple. They face economic chaos at home. Their whole economy is rotten and cumbersome. The cost of Afghanistan was too high. Now they're turning inward. They're no longer enthusiastic about the spread of Communism in Central America. We're seeing a new era. The Soviet priority is to look after themselves. Their own people are complaining bitterly about the quality of life in Russia."

"And the *rusos* throw their old allies to the dogs?"

"There will be a bone or two. But that's all. We can't look forward to a continuation of generous past policies."

"*Cochinos!* Perhaps I should make the trip to Moscow myself."

"It may make no difference."

The Lider Maximo was too proud to go cap in hand before the Russians. The begging-bowl held out for scraps! Never! Besides, he had no fondness for the General Secretary, whom he considered a capitalist. He had entertained the man during the Secretary's visit to Havana last spring. Serious talks had taken place on the subject of solving Cuba's indebtedness to the Soviet Union, and there had been a great deal of smiling camaraderie for the benefit of the world's press. But now, when the Lider Maximo needed some extra credits, when he needed cash, when he saw his Revolution founder in an ocean of debt and despair, the Soviets had abandoned him.

Nothing was said for a long time. Faintly, the piano could be heard from the lower part of the house. Outside, the breeze picked up, driving the tide a little harder on to the beach. From the courtyard came the sound of a guard sliding a clip inside his automatic rifle. They were always prepared, always checking their weapons. The Lider Maximo put on a pair of glasses and walked to his desk, where he scanned a batch of papers.

"Do you know what these are, companero? Projections prepared by our finest economists. Graphs and numbers and scientific notations. They were prepared by people in your own Ministry. They forecast continued shortages in basic items. Beef. Fish. Milk. Shoes. Medical supplies. These might be alleviated by an infusion of hard currency. But where is it to come from? Without hard currency, how do we import goods? The shortages will get worse. And our soldiers returning from Angola—how are they to be absorbed into a work force that has no work for them?"

He crunched the sheets in his hands and tossed them up in the air, swatting at them like shuttlecocks as they floated back down. He picked up those that had fallen, balled them even more tightly in his fists and threw them from the window, where they were carried briefly by the breeze. *Papeleo,* he kept saying with contempt. *Papeleo*—paperwork. Those sheets he didn't pick up he crumpled underfoot, wiping them back and forth on the floorboards as if they were dogshit that adhered to his soles. Then, his energy spent on this extraordinary display, he sat down at his desk.

"They are out to get me," he said. "Not just the Russians, companero. But there are forces in Cuba that would like to see me dead. Outside Cuba, the CIA is still sniffing after my blood. I constantly hear tales of counter-revolutionary armies forming here and there in Central America. And the exile community in Miami—there are a great many who would murder me and feel joy."

He was quiet. He was remembering the old days when La Revolucion had been his youthful mistress, the love of his heart, when she'd been bright and optimistic and constant. Now she was turning, as many loves do, into a nagging crone whose demands grew more preposterous daily. She'd become brittle, and her breasts sagged, and she was gaunt. She had all the light-hearted humor of a Greek chorus. And yet once, in the delight of her early years, those breasts had been full, and her belly smooth and tight. She had been a glory to behold. Lost inside La Revolucion, he had squandered the very best of his seed.

The Lider Maximo said, "I have few trusted friends. My brother, perhaps. But he's in Africa. My inner circle—but they're too ambitious for me to trust them wholeheartedly. My bodyguards, of course. But even guards have been known to turn. And you. My Minister of Finance. Can I trust you, Rosabal?"

There were rare moments when Rafael Rosabal glimpsed the ghost of a younger Fidel, not this curmudgeon who grew resentfully old but another Castro of flinty determination and irresistible charm. He'd once possessed magnetism enough to persuade men to embark on the frail overcrowded craft called the *Granma* and sail twelve hundred miles on a harsh sea from Mexico to Cuba, the gift of convincing them they could survive not only the voyage but the killing heat and cold and malarial mosquitoes in the inhospitable mountains of the Sierra Maestra. Triumph—you could still see that glint in Fidel's eyes when they weren't otherwise darkened by injuries and betrayals, many of them imagined.

Rosabal said, "I am on your side, Commandante. As always."

The Lider Maximo looked thoughtful. "You see, the problem is simple, but not easy to correct. When we won the armed struggle against Batista, we faced a situation that was beyond our experience. What did soldiers know of the economy? Of government? They could fire rifles, but they couldn't administer the sugar industry, or the tobacco crop, or the mines. So. Mistakes were made. Bad mistakes. The wrong crops were planted—"

Rosabal thought: *You were personally responsible for those, Commandante. You were the laughing stock of Cuba for your bizarre horticultural ideas.*

"—and essential machinery rotted on the docks in Havana because we didn't have the necessary moving equipment. And perhaps our agricultural reforms took the initiative away from small farmers. We brought capitalism to its knees, Rosabal. But what did we put in its place?"

Rosabal was very quiet. A quiet pulse beat at the side of his head. He knew this pulse, which was often the harbinger of a rage he couldn't always control, a dark sensation Castro often inspired in him. He maintained his poise with enormous difficulty, closing his eyes a moment, concentrating very hard on the black spaces inside his head. He made no answer to the Commandante's question, which had been rhetorical in any case.

The Lider Maximo said, "People live longer nowadays, and they are better educated, and they have brighter opportunities, but none of this is enough for them. Why?"

Rosabal felt the breeze come through the flyscreen and stir his hair. His bad moment passed; that sense of slippage was gone. He had control of himself again. His voice was relaxed. He said, "I wouldn't presume to know the answer, Commandante." He thought: *Because life is drab, and people feel hopeless. And now not even the Russians will support you. You have driven Cuba into disaster and bankruptcy. You stupid old fucking clown in your idiotic gaberdine fatigues.*

Castro said, "The problem isn't in the system, Rosabal. Of course there are some inefficiencies. But the real problem is that the people are self-centered! They put themselves before the Revolution. If there is a failure, Rosabal, it's because we haven't *educated* the people as well as we might. We haven't educated self-ishness out of them. They still don't understand that the Revolution requires extraordinary patience and endurance and self-denial. We've asked them for an enormous effort in the past, but we haven't asked for enough. Now we must demand even greater sacrifices."

"Greater sacrifices?" Rosabal asked. How typical of the Commandante to turn blame away from himself and apportion it to the people! If only the people had been educated to understand the shortages on the island, there wouldn't be any complaints! How laughable! The populace hadn't understood the Revolution, and in the Lider Maximo's mind that was the real failure!

Castro's lips contorted slightly. There was a swift

arc of pain in his intestines; he wondered if he might have ulcers. He waited until the feeling passed before he said, "In Cuba today, for example, we export all the lobster we catch, and most of the shrimp. As a consequence, the Cuban people don't have these bourgeois delicacies in their diet. The reverse side of the coin is that children no longer have rickets and malaria is practically dead. And if the Russians are no longer going to assist our Revolution, then we must tighten our own belts one more notch, Rosabal. We must ask for more working hours and cuts in pay. We must have more volunteers in the construction industry and in the cane fields. We must export more beef cattle."

Rosabal was filled with contempt for the Lider Maximo. He was thinking of the small room in the Palace of Congresses in Moscow where Anatoly Tal, the Minister of Finance, had talked to him at great length about how much money the Soviet Union had poured into Cuba—and he'd emphasized the word 'poured' as if he were talking about some precious liquid tossed down a sink. In currency and technical support during the last thirty years, the exact amount was incalculable, but Tal reckoned it in the region of two hundred and fifty billion U.S. dollars. And what had the Soviet Union gained? Hard questions were being asked inside the Politburo. There were members prepared to cut Cuba completely adrift.

Rosabal mentioned none of this to the Lider Maximo. It would prompt a ranting speech that might last for hour after hour, filled with bitter expletives and self-pity, bravado and chest-thumping. One of Castro's speeches, characterized by non-sequiturs and nostalgic drifts, could imprison a listener for four or five hours, and Rosabal had no desire to be locked into such a monologue. Sometimes these speeches took dangerous turns, and the threats increased with the bitterness, and Castro spoke about bringing destruction to his principal enemy, the United States. You could see it then in his eyes, a certain fiery quality, something that shone with the light of old dangers that hadn't quite died away. *There are still teeth in your head, El Viejo*, Rosabal thought. *There is still danger in you. But for the sake of Cuba, you must be forcibly removed.*

Rosabal glanced at his watch; in one hour and twenty minutes from now, the first act would begin in the depths of the English countryside.

"We will initiate a new propaganda campaign," Castro said. "Tomorrow, we will announce to the Cuban people that the Russians—who are now friendly with the Yanquis—have deserted their Cuban comrades. There will be a period of patriotic self-denial. Posters. Newspaper articles. I'll make a speech on television. I'll talk on radio. I'll go into the streets and squares."

Rosabal heard the familiar voice, but tuned out the words. He walked to the window, concentrated on the sound of the piano playing thinly from below. The tune, perhaps inevitably, was *Guantanamera*. He gazed across the courtyard, seeing small huddles of guests.

Here and there he recognized sympathizers—an old soldier who had been with Fidel in the Sierra Maestra but had lost all faith, a female journalist whose critical reports on Communism circulated anonymously, an official from the Ministry of the Interior who despised the police state he had helped create.

Rosabal turned back to Fidel, who was still talking. Did the Lider Maximo use language as a means of exorcising his doubts, of chasing despair away? Did he drown truth with the empty rattle of words? Or was it the poison systematically introduced into his system by his personal physician during the last three months that made him babble so freely and with such confusion? Not enough poison to kill, only to confuse and debilitate the bastard. Rosabal didn't want him to die that way. He wanted to look him straight in the eyes at the point of his death.

When that time came, Rosabal would kill him personally.

And then the island would be his, wrested from this pathetic dictator whose time had come and gone, whose policies had not only failed but had torn the heart out of sad, dying Cuba, a corpse barely afloat in pale blue water.

Norfolk

The Range Rover travelled slowly down a narrow lane. On either side meadows stretched toward trees. An unpromising morning sun, now white and watery, hung low on the landscape, destined to vanish behind cloud mass again. A church tower eclipsed the sun a moment, and headstones in a cemetery, damp still from the recent rain, gleamed gently. It was lovely and serene, a world of quiet, peaceful corners and birds that called softly. Even the sound of the Range Rover was absorbed by the landscape.

Flavell drove. He did so with great care. No traffic lay behind, none came in the opposite direction. The world might have been empty. Ruhr sat in the front; the two Americans and Zapino in the back. The girl, bound and gagged, was cramped on the floor. She lay very still. She'd seen the body of the policeman— barely covered with dead leaves—and the sight had horrified her. If she'd worried about her own death before it had been at one remove, like a very bad dream. But it was different now because there was no awakening. This was the reality. She kept whispering *Jesus* to herself, over and over.

Ruhr watched the road. He had no need of the map, which lay folded in the glove compartment. He knew where the turns were, the intersections that lay ahead. He checked his watch. It was eight AM. A signpost announcing the village of Hornside (pop 134) approached. A narrow main street, a pub, a grocery, an antique shop, a church, and then Hornside, in all its bucolic charm, was gone like an old postcard.

The Range Rover kept moving. Ruhr looked at his watch again. Ten past eight. The narrow lane turned this way and that. A windmill loomed up, its big blades motionless. And then the road forked. Ruhr directed Flavell to drive between trees where the vehicle would be concealed from the sight of anyone passing. Flavell cut the engine and there was silence.

Eight-thirteen.

Ruhr ordered the men to make their weapons ready. Rick, in charge of the tear gas, stepped out and began to remove canisters, which he set carefully in the damp grass. The Argentineans checked the clips in their automatic rifles. Trevaskis fingered his St. Christopher for luck, then checked his own rifle. Steffie Brough shut her eyes tightly. She didn't want to look. Not at the men, not at the guns; she wanted to be blind, freed from everything that encroached on her. *Jesus Christ, please help me. I haven't done anything wrong, not really wrong, I don't deserve this. Get me out of this and I'm yours for life.*

Ruhr looked once again at the time. Eight-seventeen.

The landscape was still quiet. But it seemed sullenly menacing now, as if something long dormant were about to emerge from a crack in the earth. Ruhr stared through the trees at the road. He raised his rocket-launcher to his shoulder. He turned his face up to the sky, from which the sun had disappeared. He listened. He could hear it faintly in the distance. The timing was exactly right. Beautiful.

And now there was another noise, a low rumble of gears that sent vibrations through the still air. It was the sound made by an engine whose enormous power was restrained.

"You all know what has to be done," Ruhr said. If they didn't, it was too late to learn. The time for rehearsals was long past.

Ruhr peered through the green enclosures of the trees. He saw a large truck covered by a dark green canopy. More than thirty feet long and cumbersome, it travelled at fifteen miles an hour. Directly in front were three jeeps, and on either side of the truck two motorcycles. In the rear a smaller truck carried a dozen armed soldiers. The larger vehicle's gears groaned, the ground underfoot trembled. Ruhr looked up at the sky once more.

There, like a flying spider, was the black helicopter, the Cobra. Unmarked, windows tinted, it came in at a low angle, barely skimming treetops and sending birds up out of branches. The sky screamed, the day gone suddenly wild; but it was merely a preamble.

Now, Ruhr thought. He pulled his mask over his face.

The first canisters, thrown by Rick, exploded in front of the jeeps. Swirling gas created an unbreathable atmosphere. Ruhr aimed his rocket launcher and fired at the jeeps even as the occupants, prepared for the contingency of tear-gas though surprised by it nevertheless, fumbled for their masks. Trevaskis let his M-60 blaze at the same time. One of the jeeps overturned and slithered into a ditch, where it caught fire.

The blades of the Cobra fanned smoke and gas fumes. Fire from the guns mounted on the chopper was directed viciously at the motorcycle escort. Fuel tanks on the bikes exploded while the chopper began to fire at the smaller lorry in the rear, where armed soldiers were scattering into the trees and firing their automatic rifles up into the sky.

Ruhr released another rocket, which blew a second jeep apart. Flame, higher than the trees around it, created a vast blue and orange column brighter than any sun. Zapino and Flavell, both masked, ran through the trees toward the long truck. Its drivers were climbing out of the cab and shooting in the general direction of the chopper. The Cobra, hunting the soldiers, eluded the shots and sprayed the woods with quick fire. It was important to wipe out the scattered squadron before radio communication could summon reinforcements. They would arrive sooner or later, of course. Ruhr preferred later. Much later.

He surveyed the action with quiet satisfaction. He saw Flavell and Zapino reach the long truck. He fired his rocket launcher again, setting more trees on fire. And suddenly, emerging from the thick orange smoke, was a green military helicopter, probably part of the original escort, scanning the terrain for just such a contingency as this.

Ruhr watched the Cobra, a huge mysterious raven, churn upward, drawing the military helicopter clear of the smoke. The Cobra fired its rocket launchers first and the camouflaged chopper tilted sideways, then downward, going into an evasive slump. The Cobra persisted like a rabid bat, pursuing the other aircraft with a tenacity Ruhr admired. The air struggle was brief. The military craft exploded and the Cobra wheeled away from the great reaches of flame.

But not quickly enough. Flame and debris blown out of the falling chopper caught the fuselage of the Cobra, which disintegrated with spectacular fury and dropped into a nearby meadow where it burned.

Ruhr, who never allowed himself to be upset by the changing fortunes of war, hurried from the cover of the trees, spraying the area before him with his M-16. He was alive now, attuned to battle, moving, not thinking, running on instinct. Zapino had already gained entry to the cab of the long truck. Flavell, dead, lay directly under the large front wheels. Everything burned—jeeps, motorcycles, trucks, the wreckage of the choppers, trees, an abandoned barn nearby. It was a landscape imagined by a pyromaniac. Everything burned except the one thing that mattered: the large truck with the green canopy.

Ruhr climbed up behind the wheel. He engaged the gears and drove over the body of Flavell and through the wreckage of jeeps and the corpses of soldiers. Gunfire still came from those soldiers concealed in the woods, sporadic, almost indifferent. It was answered by Trevaskis and Rick as they rushed toward the parked Range Rover. Rick was struck in the neck and he fell face down.

In the truck, Ruhr stepped on the gas pedal. The Range Rover, with Trevaskis at the wheel, came out of the woodland and followed. Thin gunfire still rattled behind them, growing fainter. Ruhr stamped the pedal to the floor. He couldn't get the truck beyond forty, forty-five miles an hour because of the weight of the cargo as he drove the narrow, empty lanes that led to the airfield. There was an astonishing density to the trees here. They created a mystery out of the quiet meadows and lonely farmhouses that lay beyond them.

Ruhr looked in the side mirror. The Range Rover was immediately behind. The airfield was one mile away. Ruhr tried to get the truck to go faster. At fifty, it vibrated with asthmatic severity. It began to shudder and skip and threaten to die as the airfield came in view.

At the edge of the tarmac sat the massive transport plane, the C-130, engines already running. Ruhr drove the big truck to the back of the plane, where a ramp, hydraulically-operated, angled out of a doorway in the C-130's underbelly. The Range Rover came to a stop alongside the truck and Trevaskis jumped out.

"Let's get this fucker loaded toot sweet!" Trevaskis shouted.

But Ruhr had something else to do first; he reached inside the Range Rover and lifted out the girl.

"Sweet fucking Christ," Trevaskis said, baffled and angry. Rick was dead and so was Flavell and if somebody had managed to summon reinforcements this whole place would be crawling with soldiers and Ruhr *still* found time to take this girl along. The sick fuck.

Ruhr carried Steffie Brough to the ramp. Her blouse half undone, small white breasts sadly visible, mud-flecked skirt swept to one side. Her eyes were open, bloodshot from the tear gas. If they expressed anything, Ruhr couldn't read it. Her lips, dry and cracked, appeared to have lost color. Ruhr took her school scarf from around her neck, draped it carefully over the Range Rover's back seat, then raised her small body up, passing her to the hands of the men inside the transport plane, who took this unexpected merchandise without question.

Trevaskis, puzzled by the business with the scarf, guided Zapino as he backed the truck up toward the ramp so that the cruise missile and the separate rectangular compartment, some eight feet by seven, that contained the control system, could be loaded into the plane.

It was a precious prize, the stolen property of the North Atlantic Treaty Organization.

10

It was shortly after ten AM, some two hours since the attack. Ambulances came and went in utter confusion along country lanes built for horses and carts. Spectators from nearby villages stood beneath umbrellas and some macabre souls took photographs despite the entreaties of military policemen. Physicians in wet white coats, an Anglican priest, a group of taciturn military investigators, the inevitable reporters, the general ghouls attendant on every bloodletting—it was a crowded circus, and Pagan, whose chest pain flared despite a recent ingestion of Pethidine in the fast car from London, was filled with several feelings at the same time, all of them cheerless.

Rain fell bleakly. Foxie had his collar turned up and looked like a gambler praying for a winner in the last race of a long, losing day.

"I'm angry," Pagan said quietly.

When Frank's words emerged like sand through a

clenched fist, Foxworth knew Pagan was going into his dragonlike mode. Even the way his breath hung on the chill wet air suggested fire. The business in the hotel last night with the Cuban-American woman and the man known as Rafael Rosabal, who had turned out to be a member of Castro's government, was another problem. Something there cut deeply into Frank, and Foxie wasn't sure what. Pagan had reacted oddly to Foxie's information about Rosabal, as if he were pretending not to listen at all. Was the woman an old love, a potent ghost still? Foxworth was a tireless observer of the signs in Pagan's personal landscape, and he'd developed an ability to read most of them—and even love a number of them—but every now and then Frank vanished inside himself and became camouflaged at the heart of his own terrain. Now was one such moment.

"We have half the police force of the country looking for Ruhr—and he pulls this off anyway," Pagan said. "A fucking cruise missile!"

A savage little pulse worked in Pagan's jaw. "You know what makes it even worse? We've got a couple of eyewitnesses among the soldiers who saw his face clearly before he put on his gas mask. You know what that means? He wanted people to *see* him. He wanted to be *noticed*. He's like a bloody actor who just happened to do a quick stint in the sticks here. He wants audience appreciation even in the miserable provinces! Jesus Christ! The man's bored with all his years of anonymity and now he's got a taste of fame and he loves it. Vanity, Foxie. The bastard's suddenly got theater in his blood. I want him. I want that fucker."

Foxie surveyed the team of experts sifting through the wreckage of the two helicopters. Here and there, in ditches, under trees, hidden by long grass, lay bodies that hadn't yet been taken away. It was a sickening scene. Foxie thrust his hands in the pockets of his raincoat and thought how infrequently he'd seen Frank Pagan this upset. Sirens cut through the rain, flashing lights glimmered feebly. It was a miserable day with a gray sky that might last forever.

"The missile didn't have a warhead," Foxworth remarked. A small consolation. "Without the nuclear hardware it's only a bloody twenty-odd-foot cylinder of metal."

"With dangerous potential," Pagan said. He was watching a soldier being raised on a stretcher; the boy's leg was missing below the knee. Pagan turned his face to the side. There had been a royal battle in this quiet spot whose only usual violence was that of an owl setting upon a fieldmouse, talons open, a quick dying squeal by moonlight.

An official limousine approached the crossroad and squeezed with some authority between parked ambulances. Martin Burr got out, followed by the Home Secretary, Sir Frederick Kinnaird. Both men made their way over the damp road to where Pagan stood.

Pagan had no great fondness for the Home Secretary, nor any specific reason for his dislike except that he was not enamored of politicians in general. They inspired in him the same kind of confidence as used-car salesmen. Vote for me, my Party has been driven only by an old lady and then only on Sundays and never more than thirty miles an hour. Burr did the introductions. Hands were duly pumped. Burr opened a small umbrella and shared it with Sir Freddie. This made Pagan conscious of his damp woollen overcoat and Italian shoes that leaked rainwater.

"Is it as ghastly as it looks?" Freddie Kinnaird asked.

It was on the tip of Frank Pagan's tongue, a mischief; he wanted to say *No, it's been a lovely party but we've run a bit low on the canapes, Freddie, my old sunshine.* But he merely gestured toward the demolition site.

"A cruise missile was taken, I understand," Kinnaird said.

Pagan noticed Kinnaird's black coat with the slick velvet collar; an exquisite silk tie went well with his striped shirt, made for him in Jermyn Street, no doubt. Kinnaird said something about how the missile had been on its way to Tucson, Arizona, there to be destroyed under the terms of the Russian-American treaty. He spoke in a drawling way, as if his every word were precious, to be lingered over. Now and again he shoved a strand of thin, sandy hair out of his eyes.

Pagan said, "We assume the missile was driven to an airfield nearby and flown out. There are about half a dozen air-strips in this vicinity left over from World War Two, most of them private flying clubs now. I've got men checking them out. If the missile *hasn't* been flown from the area, it wouldn't be too hard to hide. An underground tunnel, a warehouse, a bus garage."

"To where could the missile be flown?" Kinnaird asked.

"Anybody's guess," Pagan said. "I hope we'll have an answer soon. The RAF has been conducting an air search, but since they haven't told *us* anything, it means they don't have a thing to report. Otherwise they'd be crowing."

Kinnaird said, "I understand one would need a fair-sized transport plane to carry the missile. Surely that shouldn't be too hard to spot."

Foxworth replied, "And it wouldn't be, except for two things, Home Secretary. The rotten weather and the fact that there's an enormous amount of air traffic in this part of the world. London's only fifty miles away, and the pattern of traffic there and throughout the Home Counties in general is horrendous. The system is overloaded."

"Why steal a missile without a warhead anyway?" the Home Secretary wanted to know.

Nobody had an answer to Sir Freddie's question. Rain fell on Burr's black umbrella. The Commissioner asked, "What about the dead terrorists?"

"We're still working on ID," Pagan replied. "We've got four of the buggers. Two died in the assault. Another two inside the chopper." He was impatient suddenly. He was very fond of Martin Burr, and admired him, but he disliked the way Big Shots drove up from London to ask what progress had been made when it was goddamned obvious that men were bleeding to death and ambulances slashing through the rain and the whole scorched, smoking landscape looked as if a meteor had struck it.

"Rather fond of helicopters, aren't they?" Freddie Kinnaird said. "What do we know about this one?"

Pagan had one of those quirky little urges to unbutton his overcoat and show Sir Freddie that, contrary to anything he might have read in the tabloids lately, there was no Superman costume under his shirt. He restrained himself and said, "We're running checks. We know it was a Cobra and the markings had been painted black. Beyond that, nothing yet. We're working on it. We assume it was the same aircraft used in Shepherd's Bush. But that's just an assumption, and practically worthless." Pagan had a difficult moment keeping anger and bitterness from his voice. The idea of a second chopper attack, and the sheer murderous arrogance behind it, rattled him.

"Sorry, by the by, to hear about your gun wound.

Bloody tragic business in Shepherd's Bush." There was the famous Kinnaird touch, palm open on Pagan's shoulder, a slightly distant intimacy, as if between nobility and the common man there might be the merest suggestion only of physical contact. It was all right for their lordships to fuck the serving wenches but not altogether good form to become too intimate with the footmen.

Pagan walked toward the wreckage of the Cobra. The dead terrorists were covered with sheets of plastic, under which charred faces might be seen opaquely, as if through filthy isinglass. Men with protective gloves picked through debris cool enough to handle. Pagan watched for a moment. From a mess such as this, hard information would emerge only slowly—a fingerprint here, an engine identification number there, maybe a scorched photograph in a wallet. It would take a long time for this chaos to yield anything useful.

Now Foxie approached the smoking rubble in a hurried way. "Just got a message from a place called St. Giles, Frank. It sounds quite interesting. It's a few miles."

"I'd welcome anything that gets me the hell out of here," Pagan said.

"I'll fetch the car," and Foxie was gone again, nimbly skirting the small fires that still flickered here and there in the gloom.

The airfield beyond the hamlet of St. Giles had once been a rundown place, redolent of robust pilots with waxen moustaches dashing off in Spitfires to defeat the Hun, but the old hangars had been painted bright blue and the control tower refurbished in a similar shade. Somebody had taken some trouble and expense to tart the place up. A red windsock flapped damply. A sign attached to the tower said East Anglia Flying Club in bright letters. Small planes, chained to the ground for protection against the wind, were scattered around the edges of the runway.

Foxworth and Pagan got out of the car. It was a dreary open space, exposed to the elements. A thin wet mist had formed in the wooded land beyond the hangars where a group of men stood around a Range Rover. Pagan walked the runway, Foxie following. At a certain point Pagan stopped and kneeled rather cautiously to the tarmac, dipping his finger into a slick of fresh oily fluid; it was some kind of hydraulic liquid, viscous and green, rain-repellent. He wiped his hands together and walked until he reached the copse of beech trees.

Three men stood near the blue Range Rover, the doors of which hung open. Pagan recognized Billy Ewing, a Scotsman who worked at the SATO office in Golden Square. The other two were uniformed men, probably local. Billy Ewing, who had a small red nose and blue eyes that watered no matter the season, had a handkerchief crumpled in the palm of one hand as he always did. He had allergies unknown to the medical profession. His life was one long sniff.

"We haven't touched a thing, Frank," Ewing said in a voice forever on the edge of a sneeze. "It's just the way we found it."

The Rover was hidden, although not artfully concealed. Whoever had stashed it here between the trees had done so in haste, or else didn't give a damn about discovery. Pagan looked inside. Boxes of cartridges lay on the floor, a discarded shotgun, two rocket launchers, three automatic pistols; quite a nice little arsenal. He looked at the instrument panel. The vehicle had clocked a mere three hundred and seven miles. It still smelled new.

Billy Ewing coughed and said, "An old geezer who was illegally fishing a local stream says he heard a bloody great roar this morning and when he looked up he saw—and here I quote—'a monster hairyplane near a half mile long' rising just above him. Scared him half to death, he says. If you need to talk to him, Frank, you'll find him at a pub in St. Giles where he went to take some medication for his fright."

As he listened to Ewing, Pagan reached inside the rear of the vehicle. Lying across the back seat was a wine-colored scarf of the kind worn by schoolkids as part of a uniform. He removed the scarf. A small threaded motif ran through it, the stylized letters MCS. The last two might have stood for Comprehensive School.

"What do you make of it?" Foxie asked.

Pagan didn't reply. An odd little feeling worked inside him, something vague moving toward the light, but as yet indefinable. He held the garment to his nose. There was a fading scent of rose.

"Belongs to a girl," he said. "Unless boys are wearing perfumes these days."

"You'll find a few," Ewing remarked in the manner of a philosopher resigned to paradoxes. "It's a funny world these days, Frank."

"What's the scarf doing in this particular car?" Foxworth asked.

The feeling coursed through Pagan again, creating an uneasiness. "My guess is Ruhr left it there deliberately," he said.

"Why? You think he's thumbing his nose at you, Frank?"

Pagan gazed through the beech trees. Ruhr's disturbed mind, the surface of which Pagan had barely scratched during their interviews, seemed to present itself in a solid flash of light, like a hitherto unknown planet drifting momentarily close to earth. "It's possible. I think he's got himself a bloody hostage and wants me to know it. He likes the idea of turning the screw."

Pagan shrugged; how could he know for sure? The flash of light had gone out and Ruhr's mind was once again a darkened planetarium. "Let's find out what MCS stands for," he said. "Then call in the fingerprint boys and have them go over this car."

Foxworth shivered as the wind rose up and roared through the beech trees, tearing leaves from branches. He wasn't happy with this deserted airfield, or the spooky beeches, or the girl's scarf. Nor was he exactly overjoyed to see Frank slyly swallow another painkiller, which he did like a very bad actor, turning his face to one side and smuggling the narcotic into his mouth.

"Keep an eye on things here for a while, Billy," Pagan said.

"Will do," the Scotsman answered, and sneezed abruptly into his hankie.

Pagan and Foxworth walked back to their car. The red wind sock filled with air, rising quickly then subsiding in a limp, shapeless manner.

Cabo Gracias a Dios, Honduras

The midmorning was infernally humid; even the sea breezes, sluggish and sickly, couldn't dispel the stickiness. The man who stood on a knoll overlooking the ocean wore very black glasses and a battered Montecristo Fini Panama hat; he carried an aerosol can of insecticide with which he periodically buzzed the mosquitoes that flocked constantly around him.

The man was Tomas 'La Gaviota' Fuentes, a Cuban-American whose nickname, The Seagull, came from his amazing ability to fly seaplanes. Storms, whirlpools, hurricanes—Fuentes flew and landed his planes regardless. He had a madman's contempt for whatever inclement weather the gods sent down.

Fuentes looked along the beach, watching a score of fighter planes come in pairs at 1500 feet, then drop to 1200, at which point they strafed the sands, firing at bull's-eyes painted in the center of white banners. The planes, a mixture of Skyhawks, Harriers, and F-16s gathered from a variety of locations, used the inert practice ammunition known in the trade as blue slugs. Many of the banners remained undisturbed as the aircraft completed the run and veered left. Then fifty amphibious craft, each containing fifteen armed men, rolled with the tide toward the beaches. Every day the men practised wading ashore, hurrying over the sands to the cover of trees, where they disappeared swiftly and quietly.

La Gaviota took off his hat and cuffed sweat from his brow. This place was the asshole of the world, the planet's sphincter. He turned away from the beach, strutted toward his large tent. Despite the fan powered by a generator, stifling air blew in self-perpetuating circles; hell wasn't, as a certain clown of a French philosopher had claimed, other people. Real hell was a canvas tent in a Central American republic surrounded by hungry dung-flies as big as wine bottles.

He poured himself a cold beer from an ice-chest and gulped it down quickly. He was a big man and all muscle; even the way his forehead protruded suggested an outcropping of muscle rather than bone. Each of his hands spanned twelve inches and he wore size thirteen army boots. He crumpled the can like tissue paper and turned on his radio, which was tuned to a country station beamed out of El Paso. It wasn't great reception, but better than nothing.

The flap of his tent opened just as he shut his eyes and listened to the sweet pipes of Emmylou Harris singing *Feeling Single, Seeing Double.* The visitor was Fuentes's second in command, a lackey Harry Hurt had sent from Washington. His name was Roger Bosanquet and he was some kind of limey, with an accent you could spread on a scone.

"They're getting better," Fuentes said. "They're not perfect, but they're improving." Here Fuentes added the words 'old bean', which he imagined was the way Englishmen addressed one another at every level of society. His attempt at an Oxford accent was appalling. Bosanquet always responded with a polite half-smile.

Bosanquet said, "The infantry coming ashore performed with precision. They can't possibly be faulted. The pilots, however, were not as accurate as they should be. They need a little more time." He had received training at an army school in England—from which establishment he'd been expelled for reasons Fuentes didn't know, though he had absolutely no doubt the crime was faggotry. All Englishmen were faggots. It was a law of nature.

Fuentes made the basic mistake of seeing only Bosanquet's manicured manners and his quiet subordination. He missed a certain hardness that lay in the Englishman's blue eyes. Nor did he notice the determined way Bosanquet sometimes set his jaw. He consistently underestimated the Englishman, whom he considered a *boniato*, a thickhead. But at some other level, one Fuentes did not care to acknowledge, he envied Bosanquet his education and training. His cool. His *class.*

"They don't have more fucking time," Fuentes said. "The clocks are running, *yame,* and they're running just a little too damn fast. The aircraft are supposed to destroy Castro's defensive positions on the beach before the landings, correct? And if they don't, then the poor bastards coming ashore are walking into a slaughterhouse. Correct?"

Bosanquet wiped his brow with a red bandanna. He had served with Latin Americans like Fuentes before now and he disliked their sudden passions; they were brave soldiers but lacked detachment. It couldn't be expected, of course. Impatience and irrationality were programmed into them. They loved theatrics. They threw fits. They were unpredictable. They were not, when all was said and done, Anglo-Saxon. Bosanquet, who had done many dirty deeds for Harry Hurt in his life and who was here in this stinking place to provide a counterweight to Fuentes (and make confidential reports to Harry), spoke in a reasonable way. "With a little more accuracy on behalf of the planes, everything will work out superbly."

"*Cojones!* Castro's apes will shoot those poor bastards in the boats like coconuts on the midway," Fuentes snarled.

"Only if Castro's apes get the chance," Bosanquet said quietly. "And we don't believe they will, do we? All we are doing here is to prepare our men for a contingency that isn't going to arise. Besides, it keeps them from getting bored."

Fuentes, calmer now, mumbled and shrugged. He was into a second beer now, a Lone Star. Like all demanding leaders of men, he always thought the worst of his subordinates. They were misconceived sons of whores, and yet he prayed, as any stage director will, that all would somehow be well on opening night, lines would not be fluffed, and some generous magic would inhabit his actors and raise them to the status of gods. In truth, he was reasonably pleased with his forces, but he was damned if he'd ever admit this. You didn't go round handing out Oscars before the goddam performance.

He pulverized a mosquito on his green baize card table. He imagined squelching Fidel in just such a way: *schlurp*—out came the blood of Cuba.

Bosanquet opened an attaché case that contained several cashiers' checks and negotiable bonds. Fuentes looked at the stash for a second. He imagined depriving Bosanquet of the loot and making off into the hills, there to vanish and live a life of debauchery eating the pussy of coffee-colored maidens. It was a temptation easily ignored. Fuentes had been in the Cuban Air Force until 1959; he'd been promoted to the rank of Major in the U.S. Marines following some heroic feats of flying against Castro during the Bay of Pigs. But there was no way he could fit into an American officer's mess. He looked wrong and his accented speech was rough and his manners were uncouth, which added to his resentment of somebody like the well-spoken Bosanquet, who always seemed to know the correct thing to say. But you couldn't fault Fuentes when it came to loyalty to his superiors. Besides, Harry Hurt wasn't the kind of guy you wanted to cross. Fuentes had the feeling Hurt wasn't acting alone, that a powerful, wealthy organization existed around him, and Harry was just another ghost in a mighty machine.

Fuentes popped a third beer and tossed the aluminum tab into the blades of the fan, which sucked it in, rattled it, then ejected it. "You got a lot of bread there, Roger," he said.

Bosanquet shut the case. "Today's the day we spend it."

Fuentes wondered how much longer a man might live in such a shitpile as this. After his retirement from the Marines he'd purchased a six-hundred-acre spread in Texas, between Amarillo and McLean, where he raised Aberdeen-Angus cattle and studied military history in his spare time. Sometimes he thought he should just have stayed home. But lonely old soldiers, like trout, were suckers for old lures. It wasn't even the money. What it really came down to was a break in the predictable tedium of life in the Texas Panhandle. Back home he had nothing but cows. Down here he had an army to drill—mainly Cuban boys recruited with great secrecy from the exile communities in New Jersey and California. A few had come from Florida, but Fuentes had not concentrated on recruiting there for the simple reason that he believed there were just too many big flapping mouths in Miami. He also had some Mexican mercenaries and a handful of Bolivians who all claimed to have been with Che at the end and who believed Fidel had conspired in Guevara's killing. In addition, he had about twenty Americans who had been in Vietnam, at least half a dozen of whom were CIA operatives in undercover roles. There was a considerable amount of hardware too; automatic weapons, grenades, rocket-launchers, a seemingly endless supply of ammunition, and the twenty fighter-planes the amazing Hurt had somehow managed to acquire in the military bazaars of the world. The F-16s had been built in Pakistan, the Skyhawks originated in South America, the Harriers, though American-made, had been bought through South African sources.

Fuentes hated Castro for the way he'd kicked ass at the Bay of Pigs. One of those bruised asses had been

Fuentes's own. Cuba without Castro was Tomas Fuentes's dream. He had no idea who would take over the country after Fidel, because this was information he'd never been given, nor did he particularly need it. He assumed that the next president and his government would have the support of both the Americans, which in Tomas's mind meant the CIA and some powerfully rich individuals, friends of Harry Hurt and certain important factions inside the Cuban armed forces. What did it matter? Nobody could be worse than Castro. Fuentes would do his own job, and do it to the best of his ability, and the politicians would take over when all the dust had settled.

"Listen," said Roger Bosanquet.

Tommy Fuentes tilted his head. There was the sound of a small plane overhead. Fuentes stepped out of the tent. The plane, a Learjet, approached from Nicaragua. It flew toward the airstrip that Fuentes and his army had hacked out of this godless landscape. The plane came in low and silvery-gold, touched down, bounced, then ran smoothly the length of the runway. Fuentes, with Bosanquet trotting at his back, walked down the hillside to the tarmac.

The Lear rolled to the place where Fuentes and Bosanquet stood. When it stopped completely the side door opened, the gangway slithered down into place, and two men—so similar in height and appearance they might have been twins—stepped out into the insufferable weather. Both wore floral shirts and sunglasses and brand new white linen pants and they looked like novice fishermen of the kind you find drifting in the coastal waters of Florida under the questionable tutelage of some self-appointed, dope-smoking guide. They were called Levy and Possony, and they spoke English with Eastern European accents, developed in the 1960s in

Prague where they'd been dazzling physics students together at the University, brighter than all the other students and most of the professors too. They had lived for years in Tel Aviv and Jerusalem and then at a secret research institute in the Negev, where they'd been regarded as scientific treasures of a kind—even if they'd been rewarded on the same salary scale as basic civil servants. It was commonly assumed, and quite wrongly, that they were too obsessed by their little world of scientific exploration to have any interest in material possessions. What was overlooked was the simple fact that Levy and Possony, after lives of poverty and wearisome anti-semitism in Eastern Europe, followed by emigration to a strange land inhabited by people who spoke a language the two Czechs never mastered, longed desperately for something bright in their lives.

Tired of penury in pursuit of science, weary of scratching around for grants, fed-up with the bulk of their salary checks being gobbled by patriotic taxes, Levy and Possony both desired less spartan lifestyles—even, to be honest, with a touch of sin thrown in. They had come to the attention of the Society in the person of Harry Hurt, who saw in them middleaged geniuses endangered by sexual dehydration and monotony. Neither was married; both were very horny in a manner befitting secular monks who had toiled for many arduous years in the rarified, lonely atmosphere of higher physics. Levy and Possony, like two figs, were wonderfully ripe for picking, and Harry Hurt, who had all the charm of an open checkbook, plucked them carefully by moonlight.

Money, briefcases of the stuff, vacations at glamorous resorts in exotic places where access to women was made easy for them. Possony had taken to Brazilian ladies and Levy to fellatio in a hot tub. Then a little indoctrination about how Castro loathed the existence of Israel and was practically an honorary Palestinian—wouldn't it be wonderful and, yes, patriotic, to help bring down a regime such as Fidel's? Levy and Possony, anxious only that nobody be hurt on account of their participation—an assurance gladly given by Harry Hurt, who would have assured Khaddafi a Nobel Peace Prize to get what he wanted—had their consciences swiftly appeased and agreed to a form of defection. In return for what Hurt needed, Levy and Possony would spend very pleasurable lives in some tropical paradise. They would be provided with new passports under new names, and they would be rich. And, if some future urge seized them to return to research, Hurt would cheerfully provide the means.

Now Levy and Possony shook hands with Fuentes, and ignored Bosanquet completely, as if they had intuited his lower standing. They had about them the contempt of tenants of ivory towers for those who toil in the cellars and workhouses of the world. Possony wore thick-lensed glasses through which his eyes, enlarged, unblinking, appeared to miss nothing. Levy, on the other hand, had a certain myopic uncertainty about him which suggested brilliance held in some delicate neurotic balance.

"Only mad dogs and Englishmen," said Bosanquet, gesturing at the raging sun. It was his little turn at wit, but it went unappreciated. Noel Coward had never played Cabo Gracios a Dios.

"We have the merchandise," Levy said. "You have the money?"

Bosanquet opened the case. Possony counted the bonds and checks, which he did with irritating slowness, like an old-fashioned accountant who has forgotten to pack his abacus.

"Everything is in order," Possony said.

"Now the merchandise," Fuentes said.

"On board the plane," said Levy.

All four men went up the gangway. The Lear jet was air-conditioned, a blessed oasis. Fuentes glanced into the cockpit where pilot and co-pilot sat. They wore holstered pistols. Levy led the way to a compartment at the rear. He unlocked a door, switched on a light. An unmarked wooden crate, measuring some six feet by four, stood in the lit compartment. There were no markings on the box.

"This is it," said Possony. "The material is completely configured to the specifications supplied by Mr. Hurt."

"Therefore accurate?" Fuentes asked.

Levy clapped the palm of his hand across his forehead, rolled his eyes and said, "What am I hearing?"

It was clear to Fuentes that he'd somehow insulted Levy, though he wasn't sure how.

Possony, less histrionic than Levy, said, "Accurate? Laser technology, Mr. Fuentes. The finest electron microscopes. We're not making imitation Swiss watches to sell on Forty-seventh Street."

Fuentes shrugged. He glanced at Bosanquet, who was obviously amused by Fuentes's moment of discomfort. Possony took the attaché case from Bosanquet's hand and said, "Now have the merchandise removed from the plane so we can leave. Nothing personal, you understand. But obviously we're in a hurry to get the hell out of here. I don't care if they call this place Cabo Gracias a Dios. Frankly, I think this little piece of our planet was put together on God's day off by a makeshift crew of inexperienced apprentices."

"None of whom," added Levy, "had any experience in landscaping."

Paris

The hotel with the unlisted telephone number was small and expensive, hidden behind chestnut trees on a side street in the Latin Quarter. The private dining-room, panelled and hung with heavy drapes and eighteenth-century oils, was located on the second floor, a gloomy room, discreet in a manner peculiarly French. Waiters came and went like deaf mutes on well-lubricated roller skates. When the sommelier uncorked wine the pop resembled the kind of quiet belch one usually only hears in the dining-rooms of very fine clubs.

Five men sat round the table, the surface of which had been carved with the initials of various luminaries who had eaten in this room. Victor Hugo had been here, and so had Emile Zola, and Albert Camus had dropped in now and again for an aperitif after a soccer game. The literary credentials didn't impress the five diners, none of whom had much of an appetite. A particularly delicious *terrine de foie de canard frais* had barely been touched. A good bottle of St. Emilion had gone practically unnoticed and the consommé, decorated with a delicate lacework of leeks and—a jaunty nouvelle cuisine touch—yellow squash cut in florets, was ignored.

When the last waiter had departed, Enrico Caporelli sat very still for a while. Beyond the heavy drapes could be heard the traffic of the Fifth Arrondissement, but it was a world away. Caporelli tasted his wine, pushed the glass aside, sipped a little coffee, which was a roasted Kenyan, and excellent. Sheridan Perry lit a cigarette and Harry Hurt, a fervent anti-smoker, fanned the polluted air with his napkin. Across the table from Caporelli was Sir Freddie Kinnaird; on Kinnaird's right sat the German, Kluger, his face somber.

"First Magiwara, then Chapotin," Caporelli said quietly as he finished his coffee. He glanced across the room at Freddie Kinnaird, then at Kluger, then Perry. Why was he drawn back, time and again, to the face of Sheridan Perry? Did he think, at some level beyond precise language, that Perry was behind the murders? Admittedly, Sheridan lusted after the Directorship. But lust was a long bloodstained step removed from two brutal murders. Or three, if you counted Chapotin's young fluffball, who, it appeared, had connections with the English aristocracy.

"Why?" Caporelli asked. "Why those two? Did they have something in common we don't know about? Were they involved in something that went very wrong for them? What made them candidates for death?"

Nobody answered. Some silences are polite, others awkward, but this particular expanse of quiet had running through it, at deep levels, many different tides and currents. Mistrust, anxiety, fear. Caporelli looked inside his coffee cup. He shivered very slightly and thought *Somebody is walking on your grave, Enrico.*

Superstitious nonsense, you peasant! Some things you just don't lose. Your background, the way you were raised in the hills with simple people who crossed themselves whenever there was an eclipse of the moon or a calf was born with three legs. All the money and the smart tailors hadn't erased the old ways. You still tossed spilled salt over your shoulder and avoided the space under ladders and you gave black cats a very wide berth.

"Has anybody noticed anything unusual?" Caporelli asked. "Any cars following them around? Strange people prowling? Perhaps phonecalls with no voices at the end of the line?"

Nobody had witnessed anything out of the ordinary. No strange cars, no stalkers, no late night callers.

"How did these killers know the whereabouts of Chapotin and Magiwara? How did they know not only places but times?" Caporelli asked. "Neither victim led a public life, after all. They were not common names in the society columns. They were private people."

Harry Hurt sipped some mineral water. "Here's one possibility. Our Society came into existence because of the Mafia. We all know this. Had our Sicilian brethren shown more restraint and less taste for lurid publicity, we'd still be their bankers. However. We went separate ways. Our predecessors, men of some vision, expropriated certain funds many many years ago and followed their own star. The Mafia, which was making more money then than all the governments of the free world combined, didn't notice that we had 'misjudged' the stock market to the tune of some, ahem, 22.5 million dollars. To them this was mere pocket money. To the Society it was a fresh start."

"We know the history," Caporelli said.

Hurt raised an index finger in the air. "Let me finish, Enrico. Suppose some young mafioso, a kid, a soldier, wants to make his name. Suppose he delves. Suppose he sees in some dusty old ledgers figures that don't add up—what then? Would he want revenge? Would he want to wipe out the Society?"

Caporelli was skeptical. "First he'd want the money back. Then and only then he'd blow a few heads away. He wouldn't shoot first. He'd want to know where the cash was kept before he stuck us in front of a firing-squad."

Hurt shrugged. "I'm only looking at possibilities, Enrico, not writing in concrete. Here's another one. Say an agent of Castro's intelligence service is behind the murders. A goon from G-2 or whatever the hell it's called. Somebody who has heard of our scheme. Perhaps somebody who has been spying on Rosabal."

Caporelli frowned. "For argument's sake, let's say Rosabal has indeed been followed by an agent of Castro—which, I may add, I discount. The stakes are too high for him to behave like such an amateur. But so what? Where could Rosabal lead such a spy? This agent might see Rosabal and me drinking tea in Glasgow or beer in a hotel in St. Etienne—but what good would that do for the spy? Rosabal knows only me. He has no idea of the Society's existence. How could he lead some *fidelista* directly to our membership? No, Rosabal's not the poisoned apple."

Sheridan Perry sipped St. Emilion with the air of a man who has been told he should appreciate fine wines but doesn't quite enjoy the taste. "We've always taken great precautions about secrecy. We've always protected our own identities. Security has been high on our agenda at all times."

Freddie Kinnaird said, "Not high enough, it seems. For example, none of us has felt the apparent need for a bodyguard."

"It suddenly seems like a terrific idea," Hurt said.

Caporelli stood up. He walked to the window, parted the drapes a little way, looked out. Lamps were lit along the sidewalks; it was a particularly romantic scene, he thought, the pale orbs of light obscured by chestnut branches, a soft breeze shuffling leaves along the gutters. A pair of lovers walked so closely together they appeared to have shed their separate identities and fused here in the Parisian twilight.

All this talk of a mafioso, bodyguards—it left him cold. It didn't come to the point. He lowered the drape, fastidiously made sure the two hems met and no exterior light penetrated, then turned to look at the faces around the table.

"We've been ruptured," he said quietly. "And we must at least consider the unpleasant possibility that somebody in our own membership . . ." Caporelli poured himself more coffee. He couldn't finish the sentence. The faces in the dining-room were each in some way defiant or incredulous. "From within or without— the fact is, our security is broken. Somebody knows who we are, and is set on our destruction. I don't think we're going to reach a conclusion no matter how long we sit round this table tonight, my friends. We'll argue, and throw possibilities back and forth, but nothing will be accomplished in this manner."

"So what are you saying?" Perry asked. His thick eyebrows came together to create one unbroken line of fur above his tiny eyes.

Caporelli gazed at the American for a time. Again he wondered if Sheridan were capable of making a destructive play for control of the Society; and, if so, was he doing it without the complicity of his friend Hurt? Was there a rift between the two? Had Perry's greed and ambition created an abyss across which Hurt was neither allowed nor prepared to walk?

"I am saying this, Sheridan," Caporelli remarked. "I am saying that we attend to personal security by hiring bodyguards. I am saying we adhere to no regular schedule. I am saying that we change cars and travel plans as often as we can. Secrecy is a prerequisite of survival. In short, we take precautions, as many as we possibly can. And we are very careful of how we communicate with one another."

This last statement fell into the room like a stone dropped from a great height. It was unpleasant. The Society had always existed on the basis of mutual trust. Now it was being undermined. Caporelli imagined he could hear old beams creak and rocks crumble in the deep shafts.

"And does all this affect our Cuban undertaking?" Perry asked. "Do we cancel that project for starters?"

Suddenly agitated, Freddie Kinnaird made a ball of his linen napkin, which he brushed against his lips. "Have you lost your mind? The cruise missile was successfully stolen this morning and is presently in transit, and since the British police are practically clueless, I don't see any reason to cancel. The investigation, headed by a policeman called Frank Pagan, falls into my domain. When Pagan knows anything, I know it too. A rather lovely arrangement altogether. If Pagan goes too far, I can find a way to tug gently on his rein. Besides, if we take the precautions Enrico has suggested, I think we will see a general improvement in our mood. Prudence, my dear fellow, wins in the end. And whoever has taken to attacking our little Society will be flushed out finally."

Kinnaird's expression was that of a voracious realtor who has just placed an island paradise in escrow and whose plans include casinos, resorts, colossal hotels, and as much sheer, silken sin as anybody could stand.

Kluger lit a cigar. He blew a ring of blue smoke and said, "I personally do not believe that anyone in this room is a traitor." There was authority and finality in the German's tone, as if he had access to information denied everyone else. "I think we have been too lax, too complacent, in our security and now we are paying a price. The solution, as Enrico tells it, is very simple. We continue to go about our business—but with this difference. *Extreme precautions*, gentlemen. Sooner or later, the culprit will appear in broad daylight. Sooner or later.''

Kluger stood up. He filled a glass with brandy and extended his hand across the table. The toast was made, glasses clinked together, faces formerly glum forced smiles. Cuba was there for the taking. The show would go on regardless.

''To the success of friendship,'' said Sir Freddie Kinnaird.

It was early evening by the time the members left the dining-room. The last wistful twilight had gone, and the cafes were bright now, the night life restless as ever, beautiful social moths flitting after this piece of gossip or fearful of missing that particular face. Nothing had been solved in the hotel, but a slightly uncertain consensus had been reached that no Society member was responsible for the killings.

Arrangements pertaining to bodyguards were discussed, recommendations made. Sir Freddie Kinnaird knew of a reliable agency in London; Harry Hurt spoke well of an outfit in Dallas. And Enrico Caporelli, who had an apartment and a great many connections here in Paris, had already made a phonecall and had been promised a carload of armed protectors who would arrive outside in ten minutes or so.

The mood, if not exactly terrific, was not so somber as it had been before, and the news of Gunther Ruhr's successful theft took the hard edge off grief. The possibility of Cuban profits had instilled a small delight that, in the hours ahead, would grow until dead members were almost forgotten.

The five men stepped out of the hotel together. They were to be met by their security people outside a well-lit cafe across the street. They walked very close to a couple of strolling gendarmes, an illusion of protection until the real thing arrived. Kluger was attracted by a girl at a sidewalk cafe but decided to be abstemious, despite the luscious red gloss of her parted lips.

All five men crossed the street at a traffic signal. Kluger, puffing on the remains of his cigar, lagged a few feet behind, turning now and again to observe the lovely girl. He could not have seen the truck until the last possible moment, perhaps not even then. It struck him, tossed him ten or eleven feet forward, then ensnared his limp body under the front axle and dragged it another fifty or sixty feet before final release. Kluger rolled over and over toward the gutter, his coat torn, his arms broken, his face devoid of any resemblance to its former self. The truck driver's name was Luiz Dulzaides, a forty-nine-year-old long-distance driver from Madrid. His eight-wheel rig came to a halt inside the plateglass window of a large pharmacy, after it ploughed through colognes and powders and perfumes and demolished a menagerie of soft toy animals. Dulzaides, tested by the police, had drunk the equivalent of three bottles of wine that day. He'd never heard of Herr Kluger, had no recollection of seeing him in the crosswalk, no memory of striking him. Dulzaides was too drunk to stand upright. He was removed in a police car. Caporelli and the two Americans answered the usual routine questions of the gendarmerie while Kinnaird, the most public of the members, feared adverse publicity and slipped easily into the large crowd of spectators that had assembled at the scene.

Officially, it was an accident. After all, Dulzaides was blind drunk; was that disputable? Statements were taken, a report filed, a dossier opened and closed.

Enrico Caporelli and the others repaired for drinks to the Ritz, conveyed there in a chalk-white Cadillac driven by two armed men. Freddie Kinnaird joined them there. Each member was skeptical about the matter of the accident; but what was there to say? The police were convinced, the witnesses many, and Dulzaides's blood alcohol level was undeniably dangerous. Perhaps an accident; perhaps not. If an accident, then it was an ironic one, given the recent circumstances surrounding the Society.

In the morning Caporelli, who wanted the chance to speak with a sober Dulzaides and perhaps check the man's background, the veracity of his story, telephoned the jail where the driver had been taken. He was informed by a cold voice that M. Dulzaides had, *helas*, died of heart failure at 4:20 AM and the body had already been claimed by relatives. Like garbage under a violent sun, it had been removed quickly from the premises.

11

Norfolk

Middlebury Comprehensive School, located between Norwich and the ancient Saxon town of Thetford, was a new building that resembled a car-assembly plant, as if each pupil were a machine to be bolted, buffed, waxed and wheeled out into the world—which, Pagan supposed, was true in a limited kind of way. According to the headmaster, a man named Frew who had the deep fatalism of the jaded schoolteacher, a pupil called Stephanie Brough had been missing overnight. Steffie's pet horse had returned home, saddled and riderless. Country policemen, defeated by darkness, had begun a systematic search at first light. By three o'clock in the afternoon, seven hours after the theft of the missile, not only had the missing girl continued to elude detection, but a constable on the case had vanished as well.

By five o'clock inquiries made of estate agents in a twenty-mile radius of Steffie's home had revealed the recent rental of a dilapidated farmhouse. The nice old dear who told Pagan about the tenancy had the quietly confidential air one sometimes finds in people whose occupations involve discretion. She would give nothing away unless the authority that needed answers had unimpeachable reasons. Pagan's needs, backed by his imposing credentials from Scotland Yard, fell into that category.

It was the woman's opinion that the man who'd rented the house was a 'foreigner', although remarkably 'civilized' for all that.

Had there been only one renter? Pagan asked.

The agent remembered no other. Of course, a tenant could do pretty much what he liked as soon as he had a key, especially in a rural area without nosy neighbors. She would be happy to find a copy of the tenant's signature, but it would take an hour or so. Her office was not, she remarked proudly, computerized. Pagan thanked her and said he'd return.

The farmhouse was dismal, buried in a black hollow. Moss grew against walls and the chimney had partially collapsed. Tire tracks were found outside the house; on the slope behind the building were varied muddy footprints, some large, a few rather small, small enough to be Steffie Brough's. Pagan stood for a while on the rainy incline, a photo of the girl, provided by her school, in one hand. She was pretty, a lovely devilment in the face, a puckish little smile, tiny pointed ears suggesting otherworldliness. A pixie. He tried to imagine Steffie Brough on this slope, watching the farmhouse.

Was this the place where she'd come? And then what? Had Ruhr surprised her? Pagan ran a fingertip across the image of the girl's face. If he squinted, there was a very strong resemblance between Steffie Brough and the girl with whom Gunther Ruhr had been captured in Cambridge. It was an unpleasant realization: if this child were in Ruhr's possession, then he not only had a hostage but one who was practically a duplicate of somebody he'd desired into the bargain. Pagan pushed this thought aside and squelched back down to the house where Foxie—whose red hair was the only bright thing in the place—was wandering around.

"I don't doubt Ruhr and his chums found accommodations here, Frank," Foxie said. "Look at this. Presumably they kept the child here."

Foxie led Pagan inside a narrow room where an old iron bed had been placed under the wall. Lengths of rope were attached to the frame; somebody had clearly been bound here. On a threadbare bedside rug lay a small white bra streaked with hardened mud. Foxie picked it up and passed it to Pagan, who handled the garment as if he were afraid of finding blood inside it. He looked for stencilled initials, laundry marks, but found none. He gave it back to Foxworth, who folded it in the pocket of his raincoat.

Pagan gazed at the bed again, the ropes, the strict knots. The idea of the child being imprisoned here upset him. He wandered uneasily through the rest of the house. Except for the remarkably tidy kitchen, the place was a mess. The smell of dampness was overpowering. Pagan went from room to room, most of them small low-ceilinged enclosures with narrow windows. Upstairs several old mattresses lay on the floorboards. Rodents scratched in the attic.

"This must be the terrorist dormitory," Foxie said. "Not very well appointed, is it?"

Pagan moved to the window. The view was uninspiring. Flat and dead fields, stricken by the breath of coming winter, stark trees from which a couple of ravens rose. Only the big black birds created any kind of movement. Pagan pressed his moist forehead against the windowpane. The motion of the birds—floating, searching—intrigued him, though for the moment he wasn't sure exactly why.

He went back downstairs to the main part of the house. In the living-room dirty glasses stood on a ping-pong table, newspapers were strewn everywhere, spent matches, cigarette butts, beer bottles on the cracked lino. He re-examined Steffie's picture, turning it over and over before passing it to Foxie.

"Ruhr likes them pale and thin, doesn't he?" Foxworth said in a quiet voice.

"That's the way it looks." Pagan bunched his hands in the pockets of his sodden raincoat. "When they're finished with the Range Rover, the fingerprint boys better get over here next. The way I see it, nobody's been very careful about hiding their prints."

"Arrogant lot," Foxie said.

"With an arrogant leader. I'll tell you what else pisses me right off, Foxie. How could this damned place be overlooked in the general search for Ruhr? How could it be missed, for Christ's sake? It has all the necessary credentials for a hiding-place. Isolated. Recently rented. You'd think it would be obvious to any cop."

Foxie was silent. He might have said that the countryside was large, the police force relatively small, and this house well-concealed, but he could see that Frank was in no mood for platitudes, even truthful ones.

Pagan walked round the room, thinking how some places defeated the imagination—they were empty stages, and you could never imagine anybody playing on them. Other houses, by contrast, were vibrant long after their vacancy, and seemed to echo with laughter that although old was cheerful just the same. But this house was a slum, like an abandoned inner-city house where drunks came to defecate, and light could never alter it. The presence of happy people couldn't change the structural gloom. Misery claimed this house, and misery was a clammy tenant, tenaciously silent.

Ghosts, Pagan thought. He stood at the foot of the stairs. For some reason he thought of Magdalena Torrente; her intrusion into his mind was at least a bright occurrence. He tried to imagine how her laughter, floating deliciously from room to room, might make a difference to this hideous dump. He thought of how he'd kissed her before walking away from her, and he could still feel her tongue against his own—another ghost.

How had it come about that Magdalena, who despised Castro's regime, whose father had been shot down and killed at the Bay of Pigs, had become the lover of Castro's Minister of Finance? Rosabal had reputedly been hand-picked by Fidel to mend Cuba's broken finances and restore economic order to a nation allegedly going under. Castro sent him on fund-raising trips to Russia and Czechoslovakia and anywhere else a purse might be forced open for Cuban coffers. Why did Magdalena associate with such a man? Was Rosabal part of some anti-Castro movement? was that the connection with Magdalena? Had she perhaps changed and become a secret supporter of Castro? God, how unlikely that seemed. Perhaps they were simply lovers. He pinched the bridge of his nose and frowned.

Dear Christ, what did Rosabal and Magdalena matter? He had a missing girl and a crazy terrorist to deal with. Steffie Brough had stumbled on to this place, and Ruhr had seized her. A simple story really, a variation on Beauty and the Beast, with the contemporary addition of a stolen nuclear missile. He wondered if Ruhr had hurt the girl yet in any way, or whether Gunther preferred to savor such possibilities, and prolong them, getting the timing and the flavor just right before he made his move.

Or did Ruhr understand how the idea of the frail girl's life and security would go round and round maddeningly in Frank Pagan's mind? And did he enjoy the feeling? Of course he did. Ruhr had one of those instinctive minds that quickly pick up on the personalities of others, almost a mimic's skill; in their few encounters he had come to know Frank Pagan somewhat. He would also know where to open Pagan's skin and lay bare the appropriate nerve.

Pagan saw now that the German was doing more than what Foxworth had called 'thumbing his nose'; he was torturing Pagan. The scarf, the bra, these weren't mere gestures. It was as if the girl were being forced to perform a slow striptease. And Frank Pagan, like some devoted father desperately searching for his missing daughter through a maze of sleazy night clubs, was doomed to find only the girl's discarded clothes.

Impatiently, Pagan stepped to the door, looked out across the yard. The birds were on the ground now, pecking with dedicated industry at something concealed under leaves. For one dreadful moment Pagan's heart lurched in his chest as he walked across the mud. He thought that perhaps the birds were feasting on Stephanie Brough, that she hadn't been kidnapped at all, that Ruhr's clues had been cruel jokes. The girl lay here, demolished by black-feathered morticians who picked their corpses down to bone.

Disturbed, the ravens fluttered a couple of feet away, landed, observed Pagan with bleak resentment. They were patient creatures who often had to take their meals cold. Pagan kicked some dry leaves aside. The face that appeared was missing one eye, half the lower lip had been ripped away, a cheek gouged. There was a deep wound in the neck. The man wore a police constable's dark blue uniform made all the more dark by blood that had dried around his chest. Pagan turned away from the sight, picked up a couple of rocks, tossed them at the big birds, who flew quietly to a nearby tree, there to wait.

Foxie came out of the house and glanced at the corpse. All color went out of his face. "Christ," he said quietly.

Pagan rubbed his hands together. His entire body was suddenly cold.

Foxworth said, "I've had enough of this place, Frank. Do we need to linger here?"

Pagan got into the car without saying anything. He heard Foxie on the car telephone, reporting the discovery of the dead constable. The afternoon was darkening, the English autumn yielding to the coming winter with customary melancholy. Pagan sat in a hunched position, bent slightly forward to find relief from his renewed pain. Along country lanes a fresh wind blew moist fallen leaves at the car. All the little scraps of a perforated season were falling finally apart.

The office of the lady who had rented the farmhouse was located in a village seventeen miles from Norwich. It was an eccentric operation, manila folders stuffed in drawers, a big old-fashioned black telephone left over from more poetic times when exchanges had proper names. Joanna Lassiter wore her graying hair up, held in place by a marvellous array of colored pins that Foxworth and Pagan admired. It was as if her skull were a map and the pins pointers to various locations.

She was a pleasantly confused woman who mislaid files and papers. On her desk scores of yellowing receipts had been impaled on a metal spike. The presence of the two policemen unsettled her. She suggested herbal tea, which both men declined. Pagan was impatient to go back out into the darkness of the early evening.

While she searched her desk for the necessary information, Joanna Lassiter said she personally supervised the rental and management of more than a hundred houses and apartments throughout the area, that business was good, and that once—funny, weren't they, these tiny coincidences?—she'd owned a pet dog called Pagan. As she rummaged she flitted breathlessly from topic to topic as if the pins that held her hair in place had punctured the brain itself, destroying the routes along which mental signals were meant to travel. When she wasn't speaking she kept up a sequence of little noises—*mmms* and *arrumms* and *drrmms.* There was battiness here, relief from a grim world.

"He was, I recall, a pleasant sort of fellow. Wore black glasses, which I don't usually like. I only met him once, and then briefly. Our business was done mostly by phone and mail. Can't possibly imagine him connected to any wrongdoing." Joanna Lassiter poked through a thick folder from which slips of paper fell to the floor and were not retrieved. "Most of our tenants give me absolutely no trouble. Well, I always say I have an instinct about people, Mr. Pagan. I sense vibrations from them, you see. It's a gift."

And on and on.

Finally she pulled a sheet of paper out of the folder and held it aloft. "I rather think this is the naughty little chappie we've been seeking, Mr. Pagan." She held the paper directly under her desk-lamp and squinted at it. Pagan leaned across the desk with interest but the handwriting on the sheet was like Pitman's shorthand.

"The man rented the old Yardley place for six

months. Paid the whole thing in advance with a money order. I think he said he was some kind of naturalist, actually. Needed a place to assemble his notes on a book. Mmmm. He was only two weeks into his tenancy. Well. It's not an easy property to rent, I'm afraid. Has bad feelings. Don't much like going over there myself. Dreary. Spot of paint might help a bit."

"Is there a name?" Pagan asked.

"Name?" Joanna Lassiter looked surprised, as if this were a whole new concept to her.

"Did the tenant have a name?" Pagan asked a second time.

When she smiled thirty years fell away from her face. It was almost as if her bone structure altered. She put her fingertips up to her lips. "Silly me. Of course there's a name, Mr. Pagan. Couldn't very well rent a house to a man without a name, could I now?"

"I've heard of stranger things," Pagan said.

"I daresay you have." Joanna Lassiter pushed the sheet of paper across the desk. "There. See for yourself. Funny kind of name. Foreign, of course."

Pagan picked up the paper and read.

"Does it help, Mr. Pagan?" she asked.

Pagan passed the sheet to Foxworth.

He didn't answer Joanna Lassiter's question because he wasn't sure how. He stared through the black window at the village street beyond. The pub sign hanging on the other side of the road, pale and inviting, reminded him of a thirst he'd been suffering for hours.

Marrakech, Morocco

Steffie Brough's head roared and her whole body, locked

for ages in one stiff position, felt like iron. Even though somebody had stuffed small pieces of foam rubber inside her ears the great noise of the plane, like that of a locomotive infinitely screaming in an infinite tunnel, had drilled through her skull anyway. She was sick and tired, shaken by the long turbulent flight. Every now and then she'd felt the craft drop suddenly, like something about to fall out of the sky.

She didn't know how many hours she'd actually lain in the cabin of the truck, conscious of cockpit lights up ahead and the shadows of men moving back and forth. It was very weird being conveyed inside one kind of transportation that was being transported inside another.

When the plane began to lose altitude she became aware of pressure building up in the hollows behind her eyes and then rolling painfully through all the dark cavities of her head. Then the plane skimmed over land, bouncing. After that, the silence was wonderful as the craft slid slowly along the runway.

Now, when the door of the truck opened, she twisted her head back and saw Ruhr. Silently, he undid the ropes that bound her and she tried to sit up but her bones seemed to have jammed in place. Her brain throbbed and the ache in her bladder was unbearable.

"I need to go to a toilet," she said. The rasp in her own voice surprised her. She sounded just the way her Aunt Ruth did before she died last year from throat cancer. She thought *I'd rather be dead from that than trapped in this bloody awful place.*

She glanced toward the back of the big truck, whose cargo was concealed under a long green canvas cover. She didn't want to think what it might be or why Ruhr and his friends had gone to so much trouble to steal it, because then she'd start remembering all the gunfire and how tear-gas and smoke had choked her.

But she thought she knew anyway. What else could it be but a missile? What else was there worth killing for in her small corner of the world? She'd always known there were missiles as close as ten miles from her home because she'd watched people walk along narrow country lanes on protest marches—but like many things in her young, protected life, missiles were abstractions outside her own limits and interests. They belonged in a world beyond horses and rock music and boys. Now it was different. She could reach up, she could actually *touch* one of the things if she wanted.

Ruhr led her through the aircraft. She was aware of two men sitting in the half-light and how they looked at her as she passed. The air was thick with the smell of fuel and tobacco. The lavatory was tiny, filthy, the floor puddled, and somebody had removed the lock from the door, but she was beyond embarrassment.

She splashed cold water all over her face, then drank thirstily even though the water tasted stale and dusty. She pushed her wet fingers through her hair. Her reflection in a small mirror was white and dreadful. She seemed to have diminished. She looked like a pygmy, a shrunken head. She hardly recognized herself.

She dried her face with paper towels and wished the lavatory had a window so she could look out. She didn't know where she was, she had no idea where she was going. Her parents—oh Christ they would be completely frantic with worry now. Even her stupid brother would have expressed concern in his own stumbling fashion. She raised her face to the mirror a second time. The rough paper towels had at least brought some color back to her cheeks. And even if she felt like crying, she knew she wouldn't.

Ruhr had a global network of men and women who owed him favors. This airfield, for example, had been made available by an old associate, somebody close to the Moroccan royal family. Situated twenty-five miles from the city of Marrakech, it had until recently been used by Moroccan Air Force fighter planes flying against Western Saharan rebels, but its age and condition had caused it to be abandoned.

The huge transport plane taxied over potholes toward an enormous hangar made from prefabricated metal that had rotted years ago. In the fading afternoon sun the building's vastness was strangely exaggerated. Bats flew in and out of the rotted roof, fulfilling some odd rodent urge to veer close to the strips of blinking fluorescent light that hung from the ceiling.

The plane came to a stop outside the hangar, where a large fuel truck was parked. Joseph Sweeney stepped out of the flight deck and moved into the rear cabin, where Ruhr stood. The two men who had come with Ruhr, Trevaskis and the Argentinean, sat against the wall and looked sullen. Sweeney opened one of the paratroop doors and tossed a rope ladder down. Ruhr said, "Keep your eye on the girl, Trevaskis," and then swung down the ladder to the tarmac. Sweeney followed him.

When he had his feet firmly on the ground, Sweeney worked a small finger inside his ear. "That damned roar deafens the hell out of me," he said. He shook his head a couple of times, then pinched his nostrils and puffed up his cheeks.

Sweeney, born in County Cork and swept off to Boston at the age of ten, glanced a moment at the fuel truck, which was moving slowly toward the plane. He'd worked with Ruhr a dozen times all over the world and if anybody could be said to know the German it was

Joseph James Sweeney. And while Sweeney wouldn't have enjoyed a night's drinking with Gunther, nor let the man anywhere near his teenaged nieces, he had a certain admiration for him.

Sweeney gestured toward the plane. He asked a question he'd been hesitant about. "I suppose the kid somehow fits your general plan?"

Ruhr said, "She may provide insurance. Or diversion."

Sweeney nodded, then dropped the subject. He knew when to persist and when to let go. Ruhr could be incommunicative and distant when it suited him, and it obviously suited him now. Sweeney felt a passing pity for the girl, but like most of his emotions it was allowed to evaporate quickly.

"You had me worried, Gunther."

"How so?"

"When they took you in Cambridge, I thought it was all over."

Ruhr made a dismissive gesture and laughed abruptly. "You know me better than that. I have many lives."

Sweeney watched the fuel truck park alongside the plane. In half an hour or so they'd be out of this godawful place and flying the Atlantic. Frankly, he'd be glad when this one was over and he could go back to the anonymous life he'd worked hard to build for himself in the USA, a quiet house in a quiet street in Newburyport, Massachusetts. His neighbors thought he was living off land investments, an illusion he gladly encouraged.

He wasn't sure why this particular undertaking made him so goddam uneasy. The presence of the kid obviously contributed to it, but something was different about Ruhr as well. He had a cold distance about him, a weariness. Sweeney felt these were danger signals although he couldn't interpret them. He'd stay away from Gunther as much as he could for the duration.

He watched the hose from the fuel truck extend to the fuselage of the big plane and remembered the thought that had occurred to him a couple of times recently: *in his lifetime, he'd killed more men than he'd fucked women.* Somehow this realization had shocked him. He said, "I really think this is my last time, amigo."

"You've said so before. You've always come back." Ruhr was conscious of Trevaskis watching him in a hostile way from the door of the plane.

"This time I'm beginning to hear the creak of my bones," Sweeney said. "And the thrill's not in it any more. Or maybe there's too much for me to handle. I'm forty-two, Gunther. I've lived this life since I was twenty-two and that's a long time. And I'm not including the five years before that when I was in the United States Air Force. How long can a man go on? Can you imagine doing this when you're sixty?"

Ruhr had also been living this life for a long time. Unlike Sweeney, he couldn't imagine retirement. The real trick was to find new ways to keep the game fresh, to introduce new elements. Even new risks. The alternative was dullness and Ruhr couldn't tolerate that. A bat flew out of the sun and flapped close to his face and he lashed out at the thing.

Sweeney said, "I can get absorbed real smoothly into what they call the mainstream of American life."

The mainstream of American life. Sweeney must have been reading *Time* magazine. Ruhr said, "Barbecue and Budweisers and little girls with metal on their teeth and tedium without end."

"You make it sound comforting."

"All anesthetics give comfort," Ruhr remarked. "But only on a temporary basis."

Both men walked some distance from the fuel truck. In the extensive network of reliable men Ruhr had built over the years, none had proved more valuable than Joseph Sweeney. Whenever Ruhr needed something—an individual's name, or a certain kind of weapon, or in this case a plane—Sweeney always managed to find it somehow. He had become, in a sense, Ruhr's quartermaster, resourceful, reassuring.

Sweeney combined the soothing charm of a confidence man with the hardness of an assassin. Since he'd experienced at firsthand the staggering ineptitude of the military mind, he knew how to exploit it ruthlessly, how to gain access to military bases and installations; how to impersonate an officer with such authority that no guard or military policeman ever questioned his presence. He was the best at his craft.

It was Sweeney who had identified the Duty Officer responsible for the transportation of missiles at the site in Norfolk; and even if it was Ruhr who had seduced the man into treachery, nevertheless it had been Sweeney who'd first uncovered the essential information. Name and rank and serial number; date of birth; marital status; specific duties; known weaknesses.

Known weaknesses, Ruhr thought. He'd never yet found a man without a faultline to be widened; he'd never encountered a man who didn't have a purchase price of some kind. With some it was very simple—a need for money, for drugs, certain kinds of sex. With others it was more complicated—the moment of shame recaptured, the dark skeleton in the unopened closet. The Duty Officer at the site belonged in the latter category.

A thirty-five-year-old man from Nashville, the Duty Officer had a wife and child living in Tennessee. At the same time, he was deeply involved with a woman who lived in Norwich, a mistress with definite ambitions of her own. It was a situation Ruhr considered pathetic; loneliness had driven the Duty Officer into the grasp of a woman whose connivance overwhelmed the man's naivety. He was basically a nice, easy-going fellow with the kind of dull good looks essential to the success of any backyard party. What the mistress wanted was marriage and an escape route out of the damp miseries of Norwich. She was about to write a letter to the wife in Tennessee. If the man wasn't willing to talk divorce, then by God! she'd force his hand.

Lurid lives, Ruhr had thought. Especially in the quiet suburbs of boring cities, lurid lives. He felt as if he hovered above this human swamp like a minor god, indifferent. And so, after observing his victim for several days, he'd swooped down from his lofty place into the young man's life, both as savior and deceiver. He found the pub where the officer sometimes drank, engineered an introduction. He posed as a Swiss photographer who'd unfortunately lost his fingers shooting film in Vietnam. It struck a sympathetic chord in the Duty Officer, who'd served in Vietnam too toward the bitter end—a fact Ruhr already knew, of course, courtesy of Joseph Sweeney.

A quiet companionship grew; it was nothing substantial. A few beers now and again, under circumstances that appeared to be sheer chance. Once or twice they ran into each other in Cambridge as well as Norwich. It's-a-small-world, Ruhr would say, and smile his most appealing smile, the one in which his lips didn't disappear. Gradually the facts of the Duty Officer's life emerged. He was bogged down, the woman in Norwich was goddam demanding, why had he ever let himself in for this godalmighty mess in the first place? Ah, Sweet Jesus! He loved his wife and kid, he didn't want to hurt them or lose them. But his wife, Louanne, couldn't come to England because she had a sick mother in Knoxville. It was complicated, and getting more out of hand every day. Once, the Duty Officer had actually said: *I wish I was dead.*

That, Ruhr suggested, was the wrong solution; the wrong party would be eliminated in that event.

Ruhr had thought up something much better.

If there was to be a candidate for a coffin, the choice was obvious: the mistress—who else?

But how? How could that kind of thing happen? the Duty Officer had asked.

Ruhr was sly then, almost coy in his cunning. He offered a few suggestions, crumbs, nothing more. What it came down to was this simple: the woman in Norwich had to be . . . disposed of. The Duty Officer shuddered at the notion. He'd entertained it, of course. Who wouldn't? But in the end he knew he couldn't commit murder—other than in his heart, he'd added, as if to reassure Ruhr of his masculinity.

Then find somebody else to do it, Ruhr had said.

The idea, once planted, grew in the dark. Ruhr, master gardener, nurtured it, made it sprout. And when it was fully grown and luxuriant in the Duty Officer's mind, Ruhr administered the final flourish one night while he and his new American friend were drinking schnapps at a pub on St. Andrew's Hill in the center of Norwich. Ruhr needed something from the Duty Officer. Something simple really. But classified. Ruhr hinted broadly that in exchange for this small item of information the Duty Officer's life could be 'rectified'.

He wouldn't ever have to worry about his girl-friend again. Ruhr understood, of course, that the 'drastic' solution he was suggesting might be offensive, alien even, to the young man, and if he wanted to refuse Ruhr's offer, well, what difference would it make to their friendship?

Why did Ruhr want the classified information? the Duty Officer asked in the manner of a pharmacist asking a customer why he needed a restricted medicine for which he had no prescription.

Ruhr answered that it was a trifle really, a journalistic matter, an opportunity to photograph a missile in transit from a site, an exclusive. He was convincing in an odd, hypnotic way. He could use a stock shot of the kind supplied by military press liaison offices, but he resented the idea. No, what he wanted was the real thing on a real road surrounded by a real escort. The feel of authenticity—that was important. The way things truly looked, that was what he was after. For a photo-journalist, veracity was what mattered.

He needed a timetable, a calendar of forthcoming events, places and times, routes. In return for these snippets, Ruhr would ensure the total security of the young man's marriage and with it his peace of mind. And what was life when one had no serenity? How could one pursue a career distracted by emotional problems that could be clarified in an instant?

That night of beer and schnapps on St. Andrew's Hill, everything was neatly slotted in place. Ruhr knew he'd get the kind of information so exclusive it made him indispensable. He knew what the route of the missile was to be; he knew the exact time and place. Information was power, especially when it was information his employers didn't have.

It was a triumph to turn the young American

around, and yet easy too, because the Duty Officer was so vulnerable. Murder and treachery. How it pleased Ruhr to think he'd made this very ordinary young man, who was neither terribly bright nor terribly stupid, an accomplice in both crimes!

Three nights later Ruhr sneaked into the woman's house and stabbed her directly through the heart while she slept. He waited until he heard her die, then he left. By the next evening, Ruhr had the information he wanted. It had taken him exactly twenty-three days to get it. He never saw the Duty Officer again.

Now the truck had finished refuelling the plane. Joseph Sweeney lit a cigarette. He watched the sun, in a great explosion the color of burgundy, slide toward darkness on the rocky horizon. A chill was already in the air.

"It's time to go," Sweeney said.

"I am ready," Ruhr remarked. "As always."

"We should dump the cab first."

"Of course."

The cab of the truck that had conveyed the missile and the launch system was uncoupled from the trailer. It was excess weight on the plane, and useless now. It was detached from the trailer and allowed to roll down the ramp to the airstrip, there to be abandoned.

Havana, Cuba

In the early afternoon, Rafael Rosabal walked on the crowded, humid Calle Obispo in Old Havana. The breeze that blew over the sea wall, the Malecon, faded in the streets in a series of quiet little gasps that would barely shake a shrub. Today everything smelled of salt.

Today you could practically *hear* metal corrode as rust devoured it. There was rust everywhere, in the decorative iron grilles of windows and doorways, on the panels and underbodies of the old American automobiles cluttering the streets, even in the paintwork of the new Cuban-built buses and the imported Fiats and Ladas. Where rain had run through rust, coppery stains, suggestive of very old tears, discolored the facades of buildings.

Rosabal reached the entrance to the Hotel Bristol. He was jostled on all sides by pedestrians who filled the cobbled street. Rectangular posters fluttered twenty feet overhead, advertisements announcing an exhibition of modern Cuban artists at the Casa de Bano de la Cathedral. Rosabal loathed Cuban art, which he thought dull and derivative. Socialism, as it was conceived by the Lider Maximo, hadn't altogether electrified creativity.

He went inside the Bristol, passing the registration desk where a clerk was reading a copy of *Granma*, the Party's newspaper. According to the headline, the Lider Maximo was going to make a speech sometime that day on TV.

Rosabal kept walking until he came to the small dark bar at the rear, a narrow room lit by two dim bulbs. He asked for a *mojito* only to be told by an apologetic barman that lemon and lime juice were both temporarily out of stock. He settled for a beer, which he took to a table.

Apart from himself, there was one other customer, a tall, bony man in a dark blue two piece suit. This was Rosabal's contact, Teodoro Diaz-Alonso. The word that always popped into Rosabal's head when he saw Diaz-Alonso was *remilgado*, prim. Diaz-Alonso wore small glasses parked near the tip of his nose. His stiff bearing suggested a professor of the kind you no longer saw in the city. Diaz-Alonso was drinking cola from a tall glass. Rosabal sat down beside him.

Rosabal was a little uneasy whenever he had meetings with Diaz-Alonso in Havana. And yet why shouldn't there be a point of connection between Rosabal's Ministry of Finance and MINFAR, the Ministry of the Armed Forces, for which Diaz-Alonso worked as a senior advisor? Both men were government servants, after all. They knew the same people, went to the same restaurants and parties, enjoyed the same privileges of rank. Besides, Diaz-Alonso was a frequent visitor to Rosabal's apartment in the Vedado. This encounter would look perfectly natural to any casual observer. So why worry about it?

Diaz-Alonso said, "The General has asked me to convey his greetings, Rafael."

"Thank the General."

"I am also to give you a message." Diaz-Alonso paused and looked like a scholar recalling a quotation. "The General says that the conditions you require will be ready."

Rosabal sat back in his chair and tried to relax. It was extraordinary how, when you were so involved with the architecture of a conspiracy, when one blueprint had obsessed you for so long, you forgot simple pleasures—the taste of a beer, the aroma of a good cigar. It was like living in a room with the shades constantly drawn. Nothing happened beyond the shades, no cars passed in the street, no women strolled on the boulevards, no sun, no moon. The room was everything.

"Tell the General this will not be forgotten," he said. "Nor will any of the recent services he has provided."

Diaz-Alonso was expressionless as he remarked,

"The General does not underestimate the importance of his role in this whole project, Rafael. He is not a man who favors false modesty. But for himself he expects no monetary rewards, of course. He is no mercenary. The General seeks only the post of Minister of the Armed Forces."

"That's understood."

Diaz-Alonso raised his hand very slightly, as if to admonish Rosabal, in the gentlest way, for interrupting him. "The General also expects a certain seniority among Ministers, naturally. First among equals, so to speak."

Rosabal said, "The General will be accommodated. Assure him of that." General Alfonso Capablanca, second in command of the Armed Forces to Raul Castro, had always been consistent in what he wanted. Negotiating with the General through his intermediary had been part of the arrangement from the beginning. The General liked the distance. He also thought it observed a certain kind of protocol which even conspirators must obey, lest they become mere anarchists. There was such a thing as form, Capablanca said. If Rosabal was to become one day the President of this nation—with the help of the General and a number of his senior officers, of course—he would understand that form often meant more than substance. Politics, in the final analysis, was not to be confused with the real world. Politics was a matter of appearance.

Rosabal was equal to the General's cynicism. He found Capablanca an extreme bore, but indispensable. Without his inclusion, and the role of his officers, the scheme would fall to pieces. And without the General's ability to acquire the Lider Maximo's signature on a certain document, the plot—if it existed in any form— would have taken a different shape. Therefore Rosabal, out of a gratitude more pragmatic than sincere, met the General's demands, and was very polite even as he looked forward to the day when Capablanca might be 'retired' by a firing-squad.

Diaz-Alonso inclined his head a little. The gaunt, tight-lipped face yielded very little emotion. "The General will also need to know about any changes in schedule as soon as they occur."

"I expect none." Rosabal was thinking of Gunther Ruhr now, and the missile. He looked at his watch. Ruhr would be in North Africa, if all had gone well. And since there was no news to indicate otherwise, Rosabal assumed everything was in order. Anyhow, he would have heard from Caporelli if anything had altered. They usually exchanged messages by telephone. Caporelli called Mexico City, and the message was conveyed to Havana by one of the Italian's employees. Rosabal smiled a little as he thought of the Italian. Caporelli's problem was the way he deemed himself smarter and sharper than anyone else.

Diaz-Alonso said, "These are very strange times for our nation, Rafael. Once upon a time, I remember, we all had high hopes. Very high. Now, everywhere I look I see discontent." He shrugged and finished his soda. "Change must come. Every day, a little more pressure builds up, and steam always seeks an outlet. I wish there was a legal way of achieving change, but there is no longer any legality in the system. The Party is the only voice. And the Party has a big problem, Rafael. It is governed by men who cannot hear the voices of the people."

"Not for much longer," Rosabal said.

"Let us hope so, Rafael." Diaz-Alonso set his empty glass down on the table. He rose to his feet. "You know how to contact me if you have to."

Rosabal watched Diaz-Alonso cross the room, then took another sip of his beer. He put on his black sunglasses and prepared to leave. As he passed in front of the bar, the bartender asked, "Did you hear?"

"Hear?"

"On the radio a moment ago. Fidel has cancelled his speech today. They didn't say why. He must be pretty damn sick if he can't make a speech, heh?"

Rosabal, who worked to maintain a low profile in Castro's government because he found anonymity a more useful tool than renown, said nothing. He thought he saw a slight look of recognition cross the barman's face, but then it was gone.

"I heard a story he has ulcers," the barman remarked. "Maybe they're acting up. I don't remember a time when he ever cancelled."

Rosabal replied with a platitude and continued to walk, past the bar and the reception desk and back on to Obispo Street, where the breeze had gathered strength and shook the posters that hung in the air. *The Lider Maximo was too sick to make his speech.* For the first time in history, Rosabal thought.

He walked past the herbal shop, El Herbolario. The scent of mint drifted toward him, evoking an unwelcome memory of Guantanamo and Rosabal's impoverished childhood there. *Yerbabuena*, which so many people found pleasing, had grown in profusion near his home. His father had been a poor, illiterate canecutter, his house a miserable hut through which hot winds blew dust and which, in the rainy season, became flooded and filled with mosquitoes. People were said to be better off in Guantanamo these days, but that was a relative thing. Poverty, no matter what the Communist statisticians told you, still existed. The only difference was that increased life expectancy and low infant mortality meant there were many more people around to enjoy it.

Rosabal, thinking how far he had travelled from his wretched origins and how close he was to his goal, paused on the corner. He was rich now, he had access to vast sums of money and investments all over the world, and he rarely ever thought about his background. Who needed it anyway? Who needed to recall the lack of nutrition and the mosquitoes that fed on thin bodies and the sheer hopelessness that the land instilled in people? He remembered his emphysematic father cutting cane, cutting cane, on and on, season after monotonous season, stooped and burned black by the harsh sun in the cane-fields, a prisoner of King Sugar. He remembered his mother, dour, thick-hipped from too many births, dead at the age of thirty-five. She had never smiled, never. These memories bored into him, one despised picture after another, until he felt tension rise in his throat and a hammer knocking the inside of his skull.

He remembered the terrible day in 1962, two years after the death of his mother, when his father had tried to seek political asylum at the American naval base in Guantanamo; he recalled clutching his father's hand and being surrounded by Yankees in khaki uniforms who asked his father tough questions and laughed at some of the answers. Rosabal recalled the fear he'd felt at the strangeness of it all, the alien language, the unfamiliar uniforms. The cowed look in his father's eyes had haunted him ever since. The Americans turned father and son back. They rejected a dying man and his nine-year-old boy. They spoke of immigration quotas and application forms and the need for sponsors, things neither Rosabal nor his father understood.

A day later, as a direct consequence of his attempt

to flee Cuba, Felipe Rosabal was taken away by *fidelistas*. He was never seen again. For years, Rafael Rosabal couldn't decide whom he hated more, Castro or the Yanquis.

He took a handkerchief from a pocket, wiped sweat from his forehead. You had to control these memories. You had to fight them back, suppress them. They were dead and gone, they had nothing to do with you. You escaped from your childhood, from that dank brutality, from humiliation. Every now and again it reaches out darkly as if to drag you back to your beginnings, but it means nothing. It means absolutely nothing.

Thanks to the Revolution, to the opportunities given to you by Castro's regime, you fled your origins. The poverty. The futility.

The irony of this—his gratitude to the Revolution—was pointedly amusing. After all, he intended to destroy the same State that had educated and raised him at its own expense.

He was calm again as his chauffeur-driven black BMW rolled quietly toward him. He opened the back door and stepped inside where a young woman, who had the intense good looks of a flamenco dancer, smiled and reached out to him. She wore her very black hair pulled back tightly across her scalp and ribboned with red satin. Her lips, whose lipstick matched her ribbon exactly, pressed on his mouth, and she placed the palms of her hands lightly against the sides of his face. It was a gesture in part love, in part possessiveness.

"My darling," she said, a little breathlessly.

Rafael Rosabal held the woman, but not with any great enthusiasm. Her skin smelled of a perfume called Diva, which he had brought back for her from Europe.

"Can we go home for lunch . . ." She blew softly in his ear; she behaved as if the chauffeur didn't exist.

"We can go home for lunch," he said, holding her hand between his own. Later, she would make love with a kind of serenity that was in total contrast to Magdalena, with whom sex was all fire, and final damp exhaustion. Magdalena was like a magnificent whore, Rosabal thought. A wife never, a mistress always.

"Do I make you happy?" the young woman asked.

"Yes."

"You regret nothing?"

"Nothing," Rosabal said in an absent way.

The gold ring on the young woman's hand caught light and glinted. She turned her hand over, studied the band from different angles. Until three months ago, the girl's name had been Estela Capablanca Alvarez, daughter of the General. From time to time Estela still thought of herself as bearing her unmarried name. She hadn't yet become accustomed to her change in marital status. Being the wife of Rafael Rosabal was a new condition for her, and one she thought fortunate. It had all happened so quickly, a fast courtship, a very quiet wedding unannounced in newspapers—because Rafael had wanted it that way—a brief honeymoon in Mexico.

Other Minister's wives, who had sometimes contrived to play matchmaker for Rosabal in the past, considered them a marvellous couple who needed only a baby to make their marriage a perfect union. Certainly Estela wanted a child. She adored children. Sometimes she wept quietly when she read of atrocities enacted upon infants in the war zones of the world, or her heart ached when she saw some poor sad-eyed kid on the streets of Havana.

Every time she felt Rafael's sperm flood her womb she prayed for fertility. And her prayers, it seemed, had been answered. Only fifteen minutes before her rendezvous with Rafael she'd gone to her physician to learn that she was pregnant. Now, quietly joyful, she waited for the right moment to share this news with her husband, who was so often distracted these days.

A mother-to-be, yes, a clinging wife no. She wasn't at all the mindless little wife so many people, Rosabal included, perceived her to be. She had some private core to her, an independence she may have inherited from the General, a stubbornness, a native intelligence that was inviolate. She was domestic, in the sense that she enjoyed both the Havana apartment and the country house near Sancti Spiritus, but it would have been a gross underestimation to think that was the complete picture. Estela Rosabal was her own person. A fire burned inside her that few had ever seen.

For his part, Rosabal believed that being the son-in-law of General Capablanca was a profitable connection: it kept conspiracy in the family. It was a great match, even if it had been made more by power brokers and opportunists than by heaven and heart.

The weary man in the gray and blue plaid jacket carried a Canadian passport that falsely identified him as J S Mazarek. The document was a good forgery he'd been given in Miami. He had come to Havana on a cut-rate package tour from Montreal. The group with whom he'd travelled called themselves The Explorer's Association, mostly an alliance of single middleaged men and women whose only interest in exploration seemingly involved one another's bodily parts. Mazarek had already had to avoid the energetic advances of an opera-humming, large-breasted widow from Trois Rivieres.

Mazarek, a big man with hair the color and texture of froth on a cappucino, had been tracking his quarry along Obispo and Mercaderes Streets, surreptitiously taking photographs. He did this expertly because he'd been doing it for much of his life. Usually his cases involved errant husbands and wandering wives, who tended to be more paranoid than the cocksure Mr. Smooth, whose face and movements rarely betrayed a sign of nerves.

Mazarek watched the Minister of Finance open the door of the BMW. Then he got off one more quick shot with his tiny camera. He had enough data on Rafael Rosabal. His employer would be satisfied, though perhaps not absolutely happy. In this line of work—often more a probe of men's hearts than mere detection—satisfaction wasn't always followed by contentment.

12

At nine o'clock in the evening Frank Pagan sat in his office and listened to the constant ringing of telephones and the clack of printers. Despite all this incoming information, he was frustrated. What had he learned after all? The answer that came back was disheartening: damn little. He hung his jacket on the back of the chair and pressed his fingertips against his tired eyes, ignoring the bothersome sparrow of pain pecking away at his chest.

Foxie came into the room with a bunch of papers in his hand. He took a sheet off the top and scanned it. "The chopper was stolen three weeks ago from the Moroccan Air Force, who assumed it was seized by West Saharan rebels. The crew-members were Syrians. As you could predict, they didn't enter the country with a shred of legality. Known terrorists, according to the Syrian Press attaché in London."

A Moroccan Cobra helicopter, a Syrian crew; terrorism observed no boundaries. It was sovereign unto itself.

"The other men dead at the site were Richard Mayer, a native of Buffalo, New York, and one Roderigo Flavell, a citizen of Argentina. Mayer was trained by the U.S. Army in the fine art of explosives and was renowned for his demolition skills. Flavell is wanted for questioning in connection with the bombing of a synagogue in Paris a couple of years ago. A merry sort of bunch, Frank."

Pagan shifted his position. It was hard to concentrate on what Foxworth was telling him. His mind, or some dark aspect of it, kept pulling him away. Too many puzzles, each demanding his attention at the same time, nagged him.

Foxie said, "The prints we got from the Yardley farm belong to Ruhr, Mayer, and another American named Trevaskis, who has a police record in San Diego. Extortion, conspiracy to sell explosives and firearms, gun-running into Mexico. Considered dangerous. We also found prints belonging to the late Flavell as well as a fellow countryman of his called Enrico Zapino. Zapino is also wanted by the French police. Same synagogue bombing."

The Yardley farm. Now there was one puzzle that kept coming back like a bad taste. He couldn't figure out the association between the man who had rented the place and Gunther Ruhr. Impatiently he looked at his watch; the renter's wife had been sent for an hour ago—what was keeping her? She only had to come from The Connaught Hotel, which wasn't more than a ten-minute cab-ride away. Pagan hoped she might be able to cast a little light on the dark area, if she ever arrived.

Since the gunshot wound he'd felt morose, even bleak, about the fate of Steffie Brough. He'd met her parents before leaving Norwich, two very unhappy people trying to varnish their sorrow with good old-fashioned English stoicism and finding that the stiff upper lip wasn't all the advertising claimed it to be.

We'll do our best, Pagan had told them. We'll find her.

What makes you think so? Mrs. Brough had asked in that kind of ringing voice which is a cousin to outright hysteria. It was a question to which Pagan had no answer. In the policeman's almanac of platitudes, absolutely none was capable of creating a shield against grief. He kept seeing Mrs. Brough's face, which resembled an older version of the Stephanie in the school photograph. Sheer anxiety had stripped her features of any expression other than desperation. Pagan was filled with helpless sorrow and an anger he labored to control.

Billy Ewing appeared in the doorway, half in, half out of the office. He held a slip of thin yellow paper in one hand.

"Item, gentlemen," he said.

"I hope it's good news," Pagan said.

Billy Ewing shrugged. "Good, bad, I just deliver, Frank. You're the swami, you interpret. Now according to this little gem a transport plane was stolen this very morning from right under the vigilant nose of our Royal Air Force."

"Stolen?" Pagan asked.

"That's what it says here. On a routine, approved flight from Fife to Germany, an American C-130, which had flown unspecified *materiel* into a base in Fife the day before, was apparently hijacked by persons unknown. The location of the craft is also unknown."

"How did it take so damned long to provide us with that item?" Pagan said.

"Injured pride," Foxie suggested. "The RAF is awfully sensitive."

"I suppose," Pagan said, but without conviction. There was no real coordination at times between law enforcement agencies and branches of the military. Each was its own little dominion of egotism.

"Lose big plane, look very foolish," said Billy Ewing.

"How can they lose a big plane?" Pagan asked. "I can see the hijacking. Fine. Anything can be hijacked if you want it bad enough. What I don't see is the failure to find the thing."

With the authority of a man who is halfway to attaining his pilot's licence, Foxie said, "First, bad weather. Clouds, Frank. And many of them. Second, it's a big sky, and one plane is very tiny in it, no matter how big it looks on the ground. Third, the Air Force has only a limited number of interceptors at its disposal. And where do they look? The North Sea? The English Channel? The Atlantic? If the transport plane's flying low enough, radar's no help."

"Do you think the RAF has informed the Americans?" Pagan asked.

Billy Ewing said, "What a scene. The Air Marshall going on his knees to the Americans." Ewing assumed a sharp English accent, upper-class, accurate. *"Sorry, old boy. One of your planes got away from us. Damnedest thing."*

Pagan rose from his chair very slowly. He walked across the room and turned on a small portable radio. He wanted something raucous and mind-clearing, something to shake up the synapses and cover the quiet drumming noise panic made inside his head. If Steffie Brough was still alive, she was inside an airplane with

Ruhr and nobody knew where. In his imagination he saw Ruhr skywriting the words *Find Me, Frank*.

Little Richard's *Long Tall Sally* roared into the room. The sound, which to some might have been torture—Foxworth, out of Pagan's vision, winced—was balm to Pagan's troubled heart. Like most great rock music, it was meaningless if you thought about it. But meaning wasn't the point. Rock hypnotized you into a condition where you didn't need to think. That was the beauty of it. Pagan, an old rock buff, knew such arcane things as the names of the original Shirelles, the first hit song recorded by Gene Vincent, and the date and place of Buddy Holly's death.

Billy Ewing left. His musical tastes went no further than Peter, Paul and Mary and his own whisky-inspired version of Auld Lang Syne every New Year's Eve.

Pagan returned to his desk. He couldn't remember when he'd last slept. His eyelids felt heavy. He needed a brisk infusion of coffee. He was about to ask Foxworth to bring a cup of very strong brew, when the woman suddenly appeared in the doorway.

She was in her middle forties and had reached that condition known as her prime. To look at Gabrielle Chapotin was to understand the word in a way no dictionary could ever define. She had a calm confidence about her, and a style found only in women who have both the means and ambition to haunt the salons of high fashion and those expensive clinics where clever cosmetologists concoct creams and lotions to halt the ruin of the flesh. She had the air of a fortress against whose buttresses decay and deterioration may batter but make little headway.

She was beautiful in a daunting way. The high cheekbones, the hollows in the cheeks that suggested a sour lozenge of candy in her mouth, the long, groomed red-brown hair, the tailored pants suit that was pin-striped and authoritative; she was a woman who knew herself very well. She reminded Pagan of a former fashion model, somebody of well-trained elegance.

"Frank Pagan?" she asked in very good English.

"You must be Gabrielle Chapotin." Pagan rose, walked to the radio, turned it off.

Foxie scurried with a chair for Madame. She nodded to him as she would to all servants, then sat down with a very straight back. She gazed up at the big silk screen of Buddy Holly, as if she were amused.

"My regrets," Pagan said. He extended a hand. Gabrielle's clasp was slack and quick. She wanted out of here in a hurry.

"Regrets?" she asked.

"Your husband. The tragedy."

"Some marriages are in name only, Mr. Pagan," she said.

Madame Frost, Pagan thought. He cleared his throat, asked Foxworth for coffee. Gabrielle declined, saying she couldn't drink what passed for coffee in England. Pagan made a mild joke about the similarity between British coffee and transmission fluid, but Madame didn't even smile politely. Foxworth brought coffee in a plastic cup and Pagan sipped. The temperature of the room had fallen; the woman had ushered in a brisk chill.

"I have so much to do," she said. "There is tape red."

"Red tape," Pagan said. "But your way sounds more poetic."

"However you say it. Also funeral arrangements. I have to ship my late husband's body back to Paris for burial. You understand, of course."

"I don't intend to keep you for very long. A few questions, nothing more." Pagan set his cup down. "You realize my interest isn't in solving your husband's murder, don't you? This isn't a homicide operation."

She looked surprised. "Then why am I here?"

"Because I sent for you, Madame. When I learned you'd come to London, I thought it would save me a trip to Paris."

"But why, if it has nothing to do with my husband's murder?"

"I'm more interested in your husband's life than his death."

"Which life would that be, Mr. Pagan? After all, he had more than one."

It was a good point. Which life? Did they overlap? Had old Jean-Paul kept them completely separated? One world in Paris with Madame, another in London with his doomed Melody. Was there perhaps even a third life, something he kept apart from the other two? J-P Chapotin, grandmaster of deception.

"Your late husband rented a farm in the countryside," Pagan said.

"He hated the countryside."

"Just the same, the information we have is that a farmhouse was leased to him by an estate agency in Norfolk. So far as we know, he never occupied the house personally."

"Why does it interest you if he never lived there?" she asked. She was impatient. She sat defensively, as if she thought a prolonged stay in this room might contaminate her.

"I'm intrigued by the connection between your husband and the people who *did* occupy the house. They were . . . criminals. I'm simply trying to work out the relationship between these men and Monsieur Chapotin.''

''Criminals? I don't know why he would associate with such types. I can't help you, Mr. Pagan. You see, I know so very little.''

She placed her hands in her lap and looked down at them. They were excellent hands, long fingers, strong nails subtly varnished. They were made for summoning head-waiters and dismissing servants. Gabrielle may have been the spirit of winter incarnate, but she had class.

''Let's try something simpler. What kind of business was he in?''

''I paid no attention to his affairs,'' she replied, skating over—perhaps ignorant of—the double meaning.

''You must have some knowledge,'' Pagan said.

''I ran his houses for him, Mr. Pagan. That is all I did. I was his housekeeper.''

Pagan didn't think she could ever be anybody's housekeeper. Nor could he imagine Jean-Paul concealing very much from this woman. She was strong, self-willed. She wouldn't be easy to deceive. He resisted the temptation to scoff. He would press on as if he hadn't heard a word she'd said. He'd simply tuck his head down and keep charging. The battering-ram principle.

''Did he have business interests in England?''

She looked slightly exasperated. ''I do not know.''

''I assume he had a bank account here. He would have to pay household expenses in Chelsea. I could easily find out. With a little luck, I might even discover the source of his income. If there was an account, deposits had to be made somehow. There would be microfilm copies of checks. The bank manager would probably help. They usually do when I ask them.''

"I had thought your bankers were more discreet," she said.

"Nobody's discreet when you start breaking their bones, Madame," Pagan said.

"Breaking their bones?"

"Figuratively."

"How very colorful."

Gabrielle Chapotin was silent a moment. She smiled for the first time, a rehearsed cover-girl smile but gorgeous anyway. "Speaking of banks reminds me that Jean-Paul had an interest in an Italian financial institution. I don't remember the name. Commerciante something. It should not be too difficult to find if you need to. He also had, I believe, some South African investments."

Ah. Pagan found it fascinating how responsive people could be when they imagined a stranger poking around in their bank accounts. There was always something to hide, and it was usually money. Obviously Madame knew more about Jean-Paul's business than she was saying, at least enough to become communicative when she faced the prospect of Pagan interviewing a bank manager. What other financial irregularities might be uncovered? What fiscal misdeeds might be stumbled upon? Whatever they were—and Pagan wasn't interested in them—Madame surely knew. It was a great smile, though, and it warmed him.

"I'm glad to see your memory's finally working," he said.

Gabrielle shrugged. "Sometimes a small connection is all you need. A spark, you might say. Memory is a strange thing."

"Very strange," Pagan said. "What about his business interests in this country? Can we find a spark for those?"

She opened her purse and took out a Disque Bleu. Foxie found a match, struck it, held it to the cigarette. She smoked without inhaling. Blue clouds gathered around her head, making her look wistful. She gazed at Pagan and for a second he enjoyed a certain intimacy with her, the meaningful locking of eyes, the vague feeling that at some other time they might have met in circumstances more conducive to, well, mutual understanding. He was flattered.

He pushed his chair back against the wall, glanced at Foxie, then waited for Madame to go on. She held out her cigarette and Foxie, the perfect butler, produced an ashtray in which she crushed the butt vigorously. Too vigorously, Pagan thought. She was tense.

She looked away from him now. "He went to Scotland."

"Do you know why he went there?"

"He had some kind of business meeting, I believe. But I don't know the details."

"Do you know exactly where he went?"

Madame Chapotin said, "I understand he flew to Glasgow. I happened to see the airline ticket when his secretary sent it to the house."

Pagan was sure that things didn't just 'happen' in Gabrielle's life. She probably found the ticket and sneaked a look at it; she would have spied like an expert. He wondered if she'd known about Chapotin's other life all along but chose to ignore it for reasons of her own.

"Did he stay in Glasgow?"

She didn't know the answer. Nor did she know his business there, or if he hired a car, or whether he was picked up at the airport. She only knew the date of his airline ticket, which she was happy to remember. Pagan believed her. The interview was coming to an end.

Foxie, who knew what was expected of him in the light of Gabrielle's slender information, had already slipped out of the room. Pagan stood up.

She said, "You know, the more I think of this, the more I consider it unlikely that Jean-Paul rented the farmhouse. I cannot imagine him ever doing that. He hated quiet. He loathed country living. Perhaps another man with the same name was responsible. Could that not be?"

"Chapotin's a pretty unusual name," Pagan said.

"You can check it out, no?"

"My assistant obtained a photograph of your late husband from the police conducting the homicide investigation. A copy is on its way to the woman who rented the farmhouse. If it turns out that the renter wasn't your husband, why would somebody want to pose as him? What would an imposter stand to gain?"

Gabrielle Chapotin had no answer for that one. She drifted out into the hallway, where she stood for a time in thoughtful silence. Then she smiled halfheartedly at Pagan and was gone, leaving behind the faintest trace of expensive perfume.

Pagan didn't like the idea of an imposter. He'd assumed that Jean-Paul had rented the place on behalf of the terrorists, that some connection existed between Chapotin and Ruhr. Perhaps Chapotin was even the man behind Ruhr. To introduce the hypothesis of a fraud at this stage was a complication Pagan didn't need. If J-P hadn't rented the place, then why would somebody use his name to do it? Of course, there might be two different Jean-Paul Chapotins, but in England the chances were remote.

Foxworth came back into the room. "I just had a word with the Glasgow Police. They'll get back to me."

"Soon, I hope."

"ASAP. I leaned on them, Frank," Foxie said, enjoying the phrase. He had a familiar manila folder tucked under his arm, his dogeared odds and ends file. He opened it on Pagan's desk and began leafing through sheets. He found what he wanted, plucked it out and said, "When I heard Madame say Scotland, I thought I remembered this tidbit. Tell me it's mere coincidence."

Pagan looked at the sheet, spreading it on his desk.

It was one of the sheets Foxie had somehow contrived to coax out of his old school pal in intelligence. It reported the movements of Rafael Rosabal, complete with dates and times—when he entered the country, where he went, where he stayed, who he saw. There was no mention of Magdalena, which meant that Rafael had presumably given his followers the slip during that interlude or that somehow they'd lost him for a while. Busy sort, Pagan thought. Buzzing around. *London to Glasgow.*

Pagan raised his face and looked at Foxworth. "Can you tell me what's so special about Glasgow at this time of year?"

"It must have its attractions," Foxworth replied. "Chapotin went there. So did Rafael Rosabal. At precisely the same time too. Do you think they might have met, Frank?" Foxie looked puzzled. His otherwise smooth young forehead was creased with a severe frown.

"What for?" Pagan asked. "What kind of connection could there possibly be between Chapotin and Rosabal? And if a connection existed, why go all the way to Glasgow to get together? They each had, shall we say, interests of the heart right here in London, so why travel four hundred miles north to meet? Frankly, I'd hate to see any connection between them. I don't want to unravel some damned mess that involves Rosabal because if a Cuban's up to his arse in this mischief it could turn out to be a real can of worms. I'd be quite happy with just Chapotin.''

Pagan looked beyond Foxworth to the window. The darkness over Golden Square was laced with a thin rain that had begun to fall. He tried to imagine Rafael Rosabal and Chapotin meeting in Glasgow—for God's sake, why? *(He remembered the closed bathroom door in Magdalena's hotel room, the light beneath it, the presence of Rosabal: was that why he was so anxious to discount Rosabal—because it meant Magdalena had no involvement either?)* And even if he established a link, so what? How would it bring him any closer to Ruhr?

Too many questions. Too few answers. A coincidence of place and time and people he didn't like at all. He had so little to go on. Chapotin was the only thread he had to Steffie Brough and Ruhr, and a dead man's name wasn't much.

As if he'd just trespassed on Pagan's ragged thoughts, Foxie said, ''One wonders where Steffie Brough is right now.'' There was a grim note in his usually cheerful voice.

Pagan was restless. He got out of his chair and walked to the window; everything in the building had gone silent at the same time. No phones rang, no computers buzzed, no printers rattled. A fragile little island of quiet existed. Pagan looked down into Golden Square. Rain, turned to silver by electricity, coursed through the streetlamps. He took from his inside jacket pocket the small school picture of Steffie Brough, and tacked it to his cork bulletin board.

''One wonders,'' he said quietly.

Washington

It was a fall afternoon of rare beauty. Washington's monuments might have been erected less to honor some democratic ideal and more to celebrate the way leaves turned and how the smoky orange sun, larger than any ever seen in summer, burnished landmarks, seeming to isolate them in flame.

Harry Hurt always felt good in Washington. As a patriot, he considered it his true home. He loved the statues and monuments; he'd stood at the Vietnam Memorial once, reading the names of the dead and feeling a shiver of gratitude toward the fallen. The city touched him like this, made him conscious of his country, the fact he was above all else an American. He had no shame and no embarrassment in being a patriot.

As he walked along a quiet street some blocks from George Washington University, he was conscious of Sheridan Perry trying to keep up with him. Perry was out of shape. Unlike Harry Hurt, he didn't jog, play handball, eat the proper foods. He had no pride in his body.

Both men paused on a corner. Blinded, buffed by a crisp wind that had begun to blow, Harry Hurt stuck his hands in the pockets of his gray cashmere overcoat. His bony face looked more angular than usual; cords in his neck stood out. There was a question he wanted to put to Perry but he wasn't sure how. There was simply no diplomatic way of asking his compatriot if he was the man behind the murders of Chapotin and Magiwara and Kluger. It wasn't the kind of question guaranteed to promote mutual confidence.

Hurt had spent a restless few hours on the Concorde from Paris. He hated unanswered questions. Who was killing off the membership? Who had knowledge of their identities? Somewhere over the Atlantic it had occurred to Hurt that Perry, by virtue of his need for control, was as much a candidate as anyone else and that the best way to proceed was to ask a straight question and be damned. Despite the united front he and Sheridan presented to the Society, Harry Hurt didn't care all that much for Perry in any case, thinking him just a little too self-centered.

Besides, Perry's philosophy was suspect. Like Harry, he called himself a patriot, but Hurt thought he was stretching the definition. He'd once listened to Perry explain the greatness of the USA, a diatribe that caused Hurt some dismay.

According to Perry, the Constitution was a wonderful document, sure; but what made America great was the other marvellous invention it had given the world—the loophole. There were loopholes in the Constitution, in the legal system, in the tax codes; here, there, everywhere a loophole, and Perry thrived on them. America was a wonderful country just so long as you recognized the loopholes. Perry had grown quite animated at the time. Hurt often thought about the cynicism behind The Loophole Speech. The tragedy was that Sheridan Perry didn't think it cynical at all.

The midnight blue limousine that had been following Hurt and Perry at a distance of a hundred feet rolled a little closer. Three armed bodyguards sat in the vehicle. They observed the two men closely, watched the street, studied windows, storefronts, rooftops. Hurt had suggested this stroll so that he could phrase his question in private, without having to embarrass Perry in front of the bodyguards. But the car, the protection, was never very far away, while Hurt's sensitive question was further away than ever.

How could he possibly come right out and ask Perry such a terrible thing? *It's a process of elimination, Sheridan. Since I know it's not me, it either has to be you or Caporelli or Kinnaird. Caporelli's a possible, Kinnaird less so, which leaves you and Enrico as the best possible candidates.* It couldn't be asked. Perry would be deeply offended, a wedge of mistrust would be driven between them. It was, Hurt thought, a no-win situation.

The storefront at which Hurt and Perry paused belonged to a tailoring establishment so exclusive it made suits with no labels, no identifying marks save a special little cross-stitch applied beneath the collar, where it was invisible. Had the needlework been evident, it would have been recognized by only a hundred men at most. It was the apotheosis of elitism. The grubby windows were curtained. No fancy displays here. Nor was there a sign to indicate the business of the shop, simply a street number on a plain metal disc. People who came here tended to have Rolodexes filled with unlisted numbers. These men used Charles Katzner & Sons, Tailors, Established 1925, as a kind of club in which they also happened to have their suits made.

Hurt rang the doorbell; the door was opened within seconds by a tall quiet man who wore a black jacket and pin-striped pants. A tape measure was draped around his shoulders. With a slightly effeminate gesture he indicated that Hurt and Perry should follow him—between long tables covered with tweeds and linens, wools and silks, up a narrow flight of stairs and through double doors into a large unfurnished room panelled in dark brown wood. The air had the universal scent of tailoring shops, composed of the smells of dozens of brand new fabrics, all so completely intermingled they were impossible to separate. Blinds, discolored by too many summers, hung against the windows. The little light that filtered through had a strange brownish hue.

A red-cheeked man stood by the only furniture in the room, a long table on which lay a number of bulky volumes filled with fabric samples. The man wore very black glasses and a blue suit. He leafed through the swatches, pausing every now and then when one took his interest.

"This is a nice linen," he said. "I've always liked linen, more so in the pale colors." He spoke softly. He didn't have to raise his voice to make people listen to him. When Allen Falk entered a room people turned to look. Neither handsome nor trim nor elegant, he had the elusive quality known as presence.

Falk closed the fabric book. "Let me bring you up to date, gentlemen, in case you've missed anything en route. Gunther Ruhr seized the missile, as expected. A nice job too, I understand. He managed, however, to introduce a little complexity we didn't anticipate. He's got a hostage, a young girl. It's no big deal. But the unpredictable throws us off balance."

"A hostage?" Sheridan Perry had been expecting something strange from the German. "Why the hell did he need a hostage?"

Al Falk stepped in front of the table. "We'll get back to the child later. The only important thing is the missile arriving at its destination. And Ruhr's plane, I'm informed, is presently only three hours from landing."

Harry Hurt felt a little tense. He looked at his watch. Three hours seemed to him a very long time. He didn't like the notion of a hostage any more than Perry did, but only because he disliked unscripted occurrences. He had never married and had absolutely no empathy toward children. He sometimes saw them out of the corner of his eye and thought they were hyperactive and too robust, too loud. He had no real admiration for Gunther Ruhr; the man's life lacked principle. Personally, thank God, he'd had no dealings with the German. When Ruhr had supplied the complicated technical specifications for his needs they had come to Harry Hurt via Caporelli, who had received them from Rosabal. Such was the complex chain of obligations. In turn, Hurt had supplied the data to Levy and Possony. This was as close as he'd come to Gunther Ruhr, and he was grateful.

Falk continued. "There should be absolutely no problems to interfere with the arrival. Our spy satellites, which would have identified the plane, have been 'malfunctioning' for the last eight hours and will continue to do so for at least another three. Odd timing, don't you think?"

"Oh, very," Hurt remarked.

Falk smiled his famous smile. His cheeks, already plump, swelled to the size of crab apples, suggesting the face of a very jolly man, which he wasn't. He was too involved in controlling Presidents and starfucking to be either carefree or generous. The smile was secretive, and knowing, that of a man who imagines he alone has the blueprint to the power circuits of the country.

Sometimes Hurt had a suspicion that Falk knew about the Society. If so, he gave no indication that he understood Hurt and Perry were part of any organization. Perhaps he knew nothing, but only gave an impression of knowing. Or he simply thought that his old Princeton friend, Harold S. Hurt, was one half of a two-man partnership with Perry, nothing more.

"I've received information that Fidel has come

down with an unspecified illness," Falk said. "Which is exactly what we've been waiting for."

"Beautiful," Harry Hurt remarked.

Falk said, "Brother Raul, who could be a significant problem because he commands loyalty among some officers, is still in Africa. Events will delay him there until it's too late for him to return to Cuba. According to my information, South African mercenaries are scheduled to launch a border attack on Angola of sufficient ferocity to keep Raul bouncing around the continent for a few more days."

Harry Hurt was always impressed by the intricacy of the plan; it was a remarkable conception that involved not only Falk, but also the fragmented anti-Castro movement inside Cuba, a handful of terrorists under the direction of Ruhr, and the forces Hurt himself had assembled in Honduras. And behind it all, a benign overseer, a great masonic eye, the Society of Friends.

Hurt also assumed a clique existed at the CIA under Falk's control, although like most things involving that organization it couldn't be confirmed. But how else could spy satellites be manipulated? How else could the presence of a small army at Cabo Gracias a Dios be kept beyond the reach of those inquisitive journalists who were professional Central America watchers? And how could a South African mercenary assault on Angola be so precisely orchestrated?

Hurt had times when he wondered if the President himself were involved, or if he knew about the scheme but could never in a hundred lifetimes admit it, far less endorse it, for fear of alienating the allies and perhaps enraging the Soviets. It was a slippery speculation and there could never be a definitive answer. The Presidency was, as usual, a mystifying law unto itself, more myth than substance, more shadow than actuality. Besides, Hurt had all along known that the United States could only be involved in this whole project in a manner that was, so to speak, on the periphery of the periphery.

Al Falk walked to the windows, where he stood with his back to the room. "It goes well," he said. He rubbed the palms of his hands as if he thought he could strike flame from the friction of skin. Hurt had the feeling that Al Falk confidently believed himself capable of anything, walking on water, raising the dead, you name it.

Falk turned around. "You get Cuba. We get an end to Fidel. What a terrific arrangement."

Hurt smiled in his usual lean manner. He pondered the success with which different interests had been gathered together under a common banner. The last of *fidelismo,* and the control of Cuba by the Society of Friends fronted by a reasonable and malleable President in the form of Rafael Rosabal. As Falk said, a terrific arrangement. The only shadow across Hurt's otherwise undiluted enthusiasm was the way the Society was being depleted. Apart from the fact that the situation had produced paranoia, Harry Hurt didn't like being a target on anybody's hit list. Of course, new blood could be encouraged, new members carefully inducted into the inner sanctum of the Society—but that was hardly the point. What he *really* wanted to believe was that the killings had come to an end with Magiwara, Chapotin and Kluger, that these three had been murdered by a party or parties they had somehow managed to injure. A thin little hope, but he clutched it anyhow. It was better than paranoia.

Falk released a blind, which snapped up. The light in the room was tangerine now, and cold. Harry Hurt watched the Presidential advisor as the light struck him. Small reddish veins were stitched across Falk's face, like some form of embroidery. The black glasses glowed as if the eyes behind them had turned orange. Falk appeared quite demonic.

He said, "I've been watching Cuba for more than thirty years. I've watched over it the way a physician monitors vital signs. I've sniffed the wind from the place, and let me tell you it doesn't smell like sugar. It smells the way the dogshit of Communism always smells. That's what we don't need down there. So let's deodorize the Caribbean. And if the United States can't do it *officially*, then let it be done the only way it can."

Falk paused. His loathing of Communism had surfaced in 1956 during the failed Hungarian revolution, and had seized him with the passion of a first love affair. In 1968, brutal events in Czechoslovakia had strengthened this hatred. Recent occurrences in China confirmed his beliefs.

The silence in the room was broken only by the sound of his wristwatch beeping twice. He ignored it and went on, "Whenever the CIA tried in the past to assassinate Fidel, it was always ridiculed. The USA was always the oversized bully trying to push little Fidel round the schoolyard with no justification except for the fact we were bigger than Cuba and could kick its ass all the livelong day. A stinking image, friends. In the feckless court of world opinion, which is the only international court that really matters these days, we had no justification for killing the cretin and clearing the excrement out of Cuba." Here Falk puffed out his cheeks. "It's another ballgame now. This time we'll have evidence that's damned hard and incontrovertible. The trick of victory in our day and age is to present to a reproachful world a *fait accomplis* which is perceived as utterly regrettable but inevitable. We don't want to upset the Organization of American States, some of whose member countries have close relations with Cuba, and we don't want to upset our NATO allies, some of whom enjoy lucrative trade with Fidel. We need the mumble of world approval in everything we do because that's how goddam sensitive we've become. A nation of images. We're not people. We're holographs. All we want to do is look good, for Christ's sake."

Falk paused, swallowed. "Consequently, we can't go in with a big stick. No, we go in sideways, obliquely, pretending we have absolutely nothing to do with it. We use surrogates. And if by some *slight* chance we *are* associated with them, we stand in the courtroom and wring our hands, filled with terrible remorse for having helped recover a missile from a sick despot. But what were we supposed to do? That missile was being pointed directly at our goddam throat, after all. So we *gave some assistance* to a small army of Cuban exiles just to show that we weren't bullying poor little Cuba again. And we laid out our photographs of the missile for all the judges to see. Case closed. Amen."

Hurt, who enjoyed the way Falk talked, looked down into the narrow street. The limousine was parked across the way, engine running. A white Ford Taurus passed, then stopped.

Falk reached under his glasses with a finger and rubbed an eye. "Now. The hostage. I think a simple message to Ruhr is going to be enough. Something to the effect that no excess baggage is allowed. No hysterical little eyewitnesses. He knows what to do. He's been around."

Harry Hurt was about to agree when he noticed the Ford Taurus backing up very quickly until it was aligned with the parked limousine. Something was going on down there. Hurt started to mention the suspicious appearance of the Taurus in the center of the street, a great plume of exhaust hanging behind it like an angry wraith. He got out the words *I wonder what the hell* and then stopped, because the Ford moved forward very quickly, tires whining on concrete, leaving the limousine exposed to view.

But only for a second. There was a flash of extraordinary light. The limousine exploded. It rose a foot in the air. Windows shattered, metal buckled, a wheel flew off. A great sphere of smoke, dark, thick, rich, billowed around the limousine. Shockwaves blew across the street and shattered the window where Hurt stood. He managed to step away before thin razors of glass lanced into the room. Allen Falk, less nimble, received a scalpful of slivers. Perry, who stood by the table, was unscathed.

"Dear Jesus," Falk said. Blood flowed over his forehead and down his well-fed cheeks.

Hurt took out a handkerchief and helped Falk mop blood from his face. He glanced at Perry, who had moved to the broken window and was looking down into the street.

The trashed limousine straddled the sidewalk. The hood was gone, the fender mangled, the trunk crumpled. The doors had been blown open. Two motionless men lay in the back, one upon the other. In the front a man was twisted over the steering-wheel.

Hurt said nothing. Clearly somebody had been under the impression that he and Perry were inside the limo. Somebody had thought them sitting targets. Somebody had been mistaken. *This time.*

Falk touched the side of his skull with the bloodied handkerchief. "We ought to be long gone by the time the police arrive and start looking for eyewitnesses. I suggest we get the hell out of here now."

Neither Hurt nor Perry hesitated. The room was filling up with vile, rubbery smoke that drifted across the street from the ruined limousine. As Hurt walked toward the door behind Falk, he considered the question: who *knew?* Who the hell *knew* that he and Perry were travelling in that particular vehicle?

On the staircase down he was struck by a thought that would make some sense to him later: *Perry. Perry knew.*

13

Cabo Gracias a Dios, Honduras

Tomas Fuentes was in his tent when he heard the stale air around him vibrate, at first quietly and steadily, as if the evening sky were filled with the drone of a million batwings. He stepped outside and stood with his hands on his hips, listening. The sound, which originated close to the sea, had the texture of a natural force, a tornado gathering strength, say, or an earthquake forcing open a fissure on the bed of the ocean.

Roger Bosanquet emerged from the tent pitched next to Tommy's. The sound grew more profound. Among the trees yellow kerosene lights illuminated pathways between the large marquees in which the army slept. It was Tent City here.

Tommy Fuentes scanned the heavens, but saw nothing moving. Still the sound grew in intensity, a rumbling suggestive of thunder now. Tommy thought the ground under his feet had begun to tremble, but it was only his imagination. This landscape seemed to trap and amplify sounds. It was like being imprisoned inside a loudspeaker.

"There she is," Bosanquet said and pointed to the sky.

At first pinheads of light, nothing more. Then the shape of the craft could be seen as it lost altitude and dropped so low that spray rose up from the surface of the water into the lights.

Fuentes and the Englishman walked down the slope toward the airstrip. Blue electric lamps, surrounded by agitated mosquitoes, burned the length of the runway. The plane appeared over the trees, the noise so terrible now that Fuentes and Bosanquet covered their ears. They watched the craft roar down toward the strip. It seemed for a moment to stall in the air, but then it was down with a final scream, lunging across the runway, skidding slightly before coming to a halt about twenty feet from where the concrete ended in a clump of trees.

Just before the two men reached the runway, Bosanquet mentioned the message he'd received some fifteen minutes ago by radio from Harry Hurt.

"A kid?" Fuentes asked. "There's a kid on the plane?"

"Apparently."

"I don't want the blood of any kid on my hands," Fuentes said.

"It's Ruhr's responsibility, I would say." Bosanquet, forever calm, nodded toward the big plane, where a door was already opening. "Your hands will be clean, Tommy."

Bosanquet looked at the light in the open doorway of the C-130, where Ruhr stood framed in perfect silhouette. The plane's endless rocking during the flight had made Stephanie Brough queasy. All she'd had to eat was some dry fruit Ruhr had given her from a plastic bag. Ruhr, who was never very far from her, had watched her continually. His eyes had seemed to her like the lenses of some scanning instrument beneath which she was being dissected and scrutinized. She wished he'd turn away, look elsewhere, leave her alone. So long as she was the object of his brooding fascination, she was reminded of the danger he represented.

She still had no idea where she was and hadn't been able to eavesdrop on any conversations because of her earplugs. The two men, Trevaskis and Zapino, who sat together some feet away, didn't look like they communicated much and Ruhr didn't speak, so there was probably nothing to hear anyway.

Ruhr stood in the open doorway. The night air was scented in a way that was unknown to Steffie Brough, whose world had always been circumscribed by Norfolk and the fenlands. She smelled ancient moss and lichen and something else, something bittersweet she couldn't identify but which made her think of carcasses. She took the plugs out of her ears and was assailed at once by noises completely alien to her, bird sounds she'd heard only in zoos, a great clacking and squawking that echoed on and on.

Ruhr turned from the doorway. "Do you know where you are?"

She shook her head.

"This is Honduras."

She tried to remember atlases, maps, but her sense of geography wasn't strong. The Panama Canal, the Gulf of Mexico came to mind, but she couldn't quite place Honduras. Wasn't it close to Nicaragua? She wasn't sure, and this lack of certainty caused her despair. Wherever Honduras was, it was a very long way from anything familiar. And how could she even think of escape? If she got a chance to run from Ruhr, where would she go? She pictured jungles and headhunters, snakes and tarantulas.

She was aware of her crumpled skirt and soiled blouse and some oil stains on her maroon blazer. She needed a bath badly, but she'd come to think that defiance was more important than fresh clothes; not outward defiance, but another form of resistance—in the mind, the heart. Outwardly, she would try to comply with Ruhr if she possibly could. But inside, where it mattered, she'd stay hard and cold and distant. It was an antidote against falling completely apart. She had to be bloody strong, that was all. No weepy moods. No moaning. Given just half a chance, she'd get through this somehow.

Still, she hated the way his hand lay against her lower back as he led her toward the door and the rope ladder that dropped to the ground. An insufferable intimacy; she remembered how he'd undone her bra back at the farmhouse—oh God, the farmhouse was such a long time ago—and blood rose to her head. She couldn't stand his skin against hers, but she'd have to. If she wanted to survive she'd have to do everything he told her.

Just so long as she was untouchable on the inside.

She swung in mid-air, holding the ladder as it shifted with her weight. Ruhr was just above her. She looked up, seeing under the cuffs of his jeans. Around one ankle he had strapped a sheathed knife. She had an image of the dead policeman at the old farmhouse, his body half-covered with leaves and the strange empty way he stared up at the sky. She remembered how his eyes were filled with rainwater and how slicks, overflowing his lashes, ran down his face. It was pointless to remember that sort of thing. She had to survive, and survival meant thinking ahead, not back.

There were men on the ground below. In the distance, yellow and blue lights burned and a faint aroma of paraffin and scorched meat drifted through the dark. Steffie was lightheaded. She gripped the rope, fought the sensation away. Then she was down, and the ground felt good beneath her feet. Ruhr came after, and then the other men from the craft, and suddenly there was confusion, men greeting one another, languages she didn't understand, handshakes. For one tense moment, when she realized nobody was paying her any attention, she considered the possibility of flight.

Dense trees, tents pitched here and there among the lamps, shadowy figures moving back and forth, guitar music, a voice singing a Spanish song in the distance—there was nowhere to run. If she did escape, which was unlikely, she'd certainly get lost and die out there. She looked at Ruhr, who was involved in a conversation with the two men who'd met the plane. The voices were low, but Steffie could tell they were angry. Her parents argued in exactly the same muted way when they didn't want her to overhear.

Ruhr broke away from the two men—one of whom wore a Panama hat—and stepped toward her.

"Come with me."

She followed him across the concrete strip. An olive-colored tent, pitched two hundred yards from the runway, stood within a thicket of trees. Ruhr opened the flap and Steffie stepped inside the tent. He struck a match, lit a lamp. An odd bluish glow threw misshapen shadows on the canvas walls.

"Sit down."

A sagging camp bed was located in a corner. She sat, knees together, hands clasped in her lap. Ruhr stepped in front of the smoky lamp, eclipsing it with his shadow.

"They want me to kill you."

Her throat was very dry. "Why?"

"You have seen too much and now you are to be discarded. Permanently. It's simple."

Steffie was quiet for a long time. She had an image of herself dead—a pale white corpse in a mahogany box, white lace ruffles, a gown, an array of soft candles illuminating her delicate features. But it wouldn't be like that, would it? She'd be shot and dumped in the jungle, where she'd rot. And there was nothing poetic or romantic about that kind of death.

"I don't want to die," she said in a composed way; she was determined to hide her terror.

Ruhr had no problem with the concept of killing the child. What he resented was the idea of being *ordered* to do it. Nobody controlled him. Nobody told him what to do and when to do it. Fuentes would soon discover that Ruhr was very much his own man. He didn't trust Fuentes or the quiet Englishman called Bosanquet; they had something furtive about them, as if they knew something Ruhr did not. But he knew how to protect himself from them, how to guarantee his own future. Besides, he had not yet finished with this girl; he'd barely begun. And if he was going to kill her he wasn't going to do it the way any cheap assassin would. A shot in the back of the skull, impersonal and fast, wasn't his style. No; he'd been observing her the whole trip, and the more he studied her the more impatient he became.

He would have her. In his own inimitable way, he would have her.

He watched how lamplight shone on her legs. She had smooth skin, unblemished, perfect as only young skin can be. He reached out with his deformed hand and slid it under her skirt, the palm flat against her inner thigh. It was as flawless as any flesh could be.

The contrast enthralled him. The idea of his imperfect hand touching this child's perfect thigh filled him with wonder. The ugly and the beautiful welded together, the alignment of opposites, thrilled him. Gunther Ruhr, superior to most people despite being unattractive and crippled, a fugitive despised for his history of destruction, could do anything he liked with this lovely child. Anything. He had the power.

He kissed her on the mouth. She drew her face away. Ruhr smiled. She didn't understand the nature of the game, that was all. She was not permitted to resist. He slid his hand further up, stopping just before he reached the top of her legs where she radiated a mysterious warmth. There was a loveliness here he hadn't encountered before; an innocence. He'd known whores all his life. He'd known the child whores of Saigon and Mexico City and Manila, hardened ten- and eleven-year-old girls with sad eyes and tiny breasts who performed with mechanical exactitude. But what he'd never known was real innocence. Until now. She was fresh and new, unused.

He kissed her again. This time, with lips tight, she didn't turn away from him. She didn't yield to the kiss, she merely tolerated it.

"I will not kill you," he whispered. "I will not let anyone harm you."

He put his good hand below her chin and turned her face up, forcing her to look directly into his eyes. He could smell the fear on her. He gazed at her slender neck and he remembered her school scarf in the back of the Range Rover. He wondered whether Pagan had read the sign. He was surely at a loss by this time; even if he'd discovered the abduction of the child—and it didn't take a genius to get that far—he had no way of knowing where she'd been taken. Frantic Pagan. Ruhr revelled in the idea of the policeman's anxiety. The abduction of the girl was tantamount to driving a nail into the Englishman's heart.

He caught her shoulders, pushed her down on the narrow bed. She lay mute, looking past him at the lamp, which flickered monstrously and cast enormous distended shadows inside the tent. With a finger of the deformed hand he touched her mouth, forced her lips apart, caused a frozen smile to appear. He inserted the finger between her teeth, along the surface of the tongue, the gums. He drew the finger back and forth, in and out. He could feel the child's body go rigid.

And still she wouldn't look at him. She had closed her eyes. He took her hand and led it toward his groin. She made a noise, shook her head from side to side in protest, then bit the finger still inserted in her mouth. Ruhr, pained, drew away from her. There were teeth marks in his flesh.

He slapped her across the cheek with the deformed hand. She turned her face to the wall silently, hearing the slap echo in her head.

"You must do what I want," he said. His voice was quiet, hushed, kind. If you didn't know it was Gunther Ruhr speaking, you might think it the persuasive voice of a therapist. It was one of the many voices Ruhr assumed.

"I don't want to touch you," she whispered.

"What choice do you have, little girl?"

She tried to free herself but it was useless to struggle against Ruhr's strength. She shut her eyes, seeking a secret room in the mind, sanctuary. If she concentrated hard she could reach it, unlock the door, go inside. Safe from Ruhr. Safe from harm. She thought: *Somebody must be searching for me. Somebody has to be looking for me.* Be real, Steffie. How could anybody ever find you?

She felt Ruhr's ugly hand cross the flat of her stomach, like a crab moving on her skin.

"My sweet girl," he kept saying. His breathing was different now, harder, louder. "I will not hurt you. I promise you. You will come to no harm."

He stroked her breasts, unconscious of the girl's discomfort, unaware of the tautness in her body. To Ruhr, the girl's pale flesh was a soft white marvellous world for him to explore and finally exploit. He was a discoverer, a pioneer, creating a new map of engrossing territory. And, like any colonist, he would inevitably corrupt the terrain he had conquered.

A sound came from the doorway of the tent. The flap was pushed aside. A shadow fell across Steffie's face. She saw the man from the plane, the skinny one called Trevaskis. The pressure from Ruhr's body lifted as he turned his face around quickly, angrily.

Trevaskis, whose gaunt features appeared ghostly in the odd flickering light, pretended he saw nothing. "They want you at the airstrip. Something about opening a box."

Ruhr got up from the camp bed. "Have you no goddam manners?" he asked. He pronounced 'goddam' as 'gottdam'.

Trevaskis glanced down at Stephanie Brough, then looked at Ruhr. "Don't blame me. I'm only the messenger. They told me to fetch you. Here I am. Fetching. They need you because they have to open the box. Whatever that means."

Ruhr laid the palm of his hand upon the girl's face.

"Don't move," he said. "Don't even think of moving. Is that understood?"

Ruhr stepped impatiently toward the doorway and out of the tent into darkness. He could see in the lights around the airstrip the C-130's ramp being lowered. He stood very still and watched the great shadow of the missile emerge from the underbelly of the transport plane. It had a hardness of line, a cleanliness of form. Incomplete as yet, it required his knowledge, his touch, to make it perfect. The mood with the girl was ruined for the moment anyway. Later it could be recreated.

Trevaskis came out of the tent, closing the flap at his back. He followed Ruhr a little way in the direction of the airstrip. Then he walked in another direction, entering a dark place where the trees grew close together. Ruhr kept going toward the plane. Trevaskis doubled back toward the tent. He undid the flap. The girl was sitting on the bed, her skirt smoothed down over her knees and her blouse buttoned up. She turned her face toward him. She was white and scared—but how the hell was she supposed to look, Trevaskis wondered, after the sicko had been at her?

Trevaskis said, "Get the hell out of here. Now."

"Where can I go?" she asked.

"Look, you got two choices. You stay here, you die. No two ways about it. Don't kid yourself. You go out there, you at least got a chance."

"What kind of chance?"

Trevaskis said, "Five per cent better than slim."

Steffie, who didn't need time to think, got up from the bed. Trevaskis held the tent open for her. She ducked her head under his arm; the night was vast and hostile.

"Kid," Trevaskis said, and he pointed. "Go that way. You don't run into any tents over there. Keep going in the direction I'm pointing. I think there's a highway over there. Five miles, something like that. I'm not sure. But it's your best shot.''

Five miles through an unfamiliar environment. For a moment the lamp that flickered against the walls of the tent seemed positively cheerful. For God's sake, how could she even think of staying? She turned away from Trevaskis and, saying nothing, not knowing whether to thank him, headed through the trees. She must have strayed from the narrow path because immediately the foliage was dense all around her, and suffocating, like the greenery of some nightmare.

Strange forms reached out to her, tendrils brushed her arms, something small and furry flew directly at her forehead. And the night *clicked* all around her. Strange insect sounds came out· of the underbrush and the places where ancient roots gathered around her ankles. It was too much; too terrifying.

Frightened, she stopped. She looked back. Trevaskis was standing beside the tent, his shape outlined by the flame of kerosene. Ruhr, half-crouching, conjured out of the night, appeared behind him. Steffie saw Ruhr's arm rise in the air, then fall swiftly, an indistinct brush-stroke. Trevaskis cried out, doubled over, slid to his knees. And then she couldn't see him any more.

She turned and tried to claw her way through the foliage. She froze when the beam of the flashlight struck her. She could hear Ruhr breathing as he came toward her.

''He thought I was stupid enough to leave you without supervision,'' Ruhr said. ''Do you also think me stupid, little girl?''

He caught her by the hair and yanked her head

back. The blade of his knife, wet with Trevaskis's blood, was thrust against the side of her neck.

Gunther Ruhr smiled. "I am disappointed."

Steffie Brough couldn't speak.

Tommy Fuentes watched the missile, mounted on the bed of the truck, come down the ramp under the guidance of the airplane's crew members, men anxious to be gone from this Honduran paradise. The cylinder rolled slowly a couple of feet on the concrete, then stopped. A small Toyota truck drew up very carefully alongside the missile. The tailgate was lowered, and the wooden crate that had been delivered by Levy and Possony was carried out by three soldiers. They set the box down about six feet from the missile.

Fuentes trained a flashlight on the crate and two soldiers held lanterns.

"Where is Ruhr?" Fuentes asked.

Bosanquet said, "It appears that our German friend has all the worst traits of his race. Arrogance and a complete indifference to any timetable but one of his own choosing."

Fuentes turned his face to look in the direction of Ruhr's tent. Perhaps when he'd had his fun with the unfortunate girl and then disposed of her, the German genius would condescend to come down to the airstrip and do what he'd been paid for.

After all, the ship that would carry the missile to Cuba was due to arrive within twenty-four hours.

London

A deceptive autumnal sun hung over London, a hazy

disc that chilled the city more than it warmed it. At eight AM Sir Freddie Kinnaird stepped from his limousine in Golden Square and entered the building that housed Frank Pagan's operation. In the lobby he passed a uniformed policeman, who saluted him briskly, then he rode in the old-fashioned elevator to the top floor.

He entered Pagan's office without knocking. He considered it his prerogative as Home Secretary to go wherever he liked within his jurisdiction. He often contrived to conceal this presumptuous attitude with a certain upper class charm. His style in Savile Row suits had made him, according to a frivolous magazine, the ninth best-dressed bachelor in Britain last year. If Sir Freddie Kinnaird had been a book, he would have been on the best-seller lists.

Today he wore a charcoal-gray overcoat with a discreet velvet collar. Pagan, who lay on the sofa, turned his face drowsily toward the man. "Sir Freddie," he managed to say. "What a surprise."

"No need to get up, Frank. Just passing. Thought I'd drop in and see how things stand."

Pagan's shirt was undone. A fresh bandage, applied some hours ago by Foxworth, was visible around his chest. He raised himself into a sitting position and looked at Freddie Kinnaird, whose face had been reddened by the cold morning air. *How things stand*, Freddie Kinnaird had said. Well, one of the things that *wasn't* standing was Pagan himself, who had lain crookedly in sleep and now massaged the sides of his aching legs, his knotted muscles.

"What news, Frank," Sir Freddie said, glancing at the silkscreen on the wall, then surveying the chaos of the office, the litter that had missed the basket, the coffee cups, the stained saucers, the crumpled fast-food wrappers.

Pagan got to his feet, poured himself a cup of coffee from the pot that had been on a hot-plate for God knows how long. "The investigation chugs along," he said.

"How does it chug, and where?" Kinnaird asked.

"With all due respect, Sir Freddie, the details are being kept confidential in light of what happened in Shepherd's Bush." Pagan sipped the coffee, which was the most vile fluid that had ever passed his lips. Stewed did not describe it. He fought a certain turmoil in his stomach. "Any information you want must come to you directly from Martin Burr. That's the Commissioner's rule. Access is strictly limited. We don't want any more leaks, obviously."

"Admirable security," Sir Freddie remarked brightly. "Naturally, Martin keeps me informed on a daily basis. I simply thought I might drop in and see if there were any recent developments that may not have reached the Commissioner's desk yet. The overnight stuff. The lowdown, as they say. This whole business has caused me quite considerable anxiety, as I'm sure you'll understand."

Pagan smiled agreeably. He set his cup down and buttoned his shirt. "Martin Burr knows all, Sir Freddie. Everything that happens in this office comes to the Commissioner's attention. Promptly."

There was a momentary silence. Pagan looked at this rather conservatively fashionable man who had become one of the most popular politicians in the present government. Prosperous, rumored to rise even higher in his political party, Sir Freddie had come a long way. Pagan had a faint recollection of how, a dozen or so years ago, the newspapers had made much of the fact that Kinnaird was strapped for cash because of onerous death duties on the demise of his father. The old country estate in West Sussex had been sold to a Japanese electronics tycoon, farming lands in Devon had been auctioned, and Freddie himself was obliged to sit on the boards of a variety of corporations. He needed the money, the companies needed his class and style. He had obviously made a terrific recovery from those days.

Kinnaird asked, "Seen the morning papers?"

"I try to avoid them."

"What a hullabaloo," Sir Freddie said. "The press doesn't know which way to turn. First the stolen missile. Then the abducted child. And if that wasn't sensational enough, there's the hijacked plane into the bargain. They haven't had this much news in one day since World War Two, I imagine. And speculation, my God! Ruhr's in Africa. He's in Iran. He's in the Canadian Rockies. And the one I like—he never left England. He's holed up somewhere in the countryside, laughing up his bloody sleeve."

Pagan said nothing. He imagined the headlines, he didn't need to see them. He didn't need to read about Stephanie Brough in particular. Whenever he thought about her he was filled with a kind of parental dread. He couldn't even begin to understand what her real parents were suffering, although he had insights into their all-consuming worry.

He'd refused to take phonecalls from the press. They were fielded downstairs with bland, tight-lipped comments from other officers. Reporters were given items of information they could have gleaned for themselves without much trouble—the nationality of the dead terrorists, the origin of the helicopter, the number of military casualties. It was the spirit of limited cooperation: more delicate areas of the investigation were inaccessible.

Sir Freddie adjusted his black cashmere scarf and

said, "I think you're doing a wonderful job in the circumstances, Frank. You and all your men. Convey my admiration to them, would you?"

Pagan hated such speeches, which he felt were offered more for political reasons than out of genuine gratitude. A man like Kinnaird, who was always onstage, confused politics with real life. He probably made love the way he made speeches, with appropriate pauses for effect and great expectations of applause. Pagan wondered if he were ever heckled in bed.

"Keep up the good work, Frank."

Kinnaird shook Pagan's hand firmly. Then he stepped out of the office just as Foxworth, hair dishevelled, pin-stripe suit crumpled, was coming in. Kinnaird nodded to the young man before passing along the corridor in the direction of the elevator.

Pagan sat down behind his desk. Foxworth said, "Company from a lofty place, I see."

"Pain in the arse," Pagan remarked. "He drops in, fishes for some hot news, gives me a bit of a pep talk, expresses his thanks and aren't we just wonderful all round. Spare me, Foxie. Have you slept?"

Foxworth fixed the knot of his striped tie. His complexion was colorless and he hadn't shaved, but his eyes were bright and excited. "I got in an hour or two, Frank." He patted his briefcase. "I also found time to pick up a change of clothes for you."

Pagan opened the case and looked at the black and white silk jacket, brown pants, gray socks, blue and white shirt, and he wondered if Foxie had picked them out in the dark. He didn't criticize; he was less interested in the apparel than in Foxie's quietly pleased little look. "So what are you repressing, Foxie?"

"Repressing?"

"I know your whole repertoire of grins, twitches

and glances. Right now, you look like the top of your head is about to explode."

Foxie leaned across the desk, smiled. "Fancy that. Didn't know I was so transparent, actually."

"You're a window, Foxie. Speak. What's on your mind?"

Foxworth took out a small notebook, flicked the pages. "A couple of recent developments I think might interest you. First, the Norwich police and our friend Joanna Lassiter. Joanna was shown Chapotin's picture and—according to a certain Detective Hare in Norwich—responded with an emphatic denial. Chapotin was not even remotely similar to the man who rented the farmhouse."

"Did she describe the man who would be Chapotin?" Pagan asked.

"Better than that. Based on her description, Detective Hare had a composite assembled. It ought to be coming across the fax machine at any second."

Pagan looked at his watch. "This Hare's an early bird."

"Provincial living does that to a man," Foxie said. He turned the pages of his notebook. "Now for the news from bonnie Scotland. You'll like this."

Pagan sat back in his chair.

Foxworth said, "Rafael Rosabal met a man in a Glasgow hotel, according to a report from the Criminal Investigation Division, which had been asked by London to conduct routine surveillance of the Cuban."

"Was the man Chapotin?" Pagan asked.

Foxie shook his head. "No. Rosabal met briefly with somebody called Enrico Caporelli."

"The name doesn't mean anything," Pagan said.

"Caporelli, an Italian citizen, is known to Glasgow CID because he has business interests in that city, one of which—a string of betting-shops—has been the subject of an undercover investigation recently. Something to do with skimming cash off the top. Tax cheating. Happens in a lot of cash operations. Enrico Caporelli is simply a sleeping-partner in the business. He isn't involved in the daily running of it. I understand he spends most of his time in Europe and America. Probably doesn't even know some of his managers are skimming.''

''What could Rosabal possibly have in common with this Caporelli?''

Foxworth once more turned the pages of his little book; he was clearly enjoying himself. ''Cuba,'' he said quietly.

''Cuba?''

''It's a bit of a maze, actually, but according to some homework Billy Ewing has just completed, Enrico Caporelli resided in Cuba from 1955 until 1959, where he made a considerable fortune in various businesses. The Cubans took everything away from him. Expropriation is Fidel's word.''

''How did Ewing dig that up?''

''From our American pals in Grosvenor Square, Frank. Ewing called in a small favor at the Embassy. Back comes the info that Enrico Caporelli, a businessman deported from Cuba in spring, 1959, was debriefed that same year by the Central Intelligence Agency, which was assiduously gathering material on Castro at the time with the intention, one assumes, of assassination. Hence, Caporelli's name is in the files somewhere.''

A bit of a maze, Pagan thought. The phrase struck him as understatement. He was always surprised by the connections that existed between people who, on the face of it, would seem to have nothing in common.

Threads, trails left in space and time. A Cuban politician meets an Italian businessman in Glasgow in 1989, setting up a situation that creates echoes in very old files. Join the dots and what do you get? Companions in conspiracy, he thought. But what was the meat of this conspiracy?

"Where is Caporelli now?" he asked.

"The last available information came from a check we ran with the Italian police. According to the house-keeper at Caporelli's house in Tuscany, he's presently at his apartment in Paris."

"I'd love to have a word with him. I'd also like to sit Rosabal down and have a nice little chat."

"He already left the country. Presumably he's back in Cuba."

Pagan stood up. Despite the horror of it, he poured himself a second cup of coffee, which he took to the window. Drones crossed the Square, hurrying inside offices. Another day was cranking up. In the east, clouds the color of mud had begun to drift toward the city; below, a funnel of wind sucked up some brittle leaves. Strangely, an untended scarlet kite in the shape of a horse's head, probably tugged from some poor child's hand in Hyde or Green Park, floated across the roof-tops. Could a lost kite be some form of omen? Pagan watched it go, then turned back to Foxie.

"What does it all add up to?" Pagan asked. "Rafael Rosabal meets this Italian in Scotland. At the same time, Jean-Paul Chapotin arrives in Glasgow. Meanwhile, somebody using Chapotin's name rented a farmhouse in Norfolk, which became the headquarters for a group of terrorists. One solid connection exists between Rosabal and Chapotin and Caporelli: Cuba. It's all bloody absorbing if you're in the mood for puzzles and you've finished the *Times* crossword, but where does it leave us, for Christ's sake?"

Foxworth closed his little notebook. Billy Ewing put his face round the door. "Fax for you, Foxie," he said.

Foxworth took the slip of paper from Ewing. He studied it for a moment, then smiled. "Surprise surprise," was what he said. He gave the paper to Frank Pagan.

Pagan found himself looking at a police composite, an identikit creation; he thought these things always made human beings resemble pancakes. They rendered features flat and dopey. The constituent parts of the face never bore any relationship to one another, plundered as they had been from a kit of human bits and pieces. The face in this particular picture had black hair and a straight nose and a mouth that was rather tense and unreal. The face also wore sunglasses. Pagan thought of a zombie.

"What's so surprising, Foxie?" he asked.

Foxworth told him. "The man in this picture, wretched as he may appear, bears more than a passing resemblance to Rafael Rosabal, which may mean only one thing—that he rented the farm under Chapotin's name."

"What kind of sense would that make, for Christ's sake?"

Foxworth shrugged. He didn't know. He said, "You'd have to ask Rafael that one, Frank. And since he's back in Cuba, it isn't going to be easy."

"He'd deny any involvement anyway," Pagan said. "How could I prove otherwise? This wretched illustration isn't enough. Rosabal would laugh his ballocks off."

Pagan, who hadn't looked at a likeness of Rafael

Rosabal before, hadn't even wanted to, gazed at the picture. So this was Magdalena's lover, this bland face that stared back at him, this prosaic product of a technician's craft. Composites never suggested emotion, certainly not passion; those lips looked as if they might never have kissed any human being. He tossed the drawing on the desk. It was funny how, after all this time, there was a streak of jealousy in him, like the trail of a very old comet, but uncomfortable just the same.

"And what's Rosabal's connection with Ruhr?" he asked. "Why would he rent a farmhouse for Ruhr to live in?"

"Perhaps because Rosabal hired Ruhr to steal the missile."

"Perhaps, but also impossible to prove on the flimsy basis of an identikit," Pagan said. "Why would Rosabal want his own damned missile to begin with?" He was thinking of another question now, one he didn't want to ask at all, but which he knew would have to be voiced, if not by himself then surely, sooner or later, by Foxworth.

"I wonder how Magdalena Torrente fits into all this," he said.

"Maybe she doesn't fit anywhere," Foxie answered. There was some kindness in his voice, as if he intuited Pagan's difficulty with the subject of the woman.

Pagan sipped the spooky coffee. *Maybe she doesn't fit*—but he wasn't convinced and he wasn't reassured and the melody that ran through his brain was composed of bad notes. His instincts told him he couldn't consign Magdalena to some convenient oblivion. Not yet, perhaps not at all. Somewhere along the way he thought he'd have to see her again, talk to her, probe the nature of her affair with the Cuban. Hadn't she hinted in an elliptical way about the prospect of a coup in Cuba? 'Hinted' was too strong a word; rather, she'd failed to answer his direct questions, leaving room for his own speculation. Mysterious Magdalena.

He had mixed emotions about the prospect of seeing her again. But she was Rosabal's lover and there was at least a chance that she knew something about the Cuban's business. Perhaps they shared something more than each other's flesh; little secrets, the kind spoken across pillows and through tangled limbs.

Rosabal. Magdalena. Chapotin. Ruhr. Caporelli. He wondered what was secreted by those five names.

He asked, "Why Scotland? Why go up there at all? Why did all three men have to be in Glasgow on precisely the same day? Where did Chapotin go when he arrived there? Did he meet somebody? Did he meet Ruhr? Did he meet Caporelli? Did all three of them get together at some point? Is there life after death?"

Foxworth smiled. "Is there life after Glasgow?"

"Not for Jean-Paul Chapotin," Pagan said.

Both men were quiet. The sound of a printer drifted through the open door; a telephone buzzed in another room, a man cleared his throat. Pagan's head ached. Too many questions. The more information that reached his office, the more solid grew the whole edifice of mystery. It was time to be dogged, time to be systematic; take each problem as it comes. Time, he thought: did Steffie Brough, wherever she was, have the luxury of time? He was conscious of a clock ticking madly away.

"If I want to interview Rosabal, what official channels do I have to go through?" he asked.

"I can find out. I suspect they're complicated and involve hideous protocol."

Pagan shook his head in slight despair. It was a

hopeless kind of quest really. Rosabal would simply refuse to come back to Britain, and if Pagan went to Cuba,
armed with the silly composite, Rosabal would mock
him—if indeed he agreed to see him at all. Ministers
and their ministries could keep you waiting in ante-
chambers indefinitely, whether you came from Scotland Yard or not. It wasn't going to be fruitful to
approach Rafael Rosabal in a headlong manner; there
was too much tape red, as Madame Chapotin might
have said, for that. No, he would have to chisel away
at the edifice confronting him, sliver by sliver, like a
sculptor intrigued by the form concealed in a block of
granite.

"Put Billy Ewing on it. I've got something else in
mind for you, Foxie."

"Paris?" Foxworth asked.

"Glasgow. I'm taking Paris."

"Why don't we discuss it?"

"Because this isn't a bloody democracy, Foxie. I get
Paris, you get Glasgow. It's a matter of seniority,
sonny."

Foxie sighed in resignation. He doubted if Pagan
was quite strong enough to travel, but he wasn't going
to argue the point. Frank had switched into his headstrong mode and that was it.

Pagan said, "I'll see you back here tonight."

"That soon?"

"Soon? That gives you the whole day, Foxie. Use
it well. Tell me where Chapotin went and how he's
connected to Ruhr. Tell me why Rosabal would use
Chapotin's name. Tell me why they selected scenic
Glasgow for skullduggery."

Slavedriver, Foxie thought. "You want a miracle,
Frank."

"I want more than a miracle, Foxie," Pagan replied.

Villa Clara Province, Cuba

At four AM the Lider Maximo lay in his bedroom with a rubber hot-water bottle pressed flat upon his stomach. He was unable to speak because of the thermometer stuck between his lips. The physician, Dr. Miguel Zayas, checked the great man's pulse.

"Now," Zayas said. He took the hot-water bottle away and prodded here and there the fleshy stomach of the Lider Maximo. "Does that hurt? Does that? Does this?"

Castro shook his head. How could he speak with a damned tube in his mouth? It would not do for him to moan and admit pain, even though Zayas was fingering some tender spots; especially he couldn't admit anything so human as pain in front of that old buzzard General Capablanca, who was hovering in the room like a greedy relative at a will-reading.

"What have you eaten recently?" Zayas asked, and took the thermometer away.

"Shrimp," Castro said. He grabbed back the hot-water bottle and laid it over his navel.

"What else?"

"Moros y cristianos."

"Anything else?"

"Plantains."

The physician tugged the hot-water bottle from Castro's belly. "This may aggravate your condition."

"Which is what exactly?"

"Gastric influenza," the physician said.

Castro slumped back against the pillows. It was ignominious to have cancelled a speech in which he had planned to castigate the new, cozy friendship between the Yanqui imperialists and the 'soft' reformist, quasi-capitalist regime in the Soviet Union, but the attacks of diarrhea, which left him weak and helpless, were positively humiliating. He had also a fever and he couldn't concentrate. Goddam, it would have been a great speech, perhaps his best, emphasizing Cuba's splendid isolation in the world, the kind of exciting speech that would have brought Cubans together in a show of solidarity. Cuba would not be threatened by this obscene new collusion, this game of footsy, between the United States and Russia.

Capablanca, whose thick white moustache covered his upper lip, came close to the bed. Castro was annoyed by the intrusion of the General, a man he'd never been able to stand anyway. Capablanca was a leftover from a class that should have been swept away by the Revolution, but still lingered here and there in pockets despite the Party's best efforts.

Capablanca, who had a set of papers in his hand, said, "I have come to remind you, Commandante, that tomorrow's troop maneuvers require your personal authorization in the absence of your brother."

"What maneuvers?" Castro asked. He could remember no mention of troop movements. His was a life totally consumed by detail: how could he possibly recall every little thing? Nor did he trust his own memory entirely. Lately, it hadn't seemed an altogether reliable instrument. He seized the papers from the General's hand.

Peering through his glasses he saw that the documents described a huge military exercise scheduled for dawn tomorrow. It involved the movement of troops from the Santiago de Cuba Province. Infantry battalions, as well as airplanes, were to move inland from the coastal region of the province, which lay on the island's southern seaboard. Ships of the Cuban Navy were also

scheduled to sail around the tip of the island at Guantanamo, bound for Holguin Province. This would expose
the coast of Santiago de Cuba, leaving it defenseless.
Not that Castro expected an invasion force, but one had
always to be prepared.

The same documents described other military exercises in Havana Province. These were less extensive
than the movement of troops from Santiago to Holguin,
but they were impressive just the same and involved
the transportation of more than seven thousand men
from Havana Province to Matanzas; there, in the moun-
tainous region surrounding Matanzas City, exercises
would keep these troops occupied at a distance of some
fifty miles from the Central Highway.

"All this involves thousands of soldiers and reservists," Castro said.

"Indeed," the General answered.

"Why? Why this undertaking?"

"Readiness, Commandante. Alertness. A standing
army must flex its muscle, otherwise it withers."

"Readiness is important, but does Raul know of
these maneuvers?"

"Of course," said the General. "It was Raul's
idea." Lies came to him with great difficulty.

Castro tossed the papers back at the General. The
pain that shot suddenly through his stomach was like
a fierce little cannonball. He imagined it leaving a scalding trail of debris on its passage through his guts. He
spoke with some effort. "I do . . . not . . . recall my
brother ever . . . mentioning these exercises before now,
General."

"But Commandante," Capablanca said. He was
tense, slightly panicked. He hadn't expected resistance;
he'd imagined that the debilitated and confused Lider
Maximo would give his consent willingly. He needed

the Commandante's authorization of the documents; without that imprimatur, those officers loyal to the Party, and to *El Viejo* himself, would refuse to participate in the exercises. They wouldn't raise a finger unless one or other of the Castros authorized it. Such disobedience on the part of the misguided loyalists would mean chaos, disorder, bloodshed. The General pictured slaughter on the beaches. God knows, there would be unavoidable bloodshed somewhere down the road, but the ship coming from Honduras had to arrive without impediment. That was a matter of the utmost importance.

Besides, there was form to consider; and form was one of the General's obsessions. With the authorization of Castro maneuvers would have the appearance of legitimacy. This was important because the General did not want history to perceive him as a common adventurer and scoundrel. Everything he did had to be just so, everything by the book.

He had another important reason, one of sly importance, for getting the Lider Maximo's signature on these papers.

A space had been left on the third page for an extra paragraph to be inserted; this paragraph, when the General added it, would contain Castro's authorization for a cruise missile, formerly the property of NATO, to be fired from a location outside Santiago de Cuba . . .

Of course, no missile would ever fly. The authorization was the only thing required; the apparent intent was all.

Now Castro waved a hand in a gesture of dismissal. He was reluctant to give his approval to the maneuvers because he didn't like interfering with his brother's gameboard. Raul played toy soldiers, not he.

"Cancel them, General. Postpone them until Raul returns."

"Commandante," said the General, trying to conceal the small panic he felt. "You must approve these—"

"I do not have to do anything, General. Now do as I say! Postpone the maneuvers!"

Capablanca glanced at the physician. Zayas understood the look; he reached inside his black bag and took out a hypodermic syringe. He inserted the needle into a small phial of colorless liquid, filled the syringe, then held the needle close to the Lider Maximo's arm.

"What is it, Zayas? What's in the syringe?" Castro asked. His eyes opened very wide.

"A simple painkiller," the physician said.

"I am not in pain!" Castro would have decked the physician, had it not been for the terrible weakness he felt. His belly creaked like the rotted wood of an old ship and he had the feeling of hot liquid rushing through his intestines. He'd have to get up, rush for the hundredth time to the john.

The needle pierced flesh, found the vein; after twenty seconds Castro, who resisted enforced sleep fiercely, closed his eyes. His head rolled to one side and saliva collected at the corners of his lips as he snored.

The physician raised one of Castro's eyelids, then let it flop back in place. "Give me the documents, General."

General Capablanca did so. The physician, with meticulous penmanship, forged the Lider Maximo's signature. It was a passable fraud.

"I haven't been his personal physician for years without learning a great deal about our fearless leader," Zayas said. "Now open the middle drawer of the desk."

Capablanca, surprised by both the skill and gall of

the physician, went to the desk. Inside the middle drawer was the Lider Maximo's personal seal. The General removed it. He took the document from the physician, who was still admiring his own forgery, and pressed the metal seal over the fake signature.

"There," said the General, relief in his voice. "It's done."

Zayas looked down at the doped leader. "When he wakes, I'll shoot him up again."

The General said, "I'd prefer him dead. But I have my own orders to follow." He walked toward the door, where he stopped, turned briskly around. "Your role will not be forgotten, Zayas. By tomorrow night, Cuba will be free of this madman."

"I'm happy to help a new regime, General. People who love freedom must unite against despots."

General Capablanca stepped out of the room. In the corridor, Castro's bodyguards stood tensely around.

"A minor gastric disorder," said the General in a booming voice. "In a day or so he will be as good as new. For now, he sleeps."

The bodyguards relaxed. They trusted Capablanca and they trusted Dr. Zayas. They had known them for years. All, therefore, was well.

14

On this strange dawn enormous cloud formations, lit by a pale sun, formed a purple mass over Miami. Motionless, the clouds might have been solid matter, cliffs and rocky promontories afloat in the sky. Later, the day would grow warmer and the bulk would disperse in violent lightning and rain, the whole discordant Floridian symphony of weather.

Magdalena Torrente, driving her BMW toward Little Havana, took no notice of the heavens. She crossed the Rickenbacker Causeway at the speed limit. Traffic was still light. She'd been drawn out of sleep by the telephone, and had reached for the instrument with a sense of dread. Nothing good ever came from phonecalls at seven AM. Anything that happened before then had to be ungodly. She'd heard Garrido's voice. He needed to see her at the restaurant. He wouldn't say why. The old man had grown increasingly fond of cryptic behavior. He'd been playing the secret game for too many years. So, still sleepy, she'd showered, brewed coffee, dressed, left her house in Key Biscayne.

She drove on Brickell Avenue, heart of revitalized Miami, leafy between high-rise buildings, banks, commercial centers. The Bayside Market Plaza was new and bold. Drug money had infiltrated everyday life. An illicit, cocky prosperity flourished here. But this was something else Magdalena didn't notice as she drove toward Calle Ocho. What did Garrido want at this hour? Why had he called? His voice was quiet, almost a whisper—she couldn't tell much from it. On Calle Ocho she passed closed shops; a couple of druggies, locked in their own time zone, stared morosely at her.

On the sidestreet where Garrido's restaurant was situated she parked the car, got out. She wore blue jeans, soft leather boots that came just above the ankles, a black silk jacket, lemon shirt. She was incongruous in this neighborhood of steel-shuttered windows and graffiti and funky yards filled with empty wine bottles and needles and tires.

She entered the restaurant by the front door. The big empty room, which wasn't open for breakfast trade, smelled of last night's onions, chilis, fried foods. Chairs were inverted on tables. Garrido, in the white suit he always wore, sat in an alcove at the rear. Beside him was a hefty man she'd never seen before—unusual in itself because Garrido always preferred to meet her alone.

Garrido looked up when she approached. She felt a dryness at the back of her throat, a sudden pulse in her chest. Something in Garrido's face unnerved her, although she wasn't sure what—the light in the eye, the set of the mouth, something. He was different this morning and she didn't like it.

"Sit down, my dear," he said.

She eased into the alcove, conscious of the stranger

watching her approvingly. When she caught his eye he winked, smiled. She was sometimes amused by the effect she had on men; even Pagan, even dear Frank, when he'd come to see her in London, had been strangely subdued in her presence—except for his bold parting kiss, which had been interesting to her only as a memory. There was nothing left inside her for Frank Pagan or any other man but one.

Garrido kissed her hand. "My dear, I want you to meet a good friend. A trusted friend. Sergio Duran. He is with us."

Magdalena barely nodded at Duran, who nevertheless insisted on placing a kiss of his own on the back of her hand and saying how delighted he was to meet her; she was as beautiful as he'd heard, even more so. It was Latin overstatement, that blend of flattery and machismo, and she was unmoved by it.

"Why this hour of the day, Fernando?" she asked. "What's the big deal?"

Garrido was quiet a moment. He looked moody, distant, and even the chocolate-brown dye he used on his hair and moustache appeared to have shed lustre. "Sergio returned from Cuba last night," he said finally.

"And?" she asked.

"Perhaps I'll let Sergio tell you himself."

"Fine." She looked at Duran, who wore a blue and gray plaid jacket and styled his hair like frothed milk. "I'm listening, Sergio."

Duran's voice was deep and low, more a rumble than anything else. It reminded Magdalena of a radio announcer. He took out a cigar, one made by the Upmann Company of Havana, and he lit it. He had huge fat hands.

"Fernando asked me to go to Cuba on his behalf. He needed somebody to check on a few things."

"Check on what things?" Magdalena asked, and looked at Garrido, who inclined his head as if to say *Listen, Duran will tell you everything you need to know.*

Duran blew smoke upward, steering it away from Magdalena's eyes. "He needed certain information. He asked me to provide it."

"Exactly what are your credentials for gathering information, Sergio?" She was on edge now and couldn't say why exactly. The hour of the day was part of it, certainly, but she knew that these two men between them had something to tell her and there was an awkward kind of pussyfooting going on, an evasion of the point. She was impatient, almost rude in the way she threw questions at Duran.

"I am a private detective right here in Miami," Duran said.

"I see. So you're qualified to snoop around."

"Magdalena," Garrido said, a plea for patience and tolerance in the tone of his voice.

"It's okay, Fernando. Miss Torrente is right one hundred per cent. I'm a qualified snoop."

"And what did you snoop in Cuba, Sergio?" Magdalena asked.

There was silence. Why did she feel she was a patient in the presence of two specialists who have studied her x-rays with the utmost care and whose prognoses are bleak? They were about to tell her she was terminal.

"Considerable sums of money have gone to Cuba in recent years," Duran said. "Fernando asked me to ascertain, as far as I possibly could, exactly where the cash had ended up."

Ah: so it came down to that old bone, Garrido's mistrust of Rafael, his paranoia. She should have known. He wasn't happy about Rosabal—specifically her relationship with him—and so he'd sent his own personal spy to Cuba! She wanted to shout at the old man, and reproach him bitterly for his distrust, but for the moment she kept her silence.

Duran went on, "The disposition of funds was always in the hands of one man. Rafael Rosabal. It was left to him to assess the needs of the various underground groups and disperse the cash according to these needs. A big responsibility, of course. A job requiring some measure of good judgment."

"And?" Magdalena asked. Why did she feel so goddam awful all of a sudden? Something monstrous, just beyond the range of her vision, was taking shape in the shadows of this room. Her forehead was flushed and hot. She put the palm of her hand to it.

"I have discovered beyond doubt that a full accounting is difficult—"

"What does that mean? Be precise, if you can."

"Money is unaccounted for—"

"Why? Why is it unaccounted for?"

Duran sucked on his cigar; what Magdalena read in his eyes was an odd little look of pity. It was visible pity, the kind felt by a man who so rarely experiences such sensations he doesn't know how to hide them. He said, "As far as I can tell, millions of dollars are missing."

"Missing? What does missing mean? How can millions of dollars go astray? What are you saying, Mr. Duran? How can you even make such an estimate anyway? It isn't the kind of situation conducive to accurate book-keeping, is it?" Her voice was shrill and rising. She knew where Duran was headed now. She saw it as clearly as if there were a map in front of her.

Duran spoke slowly. "Rosabal dispersed funds to

the various groups, certainly," he said. "But in his own way. Sometimes he'd give money liberally to one group and deny it to another, claiming a shortage of funds. At other times he'd give very little to all the groups, and tell them there was nothing in the kitty, that cash hadn't come from the Community in Miami. He relied on the fact that no one group would know what the other groups received."

"What exactly are you trying to tell me, Sergio? That Rafael pocketed money for himself?" She made a sound of disbelief, a gasp.

"Be patient," Garrido said, and patted the back of her hand, which she drew away at once, causing the old man to look rather sorrowful.

Duran continued. "It appears that Rosabal promoted a system in which he sometimes seemed to be favoring certain groups by saying he'd managed to squeeze out a little more cash for them this time around—but he'd always ask them to keep the favor quiet. Don't tell anyone else, he'd say. Don't start squabbles. This way he created confusion and divided loyalties. Am I making this clear for you?"

"Garrido," and she turned her face to the old man. "How could you do this? How can you oblige me to sit through this?"

Garrido said nothing. That silence again; it beat against Magdalena with the certainty of a tide.

Duran went on, "A rough estimate of monies embezzled would run into the millions."

"You said yourself that an estimate was impossible." She was Rosabal's advocate now, his protector, defender.

"I said it was difficult, not impossible. It would take a very long time to be exact, I agree. My own estimate is a ballpark figure, that's all. More, less, what does it matter in the long run?"

"How can you malign him in this way?" she asked. "Both of you, how can you castigate him like this? Don't you understand the risks he's taken for our cause? He met regularly with underground representatives, people in the democratic movement, he carried U.S. dollars to these people, he went to places where discovery would have meant the death-sentence for him—how can you possibly accuse him of embezzlement?"

Duran shook his head slowly and looked depressed. "There is other evidence, Magdalena."

"Like what?"

"I'm informed he's been making investments for the last few years through banks in the Channel Islands. He always goes there briefly whenever he makes a trip to Europe. He visits discreet bankers who invest considerable sums of money on his behalf in France and Switzerland and the Far East."

"How do you know this?"

Duran shrugged. "We have reliable sources."

"Spies."

"Spies is as good a word as any."

"How do you know he isn't investing money on behalf of the cause? You don't have any evidence he's investing this cash for himself."

"Not directly, no. All I can tell you is what I already said—funds are being diverted. And the likelihood that the cash has been invested for the cause is, let's face it, slim."

Garrido, like a patient country doctor schooled in platitudes, spoke soothingly when he interrupted. "Sometimes too much money is too much temptation.

A man can find weaknesses in himself he never suspected.''

"I believe in Rafael," she said. She was hoarse; tension had dried her throat and mouth.

As if he hadn't heard her, as if he were just too
wrapped up in his own ambitions to pay Magdalena any
attention, Garrido continued in a mournful voice. "It's
more than just the money. It's the violation of the trust
we put in Rosabal. He was supposed to be our representative in Cuba. He was supposed to be spreading funds
to make the democratic underground strong. He was
the big man, the force behind the movement to overthrow Castro, he was preparing a coup, assembling a
democratic alternative to Communism, and when the
time came . . ." The old man paused and looked sad.
He touched his lips with a linen napkin. "I was a part
of it. I was going back to Cuba to serve in this new government. Now what? Now what, Magdalena? Where is
the dream now? How can we know if there is any kind
of strength or unity in the anti-Castro cause? How can
we know if Castro is ever going to be deposed? Do you
see what Rosabal has accomplished with his treachery,
Magdalena? Confusion. Disappointment. Unhappiness.''

Magdalena stood up. She'd listened longer than
she needed. What proof had these two men offered her
of Rosabal's alleged larceny? It was unsubstantiated
talk. It had its roots in Garrido's approaching senility,
his unsupported mistrust of Rafael. Probably even jealousy—Garrido resented the younger man for staying in
Cuba instead of fleeing, as he himself had done, into
the safety of exile.

"Where are you going, Magdalena?" the old man
asked.

"Home."

"Are you going to ignore what Sergio has told you?"

She didn't answer. She stood, her hip pressed against the edge of the table, her weight on one leg. *Castro's a dead man.* She remembered how emphatically Rafael had said that in London. If Garrido and his sidekick Duran had heard him then, they wouldn't have entertained any doubts about his trust, and this obscene investigation need never have taken place.

"We're not finished, Magdalena," Garrido said. "Please. Sit down."

She refused. She took small, almost spiteful pleasure in denying Garrido. He said, "I didn't want to inflict any more on you, dear girl. But since you choose to defend Rosabal still, you leave me no real choice."

Garrido nodded to Duran, who took an envelope from the inner pocket of his jacket. He opened then inverted it; photographs slid out on the table.

"Please, Magdalena, sit down," and the old man gestured in a not unkindly manner, but still she refused him. She gazed at the colored pictures that lay on the table. She had no desire to look at them closely.

"I took these in Havana," Duran said. He isolated one, pushed it across the table. As if it were alive the photograph made a quiet sound that suggested breathing; it was the contact of shiny photographic paper on the surface of the table.

Magdalena squinted down at it.

"Pick it up," Garrido said.

Why did her hand tremble? She didn't reach for it. She could make out Rafael's likeness without touching the thing.

Duran raised the picture, studied it. "This shows Rosabal getting into a car. Look at it carefully, if you will."

She saw a car, rear door open, Rafael, beloved Rafael, bending slightly to step inside. Then she looked away. She stared across the room at the window; pinkish light lay on the opaque glass. A car backfired somewhere.

"This I took at Rafael's house outside Havana," Duran said, and selected another photograph. Once more Magdalena glanced at the thing, seeing a flash of color, shrubbery, a swimming-pool filled with turquoise water, and there was Rafael seated on the edge of the pool, beautiful in his black trunks, face turned slightly away from the camera.

"Lovely home," Duran said. "He lives well."

Magdalena drifted. She floated from this table, this room; she didn't need to see photographs.

"The young woman beside him in the car, the one who is holding his hand beside the pool . . ." Duran said, then faltered just a little. "That is his wife. Estela Capablanca Alvarez, daughter of General Capablanca. They were married a few months ago."

Wife: the word exploded like thunder in Magdalena's head. And, like thunder, it rolled meaninglessly away, echoing even as it faded. Wife: it might have been a word from an alien dictionary, a signal sent out through space, travelling countless centuries before being picked up on this planet, in this city, this room now by Magdalena Torrente. How could Rosabal possibly have a *wife?*

Magdalena reached down, picked up the photographs, flicked through them. The woman was young and handsome in a way that was distinctly Spanish. The few photographs where she appeared she was invariably looking at Rafael with the eyes of an adoring wife, a new wife, one in whom love has barely flowered—the new bloom, enchantment. Magdalena, dizzy, set the pictures back down. The tips of her fingers were suddenly chill; a sensation of cold tingled upon her spine and neck. A strange pressure built behind her eyes, and her heartbeat became arrhythmic.

"I am sorry," Garrido said. "He has abused you as well as the cause. I am sorry, Magdalena."

She barely heard Garrido's voice. She was tracking her own thoughts as if they were strangers eluding her. There had to be a simple explanation. There had to be a reason. Why had he never mentioned this woman, this wife, to her? Why, with the love they shared, had he never shared this information too? Reasons, all sorts of reasons—the wife was the daughter of a General, therefore the marriage might be political, a marriage of convenience, perhaps a match that might one day be useful to the cause. How could she know? How could she know anything? Unless she looked him in the face, unless she stared directly into his eyes, how could she know she'd been betrayed? She had only Duran's photographs to go on. And photographs, at best, were limited windows into reality.

But still her heart wouldn't beat regularly, and the cold had spread like a glacier from spine to scalp. Now the pressure was not located so much behind her eyes as it was in the very air around her, as if she were descending through unlit fathoms in a faulty bathysphere. She moved toward the door. She had to get out of this room and away from these two men and their *evidence* of treachery. She needed time alone, the clarity of solitude.

Neither Garrido nor Duran made any move to detain her. She stepped into the street and stood under a sky whose clouds had become an outrageous bright pink, a carnival color far removed from what Magdalena Torrente felt.

Paris

At midday Frank Pagan arrived at Orly Airport and took a taxicab driven by a chain-smoking Parisian who complained for miles about the economic policies of the Common Market, and how migrant workers were the scourge of all Europe. Pagan nodded politely from time to time and muttered *Mais oui, mais oui,* but he wasn't interested, and the man's patois was difficult to follow.

Pagan asked to be let out on the corner of the Avenue Victor Hugo in the Sixteenth Arrondisement, a little way before his ultimate destination. His eyes watered from cigarette smoke and his head throbbed as he walked in the direction of the Bois de Boulogne, slowly, deliberately, wary of pain.

Paris was overcast, damp, locked in the leaden grip of autumn; the greenery of the Bois had faded. The gutters were choked by fallen leaves. It wasn't a city that held personal associations for him. Once or twice he'd come here on business, but he knew the place only superficially, like a tourist. He checked Enrico Caporelli's address in his notebook. It was an exclusive apartment building about a hundred yards from where the taxi had dropped him. Gray, imposing, opulent in a stately way, it overlooked the Bois with the musty dignity possessed by the old apartment buildings of the very rich.

Pagan was confronted by a uniformed doorman as soon as he stepped inside the lobby. The doorman, haughty, a *gauleiter* in burgundy cap and uniform with gold epaulets, insisted on telephoning Caporelli before Pagan was allowed access to the elevator.

Enrico Caporelli apparently was not perturbed by the prospect of an English policeman coming to call; Pagan was led promptly to the elevator by the doorman, the iron gates were closed, and the lift rose in the shaft. He got out on the fifth floor. The corridor was dimly-lit. Two men, both dark-suited and muscular in a way no subtle tailoring could ever conceal, greeted him—although there was nothing warm in their manner. They checked his identification, frisked him expertly, without apology. He hadn't brought a gun. When they were satisfied, they ushered him into the vestibule of the apartment, then withdrew, a pair of big gloomy ghosts vanishing in the dimness of their surrounds.

Enrico Caporelli appeared in a doorway. He wore a navy blue robe and carpet slippers; somebody's diminutive uncle, Pagan thought. The quick handshake was firm and cool, the skin like smooth leather.

"They over-protect me," Caporelli said. "Good men, but perhaps a little too diligent. Come with me, please."

He led the way inside a study where heavy brocade curtains had been drawn against the windows. The room was lit only by an antique desk-lamp. Pagan, a little surprised by Caporelli's calm acceptance of a policeman's presence, sat down on one side of the desk and wondered about the two bodyguards and whether they came with the territory of the rich. Caporelli drew up a chair facing Pagan and pushed a cigar box across the desk. Pagan declined to smoke.

"I have read about you in the British newspapers, of course," Caporelli said. There was a hint of New York in the Italian accent. A man without a country, Pagan thought. Or perhaps one with many countries. "You've become quite a famous man, Mr. Pagan."

Pagan brushed this aside. He'd been played up a great deal in the newspapers lately, but if that was fame then it was a kind he didn't want; it was the notoriety of a man who has survived a tragedy—an airline disaster, a sinking ship. In the circumstances, he preferred anonymity.

"First the unfortunate killings, now the business with the missile." Caporelli looked sympathetic. "I am a little surprised you have come to see me. I cannot imagine how I can help you. Of course," and here was the little shrug of a man prepared to do favors, "I will always help the police in any way I can. In Italy, for instance, I cooperate with the police beyond the call of any citizen's duty. Ask them. They'll tell you."

"I'm sure you're an exemplary citizen," Pagan said. Dark drapes drawn against the light of day, body-guards in the corridor: what was Enrico Caporelli afraid of? Kidnapping? Violence of the kind practiced by certain Italian radicals? "But I haven't come to Paris to discuss your good behavior, Signor Caporelli."

"Somehow this does not surprise me," Caporelli said. "How can I assist you?"

"You were in Britain recently, I understand."

Caporelli tipped his chair back and looked up at the dark ceiling. Painted there, but obscured by the bad light, was an impression of an angel's gold wing, vast and still. "Yes," he said. "Why is that of interest to you?"

Pagan didn't answer. He sailed straight ahead. Un-answered questions often created a useful uncertainty. He took out his notebook and used it as an actor might a stage prop, flicking pages meaninglessly, pretending to search for something in particular. "You went to Glasgow."

"I have business there, Mr. Pagan," the Italian said. "Now and again I like to check on it. I had no idea my movements would attract official attention."

Pagan longed to draw the drapes and let daylight fill the room. "Who did you meet in Glasgow?"

"What would happen if I refuse to answer you?"

Pagan allowed this question to pass unanswered also. There wasn't any sharp response to it anyway; Caporelli could refuse to say a word. That was his prerogative. The important thing, from Pagan's point of view, was to keep rolling along. "Did you meet a man called Rafael Rosabal?"

"Yes."

"Why?"

Caporelli appeared amused by Pagan's bluntness. "He keeps me informed of events in Cuba. A long time ago, I lived there. I like to have news of my old friends on the island. Call me sentimental."

Sentimental, no, Pagan thought. There was nothing soft-centered about Enrico. "The Cuban Minister of Finance, a member of Castro's government, brings you news of your friends? Isn't that an odd arrangement? How does Rosabal justify this . . . service? Does his government know he meets you?"

"You sound melodramatic, Mr. Pagan. It's all very innocent, I assure you. Years ago, I knew Rosabal's family. The connection has never been broken. Besides, Rosabal and I never, never, discuss politics. I have no interest in Cuban affairs."

Was this a lie? Pagan wondered. Caporelli had a certain easy plausibility about him, but Pagan couldn't quite get a handle on Rosabal's angle in this. Why would the Cuban ferry news to Caporelli?

"Why did you have to go to Glasgow to meet?"

"It was convenient for me," Caporelli answered.

"And for him?"

Caporelli gestured in a manner capable of only one interpretation: *I don't give a damn about his convenience, Pagan.* It was easy to see who had the upper hand between the Italian and the Cuban. Rosabal was clearly ready to be inconvenienced. But why? It wasn't adding up; Caporelli was sliding past another element, something that sent Rafael scurrying to Glasgow. A hold, perhaps; or Caporelli had something Rosabal badly wanted. Pagan pressed his fingertips into his eyelids. Guessing games, no bone-hard facts. He needed links solid enough to create a strong chain.

"Rosabal rented a farmhouse in England. Did you know that?"

Caporelli shook his head. "I do not monitor his life."

"He never mentioned this farm?"

"Never."

A quick beat. "The house was occupied by Gunther Ruhr."

"Ruhr? The terrorist? Are you sure of that?"

"I'm sure," Pagan said. *The terrorist*, as if there were other Ruhrs who might come to Caporelli's mind. "Can you see a connection between Ruhr and your friend Rafael?"

Caporelli moved his face out from the reach of the lamplight. Shadows settled around him. Only his white hair was visible. "I can imagine no relationship, Mr. Pagan. None at all. Your information surprises me. In fact, it astonishes me."

But Caporelli's face and voice didn't altogether suggest astonishment; Pagan had the feeling he was telling Enrico things he already knew.

"Why would the Cuban Minister of Finance rent a farmhouse and allow a group of terrorists to inhabit the place, Signor Caporelli?"

Caporelli folded his fine little hands on the desk and regarded them as if they were precious. He shook his head from side to side. "It defies reason, Mr. Pagan. I have no ready explanation."

Pagan was silent now. Quietness gathered in the black hollows of this spacious unlit room. A clock chimed half past the hour with the subdued sound of an expensive mechanism.

"Stranger still is the fact that Rosabal rented the farm in another man's name," Pagan said.

"Really?"

"He called himself Jean-Paul Chapotin."

It was obvious at once that Caporelli hadn't known this before. The information had an unmistakable effect on him, as if he had just discovered something bitter in his mouth but good taste prevented its expulsion, and there was no napkin at hand. He bit on his lower lip, then backed himself further out of the range of the lamp, and his face became invisible to Pagan. There, concealed, he recovered his composure with a swiftness that was admirable.

He said, "The name—you did say Chapotin?— means nothing to me. And as for Rafael's private affairs, well, I'm ignorant of them. I am sure this business is all very interesting for you, but I don't share your fascination."

Pagan had a well-honed instinct, a little worn by time, a touch frazzled by experience, activated whenever he was presented with a lie. Sometimes, like a pulse, it beat strongly, sometimes hardly at all, but he'd heard so many lies in his lifetime—some told to him by experts—that an encounter with yet another fiction was like greeting an old if unreliable acquaintance. Caporelli's lie, that he didn't know Jean-Paul Chapotin, wasn't the best Pagan had ever heard, but it was executed with theatrical skill and assurance. The little man popped a kleenex from a fancy designer box with a conjurer's flourish, as if it were the climax to his brief performance, and pressed it to his lips.

"You must excuse me now, Mr. Pagan. I don't think I have anything more to tell you. Not that I've been of very great help, I'm sure."

Pagan wasn't quite ready to be dismissed. "Are you aware that Chapotin was murdered in London, Signor Caporelli?"

"How could I be? As I already said, Mr. Pagan, I am not familiar with the man. I'm sorry if he was killed, of course. But what can I say? You really must excuse me. I have business to conduct."

Pagan rose from his chair. "Like you, Chapotin had Cuba in his background," he said. "It's one of those bloody terrible coincidences that keeps bothering me. You and Jean-Paul and Rosabal. And the common factor is Cuba. I can't get it out of my mind."

Enrico Caporelli held a hand in the air, palm turned outward to Pagan. His voice was firm. "You should know when to stop asking questions. You should know when enough is enough."

"I never do. It's one of my worst traits."

Caporelli reached for the gold-plated telephone on his desk.

Pagan stretched a hand out over the receiver, preventing the man from picking it up. "Why are you in such a hurry to boot me out of here, Signor Caporelli? I want to know a little more about you and Rosabal and poor old Jean-Paul. You can't really expect me to believe you didn't know Chapotin. He was in Glasgow the same day you were there. He lived in Cuba at exactly the same time as yourself. And he was obviously known to Rafael. Don't ask me to file all this under coincidence. Don't insult me."

Caporelli gave an odd little laugh, a brittle note like a tiny hammer falling twice on a recalcitrant nail. He got up from the desk and wandered among the shadowy furniture. "You have a fine imagination, Pagan. For your own sake, let it rest. Let it lie quietly. Forget it. A little amnesia is often a healthy thing."

Ah, Pagan thought. Was that a veiled threat, a fist in a soft kid glove? He liked the idea of being gently menaced by Caporelli; it stirred his blood, his combative instincts. He got up from his chair and grinned at the little man, knowing how utterly infuriating this look could be at times.

"Something's going on, Enrico—if you don't mind—and I want to know what. You and Rosabal, for starters. He travels thousands of miles just so you can hear glad tidings from Cuba? Give me a bloody break, Enrico. I didn't get up with this morning's dew."

Caporelli was about to object, but Pagan went on regardless. "Let's think about Gunther next. He lives in a house rented by *your* friend Rafael. What does this begin to smell like, Enrico? The whiff of conspiracy?"

"I tell you again. Too much imagination. Empty your mind. Sleeping dogs must lie."

"I kick sleeping dogs, Enrico. I like how they howl." Pagan heard a dryness in his voice. He didn't have the spit for this pursuit, the wind. His lungs seemed shallow to him, his intake of oxygen poor. He caught his breath. "Now why does Gunther steal a missile? Not because he wants one for his collection, I'm sure. He's the hired hand. But who's the boss, Enrico? Rafael? He's a good choice. After all, he was Ruhr's landlord. But is Rafael carrying out an order on behalf of some other party?"

Caporelli had crossed the floor while Pagan was speaking. Now he was pressing a wall-button mounted close to the fireplace. Bringing in reinforcements, muscle to kick Pagan out of here.

"Was it you, Enrico? Was Rafael working for you?

Did he hire Ruhr on your behalf? Was that what the meeting in Glasgow was about?" Pagan strode across the room, closer to the little man. All this was wild, like shooting from a dislocated hip. But he had a scent in his nostrils still, and it grew more and more exciting. There was joy in mad surmise, in the crazed inspiration that forced you down unusual pathways. Allegations, red herrings, hares, accusations—sometimes, Pagan thought, work could be fun.

Clearly irritated, Caporelli once again pressed the bell on the wall. Pagan reached out, removed the man's hand from the button, gave the bundle of small bones a swift squeeze. "Let me finish, Enrico."

"You have finished," Caporelli said and pulled away his pained hand.

"Not yet. Here's a fresh tack. I asked myself who else could possibly make use of a missile. Could it be Fidel himself? After all, he had a taste of missiles a few years ago, maybe he liked having them. But let's say nobody in the world wants to sell him one. Then let's imagine he decides to steal one and assigns this chore to Rosabal. Rosabal comes to you for help—old pal, old family friend you say you are—and you put him in touch with Ruhr."

Caporelli's face was expressionless. Aside from the open eyes, hooded under the white eyebrows, it might have been the face of a sleeper.

Pagan went on, "But we both know why that script's wrong, don't we, Enrico? You wouldn't lift your little finger to give Castro water on his deathbed, would you? You loathe him because he ripped you off for everything you owned in Cuba. The only interest you could possibly have in Castro is to see him either dead or tossed out of office. Therefore, if *you're* involved, the missile wasn't stolen for Fidel's sake. There's some other reason."

"You amuse me, but my patience isn't unlimited. I must ask you to leave. Now. Please."

Caporelli walked toward the door. Pagan followed, thinking how pointless it was to hope Caporelli would break down and tell all. The Italian was hard as flint. And crafty. He had trained his face to reveal very little. So far the only real surprise that had registered was when Pagan had mentioned Rafael's use of the name Chapotin. Why had that startled Caporelli? Why had that so clearly bothered him? *Because something was going on he didn't know about,* Pagan thought. *Something that really worried him.*

"I honestly don't give a damn what you're up to, Enrico. I don't care about Cuba, and I don't care about Fidel Castro. Politics leave me cold. I'm interested in them only inasmuch as they involve an escaped prisoner who happens to have both a stolen missile and a hostage with him. I want the people *and* the missile back where they belong. And I think you can help me. I think you know where they might be found."

Caporelli acted as if he were no longer listening. He opened the door, looked into the hallway, called out, "Andre. Max. Come here, please. Escort Mr. Pagan out."

There was no reply from Andre and Max. Caporelli made a small hissing sound of irritation, *tssss,* and moved down the hall. Pagan followed. They passed the open doorway of a bedroom, furnished in black lacquer pieces, like something from the pages of a chic design magazine. Next was the kitchen, the largest Pagan had ever seen, vast and tiled, crowded with appliances, slatted red blinds at the long windows, copper-bottomed pans and skillets suspended from the high ceiling, strings of garlic bulbs, a hanging congregation of red peppers.

"Andre! Max!" Caporelli, as if he were calling to two miscreant dogs, clapped his hands briskly. Still no response.

Pagan tried to get the little man's attention, but Caporelli shrugged him off as he stalked the kitchen on his quest for the bodyguards.

"If you'll listen to me, Caporelli—"

"I have listened too long already, Pagan."

"Tell me what you know about Ruhr, that's all I ask."

Caporelli smacked the palm of his hand against the center of his forehead. "How many times do you need to hear it? I know nothing. Absolutely nothing! *Prego.* Do me a favor. Go away."

Pagan stopped moving after the Italian. He leaned against the tiled wall and considered the pointlessness of further pursuit. Enrico was too good, an old fox, cunning. He was giving nothing away. Pagan stepped back into a space that was probably called the breakfast nook or some such thing, a cranny containing a table strewn with rose petals, and four chairs. He needed to sit down, think over his options, such as they were.

He moved toward a chair. Then stopped. The cranny contained more than flowers and furniture.

Andre and Max had been shot at very close range and propped against the wall in the shadowy cavity. One of the men had his big blank face turned toward Pagan, dead blue eyes open, cheek blown away, the abstract expression of sudden death. Pagan, who could still be shocked by murder, looked across the room at Caporelli and was about to tell him that his bodyguards were no longer guarding bodies—but before he had the chance to speak the kitchen door was opened.

"Ah," Caporelli said. He was waiting for his soldiers. He thought they were coming through the door, belatedly answering his call. He thought they would have the Englishman ejected in a matter of seconds. Pagan shouted at the little man, something like *Get down!* although he couldn't remember later exactly what he'd said. In the doorway stood a man with a silenced pistol; having disposed of Andre and Max, he'd presumably been roaming this enormous apartment in search of Caporelli.

And now he'd found his quarry.

Pagan had barely time to record a swift impression, and it was neither interesting nor useful—medium height, medium weight, medium everything, dark hair, dark overcoat, dear Christ description failed him in the intensity of the moment, language melted away. He was, after all, cornered in a breakfast nook, and it seemed completely absurd to be shot to death in a cranny of all places; a nook had no inherent dignity. Even the word was perfectly stupid. Objective observation of the gunman was the last thing on his mind.

"In the name of God," Caporelli said.

The gunman fired once. The sound was reminiscent of pressurized air fleeing a punctured pipe. The gunman was clearly an expert shot. Caporelli was spun round by the impact of the bullet, which had struck him directly in the heart. He clattered to the tiled floor, an unsmoked cigar in its cellophane wrapper rolling out of the pocket of his robe.

Pagan had time to see the gunman turn his face toward the breakfast area; the pistol came up once again in the man's hand. Aware of the glass door behind him, conscious too of how he was almost trapped, Pagan turned so quickly that he felt the stitches in his chest stretch. Glass would yield if he forced it, if he threw himself at it: one small corner of his panicked brain still recognized this fact. He launched himself hurriedly and without undue fear of falling from a high place because he'd seen, through the slats of the blind, a balcony, a handrail, flower pots, even an empty bird-cage.

The blind buckled and fell to pieces when he charged it, slats bending under his weight, small plastic screws popping. The door itself shattered easily, scattering angular fragments of glass across the balcony. Pagan landed on hands and knees, but he hadn't been caught by glass and he wasn't bleeding. He rose to an ungainly crouching position and surveyed the balcony quickly. Six feet by twelve, it adjoined the balcony of the neighboring apartment, separated only by an ornate wrought-iron rail, about seven feet high. Pagan rushed toward it and clambered up. Halfway, he realized he had a terrific view of the Bois de Boulogne. With this appreciation came a certain dizziness. He swayed, moaned, heard air buzzing in his ears, kept climbing. There was neither elegance nor equilibrium in the way he ascended.

He clutched the top of the rail, hauled himself up through strata of pain that were numbed for the moment by the adrenaline of fear. He glanced back once across Caporelli's balcony, seeing how the fractured blind—slats bent at all kinds of angles—hung out through the broken glass like some spindly creature that has been crushed. There was no sign of the killer; but that meant nothing. He could be striding toward the glass door even now. He could appear on the balcony at any second. He could still shoot Pagan.

Pagan made one final strenuous effort, and pulled himself over the rail. He dropped without subtlety into the adjoining balcony and stumbled just as a door opened and a man appeared. Not the gunman. He was presumably Caporelli's neighbor, this meek-looking, homely man in the tweed jacket.

"Q'est-ce que c'est?" he asked, alarmed. *"Que voulez-vous?"*

Pagan took out his wallet and showed his ID to the man, who peered at it in the bewildered way of somebody whose life, for so long a placid, plodding business, has just taken a very odd detour.

"Ah, Scotland Yard," the man said as if these two words explained all. *"Oui, oui. Entrez, entrez,"* and he held the glass door open for Pagan, who turned one last time and looked through the metal rail at Caporelli's balcony—empty and bleak, gray under the flat noon sky. Even the flecks of splintered glass reflected no light.

The detective who responded to Pagan's phonecall was Claude Quistrebert from the Surete. He was a tall elegant man who wore a black and white pin-striped suit and a splendid blue carnation in his lapel. Pagan admired his style, which isolated him from his three colleagues, rather badly-dressed men who swarmed all over Caporelli's apartment with a clumsy enthusiasm that was almost endearing. Clues were not subtle things to be coaxed forth, no, they were to be gripped hard and shaken loose from the scene of the crime. Dead bodies, beyond respect, were searched with such rude vigor Pagan would not have been altogether surprised to see them somehow resuscitated for the purposes of interrogation. Energy, the clamor of voices, filled Caporelli's huge apartment.

Quistrebert and Pagan talked in Caporelli's study. The Frenchman's English, better than the Englishman's French, relieved Pagan of having to translate.

"Your description of the gunman leaves something to be desired," Quistrebert said.

"There was nothing exceptional about him. I'd recognize him if I saw him again, I'm sure, but as for salient characteristics or features . . ." and Pagan shrugged dismally; he'd almost been shot at by a total nonentity.

"Sal-ient?" the Frenchman asked, a little puzzled.

"Prominent," Pagan explained.

"Ah. Of course."

There was a crash from the kitchen, the sound of a heavy pot or a tureen clattering to the tiles. Quistrebert seemed not to notice. Perhaps he was accustomed to conducting investigations where his men broke things in their enthusiasm.

Quistrebert, sharp-faced, equipped with a nose that might have been made for burrowing, was at the window, looking out across the Bois. "In the circumstances, I don't think we can expect to apprehend the man," he said, without turning to Pagan. There was a critical little edge to his tone; he wasn't happy with his British colleague's powers of observation. He'd read of Pagan in the newspapers and considered him, with perhaps a twinge of envy, just another publicity-chasing cop. "Why was Caporelli killed? Do you have light to throw?"

"None," Pagan replied.

"You had reasons of your own for being here, of course. I will not pry."

"Routine questioning." A blanket phrase, a clear signal that meant don't ask.

"Naturally." Quistrebert strode across the room on long, stalklike legs. He sat behind Caporelli's desk and surveyed the papers there absently. "Caporelli had business interests in France. A paper mill. A perfume company in Nantes. Also some banking. This much is a matter of public record. I understand he had many commercial interests in Italy also. On the face of it, a wealthy businessman. Such a man would inspire a number of enemies, no?"

"More than likely," Pagan said. Hadn't Mme. Chapotin said that her late husband had a banking concern in Italy? Pagan enjoyed these little correspondences.

Quistrebert stroked the flower in his lapel. "He interests me, this Caporelli. Only a couple of days ago, he was a witness to a fatal accident here in Paris. I read the report."

Pagan felt his interest sharpen. "What happened?"

"He saw a man run over by a truck and crushed. It was a very bloody affair. Very bad. As an important eyewitness, he was required to give a statement, of course. In any case, he clearly felt a personal involvement. The victim of the accident was an associate of his, a certain Herr Kluger from Hamburg."

An associate. Enrico and his associates, Pagan thought, had a knack for unhappy endings. Chapotin, this Kluger, and now Enrico himself. There was a grand design here, murderously neat.

Quistrebert said, "They were walking after dinner, it seems, when a truck hit the unfortunate Kluger and dragged him under the wheels. A terrible mess."

"You're convinced it was an accident?" Pagan asked.

The Frenchman looked unblinkingly at Pagan. "What else? Scores of witnesses say they saw the truck being driven in an erratic fashion. The driver, a Spaniard, was drunk. I may add that he died of apparent heart failure some hours later in prison."

Quistrebert was silent a moment. "I will share

with you a curious feature of the affair, Mr. Pagan. The body of the driver was removed by persons claiming to be his relatives."

"Claiming to be?"

"They had identification. They were from Madrid. The body was released to them. Again, nothing so very unusual. People want to bury their dead—a fact of life. But then the discovery was made by a diligent officer that the truck had been stolen four days before in Lyons. The driver had carried a false Spanish licence. No such person ever existed. His fingerprints are not on record. Nor can we locate the so-called relatives who came to claim him. We've been investigating the whole affair, but every avenue turns out to be a dead end, provoking what policemen always dread—too many questions. Too many gray areas. No clues."

This sounded to Pagan less an accident than a deliberate murder that hadn't worked out as planned. The killer had lost his nerve, as sometimes all men do, and needed the fiercely blind courage of inebriation to go through with the murder of Herr Kluger. The source of the killer's courage had also been the cause of his downfall. Surely he meant to escape after ploughing the victim down but was too drunk to do so. Pagan wasn't about to suggest this to Quistrebert, though. The Frenchman wouldn't take kindly to unsolicited advice; he had a streak of Gallic disdain and stubbornness.

"What do you know about Kluger?" Pagan asked.

"Another businessman. He was Caporelli's partner in the perfume company. But his interests were wide. He was the chief shareholder in a large pharmaceuticals company in Frankfurt, sole owner of a vineyard in California, the proprietor of magazines in Scandinavia—the list is long. A very rich man. Like Caporelli."

"Can I have a report of the accident before I return to London?"

"Of course." Quistrebert smiled for the first time since he'd arrived, a foxlike expression. "Perhaps when you have official business in Paris in the future you will call me prior to your arrival, Mr. Pagan?"

"Count on it," Pagan said.

He shook hands with the Frenchman just as there was the sound of glass breaking in another room, an intrusion that caused the superbly indifferent Quistrebert neither a blink nor a grimace.

Glasgow

Foxworth, who had arrived at noon in an unseasonably warm and sunny Glasgow, had one of those little breaks that make a policeman's lot tolerable. It came at about three o'clock in the afternoon after he'd spent several hours with members of the Glasgow Criminal Investigation Division—friendly men, he thought, and level-headed—going over the reconstruction of Jean-Paul Chapotin's movements in Glasgow. There was the usual dogged routine of checking taxi companies and limousine services and car-hire firms, which involved making many telephone calls and waiting for people to get back to you after they'd checked their records and logs. It was a dismal business, actually, and quite uninspiring; or so Foxie thought. He knew dull routine had its place in his kind of work, but he'd inherited something of Frank Pagan's dislike of this plodding aspect of their employment. Give me the bright moment, Pagan had once said. Give me the flash, the sudden insight when lo and fucking behold! you know beyond doubt.

While the investigation of Chapotin's movements had been taking place, a similar inquiry into Enrico Caporelli's trip to Glasgow had also been going on. This had been a little simpler than the Chapotin inquiry in the sense that there was a record, kept by the men observing Rosabal, of Caporelli meeting the Cuban at a hotel in the center of the city. Caporelli was merely the peripheral figure in this surveillance, an incidental entry in the Cuban's life. But the young detective who'd logged the time and place of the encounter had the brains to record the licence-plate number of the limousine that had picked Enrico up. Foxie liked this young man's notes, which combined the merit of plain observation with a touch of personal resentment; *subject rode off in a fat limousine, licenceplate G654 WUS; very small man with white hair and an arrogant strut.* Fat and arrogant; an enjoyable deviation from the prosaic language of police notes.

It was a start; a licence-plate number.

The limousine that had ferried Caporelli away belonged to a company called Executive Motor Cars Ltd, with offices in West Nile Street in the heart of the city. When Foxie called the number, a polite female told him she 'needed a wee minute' to check her log—how often had he heard the word 'log' since he'd come to Glasgow?—and get back to him. Foxie, during his routine telephoning, had already asked this same woman about Chapotin. My, you're awfully busy, the woman had said on the second call. She had a lilting, liquid accent.

The Break itself happened while Foxworth was drinking tea from a thick china mug and waiting for return phonecalls. The woman from Executive Motor

Cars Ltd called back to say that the driver of G654 WUS had transported Enrico Caporelli to a house 'somewhere in Ayrshire'. As for Foxworth's other inquiry, the one concerning Chapotin, the woman told him that one of the company's other drivers had picked up a man by that name at Glasgow Airport and had taken him *to the same place in Ayrshire.*

Ah-hah! Foxie had one of those rare moments, given only to cops, poets and fishermen, when the object of a search suddenly materializes. Caporelli and Chapotin, transported by the same limousine company, went to the same address in Ayrshire. Since working-class Glasgow wasn't what you'd call Limousine City, it wasn't such a coincidence that both men had been serviced by the same car firm.

"Can I have an address for the house?" Foxworth asked.

The woman was silent a moment as she leafed through papers. "Actually, sir, I don't have an address. Only a Post Office box number in Ayr. That's where we sent our bills. Payment always comes from a company in London. This is an account we've been servicing for about a year."

"One of your drivers could give me directions," Foxie suggested.

"Of course," said the woman. "Always happy to oblige, sir."

When Foxie telephoned Golden Square to report his progress, Pagan was still in Paris, so he left a brief message with Billy Ewing. Then he drove an unmarked police car to West Nile Street. Executive Motor Cars Ltd was located above a philately shop in whose drab window there was a display of stamps from Third World countries. Cambodia, Togo, Rwanda. (He wasn't sure he'd ever heard of Rwanda.) He entered the building and climbed up to the second floor where he was greeted by the woman, Miss Wilkie, who turned out to be perfectly lovely—late twenties, curvaceous, gorgeous features and skin. In other circumstances Foxie might have been inclined to linger.

She introduced Foxie to a dour man called Roderick McNulty—Rod, as he seemed to prefer—who had actually chauffeured Caporelli to Ayrshire. Rod was the kind of person, socially rather stunted, who obliges the requests of other people only reluctantly. With thick, nicotine-stained fingers, he very slowly drew a detailed map for Foxie, and then handed it to him in a grudging manner.

Foxie looked at it a moment. The woman, Miss Wilkie—who had neat little breasts the merits of which were not entirely concealed by a green silk blouse, smiled at him. Terrific teeth, Foxie thought.

"I hope we've been able to help," she said.

"You've been wonderful." Foxie meant it too. He thought he might come more often to Glasgow.

She stepped close to him, inclining her head near his shoulder to glance at the map. "Out of the way sort of place," she said. "Who'd want to live there?"

Foxie caught her perfume just then, a delightful musk. Unashamedly romantic in affairs of the heart, given to falling in love with women he spotted only briefly on the street and could never hope to know, he wished Miss Wilkie would ride along with him to Ayrshire.

Rod McNulty said, "Aye. It's an isolated spot all right."

"Who lives in the house?" Foxworth asked.

"I wouldn't know," McNulty said, again hesitant, as if his whole life were one mass of confidences he had to keep. The chauffeur who sees all and says nothing.

With one last smile at Miss Wilkie, who raised a delicate hand in response, Foxworth left.

He drove out of Glasgow under a sunny sky. According to the car radio the weather was fine all across Southwest Scotland, although the inevitable cold front was on its way. Outside the city, green fields were bright in the sunlight. Along the coast waters sparkled, suggesting another season altogether.

He stopped briefly in the seaside resort of Ayr, a town of whitewashed cottages, a harbor, a busy High Street, a racecourse. He had a dinner of marvelous fish and chips then headed south again in the direction of Ballantrae. He wanted to reach his destination before dark.

As he drove through the small town of Girvan, the rocky hump of Ailsa Craig appeared ten miles offshore. Crowded by thousands of gulls, it looked as grim as a penal colony. When he reached Ballantrae, an old fishing village that seemed just a trifle despondent, he examined his map. The road he had to follow went inland. Road was hyperbole. It was a rutted path between tall hedges. His car thumped and rattled and the setting sun dazzled in his rearview mirror. The shrubbery became darker, denser. Now and then he had a sense of flat fields beyond the hedgerows, but he saw nothing of interest—neither farmhouses nor haystacks nor grazing cows.

He pulled the car over, turned on the interior light, examined the map. The house was about a mile away now. He drove the last stretch slowly. What was he supposed to say when he got there? *I am making inquiries. I am sorry to inconvenience you.* Standard police procedure. He thought a better ploy might be the Lost Tourist Strategy; after all, he didn't have a local accent.

He was obviously a discombobulated stranger. Feigning that particular pathos of the misguided traveller was always amusing, the doglike eagerness to get back on the right path, the profuse apologies. Why not?

But when he saw the house he wasn't sure. He had somehow expected a farmhouse, at best an old Scottish lodge, perhaps a renovated manse, not this sandstone monstrosity, which seemed ill-defined, uncertain of its own boundaries. Turrets, by God! Neither house nor castle, it managed to suggest one of those late nineteenth-century follies erected by an ambitious whiskered Victorian as a monument to his own—and his age's—enlightenment. Foxworth smiled to himself as he turned the car into the long driveway.

Twilight blurred the edges of the unlit house. Now it looked positively spooky, a place of creaking floorboards and squeaking doors and secret passageways. Not your inviting prospect, Foxie thought. But policemen, like plumbers, were obliged to go where the job took them. You couldn't just say *I don't like the look of the place, I refuse to go near it.*

Foxie parked the car. It was the only vehicle in sight. He stepped out. The house was deeply quiet. No TV sounds, no piano playing, no shadow at the window peering out.

An echo of Miss Wilkie's question came back to him. *Who'd want to live there?*

Aye, who indeed?

Foxie crossed the driveway. He didn't approach the front door at once. He went instead to the side, wondering if there might be lights at the rear, some sign of life. But he found none. It was indeed possible, he thought, that the place was empty, in which case he'd go back to Ballantrae and ask at a local pub if anybody knew the name of the owner and where he might be found.

The sun slid behind trees, its last light diffused by wintry branches. Twilight was going rapidly. No soft, sweet lingering here. No nightingale tunes. Foxie moved between the bushes.

He neither saw nor heard the parting of bushes to his right. Nor did he hear the quietly hostile *skweeee* made by the barrel of a shotgun forced between resistant branches of shrubbery. Some instinct finally made him turn round. His heart felt like a ball dropped from the roof of a tenement, down, unstoppably down, a slave to gravity.

"I lost my way," he said to the shadowy figure who stood half-hidden in the foliage.

The barrel of the gun, suddenly massive, came out of the bushes and was thrust against Foxworth's chest as if to say, with vigorous agreement, *You certainly have, chum*.

15

Cabo Gracias a Dios, Honduras

Steffie Brough, dreaming of her own death, woke when a spider crawled over a closed eyelid. She sat upright quickly and swatted the creature aside. Curled defensively inward, it created a huge black furry ball that flew across the air and struck the far wall of the tent then dropped in long-legged disarray. It took Steffie a moment to assemble her thoughts and remember where she was, and the recollection depressed her. *There were men here who wanted to kill her.*

She heard rain strike canvas overhead. The tent sagged in the center where it had gathered water during the hours of darkness. She got up, glanced at Ruhr who lay on the cot. She parted the flap, looked out, saw a dismal steamy morning. Rain weaved a mist in the trees and the density of the forest was overwhelming. Unseen insects kept up their constant click-clicking. How could she possibly have imagined escape last night? There was no way out of this place unless Ruhr said so. If she ran now he'd simply find her and bring her back. She was trapped.

Ruhr still slept quietly, and yet she had the odd feeling he could wake at will, that he'd trained himself to sleep only in the most shallow way. Any unusual noise would bring him around.

Last night, when it had seemed inevitable that he'd overpower her after the pointless attempted escape, he'd suddenly and strangely lost interest, pushed her away, tossed her a blanket and told her to sleep on the floor. It was almost as if she were a game he didn't want to finish, something he needed to linger over because there was more pleasure in it that way. She clenched her hands and stood in the center of the tent and realized that if she could see herself from a point outside she would probably look like some kind of animal with her stringy, dirty hair. I smell, she thought. I smell horrible.

Ruhr woke. Steffie had never seen anybody who rose quite like him. One minute asleep, the next fully awake, no transition between. He tossed his blanket aside and got up. He wore white underpants, white t-shirt. He dressed without talking, without even noticing her. He brushed his teeth, using water from an old pail, and spat toothpaste out on the floor. He combed his thinning hair and studied his face in a small corroded mirror. There was intense self-interest in the way he did this, a vanity.

He took his knife from under his pillow. He ran the tip of one finger along the blade, testing its keenness, then sheathed the knife and strapped it to his shin. Only then did he look at Steffie Brough, as if the weapon had reminded him of her existence.

"Hungry?" he asked.

She didn't say anything even though she was famished. Ruhr produced a plastic bag from which he took some dried fruit—God, that was all she'd had to eat since leaving England. He gave her two brown rubbery discs that might have been dehydrated apricot or pear, you couldn't possibly tell by their taste. They were awful, but she ate them anyway. When she was finished she understood she felt a vague though sullen gratitude toward Ruhr for the food.

But then she remembered how he'd touched her, that humiliating invasion of her privacy, his awful lips on her mouth, his hands all over her body, and her brief gratitude dissolved.

"More?" Ruhr asked.

She declined. She was still hungry but she didn't want him to know it. He had too much power over her already: why give him more? He took out a metal flask from a canvas bag. It contained lukewarm water. She drank. It was ghastly, gritty, tasted of iron.

"Things here are a little different for you," he said. "You're used to something else."

"Yes."

"No pleasant bedroom. No nice bathroom for you here." Ruhr smiled. He rubbed his face with the bad hand. Steffie barely noticed the deformity. She certainly wasn't repelled by it in quite the same way as before. *You can get used to anything,* she thought.

"You would like to go home," Ruhr said.

Why had he said that? she wondered. There was some sly quality in his voice. He was teasing her, only he wasn't very good at it. He wasn't much good at any kind of social interaction, she'd noticed. Even when he moved he did so without poise, like a man who knows he's ugly and feels people are watching him critically. There was an aura about him of loneliness, the same pall she'd seen around those sad, solitary figures who sat for motionless hours in the drafty reading-room of her local library, sometimes leafing newspapers but more often staring into space at nothing. Steffie, raised by decent people who tended to see the best in the human race and the bright side of everything, almost felt sorry for him.

Almost.

He kills, she thought. He kills casually. She remembered Trevaskis and his unfortunate kindness.

"Perhaps policemen will rescue you," he said, still teasing in his awkward manner. He opened the flap of the tent. There was the pungent smell of wet canvas. "Perhaps even as we speak, some kind English policeman is closing in on us. Somebody good and cunning. Perhaps Sherlock Holmes, eh?"

"Perhaps," she said.

"Hope is so wonderfully human, little girl. What person has not been completely betrayed by hope at least once in his or her lifetime?"

She sat on the floor, and hung her head. It was important to fight despair. Sometimes you couldn't find the strength to do so. Nobody was looking for her, nobody was closing in. It was stupid to think so.

He kneeled alongside her, cupped her chin in the palm of his hand. "Do not be so despondent, child. Keep hoping. What choice do you have?"

She hated him then more than ever before. The way he touched her under the face was awful in itself, but his words were the real killers—*don't give up hope. Don't be despondent.* Should I sing for you, Ruhr, and dance? She closed her eyes, blinked back tears and thought *Fuck you, you won't see me weep, you rotten bastard.*

He stood upright. She didn't look up at him. He said, "I have some business to attend to. You will stay here, of course. It would be pointless to run again. Where would you go in any case? I expect to be back very soon.''

She heard him push the open flap aside and then he was gone and the tent was silent save for the metronomic ticking of the rain and the murmur of hatred her own heart created.

The girl could wait. Delayed satisfaction only heightened anticipation. Ruhr walked down through long wet grass and mud to the landing-strip. The transport plane had gone at first light. He wondered briefly about Sweeney, but Ruhr wasn't sentimental about friendships. He simply didn't have any. All human relationships were inherently doomed, whether by death or declining interest. Why make any kind of commitment?

He had never loved in his life. On those few occasions when he'd felt the tremor of affection for another, he'd dismissed it as a chemical anomaly, a flaw in his system, something to be rooted out. It was simpler to destroy than to love. Destruction was quick and fevered and exciting. By contrast love, as he understood it, could be a protracted torture, a bundle of insecurities, a murderous game of the emotions.

He paused on the edge of the runway, enjoying the rain against his face. Then he crossed the concrete, passing the missile that sat in the truck at the edge of the runway. The green waterproof tarpaulin, running with rain, still covered the weapon. In the distance, their sounds muted by foliage, soldiers went through tedious drills designed simultaneously to dull the critical faculties and raise the temperature of enthusiasm. Pumped up for the overthrow of Castro, they would set sail with an effervescent sense of purpose and a determination sharpened by weeks of preparation here. The idea of discipline, with its unambiguous rules and codes and the geometry of its repetition, pleased Ruhr.

He went up the slope to the place where Fuentes's tent was situated. Tommy was inside with the Englishman, Bosanquet. They sat on either side of a card-table on which a map was spread. Ruhr ducked his head, went inside. The air was thick with cigarette smoke. Inverted lids of old coffee jars were being used as ashtrays by the chain-smoking Fuentes.

Fuentes looked up. Bosanquet took off his reading-glasses.

"His majesty," Fuentes said. "See how he condescends to visit us in my humble dwelling, Bose *old bean.* Are we flattered? Beat the drums. Roll out the red carpet. The king comes!"

Bosanquet, who thought poorly of Fuentes's heavy-handed sarcasm, stared at the German. He was really a disgusting shit as far as Bosanquet was concerned. Up there with the schoolgirl in his tent—very bad form. It was child-molesting, no two ways about it. He would gladly have cut out Ruhr's throat, and in other circumstances might have done just that. As it was, it was the child who would have to die, because that was how the order had come down from Harry Hurt. In Bosanquet's scheme of things, whatever was sent down the pipeline from Harry had top priority. Harry signed the paychecks and Bosanquet's loyalty was the commodity he bought with them.

"You didn't appear last night," Bosanquet said. "We waited for you. You were supposed to perform a task and you failed to show up, which is unforgivable."

"I fell asleep," Ruhr said drily. He enjoyed the Englishman's restrained display of temper. "I had had a busy day, you may recall."

"What about the girl?"

"What about her?"

"Is she alive?"

"For the moment," Ruhr said.

"For the moment," Bosanquet remarked. He really had no stomach for the idea of the girl dying. He got to his feet. Her death wasn't his business. Nor was the murder last night of one of Ruhr's henchmen. These things were Ruhr's own affairs. He changed the subject. "Are you ready to do the work you should have done last night?"

"It's raining," Ruhr said, as if this might prevent him from working.

"Does that make a difference?" Bosanquet rubbed his sweaty face with his red bandanna. He remembered how Harry Hurt had said that the German's needs were to be met at all times, because he was a very important part of the operation. Presumably this dictate included pandering somewhat to the German's sense of his own shattering superiority.

"Perhaps not," Ruhr said. "The tools."

"Of course." Fuentes removed a canvas bag from under his card table. It rattled as he handed it to Ruhr. "Everything you have requested is in there."

Ruhr unzipped the bag, looked inside, apparently satisfied.

All three men walked to the airstrip. Ruhr glanced at the covered missile on the truck and the large tarpaulined rectangle that contained the weapon control system. He had no intention of doing the work under the eyes of the other two.

The key to survival was the same as it had always been: he had to be indispensable. He'd known all along that this point would be reached, this place where his future was in the balance. It was always this way. Many of his employers had tried to shaft him in the past, to cheat him after the event. None had ever succeeded. He was always prepared, always kept something in hand. He had the documents in the care of the lawyer Herr Schiller in Hamburg, of course, but Ruhr liked to take out even more insurance policies. In this case, he was essential to Fuentes and Bosanquet and Rafael Rosabal and their scheme because of his specialized knowledge. That was the key and neither of the other men possessed it. Only Ruhr.

Fuentes pointed to a wooden crate, sheltered from wetness by sheets of plastic. He said, "This is what the Israelis delivered."

Ruhr glanced at the box, then turned away from it. For the moment he wanted to look at the missile. He unrolled the green tarpaulin a few inches, revealing the blunt gray canister. Without the nose cone the weapon lacked a dimension. Armed, it would have a range of approximately fourteen hundred miles; it could travel at five hundred and fifty miles an hour.

Ruhr walked to the wooden crate, asked Fuentes for a tool, a tire iron. Tomas found one inside a jeep parked nearby. Ruhr gently opened the crate.

Inside was a layer of packing material, which Ruhr removed.

There it was.

A nose cone of dull silver contained the nuclear warhead. A series of metal connecting pins studded the warhead. These fitted corresponding slots in the housing of the missile. Ruhr stared at the thing for several seconds. Instruments of destruction, from the flick-knife to the warhead, had always exerted great fascination for him. In the war museums of the world he'd been hypnotized by displays of old lances, maces, swords, blackpowder muskets, grenades from World

War I, tommy-guns, sophisticated automatic rifles. He believed that man reached his creative peak only when the design and manufacture of aggressive weapons was his goal. All the rest, the other products of creativity, the symphonies and poems and philosophical thinking, the computers and scientific theories, all that was just so much dross in contrast to the creation of devices meant to maim and kill.

Slicks of rain slid over the cone. Ruhr replaced the lid of the box. The beat of his heart was just a little faster.

"Now what?" Fuentes asked.

"I will wait," Ruhr replied.

"For God's sake, what for?" Bosanquet asked.

"For the ship." Ruhr stepped back from the wooden crate. "On board the ship I will make the final marriage."

"The marriage?"

Ruhr smiled. "Have I used the wrong phrase?"

Bosanquet loathed this smug character. It was damned hard to stay calm. "You are supposed to attach the warhead to the missile and make all the connections now, Ruhr. That is the plan. The missile is to be loaded in an armed state."

Ruhr shook his head. "If you are unhappy, do it yourself." He knew neither man could possibly perform the task. Even if they brought in an expert, the newcomer could not easily fathom the connections between the warhead and the missile because Ruhr, with the foresight of the survivor, had had the warhead built to his own specifications, which had been given to the Israelis, Levy and Possony. Changes in the wiring inside the missile were required to make it compatible with the warhead, which was a brilliant modification of the device known in the nuclear arms trade as the W84.

A wrong connection, a minor mistake, and the fusing would burn out, rendering both missile and warhead useless. And Bosanquet knew that: Ruhr had once again made himself indispensable.

Ruhr had acquired his extensive nuclear understanding from a homosexual West German technician employed by NATO at Wueschein, a base in Germany. He'd learned how the missile worked, and the principles behind it. He'd absorbed this with the ardor of a man in love with his subject. The technician, menaced by blackmail, had been a wonderful teacher, Ruhr an even more marvelous student. The arcane terms, the payload, the velocity, the range, the connections between warhead and missile—Ruhr took it all in without needing second explanations.

Now Fuentes tore off his hat and flung it to the ground. *"Tronco de yucca,"* he said to Ruhr. "That's what you are, Ruhr. A goddam *tronco de yucca.* Why don't you do the goddam job now?"

"I don't speak Spanish," Ruhr replied. He enjoyed Fuentes's primitive display of irritation. "Is that a compliment?"

"I don't think it is," Bosanquet remarked. He breathed deeply, staying calm. After all, did it really make a difference if Ruhr armed the missile here or on board the ship? So long as the device was ready to fly when it was placed in Cuba—that was the thing of consequence. Ruhr could make 'the marriage' on the ship, if that was how he wanted it.

"It's okay," Bosanquet said. "It's going to be fine."

"I know it is," Ruhr responded.

He walked across the runway and back up through the long grass to his tent. Guns fired in the misty distance. Target practice. He entered the tent. The girl was lying on the camp bed, her eyes closed.

He watched her. He was ready for her now.

He moved toward her quietly, with a weightless-ness years of stealth had taught him. He was about a foot from the bed when she opened her eyes and drew her hands out from under the blanket. She held a piece of broken mirror, a scabbard-shaped length she held like a dagger, and she thrust it at him. He stepped away, watching how the makeshift blade drew small reflec-tions from within the tent—the girl's lips, one of her determined eyes, Ruhr's own face, fragmented images.

She raised her weapon in the air and slashed again and this time he seized her wrist and slammed it down across his knee, forcing her hand to open and the length of mirror to fall to the ground. She wasn't beaten even then. She pulled herself free of him, twisted, kicked, lashed air with a foot that had never been meant to in-flict damage, a long foot, a dancer's foot, and he caught the ankle easily, and twisted it, and pushed her back across the bed.

She lay there, breathing hard.

He stood over her.

And smiled.

London

The physician, Ghose, examined Pagan's chest with his head cocked, like that of a bird, to one side. He kept up an ongoing stream of chatter while he studied the stitches. The human body, Mr. Pagan, is a miracle of design and efficiency. Consider for instance the lung, the robust delicacy of that organ, the bronchi, the bron-chioles, the whole system of highways that we call alve-olar ducts. Easily damaged, Mr. Pagan, but they mend under the right circumstances. And these include bed rest, no needless activity. Think of yourself as sedentary for a while.

Pagan liked Ghose and the cheerful manner in which the physician chided him. This lecture on the lung was Ghose's way of telling him to quit whatever it was that had loosened the stitches in the chest-wound.

"Tennis, Mr. Pagan? Soccer? Sex? In which of these otherwise laudable activities did you foolishly indulge?"

"I found myself in a situation where I was obliged to move quickly," Pagan said.

"In future you will move, if at all, only slowly," Ghose said. He replaced the damaged stitches after cleaning the wound thoroughly.

Pagan disengaged himself from the proceedings by thinking about the report of Herr Kluger's death in Paris. He'd translated it slowly on the plane back to London, skipping vocabulary he didn't know. The gist of the thing was that Caporelli and a couple of his acquaintances—the detailed report named them as Harold Hurt and Sheridan Perry, American citizens—had witnessed the event. Were they simply out strolling, taking the night air, four old pals crossing a street when —*wham*—one of them is dragged under a truck? Perhaps they were headed somewhere, a meeting, a cafe. It was a dead-end. He could check out Hurt and Perry, which would take time unless they had records of some kind at the American Embassy or were otherwise noted in some central law enforcement computer—if they had ever broken any laws in their time. Time: there it was again, an intolerably demanding master.

Ghose bandaged him. "There. Almost as good as new. I underline the almost. Now go home. Behave yourself. Don't play in the streets. Cars are quicker than you, Mr. Pagan.''

Pagan told Ghose he was going directly to bed, but when he left the hospital he took a taxi, through clogged West End traffic, to Golden Square. It was after seven o'clock when he reached his office. He took the bottle of Auchentoshan from his desk, poured a very small shot into a glass. He sifted his messages. There was one from Foxworth, who hadn't returned from Glasgow. Something about a car-hire company he was going to check out. Pagan could hardly read Billy Ewing's handwriting. Steffie Brough's mother had called, just checking. *Just checking.* This terse message, between whose lines lay a world of pain, caused Pagan to feel as if his heart had been squeezed. He glanced at the child's picture pinned to the wall. The elfin features of the kid neither accused nor derided him for his failure to locate her. They seemed indifferent suddenly, as if resigned to exile.

Just checking. Pagan imagined he heard death in those words. He felt as if he'd entered a memorial chapel to find Steffie's mother looking down into her daughter's casket and whispering to herself those two dreadful words *Just checking, just checking,* a hand laid softly on the child's cold cheek.

I'll get her back for you, Pagan thought. Some way.

He called Billy Ewing, told him to run a check on Harold Hurt and Sheridan Perry. Ewing had some information of his own, which concerned the protocol of Frank Pagan interviewing the Cuban Minister of Finance. It required a shit-load of paperwork, Ewing reported. Reasons had to be spelled out, justifications given. Documents were then submitted to the Cuban attaché in London, with copies to the Foreign Office. The government in Havana would review the request in due course. To put it bluntly, said Ewing, it might take six months, perhaps a year, and even then it didn't sound promising.

Pagan thought about the great bureaucratic mire into which human intentions, reduced to paperwork, were sucked and invariably lost. He hung up. His next call was to the Commissioner. Pagan asked for a meeting as soon as possible. Burr agreed. They chose a pub in Soho because Burr had an engagement at a restaurant in Greek Street at eight. Pagan then made one other call, this time to an airline company.

On his way out of his office, he encountered Billy Ewing, who had his face buried deep in a big white handkerchief.

"By the way, anything new from Foxie?" Pagan asked.

"Not yet." Ewing came up for air from the folds of the handkerchief. "Bloody pollen."

"If he gets in touch I'll be at the French pub."

"Then what?"

"We'll see."

"There goes a man of mystery," Ewing said, more to himself than to his boss, as Pagan headed for the door with an agility Ghose would not have recommended.

The French pub, so-called because in another incarnation it had been the headquarters for the French government in exile during World War II, was crowded with West End types, a few tourists, theatergoers finishing drinks hurriedly, and some dubious characters Pagan recognized as having been acquainted with Her Majesty's prisons at one time or another. He squeezed into the bar, careful to avoid potentially painful contact with anyone, and ordered a scotch.

Quite suddenly he remembered having been in

this same bar thirteen years ago with Magdalena Torrente. They'd drunk anise from a large glass urn on the counter and then they'd gone deeper into Soho, strolling hand-in-hand down Old Compton Street, up through the food stalls in the Berwick Street market. They'd eaten dinner at a small Greek restaurant on Beak Street. He'd gotten quite drunk that night. Drunk and passionate, and probably silly in his passion. The touching evening came rushing back to him in little particles of memory that had been scattered and overlooked.

Martin Burr arrived five minutes after Pagan was served. Unlike Pagan, the Commissioner waded into the throng, nudging with his stick wherever appropriate. He was an imposing man. The eyepatch, the bulk of his body, gave him presence and set him apart. He didn't want a drink. Since the place was crowded, he and Pagan went outside into the street. A snappy little breeze blew up from Shaftesbury Avenue and Pagan turned up the collar of his coat.

"How is the wound?" Burr asked.

"I'll survive," Pagan remarked. He drained his scotch and set it down on the window-ledge of the pub.

"Don't overdo it."

"I don't know how, Commissioner."

Martin Burr smiled thinly. Frank was the kind who'd soldier on regardless. Either one admired this attitude or criticized it for being headstrong. Burr was never sure which side he took.

He put his hands in the pockets of his tweed overcoat. "I'm getting flak, Frank. All the bloody time. This damned commission of inquiry has its first meeting tomorrow. I'm going to have to talk to them about the leak that led to the calamity in Shepherd's Bush. What can I tell them? I know absolutely nothing new about it.'' Burr looked up at the night sky over Soho, looking like a one-eyed country squire sniffing the air for weather changes. ''I also just received some other news that may or may not have something to do with the bloody missile. According to an intelligence report that came to my desk, the Israelis have reported two of their most highly-rated nuclear physicists as missing, as well as sufficient *materiel* to make a warhead compatible with the cruise missile. Both men are said to be somewhere in South America. The Israelis are blaming professional burn-out for the theft. Both men were said to be, and I quote, 'highly-strung'. But who knows? The information is vague.''

''If there's a connection with Ruhr, then the cruise might be armed by this time.''

''It might be.''

''Which makes the picture even more gloomy.''

''Gloomy indeed. Who is going to blow up what, I wonder.'' Burr slipped fingertips under his eyepatch and scratched. ''If it weren't for the fact that I'd feel like some rotten little bugger sneaking off a sinking ship, I'd tender my resignation in a twinkling. No messing about. But I'm like you, Frank. I keep going. Kinnaird's been supportive, I must say. Which I appreciate.''

A roar of buses was blown on the breeze from Shaftesbury Avenue and the theater district. This was a transient, brightly-lit little corner of London, streets filled with drifters, people who idled in the Haymarket and around Piccadilly Circus and wandered toward Leicester Square.

''Kinnaird's the conscientious sort,'' Pagan said.

''Calls me three, four times a day, Frank.'' Burr looked as if he were wearied by the Home Secretary's attentions. ''What did you want to see me about?''

Pagan arranged his thoughts. He expected an argument from the Commissioner, or at least an objection. He talked quickly, hoping Burr wouldn't interrupt him. He went lightly on the details, his past relationship with Magdalena. He talked about the connections between Rosabal and Ruhr, the evidence of the rented farmhouse. He sketched his conjectures, trying to give them solid weight, about the threads that linked Caporelli and Chapotin to Rosabal, and thus to Gunther Ruhr. *En passant,* he spoke about the deaths of Caporelli and the others. Now, if there was only the vaguest possibility that the stolen missile was armed, it gave the whole investigation even more urgency.

"There are some iffy bits in there," Burr said.

Pagan agreed and muttered something about the nature of all hypotheses. He glanced down the busy street.

"What do you propose, Frank?" Burr asked. Sometimes he adopted an attitude toward Pagan similar to one that might be held by an uncle toward a favored if slightly willful nephew. He was tolerant, bemused, gently critical; he knew that Pagan always did his best no matter the circumstances.

Pagan said what he had in mind.

Martin Burr put one hand up to his dark green eyepatch. "Are you really sure that this person—this Magdalena—will tell you anything, even if she's in a position to do so?"

Pagan wasn't sure. He thought about the mysterious coup she'd been so reluctant to discuss: if he knew more about that, there might be progress. "She's the only real connection I have to Rosabal. And I think the road to Ruhr leads through the Cuban."

"You could travel a long way and have nothing to show for it."

"I could also sit on my arse around London and have even less."

"True," Burr said. A certain look sometimes came to Frank Pagan's face, and the Commissioner recognized it now, determined, and hard, the slight forward thrust of the jaw aggressive. "May I remind you, Frank, that you're not in great shape for travelling? On top of that, your activity in Paris today hasn't improved your condition."

"I feel fine," Pagan said. And, for the moment, that was true enough. How long this transitory well-being would last was another matter. He had the feeling he was held together by nothing more substantial than Ghose's stitches.

Burr said, "Very well. Make arrangements to go."

"I already made them."

Burr smiled. "I should have known." He was quiet a moment. Pagan's confidence was sometimes an impressive thing. "There's an old contact of mine in Dade County. A certain Lieutenant Phillip Navarro. You might need him. He knows his way around."

Pagan memorized the name.

"I hope you bring something back, Frank. God knows, we could use a break."

The Commissioner shook Pagan's hand, then turned and walked in the direction of Old Compton Street. Pagan didn't watch him leave. He didn't have time to linger. He had to go to his apartment, toss a few things together, get his passport and his gun, and be at Heathrow Airport within the next two hours. He was pleased to have the Commissioner's blessing, the official imprimatur.

With or without it, he'd have gone anyway.

Washington

Harry Hurt kept an expensive apartment in an area of Washington that afforded a splendid view of the Potomac. It was a rich man's view, designed to instill in its owner a sense of unbridled superiority. High above the riffraff, Hurt indulged his patriotism, which fostered the illusion that anyone—anyone at all—could rise to wealth and prominence in these United States. Any Appalachian dirt farmer's boy, any steelworker's son from Bethlehem, PA, could—God, hard work, and the machine willing—ascend to the highest offices in the land. Harry Hurt believed this without question. While he was not an innocent in world affairs by any means, he was nevertheless naive when it came to some areas of understanding. His romanticized America eclipsed the hard reality.

The apartment had an exercise room fitted with an electronic bicycle, stretching devices, a Nautilus machine, a variety of weights and a rowing simulator. In this room Hurt burned off calories and kept himself tight and lean. Sometimes he had a svelte Icelandic woman come in and massage him. Such sessions usually ended in mutual oral sex, the sixty-nine position at which Hurt considered himself an adept.

A spartan bedroom with a certain Polynesian flavor adjoined the mini-gymnasium, and beyond was a large living-room where he sometimes entertained people. A glass-panelled cabinet, centered against the main wall of the living-room like a shrine, contained a variety of weapons—automatic rifles, shotguns, pistols—as well as photographs of Hurt in crumpled fatigues and black glasses when he'd been a 'military advisor' in Central America. A clutch of shrunken heads, gathered in Central American villages, hung alongside the cabinet like a spray of discolored garlic bulbs. All were reminders of his glory days.

The door of the living-room led into a vestibule furnished in soft white leather chairs and sofas. This room was presently occupied by new guards Hurt had hired. There were three in all, one a former Secret Serviceman. They wore dark blue suits.

On this particular evening, more than twenty-four hours after the limousine had exploded, Hurt was in the living-room pouring small shots of an inexpensive scotch called Passport from a bottle labelled Glenfiddich. He had some miserly ways and, like most misers, thought he could fool people with transparent deceptions.

Freddie Kinnaird, who had arrived an hour ago on the Concorde, sipped his drink and pretended to enjoy it. Sheridan Perry, knowledgeable about malt whiskies, made no objection either. He was accustomed to this odd streak of niggardliness in Harry. The more wealth Hurt accumulated, the more thrifty he became and the more energy he spent jogging and rowing and heaving weights around. It was almost as if he were obeying some strange axiom of his own: *great wealth leads only to parsimonious guilt which can be reduced only through endless exercise.*

Freddie Kinnaird, who had just finished relating the death of Enrico Caporelli, set his glass down a moment. Hurt deftly slid a coaster, filched from the Stanhope Hotel in Manhattan, under the Englishman's drink.

"When does it end?" Hurt asked. He'd already told Freddie about the attack on the limo, glancing all the while at Perry, as if for some sign of his compatriot's guilt.

"When we three are dead, I daresay," Kinnaird remarked.

"Hold on, hold on," Hurt said. "Let's be logical. Let's take this thing apart and put it back together again. It has to lead somewhere."

Kinnaird picked up his glass and finished his drink. He had so little time to spend here. There was business to conduct back in England, the affairs of his office not the least of it, but he'd come here to show a sign of solidarity with Hurt and Perry. After all, they were members of the same exclusive club. He detected some mild tension between the pair. Had there been a squabble? In the circumstances, though, nervousness was inevitable.

Freddie Kinnaird also had some information to impart at the appropriate moment, which would come when Harry had played out his little string of paranoia.

"For a while, I thought Enrico himself might be behind it," Hurt said.

"How wrong you were," said Kinnaird.

"Now, if it's an inside job . . ." Harry Hurt didn't finish his sentence.

"We three," Freddie Kinnaird said.

"Right," Perry said. "If it's an inside job, it's one of us."

Freddie Kinnaird played with his empty glass. A lock of hair fell across his forehead, creating the impression of a rather red-faced, ungainly boy. He swept it back with a toss of his head. "Consider the explosion of the limousine," he said to Perry. "Who had the information that you and Harry were travelling in the vehicle?"

Perry said, "Only Harry and me. That's it."

"Unless *you* knew, Freddie," Hurt said.

Kinnaird laughed. "I was many miles away, Harry.

I have no crystal ball, something my political enemies in the House of Commons discovered some time ago."

"You're saying . . ." Perry stopped, looking both indignant and somewhat despondent at the same time.

"It's either you or me." Hurt turned to Perry. "That's what Freddie's saying."

"Wait a minute there," Perry said.

Kinnaird interrupted. "It's only one possibility, gentlemen. Consider this as an alternative. Parties unknown to us, parties seeking the destruction of the Society, might be responsible."

This was what Hurt wanted so badly to believe. But was it really preferable to ascribe the killings to some faceless organization rather than to Sheridan Perry? Perry he could deal with. An unknown outfit was more spooky. How the hell did you begin to fight back at a shadow? His thoughts returned to the fiery limousine and the striking little perception he'd had when he'd been obliged to flee the tailoring establishment. *Perry knew*, he had thought then.

Now it made some kind of sense to him.

Consider: Perry knew.

Assume: Perry arranged the hit.

The killers Perry had hired to strike the limousine had erred. Maybe they were supposed to blow up the car later, at some time when Perry—perhaps on the pretext of buying a newspaper, something like that—had stepped out of the limo. It made simple, stunning, logical sense. Perry's killers, in their enthusiasm to do the job, had mistimed the affair.

This is what it came down to: Perry wanted it all, the whole ball of wax. He wanted the Society for himself. He wanted Cuba for himself.

Hurt switched on the light in the aquarium standing against one wall. Sudden fluorescence illuminated a clan of silken Siamese fighting fish. When they moved they did so with a kind of narcissism, as if studying their reflections in an infinity of mirrors. Hurt peered into the aquarium. His own image, the angular features, the great bony jaw, the steely close-cropped hair, shone back at him. Seeing himself thus, he remembered that control was one of his strengths, that he wasn't the kind of man to leap to unfounded conclusions. Perhaps he was judging Perry wrongly.

He turned to look at his fellow American. Sheridan Perry was pouting very slightly, the shadow of an expression left over from a spoiled childhood. Little Sheridan Perry had been the centerpiece of his parents' marriage. Fawned over, bestowed with riches, his life an endless cycle of tearing apart wrapping-paper to get to the goodies, young Perry had reached his tenth birthday before he realized that in most other houses Christmas arrived but once a year.

Perry said, very quietly, "It wasn't me. I'm not behind it. I wish you'd quit staring at me, Harry. I'm no traitor."

He looked convincing to Hurt. He sounded like a man telling the truth. Kinnaird's hypothesis of an unknown party seemed suddenly feasible to Hurt, who couldn't stand the pained expression on Perry's face. How could Perry, no matter the unfathomable extent of his greed, be responsible for wiping out the Society?

Hurt shook his head, astonished by his own ability to vacillate. You simply couldn't have it both ways. Either Perry was guilty or he was not. Indecision was a sin in Hurt's eyes.

"Let us set all this unpleasantness and mutual suspicion aside for the moment," Kinnaird said in a firm way. "There's something else that complicates our lives—the fact that a certain London policeman is presently on his way to the United States. A man called Frank Pagan. Pagan is the one who interviewed Enrico in Paris. He was present at Caporelli's unfortunate death.''

''Do you think he knows anything?'' Hurt asked.

''Very little, I imagine. At this present time. All I can tell you is the information I myself get from Scotland Yard.''

''How did he get on to Enrico?'' Sheridan Perry asked, frowning, looking oddly pale and anaemic in a way no hearty carnivore ever should.

Kinnaird replied, ''Through Rosabal, I gather. I haven't seen Pagan's report yet on his meeting with Enrico.''

''But how the hell did Pagan get on to the Cuban?'' Hurt wanted to know.

Freddie Kinnaird stretched his legs, clasped his hands at the back of his head, and tried to look relaxed, but he was faintly nervous here. ''British domestic intelligence has an occasional policy of observing members of the Cuban government visiting Britain—diplomats, ministers, etcetera. Now and then, a Cuban is selected for surveillance. Rosabal's number came up. He was watched in Glasgow. He was seen with Enrico.''

While Hurt absorbed this information, he could hear various doors squeak open in the long murky corridor of his mind. The idea that Rosabal had been followed in the United Kingdom worried him deeply. Perhaps Enrico had also been placed under surveillance on account of his association with the Cuban. And where could that have led?

''Is it possible that British intelligence is responsible for the deaths of our members?'' he asked.

Kinnaird smiled. ''I don't think it's likely. That

kind of information would have come to my attention one way or another.''

"Unless they're on to you, Freddie."

"Nobody is on to me, Harry. Believe me." Kinnaird smiled. The very idea of his exposure was preposterous.

The silence in the room was disturbed only by water passing softly through the aquarium filter and a faint *plup* as a fish briefly broke the surface. Then Hurt asked, "How good is Pagan?"

"His determination is notorious. He's also known for overlooking the book when it suits him," Kinnaird said. He recalled the hurried telephone conversation he'd had with Martin Burr just before boarding the Concorde. "Right now he's on his way to Miami. He has a contact inside the Cuban exile community. Mind you, I don't think Pagan knows very much. Nor do I imagine he's remotely interested in Cuba or anything that might happen there. He wants Ruhr and he wants this young girl Ruhr was silly enough to grab. He also wants to know the whereabouts of the missile."

Hurt walked to the window. He surveyed the blocks of apartments that, like his own, overlooked the Potomac. Lights burned in windows and a passing yacht created a bright yellow band on the dark waters. Hurt felt suddenly crowded. It was more than the deaths of his associates, it was the idea of this Frank Pagan. He looked at his watch. Everything was so damned close to completion. How could he allow some British cop to interfere? If Pagan was headed for Miami and the Cuban community there, he was getting a little too close. He was trespassing on Harry Hurt's zone of comfort.

"Who's his contact in Miami?"

"This is the interesting part, Harry. According to

my information, Pagan's friend is a woman called"—
and here Kinnaird consulted a small morocco-bound
notebook fished from his inside pocket—"Magdalena
Torrente."

"So? What's so interesting about that?" Hurt
asked.

Kinnaird was quiet a second. Then he said, "Magdalena Torrente is an intimate friend of Rosabal's."

"Intimate?" Hurt asked, alarmed by this new connection. "How intimate? What does that mean?"

Kinnaird gazed at the shrunken heads. They really
were monstrous little things. Their mouths hung open
as if these were the faces of people who had died in un-
speakable pain. "My dear Harry, I can only tell you
what I read in the reports. And police reports are not
renowned for their pornographic details. She's a friend,
a close friend. Perhaps a lover."

"What does she know? Did Rosabal tell her anything?"

Kinnaird shrugged. "I don't have the answers. My
information isn't complete. Pagan won't tell me anything directly. And since he's not the quickest person
when it comes to compiling reports for the Commissioner, I am sometimes not altogether *au courant*. But
I rather doubt that Rosabal would confide in this
woman anything so important as our undertaking,
don't you?"

Hurt nodded, though a little uncertainly. "I don't
like it anyway you cut it. The fact that Pagan's contact
in Miami is an intimate friend of Rosabal—this is not
good news, Freddie."

Sheridan Perry said, "It's very simple. I've always
followed the old line that it's better to be safe than
sorry."

"You mean what I think you mean?" Hurt asked.

Perry nodded but said nothing.

"You'd eliminate the pair?" Hurt asked.

"Eliminate's a good word," Perry remarked.

Hurt wondered if Perry's suggestion, lethal and yet so simply phrased, was Sheridan's attempt to turn attention away from any suspicion of murderous betrayal that might have gathered around him. Kinnaird had deftly changed that subject a few minutes ago, putting into abeyance the question with which this meeting had begun. Sir Freddie, diplomat, smoother of tangled paths, had focussed attention on another problem, one more easily solved than that of identifying the killer behind the murders of the Society members.

"Who would you get to do it?" Hurt asked.

Sheridan Perry shook his head. "Harry, come on. I don't have an inside track with the criminal fraternity. I thought you might know somebody. After all, you're the man with connections when it comes to guns and guys that know how to use them."

Hurt had the feeling that Perry's last remark was a way of casting a little light of suspicion on Harry himself. It was undeniably true that he had contacts among ex-soldiers and mercenaries, men who considered killing as natural a function as, say, screwing. Hurt had kept some bad company in his time, also true. Was Perry trying to damn Hurt by association? Was he trying to say that Hurt was the logical candidate if the murders were an inside job?

Sweet Jesus, Hurt thought. When you stepped on board that great rolling locomotive of doubt and suspicion it just gathered speed and kept moving, never stopping at any stations, it rattled and screamed past objectivity and sweet reason in its frantic journey to confusion and madness. He took a couple of deep breaths, seeking the calm center of himself.

"I could make a call, I guess," he said. Why deny it? He had the contacts.

"I wish there were some other way." Kinnaird's voice was quiet.

"There isn't," Perry said. "You let this character Pagan go where he pleases—what then? And if the woman happens to have information . . . No, Freddie. There's no other way. We can't afford to take chances now."

Hurt stepped inside the kitchen. Kinnaird and Perry could hear him talking quietly on the telephone. He spoke for a few minutes, then he returned to the living-room.

"It's done," he said flatly.

There was a silence in the room. In the entrance room, behind the closed door, one of the bodyguards coughed. Hurt strolled to the window. The view was breathtaking. There was more traffic on the river now, launches, yachts, one of which was strung like a Christmas tree. In the windows of other apartment buildings lights were dulled by drawn drapes or tinted glass.

He said, "Ever since we became involved in this Cuban business, we've had nothing but problems. I remember when everything was easy. Plain sailing. No clouds. Full membership. We didn't have deaths, killings. We weren't involved in all this . . ." He waved a hand. The appropriate word had eluded him. "Mainly, though, our associates were still alive and well."

He stared across the expanse of the Washington night. Because of the vast electrical glow of the city, the stars were dimmed in the sky. He was about to turn his face back to the room when a bullet, fired from an apartment tower nearby, pierced the window in an al-most soundless manner.

It penetrated his skull.

Harry Hurt put his hand up to his head, thinking for the shortest time possible, the kind of time only a sophisticated atomic clock might measure, that he had a migraine. It was his final perception, quicker than quicksilver. He neither heard nor saw Freddie Kinnaird and Sheridan Perry rush to the place where, facedown, he had fallen.

The Caribbean

The freighter, an old vessel badly in need of fresh paint, flew the red, white and blue flag of Cuba. It was not of Cuban origin. Built in Newcastle, England, some forty years before, it was registered in Panama and named—at least for this voyage—*La Mandadera*. It was a vessel of formidable shabbiness. Rust seemingly held the ship together, creating brown bands around bow and stern.

The captain was a mustached Cuban-American called Luis Sandoval who lived in Florida. He had fled Cuba in 1964 with his wife and family at a time when rumors concerning the removal of children from Cuba to Russia had been rife on the island. It was said that Fidel was going to send Cuban kids to the Soviet Union to be educated and raised there as good little Commu-nists. Luis, like thousands of others, had left Cuba for good. For more than twenty-five years he'd plied his trade as a fishing-guide around Miami, impatiently waiting for the moment of his return to the homeland.

Now he was in the vanguard of the liberation movement.

He stood on the bridge of *La Mandadera*, his binoculars trained on the dark shore five miles away. There was a half-moon and some low cloud and the sea was tranquil. Sandoval scanned the shoreline slowly. He wasn't nervous.

There! To his right he saw the sign he was looking for, a red-orange flare that ripped the darkness like a wound opening. It was followed by a constant flame, a bonfire burning on the beach. Luis Sandoval gave his crew the order to proceed. Within a mile of the place known as Cabo Gracias a Dios he would drop anchor and wait for history to take place. It did not escape his vanity that he was one of many co-authors helping to shape forthcoming events.

Twenty-three thousand miles above *La Mandadera*, a United States spy satellite that until recently had been bugged by a mysterious malfunction began to take photographs, hundreds of them, thousands, pictures that would be relayed back to a deciphering station deep in the green West Virginia countryside, where they would be processed and analyzed and, like little coded mysteries from space, broken wide open. These same photographs also showed a stormy cloud formation, as menacing in its darkness as a black hole, moving across the Gulf of Mexico and the Yucatan Peninsula toward the waters of the Caribbean.

16

On its descent into Miami the plane was buffeted like paper in a wind-tunnel. Pagan was the first person off. He entered the stuffy terminal, ploughed through customs and immigration, explained the gun and holster in his overnight bag to an ill-mannered officer who wanted to confiscate it, Scotland Yard or no Scotland Yard identification. A quick phonecall was made to Lieutenant Phillip Navarro of the Dade County Police, the name of Martin Burr was dropped, and Pagan was let through grudgingly.

He found a cab driven by a cheerful Haitian called Marcel Foucault, whose English was as thick as bouillabaisse. Pagan had Magdalena's address from the forms she'd had to complete for British immigration. It was a house in Key Biscayne. Foucault, who howled appreciatively from his window at passing women, and shook with irrepressible mirth when they responded, claimed to know Miami like a native.

Pagan had never been in this city before. Downtown was bright—office blocks blazed and hotels rose like lit glass slabs. Palm trees, tropical shrubs alongside the road, these surprised him with their alien lushness. He rolled down his window, smelled the salt air. Small man-made islands, loaded with mansions, sat in the dark of Biscayne Bay: Palm Island, San Marco, Hibiscus.

Suddenly the taxi was out over black water, suspended impossibly in the air. A bridge, of course—what else? Pagan shut his eyes, fought off a certain dizziness that assailed him. The turbulent flight, a glass of awful Sauterne on the plane, the ache in his chest—all elements that had unsettled him.

Marcel Foucault nodded toward a cluster of lights at the end of the bridge. "Zat's Key Biscayne."

The night air rushing through the window helped Pagan feel better. He thought about Magdalena. What was she going to say when he turned up on her doorstep?

He looked at the growing lights of Key Biscayne. Launches along the shoreline were tethered to private jetties that led to expensive houses. American opulence always impressed him; he thought Americans did wealth better than anybody else. They purchased more, collected more, stored more. They also produced more, ate more, drank more, and divorced more. Rich people here lived as if all America were a going-out-of-business sale.

"Yo street, ami," Marcel Foucault said. He stopped the cab outside a large house barely visible beyond dense shrubbery. Prolific plants obscured the yellow light burning beside the front doorway; thousands of moths threw themselves at the bulb, frenzied participants in mass suicide.

Pagan, a little surprised that Magdalena lived in

such a well-heeled neighborhood, stepped out. Had he expected some crummy cellar filled with anti-Fidel radicals running a leaky old printing-press? He paid the driver, then watched the cab pull away. He was apprehensive now. Given that Magdalena knew anything, was she likely to tell him? What had seemed a good idea in London now felt insubstantial to him. He wondered if painkillers had fuelled this whole transatlantic crossing, if the idea had been inspired by the actions of the chemicals absorbed in his system—a junkie's trip.

Picking up his overnight bag, Pagan moved along the pathway to the front door. He rang the bell, waited, rang again. He was aware of the malicious little eye of the peephole: somebody was watching him from inside. He heard a chain drawn back, a bolt sliding, then the door was opened.

''Frank.''

She appeared in shadow, motionless only a second before she stepped forward and, to Pagan's surprise, threw her arms around him. The embrace, unexpectedly fierce, threw him off balance. He supported himself against the door jamb even as Magdalena held on to him tightly. It was a welcome he could never have anticipated. In a black suede mini-skirt and white silk blouse, she was barefoot and delectable. She whispered his name very quietly almost as if she were afraid of breaking some spell.

She led him inside, across a large tiled hallway to a sitting-room. She switched on a soft light. The room was starkly furnished—a sofa, a chair, a table, the lamp. One of everything, he thought. She clearly didn't use this room much. It had the waxen quality of a window-display.

Still holding his hand, she led him to the sofa, then sat alongside him, curling her feet up under her body.

He noticed some slight puffiness beneath her eyes, as if she might have been crying before.

She took a cigarette pack from a pocket at the side of her skirt and lit one with a black Bic. He couldn't remember seeing her smoke before and she did it in an unpracticed way, like a thirteen-year-old schoolgirl. Something was wrong here, he thought, a sadness, a change. Her smile was a terrific effort, but it was more teeth than pleasure.

"You don't seem overwhelmingly surprised to find me on your doorstep," he said.

"The weird thing is, I just happened to be thinking about you. Lo and behold, here you are. Is it an omen?"

There was a strangeness in her manner. She was present yet absent, here yet elsewhere. "What exactly were you thinking about me?" he asked.

"How nice it would be to see you. How nice it would be to see a friendly face. I need one."

"Why so gloomy?" He laid a hand gently on her shoulder.

"I've had better days."

She blew smoke up at the ceiling. She had a wonderful throat; lined a little now—what didn't time touch?—it was still marvelous and feminine. It needed no adornment, no choker, no scarf, to make it enticing.

"You didn't come all this way just to see me," she said.

"Who else do I know in Miami?"

"You must have some business here."

"Business and pleasure. The lines get blurred where you're involved."

The telephone rang. Magdalena excused herself, rose from the sofa, and crossed the room. She turned her back to him as she picked up the receiver; when she spoke she used Spanish. The conversation was brief. She hung up, glanced at her watch, then walked back to the sofa. She didn't sit this time. Instead, she kneeled on the cushion and faced him. She lit another cigarette. Her short skirt slid up her thigh. Her black eyes were blacker than ever before. You could see all manner of sorrows in them.

"You were saying something about business," she said. There was a new note in her voice, perhaps a little impatience. Maybe the phonecall had reminded her of an appointment.

He suddenly felt scattered, weary. "I need coffee. Do you mind?"

"I made some before. It's probably still hot." She went out into the kitchen, and returned with a cup. Pagan took it, sipped slowly.

"Now," she said, and she touched the back of his hand. "Speak to me."

Pagan set his cup down. "It's a tough one."

"I'm a big girl."

"It concerns Rosabal."

"Rosabal?" She feigned innocence, her acting amateur and half-hearted.

"Ground rules," Pagan said. "No bullshit. I know more than you think. If we can both tell the truth from the beginning, it's going to save time."

She was quiet a moment. "How long have you known about him?"

"Since you were in London," Pagan said. "He was concealed—a little ignominiously, in my opinion—inside the bathroom in your hotel room."

Magdalena smiled. "I thought that was amusing. But he likes anonymity. He didn't want anyone to see him."

"A few people did. Including British intelligence.

He was followed. Not always carefully. But he was followed.''

Magdalena crushed out her cigarette in a small glass ashtray. "Okay. You know about Rafael and me. It still doesn't explain why you're here.''

Pagan told her. He did so briefly, without incidental detail. He left out the deaths of Caporelli and his associates, sketching a mosaic in which certain pieces were omitted. Halfway through the narrative Magdalena walked to the unlit fireplace and stood, legs slightly apart, hands on hips, a defensive attitude.

She waited until Pagan was finished before she said, "One thing I always liked about you, Frank. You have more imagination than a cop should. But this time I think you've gone overboard, baby." She smoked again. The small black lighter flashed; Magdalena's cheeks hollowed as she drew smoke into her lungs. She crossed to the couch and sat down.

"Overboard how?" he asked.

"Rafael and Ruhr. That's a hell of a connection. What could Rafe have in common with that maniac? And I don't see where a stolen missile fits Rafe's life, Frank.''

Rafe—the lover's abbreviation, the intimacy. The magic word that opened doors onto private worlds. Pagan stood up. His circulation was sluggish. He walked round the room. On the mantel were photographs of a man and a woman, presumably Magdalena's parents. Pagan glanced at them. Magdalena more closely resembled her father.

"When you were in London, you mentioned a coup of some kind in Cuba," Pagan said. "Is Rosabal involved?''

"You misheard me, Frank.''

"Let me rephrase it. You *hinted* at a coup.''

"I don't think so, Frank. You misunderstood."

Pagan stepped toward her, looked down at where she sat on the couch. "We agreed. No games. No bullshit."

"*You* agreed. You play by your own rules. I don't remember saying I'd comply."

"Don't fuck around with me, Magdalena. I don't have time for crap."

"Keep talking rough. I like it."

Pagan had to smile. His history with this woman, the passion locked in the past—how could he be anything other than transparent to her? How could he act demanding, and tough, and hope she'd be swayed?

She stood up, gazed into his face, then put her arms round him. Her body was limp. This was another little unexpected act. She was full of surprises tonight. What he detected in her was an unhappiness for which she hadn't found the appropriate expression, and so she held him this way, clutched him for consolation, security, light in some dark place.

He said, "Look, there's a hostage involved. A child who's only fourteen years old. There's a terrorist responsible for more deaths than I want to think about. He may hurt the kid. He may kill her, if he hasn't already. Too many people have died, Magdalena. I want the kid back. I want to know what plans there are for the missile. And I want Gunther Ruhr. I'm betting Rafael knows where to find him. You might call it a long shot, but it's better than nothing. I need to know what you know. I need anything you can give me."

Magdalena Torrente was very quiet. She disengaged herself from Pagan and walked away. She stopped at the curtained window on the other side of the room, beyond the reach of the lamp. Her features were indistinct. Ash, untended, dropped from her cigarette to the rug. *He may hurt the kid;* she couldn't stand that idea. She couldn't take the notion of any more hurt.

Pagan went to her and touched the back of her hand. She didn't look at him. She spoke in a voice filled with little catches, as though she were having trouble getting air to her lungs. Flatly, without tone, she said, "Okay, you've come a long way, you deserve to know something. I don't know a damn thing about Ruhr or any missile. All I can tell you is how things were *supposed* to be. Army officers and their troops opposed to Castro were to seize various strategic barracks. This act was intended to galvanize the democratic underground—we're talking about thousands of people, strikes, demonstrations, the occupation of public buildings, public disobedience, armed insurrection. Everything was supposedly well-orchestrated. Rafael was the leader, the organizer. The plan called for him to head the new government after Castro was deposed. The new *democratic* government, I should say. People, myself included, intended to return from exile to participate in this . . . this brave new Cuba. It was neat, simple, and it might have been relatively bloodless. But it changed."

"How?"

"The information I have indicates that Rosabal betrayed the cause." It was in her voice, her face, the burden of terrible disappointment. But more than that, Pagan thought, there was another emotion, and for want of a better word he called it grief. Magdalena wasn't grieving only for a lost cause. She'd been bloodied in love, and cut where it pained her, in her heart.

Pagan had to press on, he had to get beyond her sorrow. He hadn't come all the way to Miami to learn about the failure of a counter-revolution. He wasn't interested. He didn't give a shit about Cuba. The world stage didn't enthrall him. His own world was small, its boundaries well-marked, a specialized place in which wrongs were righted whenever that was possible and justice was more than a dry textbook notion.

He said, "Did Rosabal ever mention Ruhr to you?"

She shook her head. "Ruhr! You're obsessed, Frank. I still don't see how Ruhr comes into it. I've heard of people barking up wrong trees before now, but you get the blue ribbon."

Pagan ignored this. "What other people did our pal Rafe meet in Britain?"

"I don't have a clue, Frank."

"Think hard."

"I *am* thinking."

Now there was an impatient edge in her voice; she was tired of questions. She'd been asking them of herself all day long, ever since the meeting with Garrido and Duran. Question after question; they distilled themselves into one simple inquiry: Why had Rafael betrayed her?

She clenched her hands and strolled the room, confined by walls and ceilings. She'd gone over her relationship with Rosabal for hours, tracing it from the first meeting—Acapulco, instant attraction, common political convictions, sex marked as much by passion as by tenderness, the kind that grew, at least as far as she was concerned, into love—to the last encounter in London. *I love him*, she thought. And she wanted to believe, despite her weakening conviction, that he loved her, that he had justifiable reasons for his apparent treachery, that the democratic revolution was still a possibility. But the obstacles were so damned hard to overcome.

That day she'd walked the streets of Little Havana with dear old Garrido, arm-in-arm under the noonday sun. Solicitous Garrido, old family friend. Kindly Garrido, his spindly hand wrapped around hers. He talked of love in an airy way, as if it were a book he'd read seventy years ago and all he recalled were pages of parchment now crumbled. He spoke of the manner in which love was often victimized, brutalized, how there were demarcation lines of the emotions across which warring lovers skirmished, leaving the losers battered.

This was not language to which Magdalena Torrente was accustomed. She was no loser. No victim. And she had no intention of becoming one so long as there was a chance still that Rafael loved her; and in that inviolate part of her, free of shadows and doubts, her knowledge was certain: *Rafael loved her.*

The great trick was to keep reality from intruding.

In a situation like this, where trust has been so badly violated, there are not many choices; something has to be done, Garrido had said when they were drinking coffee in the Versailles restaurant. He had shrugged then, an eloquent gesture of disappointment and hatred, and yet there was nothing of surprise in it, as if he'd plumbed the human condition so deeply there were no astonishments left to him. He had been cheated, and his dreams abruptly ended.

Pagan held both her hands and said, "I wish I didn't have to ask you all these bloody questions."

"I don't have answers, Frank."

He was silent for a time. "How exactly did Rosabal betray you?"

"Begin with the matter of his wife."

"Wives tend to be problematic. Maybe he intends to leave her. Who knows?"

"I'm told he only just married her, but I love you for your optimism, Frank." Magdalena looked down at how her hands were firmly held by Pagan's, and she enjoyed the sense of security in the touch. She raised her face, tiptoed, kissed the side of his mouth.

She said, "I'm just a casualty of the heart. Other people were shafted in their pocketbooks. He's pretty generous when it comes to spreading treachery around. Over a period of three or four years thousands of exiled Cubans in Miami and New Jersey contributed millions of dollars to the overthrow of Castro. Most of it ended up—guess where?"

"In Rafael's pocket?"

"That's what they tell me, Frank."

"Here's what I don't get. If he's a common embezzler, he'd take the money and that would be it. End of. But what the hell is he doing involved with Gunther Ruhr? And this whole missile affair—what is his part in that?"

She shrugged. "You've come three thousand miles for nada except to see a poor confused woman whose brain is scrambled eggs. I don't have answers for you."

Pagan stepped away from her, finished his coffee, set down the cup. He had a hollow moment of sheer fatigue. He went to the kitchen and poured another coffee, then returned. Magdalena stood in the center of the floor, hugging herself as if she were cold. She seemed smaller now, diminished in a way, as if Rafe, Captain Charm, had stolen more than her love.

He sipped coffee. There was a key here, he was sure of it, a key that would unlock all the doors that puzzled him, that would allow him access to the room that contained Ruhr and Stephanie Brough. And that key was Rafael, pretender, embezzler, pirate of people's money, swindler of feelings.

Rafael had played along with this democratic underground in Cuba and the great outswelling of patriotic sentiment in the exile communities for his own ends, obviously.

But what were those ends?

Frank, what did all ambitious men seek, for God's sake?

Control. Beyond money, that's what they lusted after, dreamed of, salivated over, schemed and cheated for, maimed and killed for. That's what obsessed them and drove some of them to an odd vindictive madness. They became possessed by the very thing they'd tried to own: solitary control, the chance to shape their little corner of the world to their own liking.

Was that it? Did Rafael want Cuba in such a way that he didn't have to share it with any squabble of exiles who believed in something as primitive and muddle-headed as, heaven forbid, *democracy?* His own private sand-castle, his own fantasy, a place where he could rule the tides. Did it come down to that in the end?

Only Rafe would know.

Where did the missile fit? Where did Caporelli and Chapotin and Kluger come into this picture? Why were these men dying?

Missiles weren't for firing in this day and age. They were playing-cards, toys owned by the richest kids on the block, useful when you needed to flex a little muscle, make a demand, or simply just threaten.

Pagan shut his eyes. *Had Caporelli and friends wanted their bit of Cuba too?*

In the late 1950s Caporelli already had a taste for the place; so, presumably, had Jean-Paul Chapotin. Maybe they liked the island the way it used to be—after all, hadn't it made Caporelli wealthy? It probably hadn't exactly hurt Jean-Paul either. But they couldn't turn clocks back as long as Fidel ran the country.

Solution: get rid of Fidel. How?

A missile on the island would have the effect of—

Of what?

Of making a whole lot of people in this hemisphere rather unhappy.

So what?

Shit, it was slipping away from him.

Fatigued, he sat down on the sofa.

Magdalena sat beside him. "You look exhausted. Why don't you rest for a while? Stretch out here."

Pagan had the feeling again that he was missing something simple. But Rafe had the answer. Only Rafe.

"I don't have time to rest," he said. He stood up. Bones creaked: the small embarrassment of age.

She looked at her wristwatch. "I have to go out, Frank."

"A late date?"

"Something like that. You can stay here if you like." She walked across the room to the stairs leading to the upper part of the house. After a few minutes she came back down, dressed now in a tan leather jacket and blue jeans and looking in her paleness rather fragile.

"Where are you going?" he asked. She didn't exactly look dressed for any commonplace date.

"Out." She had an ambivalent little smile. He noticed a slightly crooked molar, a tiny flaw he'd quite forgotten, and he remembered how he'd once been enchanted by this trifling imperfection because it humanized her beauty. *Smile for me, come on:* had he really said such things back then and loved her so insanely that the sight of a crooked tooth drove him out of his skull?

"And I twiddle my thumbs? Wait for you to come back? I don't have time for that."

"I don't know how long I'll be gone. And I can't help you. I can't tell you any more than I already have, and even that was more than I wanted."

He was irritated by her furtive manner, her secrecy, the way she was dismissing him.

She made to move past him. He placed himself in her way.

"Why the great hurry?"

"I'm sick of questions, Frank. I'm sick of the ones you've been asking and I'm sick of the ones I've been asking myself."

He moved to one side and she crossed the hallway to unlock the door to the garage. Pagan followed her. There was a gray BMW in the garage.

"I'm leaving alone, Frank. I don't want company."

"And I don't want to be stranded here."

"Call a cab."

"I'll ride with you. Take me back to Miami. Drop me off at a hotel. I won't get in your way."

She sighed. "You're a determined bastard."

She got in on the driver's side; Pagan slid into the passenger seat. The garage doors opened by remote control. They slid up, revealing the dark garden in front. She steered forward, the door closed behind her. Then she was out on the street, driving with a carelessness that didn't thrill Pagan, who hated being the passenger anyway.

The BMW approached an intersection, darkened houses, dim lamplights. Magdalena slowed just a little when a large Buick entered the intersection out of nowhere and wheeled straight toward the German car; surprised, Magdalena shoved her foot on the gas pedal and the BMW thrust forward, avoiding the larger car by a couple of feet. Pagan turned his head, saw the Buick brake, swing in an arc, clamber up on the sidewalk in a series of small sparks, then come back again—directly at Magdalena's car. She evaded the Buick a second time, but only just.

"Jesus Christ!" Magdalena said. "What the hell's going on?"

Pagan didn't answer. He looked back at the big, powerful Buick as it passed beneath a streetlight. Two figures occupied the sleek vehicle—a gunman and a driver. The gunman leaned from the passenger window. The weapon he held was a magnum. A single shot cracked the air; it struck the rear bumper of the BMW, ricocheted.

The Buick roared, veering from side to side in an attempt to draw level with the BMW, striking curbs, scraping the sides of parked cars, propelled by one murderous purpose. The gunman was still hanging from the window, but the Buick was shuddering in such a way that accuracy was out of the question. When he fired a second time he hit the trunk of the BMW, a dramatic noise like that of a drum struck hard.

Now Magdalena was approaching the Rickenbacker Causeway which linked Key Biscayne with Miami, a long stretch over black water. The Buick persisted, tracking the BMW at a distance of some fifteen or twenty feet. It had all the reality of a dream, Pagan thought—this absurd chase across Biscayne Bay, the gunman in the Buick, the salt wind that rolled through the open windows of the BMW. Indisputably real was the next gunshot, the bullet that smashed this time through the rear window and whined inside the BMW and passed between Magdalena and Pagan and departed by way of the windshield. As close as you want to come to death, he thought.

There was other traffic on the bridge but sparse at this time of day. A few cars came to a halt as the BMW and the Buick screeched past. Halfway across the Causeway the Buick found reserves of speed and moved up alongside the BMW and the gunman fired directly through the passenger window. Pagan heard it, felt it, understood that this particular bullet might have had his name and number on it; but it ripped the air around his neck and sliced harmlessly past Magdalena, who gasped at the proximity of death.

It was time to shoot back. He'd been delaying in the hope that Magdalena would outrun the other car and thus make it unnecessary for him to fire his gun— he hated the combustible mixture of stray bullets and innocent onlookers in their parked cars—but the Buick clearly had muscle and wasn't going to be outmaneuvered.

The faces of the men in the American car were plainly visible to Pagan under the Causeway lamps. The gunman was square-jawed and blond; he might have been a man peddling door to door some religion or sectarian magazine—Mormonism or *The Watchtower*. The driver was a contrast, dark hair, a brutal little mouth.

Pagan shoved his gun through the window and fired. He missed first time. His second shot must have struck the driver because the dark-haired man raised his hands from the steering-wheel as if it had become suddenly too hot to touch and the Buick, without guidance, skidded out of control. There was one heart-chilling moment in which the laws of physics appeared to have been contravened when the Buick went sliding toward the edge of the bridge and rose a couple of inches before rushing through the barrier and soaring out, like some doomed flying-machine from Detroit, into the air above Biscayne Bay. With its horn sounding in panic, it twisted as it fell, as if trying to right itself in midair. It struck the spooky black waters, tossed up a vast white garland of foam, and then sunk hood-first into the wet darkness. Its tail-lights, lit still, went under like the red eyes of a creature resigned to drowning.

Pagan sat back in his seat, stretched his legs, and caught his breath. He shut his eyes.

At the end of the Causeway, Magdalena turned the car into a quiet street behind Brickell Avenue, a place of darkened office buildings. She laid her face upon the rim of the steering-wheel. Her knuckles were the color of ivory. She was drained.

"Were they after you or me?" she asked, a breathless quality in her voice.

"I don't know," Pagan replied.

Magdalena slumped back in her seat, turned her face toward him. "If they were after you, how did they know you were here? Did you tell anyone you were coming to Miami?"

"Only the Commissioner."

"And you trust him?"

"Beyond a doubt." A leak, Pagan thought, even as he answered Magdalena's question. A leak had led to the horror of Shepherd's Bush. Perhaps the same mysterious source was behind the gunman, somebody no scrambled telephones could ever frustrate, somebody privileged, somebody with an inside track.

"If nobody knows *you're* here, it follows that I was the target," she said.

"Maybe. But who sent the hit man?"

"Christ, I don't even want to speculate," she said. And she didn't; thinking led to a cerebral boulevard on which all traffic was stalled. Magdalena was afraid, but she didn't like to show fear. She could collect herself only if she shut out of her mind the unpleasantness on the bridge. Her brain was running on empty. She'd done nothing but think and brood ever since she'd gone that morning to Garrido's restaurant.

Who could have wanted her dead anyway? The only candidate that came to mind was the last one she wanted to consider: *Rafael*. If he was really through with her, maybe his next step was to get her out of the way permanently. Maybe he thought her a potential embarrassment to him, a risk. She pushed these ideas aside. She had to believe that the intended target was Pagan, not her, to believe without question that Rafael had nothing to do with it.

For his part Pagan was weary of puzzles; he yearned for solutions. Hard answers. Facts. Puzzles became jungles, overgrown and mazelike; he needed a pathway through the thickets, a machete.

"You can get out here," she said. "You'll find a hotel within a couple of blocks."

"Maybe we should stick together. The waterlogged pair in that Buick might have friends in the vicinity."

She reached across him, opened the passenger door. "Don't worry about me. I'm just sorry you came all this way, Frank." She kissed him quickly on the side of his face. "Good luck."

Pagan stepped out with great reluctance. No sooner had he moved than she pulled the door shut behind him and slipped the car into gear. He gazed at her face behind glass, thinking how forlorn she looked; she stared at him, smiling in an ungenerous way, a distracted little expression. He was irritated for having given in to her without an argument. He should have insisted, stayed with her no matter where she was headed.

But how could he? There was an urgency in him still, a drive to explore his only other connection, even though he thought he might be too late. What had

Magdalena told him anyway? Nothing he could use. Nothing that would bring him closer to what he sought.

He watched her gray car pass under dull streetlamps until it turned a corner and disappeared.

The street was now vaguely menacing like all empty streets that lie behind major thoroughfares. Pagan walked in the direction of Brickell Avenue, where it was brighter and busier and the shadows less complex. He found a hotel. As soon as he entered the vast lobby, where enormous palms and ferns reached up to a tall ceiling, he walked to the bank of public telephones beyond the registration desk.

As he flipped through the pages of the phone directory, he realized he'd left his overnight bag at Magdalena's house. What the hell. He still had his gun, wallet, passport, painkillers; the rest was just luggage.

Havana

Rafael Rosabal left his pleasantly spacious apartment in the Vedado at one AM. His wife Estela, her long black hair undone and spread upon her lace pillow, woke when she heard him move quietly across the bedroom. She whispered to him, but he didn't hear, or if he did he was in too much of a hurry to pay attention. They'd made love some hours before, Rosabal curiously mechanical, distracted, Estela unpracticed and still shy with her own and her husband's body. Sex was a disappointment to her; Rafael, who had known many women, loved her as though his mind and body were elsewhere.

Now he was leaving and still she hadn't mentioned the miracle of her pregnancy.

She listened to the sound of a car arrive outside, then the front door of the apartment closed softly. Sometimes Estela suspected a mistress, someone to whom Rafael hurried, someone in whose heated embrace he found the passion he so clearly hadn't discovered in his marriage. The thought terrified her, all the more so because she could never imagine this woman's face. Once, waiting in this apartment for Rafael to come home, she'd envisaged a face without features, smooth and eyeless and terrible.

At other times Estela believed her only true rival was Rafael's ambition, a far more dangerous enemy than any woman would have been. He restlessly drove himself, spurred himself on, pursuing furtive goals; there was that strange, secretive business involving her father, the General, and his intermediary Alonzo-Diaz—who came to the apartment late at night to whisper with Rafael—but Estela, though she eavesdropped, pretended to have no interest in politics and all the intrigues and gossip it entailed.

However, absolutely nothing that happened in this apartment escaped her. Everything she heard she stored away at the back of her mind. She was never noticed eavesdropping because she was never really noticed at all—she poured wine, made coffee; a walk-on role, a serving girl, the Minister's young and rather vapid wife, pretty but awfully sentimental. But she was smaller than anyone knew. She listened as thoroughly as any bug planted inside a telephone receiver or under the lip of a table or smuggled at the core of a rose, and she memorized what she heard. In a life that was mainly empty, rescued from total vacuity by visits to beauty parlors and hairdressers and those infrequent times when Rafael deigned to screw her, listening and storing up items of information were her principal pastimes.

Whatever was going on, the quiet phonecalls, the late-night conferences, the mysterious comings and goings, the talk of ships and military movements, and the mention of this man Ruhr, whose name was whispered as though it were too evil to pronounce aloud, made her uneasy. She worried about her husband; she worried too about General Capablanca, whose most recent utterances in her company were venomously anti-Castro.

She despised Castro as much as anyone, but she understood the dangers involved in plotting against the *fidelistas.* People vanished abruptly in the middle of the night and were never heard of again; friends and acquaintances, even those who had once been close to Fidel himself—nobody was immune. She wanted nothing to happen to either Rafael or the General. Nobody had succeeded in overthrowing El Viejo, and Estela doubted that anyone ever could.

She had been a young woman of privilege in a country that had officially abandoned elitism; unofficially, by rewarding those in favored positions of power, the system had created a new set of inequities, and Estela had benefitted—a school in Switzerland, a year in France, a summer in Spain. She'd been exposed to freedoms in other countries, and ways unthinkable in Cuba, which she saw now was something of a silly little backwater, crude and unfashionable, a slab of miserably humid land in the Caribbean run by ruffians and gangsters and fought over as if it were Eldorado by men who put vanity before peace, martyrdom before liberty.

But nothing in her experience had prepared her for this undertow of doom that racked her as she walked to the window and looked down. Absently she stroked her stomach, flat now but soon to be big like a flower newly opened; and yet even the notion of this beautiful baby did not diminish the sense of dark fate she felt. Moonlight lay across the surface of the swimming-pool. The lights of her husband's car faded between palm trees, and then were gone out of sight. She crossed herself because she wanted divine protection for her husband.

Had Rafael seen her, he might have mocked her idiot superstition.

The car, driven by Rosabal's chauffeur, went as far as Havana harbor, where Rosabal got out. He carefully descended a flight of old stone steps, slippery, studded with barnacles. He paused where the water lapped this ancient stonework. The boat that awaited him was a black, high-speed cigarette-boat, the kind favored by gun-runners and dope smugglers. It was occupied by two men in shirtsleeves; Rosabal recognized them as attachés to Capablanca. They seemed undignified out of uniform.

He stepped into the boat. The motor started. The craft speeded across the harbor. Rosabal looked up at the sky; the moon was behind clouds. A brisk wind cuffed the surface of the sea. He turned to gaze back at Havana, which was mainly dark. Now and again measures were taken to save electricity. Elevators failed to work, streetlights went out, homes were deprived of power. This, Rosabal thought, was Communism in the late twentieth century, a compendium of broken promises and lies, a putrefaction held together by the weakening glue that was *fidelisma*.

No more. Before this day was out it would be boxed for burial, with nobody to weep for it.

President Rafael Rosabal. He liked the sound of it, the ring, the pleasing timbre. Rosabal's regime would be neither democratic nor, like that of Castro, puritanical and prohibitive. It would be a benign dictatorship, at least in the beginning; somewhere along the way, years from now, there might be a measure of popular participation. But first the people had to be weaned from the mindlessness in which Castro had raised them, they had to be freed from the shopworn cant of Marxism. The citizens were like little kids who'd never chewed on anything but the mush provided to them by Fidel. They had to be led to the table and shown how to use a knife and fork and eat real food.

Those disgusting agencies of grass-roots espionage, the Committees for the Defense of the Revolution, would be abolished and their leaders jailed. The ministries, bureaucracies gone mad with that special insanity of paperwork, would be stripped to nothing and the ministers demoted or incarcerated. He would be cautious at first about the use of firing-squads: why alienate the West as Fidel had done thirty years ago? The nightclubs would open again and there would be gambling and if a man wanted a prostitute in Havana, that was his own business; the government would take its cut. Sin would be highly taxed.

American and European investors would be courted avidly, Soviet advisors ejected. Nor would Rosabal be blackmailed by the demands of the United States for representative democracy and human rights legislation; in any event, the Americans would be so gratified, at least for years to come, by the end of Cuban Communism, that political and social 'irregularities' would be overlooked.

Rosabal thought of Cuba as a big dark arena; and he had his hand on the generator that would set it brilliantly alight. His hand, nobody else's. And because he controlled the generator, he had access not only to light but wealth, great wealth, obscene wealth, the kind of riches that a boy from Guantanamo Province should not even dream about. He'd milk Cuba; he'd plunder it as it had never been plundered before. And he'd do it with a benefactor's smile on his face for an exultant populace that considered him a hero, the one who had rid Cuba of Castro.

Havana dwindled, the shoreline receded. Twelve miles out a yacht appeared, a dark-hulled fifty-footer equipped with communications hardware and a mass of antennae. A light blinked three times. Rosabal knew the signal. He was to board the yacht, *La Danzarina della Mar.*

The cigarette-boat moved alongside *La Danzarina.* Rosabal reached for the rope ladder that hung from the side of the yacht and climbed nimbly up to the deck.

"Rafael, my friend."

The man who stepped toward Rosabal had a pleasant smile, although not one that Rosabal readily trusted. Despite the fact it was night, he wore tinted glasses. He was dressed in a double-breasted blazer and smart gray flannels and expensive sneakers which looked as if they'd never before been worn. They squeaked on the teak deck.

Hands were clasped, warmly shaken. Both men walked along the deck; in the shadows white-shirted crew members kept careful watch, as if they expected a murderous assault from the ocean. Rosabal leaned against the handrail. Havana was almost imperceptible now. There were brief flickers of lightning from the Gulf of Mexico far to the west.

"It doesn't look like much from here, does it, Rafael?"

Rosabal agreed.

"Just the same, a whole lot of people have gone to a whole lot of trouble over that island, Rafael. A speck on the globe, nothing more. And it gets all kind of people in a lather."

"A hundred thousand square kilometers of real estate," Rosabal said.

"Which makes people very greedy."

"As you say."

The man took off his tinted glasses. "Are you going to give me what I want, Rafael?"

"Of course. You have my word."

"No Communist experiments. No flirting with the Soviet bloc. You want loans, you want agricultural machinery, you want certain types of weapons, you want technical advisors, you come to Washington. I don't expect you to smell like a rose, Rafael. You're going to be a very rich man, and very rich men never smell quite right somehow. But I expect you to play fair with me and my government. We're prepared to overlook some things—after all, you've got a long teething period to go through. Just don't overdo it. No excesses, no blatant transgressions, and we'll all be happy." The man was silent, gazing toward Cuba with a proprietorial air. "Let's face it, the Caribbean is America's swimming-pool, Rafael. Nobody wants litter in their pool, do they? Nobody wants to swim in dirty water."

"We have a firm agreement. I will not go back on anything." Rosabal looked closely at the other man. He noticed for the first time a flesh-colored strip of Bandaid at the side of the man's forehead.

"Been in the wars, Allen?"

Allen Falk patted the back of Rosabal's hand. "Your people got their timing wrong."

"I heard about it. What can I say? They're zealous men."

"They blew up the limo before they were supposed to. I happened to be a spectator. It's nothing."

Rafael Rosabal smiled. "We made amends, of course. Harry Hurt was shot some hours ago in Washington."

Falk slid his hands into the pockets of his blazer. He looked like an amateur yachtsman readying himself for a photograph. "Poor Harry and that goddam society of his. Greedy men. Men like that always want more. They don't know when to stop."

"They were very useful. They served a purpose."

Both men were silent. The wind blew again, flapping Falk's pants against his legs, tossing Rosabal's collar up against his cheek, shaking the antennae on board.

Rosabal enjoyed how he'd played the Society for all it was worth, how he'd borrowed men from General Capablanca's Secret Service, his private corps elite killers, shadowy, lethal men who had all the feelings of machines, how they'd murdered the members of the Society—each of whom thought his membership such a big secret—one by one. Now the Society was dying, and with it all its hopes of controlling Cuba. Hurt and Caporelli and the others had been used, deceived in the most brutal way; they'd financed an army, stolen a missile, purchased a counter-revolution—and for what?

So that Rafael Rosabal could become the new President of a new Cuba.

Falk said, "There was one tiny fruit-fly in our nice shiny apple, Rafael. A British cop called Pagan." Falk looked at his watch, a slender disc on his wrist. "He wanted to talk to you about Gunther Ruhr, as I understand. Keen sort of guy. Anxious to get Ruhr."

"Pagan," Rosabal said, thinking of London, of Magdalena, the hotel room. He remembered Frank Pagan. "I notice you use the past tense."

Al Falk, city dweller, accustomed only to the copper-tinted broth of pollution, took an exaggerated lungful of sea air. "One of Harry Hurt's last acts was to arrange for Pagan's demise. He knew all these Soldier of Fortune nuts who kill for five hundred bucks and a new subscription to that magazine. Good old Harry. Reliable to the end. Frank Pagan is probably dead by this time."

Rosabal frowned. Why did he feel a small cloud cross his mind just then? He thought of Magdalena and wondered if she had been a source of information for the English policeman—but what could Magdalena possibly tell Pagan anyhow? Nothing that could ever be proved. She could at best babble about how democracy was on its way to Cuba, and perhaps how she had ferried money for the new revolution, and the part she expected to play in Cuba's future; that was it, that was all. Silly chatter. *Balbuceo,* nothing more. And Magdalena was good at it; she was just as good at babbling about her Cuban dreams as she was in bed.

He asked, "How did Pagan connect Ruhr to me?"

Falk drummed a hand on the rail and said, "It's my understanding that you rented a house for the German. You were remembered. Bad move, Rafael. You could have found somebody else to rent the place on your behalf."

"There wasn't anybody else. Who could I have trusted? In any case, it had to be done quickly. There was no time to think. Every policeman in Britain was looking for Ruhr."

Rosabal remembered the haste with which he had to find an isolated house where Ruhr could be hidden.

He'd been moving too fast to think with any real clarity. When he'd rented the farmhouse he had done so under Jean-Paul Chapotin's name, believing that if the cops discovered Ruhr's hiding-place they would never associate Gunther with the Cuban Minister of Finance. Instead, they might dig into Chapotin's life and find their way into the Society of Friends, which would have served its purpose by that time and become excess baggage. One of those moments, rare in Rosabal's life, when he'd mistaken quick thinking for cleverness; the crazy old broad who'd rented the place to him had a sharper memory than he'd thought. She must have described him at least well enough for him to be identified.

But none of this mattered now.

In a few short hours, dawn would be breaking.

Falk said, "What about Freddie Kinnaird?"

Rosabal was quiet for a moment, as if he were deciding, in the manner of an emperor, Kinnaird's fate. "Freddie has been very helpful. He always kept us informed of the Society's plans and the members' movements. Friends in high places are usually useful."

"I hear a but, Rafael."

"Your hearing's good. It has to come to an end for Freddie. It's over. I'll issue the order personally."

"He expected a generous slice of Cuba," Falk said.

"Then his expectations are not going to be fulfilled. He knows too much. A man with his kind of knowledge can be a nuisance."

Falk paused a moment, as if Kinnaird's fate troubled him. Then he said, "Speaking of friends in high places, your friends in Washington send their greetings and look forward to your success."

"I'm grateful," Rosabal said.

He turned his face to Florida. Miami was where

those troublesome *idiotas* gathered, those roaring political dreamers who banged their drums for freedom and
talked in the cafes in Little Havana and in large houses
in Key Biscayne about taking Cuba back. They were
fools, and potentially bothersome to Rosabal. Men like
Garrido and his large network of cronies, the bankers
and politicians and restaurateurs, the TV station propri-
etors and Hispanic newspapermen and rich physicians,
all the money men who were in the vanguard of the
Committee for the Restoration of Democracy in
Cuba—they were his future enemies. After all, he had
stolen from them; and what he had taken was more
than just cash.

Were they likely to leave him alone after Castro
had been toppled?

Of course not. They would turn against him when
they understood he had no intention of bringing their
kind of democracy to Cuba. Left to themselves, they
would go on raising funds and promoting their moronic
ideals and stirring up endless trouble for him; they
wouldn't leave him in peace.

And Magdalena. Don't forget Magdalena.

She would come to haunt him in time. When she
discovered how she had been betrayed, she'd find a way
somehow to make his life difficult. These were not
guesses; these were certainties he had understood from
the very beginning.

He couldn't allow anyone to trouble him. He had
come too far. Everything was within his grasp; he had
only to reach a little further.

Falk said, "We have detailed satellite photographs
in our possession. All we need now are photographs of
the missile *in situ* on Cuba. I don't want anything that
looks faked. I want good clear pictures of the missile
on its launcher. I don't want anybody to be in a posi-

tion to accuse us of doctoring anything, if such a situation should ever arise."

"You'll have wonderful pictures," Rosabal said.

He turned his face away from Florida. Lightning came out of the west again, illuminating sea and sky with bright silver. Rosabal enjoyed the stark brightness, the light-show. A storm was gathering in that direction and the wind that sloughed round the yacht was stronger than before. He thought briefly of the signed order, purportedly from the Lider Maximo, that Capablanca had in his possession. The signature was a forgery, but what did that matter? Good forgeries went undetected as long as people were desperate to believe they were the real thing. How many forged paintings hung in museums? How many fake historical documents lay in glass display cabinets?

Falk said, "As soon as the pictures are taken, I expect to receive your message that the missile has been destroyed."

"I see no problem with that. It's exactly as we agreed."

"I'm still just a little worried about your technicians, Rafael."

"Why? They know how to disarm a nuclear warhead. After all, they learned something from their Soviet masters. They're good men. They know exactly what to do. Believe me. Besides, what is the alternative? To send in some American technicians? Direct U.S. involvement?"

Falk, his hair made unruly by wind, leaned against the rail. Open U.S. involvement was not an option. If Rafael was convinced of his technicians' qualifications, why should he bicker and worry? He said, "Expect the full media treatment, Rafael. The man who dismantled Castro and his missile. You'll be a hero."

Rosabal said, "I expect nothing for myself. Only for Cuba."

Bullshit, Falk thought. "A certain amount of fame is inevitable, Rafael."

"Possibly," Rosabal said. "But Cuba comes first."

Falk looked toward the island. His heart fluttered in his chest, as if he'd been given his first French kiss; after more than thirty years of longing, and watching, and waiting, he was going to see Castro fall. In the intensity of his desire he was blind to any other possibilities; failure was not even a consideration. Everything was going to fit together and function. He believed in cycles of history; the circle in which Castro would be crushed was almost closed.

He turned his face back to Rosabal, remembering now how they had first met during a conference of the Organization of American States in Costa Rica five years ago. The subject of the conference had been the economics of Central American republics, and the massive debts most of them had incurred. Far from the public arena, from the podium where delegates made their angry official speeches and railed at the unjust practices of the World Bank, they discovered a common interest in the future of Cuba after Fidel. They spent many hours together in a quiet resort hotel near the coast, enjoying the excellent pina coladas, the late-night visitations of exquisite call-girls, and—above all else—a sense of conspiracy that was aphrodisiacal. Although both men were initially discreet, circumspect to the point of obscurity, their mutual confidence grew and they talked more openly as the days passed; it was vividly clear to each of them that unless Fidel were 'removed' then Cuba was doomed.

It started with that simple notion: the replacement of Castro with a non-Communist, democratic regime in which bankers and investors might have faith. If the proposition was simple, the execution was not. It required all of Falk's cunning and patience to hammer together the strategy that would bring down Castro and elevate Rosabal. It required financial partners, men like Harry Hurt and Sheridan Perry and their Society, money men whose greed could always be counted upon to overwhelm their misgivings. Hurt and the others had to be brought into the scheme in such a way that they might eventually credit *themselves* with the glorious idea of bringing down Castro in the first place. But the plan required more than Hurt's merry gang—there had to be cooperation in certain Government and intelligence agencies, there had to be a force in Cuba itself that Rosabal could galvanize when the time came. So many elements, so many different instruments; but Falk, concertmaster, conductor, knew how to syncopate the music and make it coherently sweet.

Falk stared back in the direction of Cuba. He was under no illusion that Rosabal's regime would exist three or four years from now. All Cuban administrations, no matter how sound in the beginning, sooner or later deteriorated into ill-tempered factions and violence and corruption of a kind the United States could not officially tolerate. But in the meantime President Rosabal would be tolerable, and friendly, and the honeymoon between the U.S. and Cuba would vibrate with fresh enthusiasms and some satisfying intercourse. A pro-American government, corrupt or otherwise, was forever preferable to Communism in any form.

Rosabal looked at his watch. "It's time for me to leave. When we meet again, Allen, it will be in Havana."

"I look forward to that," Falk said.

"A new Havana," Rosabal added, smiling his best and brightest smile, which flashed in the dark.

Miami

Magdalena Torrente parked her car behind the Casa de la Media Noche in Little Havana. The restaurant was closed for the night, although lights were still lit in the dining-room and the jukebox was playing a mambo and a fat man was dancing with a hesitant skinny woman between the tables. Magdalena stepped into the alley behind the building. Garrido, who had been expecting her, opened the door before she knocked. In his white suit he seemed to shimmer. An hallucination, she thought. Like everything else that had happened.

He held the door open for her, then closed it. They went inside the windowless box room stacked with cans of tomatoes and sacks of rice. She suddenly longed for a view of something, anything at all. A vista. She clenched her hands and said, "I love him. I've worried it every way I can and I come to the same conclusion every goddam time. I love him."

Garrido nodded his head. "I know," he said quietly. He thought: *It is your love that makes you the only choice, Magdalena. It is your love and pain.* He was filled with melancholy suddenly, as if he were remembering the lost love of his own life, Magdalena Torrente's mother Oliva; it was all so long ago, ancient history. Just the same, he was glad there was so little resemblance between the dead woman and her daughter.

"You look tired," he said.

"I'm fine, really I'm fine."

Garrido caressed her hair with his hand. A small electric shock flashed across his palm. "Are you sure? Absolutely sure? Do you have the energy, *querida?*"

For a second she gazed up into the bare lightbulb that illuminated the room. She remembered the lights of the Buick on the causeway, the way they burned in her rearview mirror; she heard again the noise of the big car going through the barrier and over the side.

She blinked, then looked at Garrido. She said, "I'm sure."

He went to his secret compartment in the wall behind the shelves. He removed a green pouch, which he handed to her. "Some things you may need."

She took the pouch but didn't open it.

Garrido kissed her on the forehead; the touch of his lips was dry and avuncular and his cigar breath not exactly pleasant and the scent of brilliantine on his hair cloying. But she had the thought that at least there was no treachery, no betrayal, in the old man's gesture.

17

Miami

Lieutenant Phillip Navarro of the Dade County Police was an uncommon kind of cop, articulate, smart, inquisitive, loaded down with none of the weariness and cynicism, the suggestion of emotional numbness you sometimes find in forty year old policemen. He had enthusiasm still, a vitality Pagan liked. He was short and slim, his face boyish; to offset this impression of youth he'd grown a thick moustache and wore a somber three-piece suit of the kind you might encounter in the lobby of a Hilton during a bankers' convention. He listened to Pagan's convoluted story with the look of an impartial but kindly branch manager about to make a loan to somebody with no collateral.

Navarro was a big fan of Martin Burr, who had apparently deported a notorious Colombian drug lord from the United Kingdom some years ago, a man Navarro wanted for a variety of crimes in Florida. Burr had smoothed the extradition process, over-riding paperwork and red-tape, and Navarro had always been grateful. It was this gratitude that Frank Pagan hoped to tap now as he sat in the Lieutenant's cramped office, whose window looked over a lamplit yard containing impounded cars. On the wall behind Navarro's desk hung framed awards commending him for his civic work and his marksmanship.

Navarro said, "With your British passport you can enter Cuba legally. Fly out of Miami to Jamaica or Mexico City, get a visa, fly to Havana. I don't see any problem there."

"That takes too much time," Pagan said. "I'm looking for a fast alternative."

"The age of immediacy," Navarro said, and sighed, as if he longed for slower eras. He rose from his chair and walked to the window where he leaned his forehead against the pane a moment. "When I got your call, first thing I did was check you out with Martin Burr."

"And?"

"He asked me to extend the hand of cooperation. Said you were sometimes on the headstrong side but otherwise okay."

"Good of him."

"Also you were less than objective at times."

"Character analysis isn't Martin's strong point," Pagan remarked. "Besides, objectivity's overrated. I get involved."

"At the gut level," Navarro said.

"Usually."

Navarro, who had no great regard for professional detachment himself, liked Frank Pagan. He turned from the window. "I'm happy to extend the hand of cooperation. I'm just not sure how far it should go. If I understand you, what you're asking me to do is break the law."

"Purely in a technical sense," Pagan said.

"Easy for you to say, Frank. I live here. You don't."

"I don't have your connections in this town, Phil. I don't know where to go, who to ask. If I did, I wouldn't have come here and bothered you."

Navarro remembered now that Martin Burr had mentioned something about how persistent Pagan could be. Worse than a bloody door-to-door salesman, Burr had said. "What makes you sure Rosabal can help you?"

"I never said I was sure. Put it another way. I'm running very low on options, Phil. I have to talk to Rosabal. It might be a dead end, but right now I don't have anywhere else to go."

Navarro sat up on the edge of his desk, swung one leg back and forth, looked sympathetic. He had been in predicaments similar to Pagan's, when you had nothing more than some bare hunch to base your actions on and your superiors quibbled about the adequacy of your instincts. *You can't make a case on your intuitions, Phil*—he'd heard it all before.

Another reason he was sympathetic to Pagan was because the man had been at the very center of the Shepherd's Bush Massacre, which—according to Martin Burr—had made Pagan understandably anxious, some might even say overly so. A smidgen of kindness would not go amiss, Burr had added. Phil Navarro, surrounded every day of his life with news of murdered colleagues in the continuing drug wars of Dade County, hadn't grown immune to the shock of loss he felt when he heard of policemen slain on duty.

"What you want is tricky," he said. "Also risky."

"I expected that," Pagan remarked.

Navarro, who had recently quit smoking, took a

wooden toothpick from a container on his desk and poked his lower teeth with it. "Costly too, Frank."

"That might be a problem," Pagan said. He had about four hundred dollars in traveller's checks and a Visa card whose limit was dangerously close. "I assume that nobody in this clandestine line of business takes plastic?"

Navarro smiled and said, "The only plastic they understand is the kind that explodes. But my credit's always good in certain circles. There's always somebody happy to please Lieutenant Navarro. You know how it is."

"I know exactly how it is," Pagan said. In London he had his own pool of shady characters who were always delighted to score points with him. They reasoned, quite rightly, that it was better to have Pagan on your side than against you.

"Okay." Navarro snapped his toothpick, discarded it. "I'll make a phonecall. I'm going to have to ask you to wait outside, Frank."

Pagan understood. He found a chair in the lobby and slumped into it. He shut his eyes. Through the thin wall he could hear the low mumble of Navarro's voice, but the words were indistinct. Two uniformed cops went past, glancing at him with looks of surly curiosity; he felt like a suspected criminal. He sat for ten minutes, then Navarro called him back into the office.

"I'll drive you to meet a man called Salgado. He'll take you."

"I owe you one, Phil."

Navarro raised a smooth well-manicured hand in the air. "Don't thank me too soon. You ever been in Cuba?"

Pagan shook his head.

"It's not terrific under the best of circumstances,

Frank, and the way you're entering the country isn't the best by a long shot. You don't have a visa. Your passport hasn't been stamped at any point of entry. You have no return ticket. No hotel booking. Worst of all, you're carrying a gun. You've got to watch for police. You've got to be very careful you aren't seen behaving suspiciously by those charmers who call themselves the Committee for the Defense of the Revolution—they watch everything that goes on. Some of them are old ladies who sit in their windows all day long to see who's coming and who's going. They report strangers immediately. Be careful. Act normal. Act as if you know where you're going. And for Christ's sake don't get caught.''

Navarro paused and looked at Pagan with concern. ''I can get you in, Frank. When it comes to getting you out, I don't know how I can help.''

''I'll take my chances,'' Pagan said. What else could he do?

Navarro was quiet for a time. ''I was born in Cuba. My parents took me out when I was eight and I haven't been back. I've got family still there. It's an unhealthy place, Frank, like any police state.''

They left the office. When they were out in the lobby Navarro said, ''Salgado will deliver you to somebody who can provide you with a car and the address you need in Havana. After that, buddy, you're on your own.''

''I realize that.''

''You get into any trouble, you never saw me, you don't know who I am, you don't know who flew you into Cuba, you know absolutely nothing. You're a clam. Pretend amnesia. Pretend lunacy. But give nothing away.''

''Lunacy should be easy,'' Pagan said.

Navarro drove through North Miami and past Florida International University. Pagan was very quiet during the ride. He felt an odd kind of tension, as if Cuba were a haunted house he was about to enter—a strange creaking in the attic, something soft dragging itself across the cellar floor. Navarro spoke now and then about his vague memories of his birthplace—little things, a horserace he'd seen at Oriental Park in 1958, going with his father to a baseball game played between something called the Hershey Sport Club and the University of Havana in 1957, a brief adventure in shoplifting at a Woolworth store in Havana. Pagan had the feeling that Navarro might have been reminiscing about life in the United States in the 1950s, almost as though Cuba, in the doomed reign of Fulgencio Batista, had been nothing more than an unofficial American state.

Dark fields loomed up. Navarro became silent as he drove over a rutted track between meadows. He stopped the car, got out. Pagan followed him over the field. Beyond a stand of trees a small plane idled. A dim light glowed in the cockpit.

"This is it, Frank," Navarro said.

Pagan shook the man's hand, then glanced at the plane. The propellers turned, the craft rolled forward a little way. To Pagan's anxious ear the engine sounded erratic, a heart missing a beat; you're afraid, he thought. Dead scared and hearing things.

"I'm not convinced this is right," Navarro said.

"Maybe not."

"What the hell. Sometimes the wrong thing turns out to be right. In your place, I'd do exactly what you're doing. I justify it that way."

Pagan understood that he was meant to find some comfort in Navarro's approval. What he felt instead was a kind of clammy apprehension and a tightness coiled around his heart.

Honduras

Two hours before dawn the cruise missile and the tarpaulined missile control module were transported to the freighter *Mandadera*. They were raised by shipboard cranes and lowered into the hold of the vessel. Ruhr, demonic by lamplight, supervised every movement, scolding the crew, hovering over the cylinder in a way that reminded Captain Luis Sandoval of a fussing *abuela*, a grandmother. The German, who carried a canvas bag he would not let out of his sight, checked the strength of the crane cables and the integrity of the winch; he was busy here, busy there, vigilant, energetic, fastidious.

Luis Sandoval, anxious to begin the five hundred mile voyage to Santiago de Cuba, fretted impatiently, especially over the child in the entourage, a teenage girl whom Sandoval had not expected. He showed her to a small cabin, where she sat on the edge of the bunk with her knees jammed together and her eyes flat and dull. Why was this child aboard, this urchin, this unsmiling *granuja?*

It was not only the sad-faced child that made Luis Sandoval uneasy. A conspiracy of nature also contributed to his discomfort; he had heard over the ship's radio news of a storm front moving across the Gulf of Mexico toward the Caribbean. Scanning the dark sky proved nothing. He saw only a certain starry clarity. But in this part of the world he knew storms could spring up out of nowhere, streaking darkly from skies that only minutes before were clear. They could race across the heavens, dense cloud masses blown by great winds, rains that fell without apparent end, coastal regions submerged under insane tides. He'd seen it many times and, in those circumstances where science was impotent, a man was thrown back on older gods; Luis Sandoval often crossed himself during storms.

When the missile was safely lowered in the hold, Fuentes and Bosanquet disembarked and reboarded the launch that would take them back to the shore. Luis Sandoval gave the order for the freighter to sail a northeasterly course between the Cayman Islands and Jamaica to Santiago de Cuba, a journey of more than nine hours. Not a difficult trip normally, but there was a nervousness about his ten-man crew that Sandoval disliked.

Anchor was weighed, the ship's engines came rambunctiously to life as if iron bones were shaking beneath the decks. The *Mandadera* set sail, turning in a wide, ungainly arc away from the Honduran coastline. Sandoval observed Gunther Ruhr go down inside the hold. A pistol in the German's belt was visible beneath the blue denim jacket he wore. A great square of light rose from the hold, traversed now and then by Ruhr's enormous shadow.

Luis Sandoval stood on the bridge. The ship's awful cargo was something he didn't want to ponder; the cause of freedom sometimes involved undesirable things. He turned his thoughts instead to the child in the cabin, the scared little girl who sat on the edge of the bunk and had, by all reports, refused water and food.

Sandoval had a daughter of roughly the same age as that sad girl who wouldn't eat and wouldn't talk. He sympathized with the waif, even if he didn't understand her predicament entirely—but what could he possibly do to help her? She was Ruhr's property, or so Tomas Fuentes had hinted during the loading process, and she was to be left completely alone. And Sandoval would never interfere with a man like Gunther Ruhr.

In her coffinlike cabin Steffie realized that it was the blood that so appalled her. It had run down her inner thigh and she'd cleaned it with the sleeve of her jacket but now she thought she could feel it again, warm upon her flesh. She wondered if she were damaged inside somehow. For her age she was lamentably ignorant of her body and knew only what little her mother had told her and what she'd picked up from her friends—a mixture of fact and foolishness. She'd never paid much attention in biology class except when Charlie Hapgood, the blushing, timid teacher, had shown nude illustrations. Now she wished she knew more.

She shut her eyes, laid her small white hands in her lap, tried to forget how Ruhr had undone the buckle of his belt and stood over her, how even then she'd scratched and fought and kicked to no avail, how she hadn't been able to avoid seeing him and the way he was aroused.

She'd bit into her lip to keep from screaming as Ruhr forced her to accept him. He was whispering kindnesses, tender words she couldn't understand because they were in German, but she knew he was speaking to her from his innermost self, as if a part of him was untouched by cruelty—

But the pain! She'd stuffed her mouth with the edge of a blanket as he crushed her into the cot and moved inside her, growing harder and bigger with every motion—and then he gasped, and his words had come faster then, less tender, harsher, and his nails had dug into her hips. He rolled away from her almost at once and lay in silence looking up at the roof of the tent.

Puddles gathered in folds of canvas. Olive puddles, olive light. She'd closed her eyes and turned her back to him, smoothing her skirt down, trying to show she felt no pain. Trying to be brave.

She heard him rise and go out of the tent. When he'd come back it was dark and he told her they were leaving at once. She found it hard to walk, legs unsteady, muscles stiff. He helped her board a launch; the black sea scared her almost as much as Ruhr's touch.

When she was obliged to climb the scary ladder into the freighter, she thought: I hate you. I'll kill you one day. He was immediately beneath her, climbing, looking up her skirt—but what modesty did she have left?

Now she sat without moving. There was a tiny porthole but no view. What difference would a view make anyhow? Sea was sea. She studied her hands. Broken fingernails, colorless, unvarnished. She'd broken them in the struggle against Gunther Ruhr. Once she'd been proud of her fingernails, attentive to them, painting them this color and that—how long ago and silly it seemed to her now, such a petty vanity.

She got up, walked around the cabin, and felt the ship lurch briefly. She lay down, closed her eyes, listened to the rhythm of the engines, *dahda dahda dahda*. On and on. She rose again, went to the cabin door, found it locked; surprise surprise. She walked back to the bunk and lay face down, head buried in the smelly gray blanket.

She felt so incredibly lonely. But she wasn't going to get weepy about it. That wouldn't serve any purpose. She listened to the ship, couldn't really help listening.

Ruhr would come back, she knew that. He'd come back and unlock the door and step inside.

She knew he wasn't finished with her.

Something echoed in the back of her mind from days and days ago, a whole lifetime, something she'd glimpsed in a newspaper, the kind of paper with pictures of tits on page three, a paper her parents never purchased, a story about some girl in Cambridge, a prostitute Ruhr had picked up, a sensational tale of how he'd tried to do this terrible thing to her, shove something sharp up inside her, and that was all she'd read because her father had confiscated the paper. She remembered the girl had been reported as saying *I thought he was going to kill me.*

Now she thought, *Something sharp.*

What came to her mind was the sheathed knife that lay strapped to his shin.

In the dank hold which contained the relics of a past cargo—shapeless bananas turned to foul mush—Ruhr worked under a bright lamp. Now and again an inquisitive crew member peered down into the hold, and Ruhr would curse and gesture with his pistol.

He worked with the kind of concentration one might see on the face of a zealous bible scholar studying gospel. It was exacting work and required all his patience. He used wrenches and special screwdrivers from his precious canvas bag. He removed a plate from the side of the cylinder, exposing a confusing bundle of different-colored wires—red, whites, yellows, blacks, purples. There was nothing simple in the nuclear world.

These wires were connected to a variety of receptacles, openings into which the pins of the armed nose-cone would fit. Male, female. Since Ruhr had had the warhead specially assembled for him, the regular correspondence of male to female, of pin to receptacle, the precise sequence mandated by a classified technical manual was not going to make the missile functional.

Peering into the guts of the thing, Ruhr began to make his adjustments, carefully severing certain wires and splicing them with others. He did it without reference to any diagram but schemata he carried in his head. He was conscious of nothing except for what lay beneath his hands. Even the bad hand, limited as it was, seemed to shed its deformity and take on new agility as he explored and snipped, spliced and joined—a surgeon, he thought, somebody repairing arteries and redirecting them; an inventor modifying a tested device; an artist bent over a demanding sculpture whose finished intricacy he alone knew.

Erected, ready to launch and travel the distance from Santiago de Cuba to Miami, Florida—some five hundred and fifty miles as both crows and missiles flew—this lethal tube would, if released, destroy the downtown, the bridges, the water supply, the freeways, hundreds of thousands of people in an area that stretched from Coral Gables to Miami Beach. This warhead would inflict upon Miami more devastation than that wrought on Hiroshima in 1945 by the atomic bomb.

If it were ever released.

Of course it would not be, a fact that caused Ruhr a moment of regret. The responsibility for destruction on such a vast scale was something he would have accepted gladly. But he had been paid only to deliver an armed missile, not to light its fuse.

A slick of sweat ran over his eyelids. The intimacy he forged between himself and the missile was more rewarding than any he'd ever shared with a human. He wiped his forehead with his sleeve, thought of the child locked in a cabin above him. She'd fought him, resisted. He admired her spiritedness. He stared into the body of the cylinder, the veins, the sinews, and he thought of how he'd laid this complex machine wide open with simple instruments. There was a parallel here, a correspondence that couldn't possibly escape him—when he was finished with this operation, he'd go upstairs to the locked cabin.

He picked up a screwdriver; it glinted under the powerful lamp. The slight scratch the girl had inflicted under his right eye with her fingernail began, some two hundred and fifty miles out from Cabo Gracias a Dios, to throb.

Pinar del Rio Province, Cuba

It was not a comfortable flight. The black twin-engine Cessna (a doper's plane painted the color of night) bounced through layers of turbulence like a shuttlecock in an angry game of badminton. Salgado, the pilot, a Cuban-American with the physique of a linebacker, was imperturbable, a fatalistic observer of the elements. "If we don't have no fucking control, man, what's the point of worrying?" he'd asked a concerned Pagan who sat in the front passenger seat.

The Cessna dropped through clouds; the sea was agitated. Lightning flared over Key West and the Straits of Florida.

"Hey, something nasty's on its way, man," Salgado said with the confident air of a hardened weather-watcher. Pagan saw the moon being sucked behind speeding clouds. The lights of the Florida Keys vanished. The plane flew southwest toward the Gulf of Mexico where more lightning lit the sky with hard white electricity. Some fifty miles north of Pinar del Rio, Salgado turned south.

Cuba was visible, mysterious and mainly dark. The Cessna tipped, tilted, battered by a sudden uprising of air currents. Pagan stared at the green instrument lights, which meant nothing to him; how absurd it was to be suspended in black air, kept aloft by a device one didn't understand and whose instrument display was baffling.

He nervously pressed the palms of his hands together. It wasn't altogether comforting to know that Salgado, according to his own boasts, had flown surreptitiously into Cuba more than fifty times. A piece of cake, man, was how he put it when he detected Pagan's misgivings. He knew how to outfox Castro's observation posts. Just the same, Pagan's throat was very dry. He wondered what the penalties were for armed illegal entry into Cuba. He assumed Communist countries were not in the vanguard of charitable treatment toward prisoners, especially those who violated borders with Pagan's disregard.

The Cessna began to come down more rapidly now. How Salgado knew where he was going to land mystified Pagan. There were no obvious markers, no well-defined runways. The airstrip, such as it was, had been hacked out of a tobacco field. Salgado's guides were thin moonlight and instinct. He flew as if navigating blindfold. The wings of the plane brushed branches and shook foliage before it came finally, thankfully, to a safe landing.

Pagan stepped down. There was a scent of tobacco in the air, strong and vaguely bitter. What was supposed to happen next? Did Salgado fly out and simply leave him here in this dark, lonely place? No sign of habitation anywhere, no lights, just unbroken night. In a few hours it would be dawn.

Salgado came out of the cockpit. "This is goodbye, man. I gotta get back before that storm becomes real bad. Somebody's gonna meet you here."

"When?"

"This is Cuba, friend. Time ain't measured by watches in this place. They got their own system. It's no Rolex world here, pal."

"Terrific." Pagan didn't care for this information at all. He wanted to hear that Cubans were punctual and reliable and kept all their appointments.

"Adios," Salgado said.

"Wait—"

"Relax, man. Somebody's gonna show. Count on it."

Pagan was silent. He watched Salgado climb back up into the cockpit. The Cessna turned around, stopped, then began its run, taking off over the field, skimming trees, vanishing, a black plane in a black sky. With the departure of Salgado the night was emptier than before, as if Pagan's one thread back to safety had been snapped and here he was, stuck, uncertain, in an inhospitable country.

The night yielded nothing. The call of disturbed birds, frogs croaking, the wind occasionally rushing through plants, nothing else. He felt blind, robbed of any sense of direction.

Ten minutes, perhaps fifteen, passed before a lantern appeared on the edge of the field, swinging slightly from left to right as it came closer. It illuminated the broken-nosed face of a middleaged man who wore a black shirt and blue jeans and a straw hat.

"You are Pagan?" Pronounced *pah-gan*.

Pagan said that he was. The man came closer, shining his lantern directly into Pagan's eyes. The stench of kerosene was overwhelming. Pagan stepped away from the flame.

"My instructions are to take you to the highway. A car waits for you there." The Cuban, who said he was known as El Boxeador, spoke an English that was understandable if slowly enunciated.

"How far is the highway?"

"Two miles. Not far."

Pagan, wondering about the nature of the network that had made this trip possible, the collusion between Salgado and El Boxeador, walked behind the lantern. He decided they had to be part of some drug-smuggling ring that Navarro had exposed but chose, for his own reasons, not to prosecute.

The air was stuffy. The ground underfoot became marshlike. Here and there a darkened hut was visible, and once a dog barked inquisitively, but nobody appeared to investigate. El Boxeador, who said he was the former welterweight champion of all Cuba—he emphasized all with a sweep of an arm—explained that there were many Castro loyalists even in rural areas, some of them important members of the Committees for the Defense of the Revolution—a name that caused him to hawk up a quantity of phlegm and spit with contempt.

On and on they slogged, through fields and between trees and dense foliage. Pagan felt the familiar ache in his chest and pondered the notion of a painkiller then decided against it. Now and then El Boxeador switched off his lantern when he heard a noise; then he had to relight it, which was a seemingly complicated task because either the wick was burned low or kerosene was running out, Pagan wasn't sure which. Finally the highway was reached, a narrow, isolated road with a rough surface that had been patched time and again.

Pagan looked along the highway, which twisted just into the blackness on either side of the road, half-expecting a military patrol, rifles, the indignity of arrest. But nothing moved, no traffic passed.

Finally, they came to the place where a car was parked in a grove of trees. It was a late 1950s Oldsmobile, finned, rusted, painted many times, and, like the narrow highway, patched. It had once clearly been in a collision; a clumsy attempt had been made to fiberglass the hole in the trunk, but it looked like a scar. There were still thousands of American cars in Cuba, relics of pre-Revolutionary times, loved and cared for by their devout owners.

El Boxeador gestured to the vehicle proudly and said that it ran like a *campeon*; a little quirky, maybe, but it had more than four hundred thousand miles on the clock and the Cuban expected it to run for the same distance again. The upholstery was torn. Springs came up through the seats, bypassing the greasy duct tape used to repair the material. Pagan, a hopeless lover of American cars, looked at the dashboard affectionately.

"In the glove compartment, you will find a flashlight and a map," El Boxeador said. "The address you need is there also." He reached inside the car and pointed to a scrap of paper taped to the back of the glove box, where it was barely visible. "There is also a map of Havana. In the Vedado, Rosabal lives on the top floor of a new three-story apartment building. A place for big-shots, you understand. It is guarded usually by an armed man in the hallway, sometimes more than one. You will have to deal with that situation on your own, my friend."

Pagan didn't want to anticipate trouble. If and

when he encountered an armed guard he'd cope with it somehow. He shook the Cuban's hand and then got behind the wheel.

El Boxeador tapped the window and said, "The road goes all the way to Havana. Good luck!"

Pagan forced a little smile of gratitude, then stared through the glass at the bleak highway ahead. He had come a long way, but suddenly it seemed to him that the three thousand miles behind him were nothing compared to the hundred that lay directly ahead. Neither tourist nor legitimate visitor, he had absolutely no rights in this country. He started the car, which hummed rather smoothly.

This is it, he thought. A point of no return had been passed.

In slightly more than an hour and a half he would be in Havana.

Ohio

Before dawn, Sheridan Perry had left Washington for what he considered his safe retreat, his private sanctuary, the place he felt most at home. Now, terrified by last night's murderous attack and the memory of how he and Kinnaird had fled the scene before the arrival of police, he sat in the back of a Cadillac limousine as it headed through autumnal Ohio. A leafless monotony prevailed in the landscape, a sense of the year moodily turning. A great cold sun the color of a brand-new penny appeared low on the horizon, sending chilly light across wasted fields and stubble.

Perry, who saw Harry Hurt each time he shut his eyes, and heard once again that dreadful gasp Hurt had made as he turned from the broken window and fell to the floor, his skull shattered like a hammered pumpkin, stared at the fields as if hypnotized. He asked his driver to stop at Youngstown because he wanted coffee. A sleazy little roadhouse that served hard donuts and thin coffee was found, but Perry didn't care about culinary matters. Accompanied by his overweight chauffeur and a stout bodyguard he'd hired from the entourage at Hurt's apartment, he sat on a stool at the counter and sipped coffee with a hand that shook and listened to Raving Dave Dudley sing *Six Days on the Road* on the jukebox. Today was the day, Perry thought. Today was the day when things happened in Cuba. Too bad Harry Hurt wasn't going to be around to see the fruits of his work.

Perry finished his coffee. He got up from the counter. Shielded by chauffeur and guard, he walked back to the limo.

North of Youngstown, in the vicinity of Ashtabula, was a house Perry had bought some years before, his secret place. Located on the shore of Lake Erie, the house was set amid dense trees and surrounded by an electrified fence. He'd never taken visitors there, never had a woman out at the house. Only a cleaning lady, a fastidious old bat from Ashtabula, and the Polynesian servant Paco, knew Perry lived there.

Now, as he travelled north, Perry flicked through business papers he'd lately been neglecting, but found it hard to work up much interest in the cash-flow problems of a lumber company located in Vittoria Conquista, Brazil. He shut the case, poured himself a small snifter of scotch from the bar, gazed back at the road again.

The car was only twenty miles from Lake Erie. He began to feel more comfortable the closer he got to his home. Insecurities didn't fall away, rather they diminished. Fear didn't disintegrate, it decrystallized.

The placid waters of Lake Erie appeared. It wasn't the most beautiful stretch of inland water in the world, but just then it looked marvelous to Sheridan Perry.

His house came in sight beyond stripped trees, mainly cottonwoods whose denuded branches suggested fragile clouds of smoke. The house, constructed of fine stained pine, stood on a knoll. A remote device opened the electrified gate in the fence and the limousine went through, then climbed the driveway up to the front door.

Perry was glad to be here. He stepped out of the car.

Mrs. Stakowski from Ashtabula appeared on the porch, and so did the manservant Paco in his snow-white jacket. They looked nervous. They never expected Perry to visit this house in late fall. Usually he came only in mid-spring, sometimes very early summer, because he disliked the climate during other months. He stepped up to the porch. The fat chauffeur and the stout bodyguard followed.

Home, Perry thought. Here he had his computers, his modems and fax machines, and current stock-market prices flashed across his TV screens, he had his sizeable hot-tub and vibrating bed and his library of pornographic movies from the Philippines, he had his electronic games and his collection of rifles.

"Welcome," said the houseboy.

Mrs. Stakowski opened the door for Perry to enter. She did so with noticeable reluctance and a slight frown whose meaning Perry could not read. The room was dim; he couldn't make out anything but the shapes of three men who stood near the fireplace. Perry dropped his briefcase. He heard Mrs. Stakowski groan and say she was sorry, but she hadn't had any choice, the strangers were armed; then there was a flash of white as Paco scampered across the porch and headed for the woods. Perry, terrified, turned toward the open door, the porch beyond, where the overweight chauffeur stood motionless.

Sheridan Perry was cut down by gunfire from automatic pistols. It was over in seconds. He was shot in the throat and chest and groin and although he made a valiant effort to turn and flee, the attempt was hopeless; he staggered on to the porch, slipped and fell against the thigh of the chauffeur, rose again with a kind of instinctive strength, then toppled over the porchrail into a pile of raked leaves.

Mrs. Stakowski was shot once through the skull and fell to the bottom of the steps. The chauffeur tried to flee and was shot in the back of the neck. The bodyguard freed his pistol from a shoulder holster and returned the fire into the dim recess of the house, but he was caught by several bullets in the windpipe and one in the eye.

The three killers conferred in Spanish. It was decided that the houseboy, Paco, was barely worth pursuing. What could he tell the authorities anyway? Besides, as the Cuban killers guessed, he'd never go to the cops for one simple reason: he had no green card.

Santiago de Cuba Province, Cuba

Before daylight, the first Cuban troops began to move through the countryside around the city of Santiago. They travelled in Soviet trucks. The convoys passed under the shadows of the Sierra Maestra mountains where, more than thirty years ago, Fidel Castro had gathered his revolutionaries together for their assault on the regime of Batista. In the pre-dawn dark these mountains seemed indomitable and mysterious, lost in shadows and vapors, legends and myths, more iconography than geography.

The troops, a battalion of them in fifty-three trucks, went by road through the ancient city of Bayamo, where the vibrations of the vehicles rattled shop windows and stained-glass and trembled the old bell in the tower of San Juan Evangelista. The convoys, enlarged at Bayamo by thousands of reservists from the Territorial Troops Militia, passed propagandist billboards with pictures of the blue-uniformed teenagers of the Youth Brigade and captions like En La Educacion Y La Salud. From Bayamo the convoys would eventually reach Holguin, where maneuvers would begin near Guardalavaca Beach, which would be closed to visitors and tourists for a day or two.

At the same time as the convoy rumbled through the countryside, four battleships of the Cuban Navy— built in Odessa twenty years ago and obsolete by Soviet standards—sailed around Guantanamo toward Guardalavaca Beach. Shortly after dawn, ten airplanes, modified versions of Russian MIGs, flew over Santiago toward Holguin. These too were to play a role in the maneuvers.

Thus was the province of Santiago de Cuba laid defenseless. And the site for the placement of the cruise missile, a mere fifteen miles from the historic Morro Fortress on Santiago's shoreline, was occupied by a score of anti-Communist officers and more than two hundred men, some of them Soviet-trained missile technicians, who had remained behind on the specific orders of General Capablanca. They would be joined later by the invasionary force from Honduras with its sophisticated weaponry and advanced fighter aircraft that would destroy Castro's air force on the ground; and later still, on the road to Havana, by other disaffected officers and their battalions, a number that Capablanca estimated would total more than ten thousand fighting men. Backed by popular support, by peasants prepared to take up arms against Castro, by disenchanted men and women willing to strike and block highways and occupy public buildings, by the whole underground movement Rosabal said was firmly in place and ready to rise, how could there be any doubt about the outcome?

West Virginia

The near-sighted technician at the isolated tracking-station, which was dome-shaped and stood in wooded privacy like a very large boiled egg, had analyzed the early photographs transmitted from the satellite twenty-three thousand miles above the earth. Magnified many times, enhanced by computers, these images depicted various blobs that to any untrained eye would suggest absolutely nothing. The technician was skilled, however; he also knew what he was looking for.

He telephoned a number in Washington, D.C. A young lady named Karen answered in a silken voice that made the lonely technician experience a certain sexual longing. She asked for the pictures to be sent at once by courier to the office of Allen Falk. The technician, who spent far too many hours without human company, and who found Karen's voice delightful, offered to deliver them personally.

18

Havana

Magdalena Torrente's driver was a thin nervous man named Alberto Canto, a physician. He met her at the darkened airfield between Havana and San Jose de Las Lajas where her plane from Florida touched down. She hadn't flown the small Piper herself. She had the experience to do it, but if she was having a hard time keeping herself under control, how could she expect to control an airplane? Besides, she knew nothing of the terrain, the destination. Both plane and pilot—a tough, leathery little man who worked in Havana as a tourist guide for Cubatur and pretended to be a happy Communist—had been provided by Garrido, who had made Magdalena's travel arrangements with meticulous care, including the arrival of Canto in his small Lada automobile.

Garrido had pulled all the strings in Havana he still could. Old favors were called home; old friendships had new life breathed into them. Long-distance calls were made, surreptitious conversations took place, places and times were synchronized in Garrido's own fastidious way. The process electrified the old man; the discovery of Rosabal's treachery excited him in a manner he hadn't felt since his heyday in Santiago. Instead of bickering with his fellow exiled democrats, and raising funds for a new revolution whose date had always been annoyingly vague, he had something concrete to deal with at last, something with a hard center: Rosabal had betrayed everything and everybody, and there could only be one kind of justice.

Now, at the edge of the deserted, windblown airstrip, Magdalena stepped into the car and Alberto Canto rolled down the window as soon as he saw her produce a cigarette. She lit it anyway. Her hand trembled and she hoped Canto wouldn't notice. She held Garrido's green pouch in her lap, still unopened.

Canto said, "I will drop you as close to the place as I can. Sometimes there are extra police patrols in that neighborhood. They make me uneasy. This whole undertaking upsets me."

"So why did you agree to pick me up?"

"Because I'm on your side. Which is not to say that I have the constitution of a hero. Quite the contrary. I'm just a scared general practitioner. I don't take risks. I don't have the guts. I couldn't do what you just did. I couldn't fly illegally into a country in the dead of night. Especially a country like Cuba."

You do what it takes, Magdalena thought. *And sometimes it surprises you.* She said nothing, looked from her window. Havana loomed up around her, neighborhoods of small houses, shacks, apartments half-built, scaffolding and ladders and cement-mixers in disarray. Unkempt suburbs gave way to another Havana, the central part of the city where imposing buildings and monuments crowded the night sky. Here and there new architecture appeared among the old, the occasional dreary high-rise block overwhelming some decrepit colonial mansion.

Her memories of this place, which she'd last seen at the age of ten, were different from the present reality. What she recalled most were warm hazy nights and palm trees and crowds of students, usually arguing politics, strolling along San Lazaro Street. Nobody argued politics in public anymore. She remembered the stands that sold hamburgers and oysters on Infanta Street and the delicious smells that rose in the humid air. The stands were probably gone by now; the oysters almost certainly. She recalled enviably beautiful, well-dressed women on San Rafael and how she longed to grow up and enter that glamorous life, exclusive night-clubs and dance-halls with tuxedoed orchestras.

She glanced at Alberto Canto. Sweat ran down his neck and dampened the open collar of his white shirt. He took a linen handkerchief from his jacket and pressed it against his face.

"You've got a lot to lose if you're caught in my company," Magdalena said.

Canto looked grim. "I wonder if there's anything left to lose in Cuba these days. Life doesn't have much quality. It's mostly dreary but one goes through the motions, because suicide isn't an alternative. I'd like some joy, I think. Even a prospect of joy would do. Perhaps I should flee to Miami and play the exile game."

Was that how Canto saw her and Garrido and all the others in the U.S.—just players in a game? It was a bleak little thing to say, almost an accusation. Magdalena made no response. How could she object? She didn't live here. Her Cuba hadn't been the daily grinding reality of Canto's; perhaps hers had been no more than a dream place, a state of mind, something she thought she could help shake and remake in quite another image.

A state of mind: was that all? A delusion? She wasn't sure. She understood only how odd it was actually to *be* here in her native country after thirty years. Her sense of exile had always been strong and melancholic. What was more terrible than being forced out of your own country and obliged to live in another just because you disagreed with certain principles? Exile was a wretched condition—the yearning, the way you tried to laugh the longing off as some kind of silliness, but you were never convincing.

Now she smelled the Cuban night as if she'd never smelled anything before. This was where she belonged, the place Rafael Rosabal had promised her and then stolen. She was suddenly aware of his nearness. He was ten, fifteen minutes away, she wasn't sure, her sense of direction had eroded with time, amnesia, confusion. What did she feel? What did she really feel? She didn't know.

Canto slowed the car in the neighborhood of Vedado. Under the outstretched branches of a palm in a dark street, he parked the Lada, turned off the lights but left the engine running.

"Go right at the next corner. Halfway down the street there's a new apartment block. Very small. Exclusive. Rosabal lives there on the top floor. I understand there is usually a security guard in the entrance. However," and Canto paused, wiped his face with the handkerchief again, "because we have a few friends here and there, somebody was able to persuade the usual guard to call in sick. Unhappily, his replacement never received the order to substitute for him. A bureaucratic oversight. One of many in Cuba."

"Convenient."

"We have our moments." Canto stared through the windshield. Wind lashed suddenly through the fronds of the palm and they made hard slapping noises on the roof of the car.

"What about Rosabal's wife? Does she live in the apartment?"

"I didn't know he had a wife," Canto said.

Welcome to the club, Magdalena thought.

She opened the passenger door.

"I'll come back to this spot in ten minutes," Canto said and looked at his watch. "If you're not here, I'll come back again in another ten minutes. If you still haven't shown up, I'll make one more attempt ten minutes later provided it's safe to do so. If you're here I'll take you back to the airfield. If not . . . well, I prefer to be positive."

Before she got out of the car Magdalena opened Garrido's pouch. The gun inside was a loaded lightweight Fraser automatic with a handle of imitation pearl. She slipped the weapon in the pocket of her leather jacket, then reached inside the pouch again. She removed a small brown bottle that contained two unmarked white capsules, which puzzled her for a moment. And then she understood. Garrido, in a melodramatic gesture, had provided her with failure pills, suicide capsules. *Swallow two, lie down, oblivion guaranteed.* He obviously had no doubts about her business in Havana. It was all black and white to him. Either she'd do the job and come back to Miami, or she'd fail and be captured and take the pills. He didn't see the complexity of emotions involved. He couldn't imagine how there might be any indecision on her part. He didn't want to know. As he got older so did his need grow to make the world more simple, more manageable.

She stuck the bottle in the pocket of her jeans, got out of the car. Canto drove away. She walked quickly, then paused in the shadows as if frozen.

Illuminated by a solitary streetlight, two men were talking together on the sidewalk opposite. One wore a uniform, the other a white *guayabera.* The uniformed man removed his cap, tossed his head back, laughed at something. He had a pistol at his hip and was obviously some kind of cop; she had no way of knowing who his companion might be. Both men laughed now, heads inclined together like conspirators. Then the cop turned and walked away with a wave of his hand. His companion went inside one of the houses on the street, an old baroque structure carved into expensive apartments. The riffraff didn't live in this neighborhood.

Magdalena waited until the street was empty before she moved. The apartment building where Rafael lived was small and rather unassuming; presumably the Minister of Finance in an allegedly Communist society had to keep appearances down as much as possible.

Outside the entranceway she stopped to gaze up the short flight of steps to the glass doors; there was a desk in the lobby, and a lamp was lit, but nobody was present.

She pushed the doors open, entered the lobby. There was an elevator to her left, but she chose the stairs instead. She climbed quietly, swiftly, possessed by an odd light-headed feeling, as if this were not really happening and she was some kind of wraith and the real Magdalena Torrente was back in Key Biscayne. The gun in her pocket knocked dully upon her thigh as she moved. The fourth floor was at the top of the building. Since there was only one door on each floor, finding Rosabal's apartment was easy.

She stepped toward the door, which had no number, no nameplate.

You will have the pleasure of killing him, Garrido had said.

You have earned that right more than anyone else.

She knocked on the door in a gentle way.

Then she waited.

Pagan drove uneasily on the central highway that linked Pinar del Rio with Havana. Yellowy moonlight on the range of the Sierra de los Organos rendered the landscape unreal. The Oldsmobile was more invalid than automobile, and had begun to make the kind of clanking sound common to terminal cars. But it hadn't died yet.

Near San Cristobal—where in 1962 the Soviets had installed the SS-4 missiles that had led to the Cuban missile crisis—he parked the car beneath trees because a convoy of army trucks was lumbering past with no particular attention to the conventions of the road. They wandered from side to side on the highway, their dim lights menacing. When the last truck had gone past Pagan drove on.

On the outskirts of Havana he came to the district of Marianao. In a silent sidestreet he stopped the car, consulted the map he'd been given by El Boxeador. He played the dim flashlight over it; Rosabal lived in the Vedado district of the city which so far as he could tell lay in the streets behind the Malecon, the sea wall along Havana's coast.

He drove past darkened houses and unlit shops, a Coppelia ice-cream parlor, a shuttered bar; Pagan had the fanciful thought that a plague might have closed the city down. There were no pedestrians save for a noisy clutch of women who came out of one tenement doorway and immediately entered another, leaving the sound of shrill drunken laughter behind.

Streetlights were practically nonexistent and where he found them were about as bright as candles. Lush trees stirred in the dark; here and there large ornate buildings stood like neglected palaces. Some of them had been religious colleges or the business headquarters of dispossessed *norteamericano* corporations or the homes of the exiled rich. He drove with uncharacteristic caution, hearing the way the worn tirewalls, as delicate as membranes, screeched whenever he turned a corner.

He reached the avenue known as the Paseo, which was filled with trucks and private cars and people arguing over the cause of an accident in which a '56 Chevy had ploughed into the side of a van. He didn't like all this activity. He turned left, then right, crossed the Avenue de los Presidentes, found himself back in narrow streets again, some of them without names. Finally, inevitably, the Oldsmobile accomplished what it had been trying to do for the last fifty miles—it gasped and shuddered and came to a halt outside a vacant lot behind tenements. Pagan, struggling with a certain panic, pressed the starter button a couple of times. The engine wouldn't even turn over. The car's silence was final.

Dead. What bloody timing.

He got out of the vehicle, kicked a front tire in frustration. Then by flashlight he studied his map, trying to memorize the way to Rosabal's street.

He walked for ten minutes, staying close to shadows as he anxiously sought street signs, landmarks, anything that might correspond to his map. Once, from a window over a butcher's shop in which hung an unrealistic slab of plastic display beef, he heard the noise of a guitar playing lazily and a woman's reedy voice singing *Una desgracia unfortunada* and elsewhere a caged bird squawked as if in competition. Down cross streets came the damp scent of the sea and very old stone and air that seemed to crackle with the sound of water dripping on salt. He passed under the signs of closed businesses. *Farmacia. Casa Joyeria. Restaurante Vegetariano.*

Once or twice taxis went cruising past. A smell of bread drifted from some distant bakery, arousing Pagan's hunger. When had he last eaten? On the flight from London to Miami. Now he couldn't remember what the food had been. Something awful. The smell of bread teased him. He kept walking, concentrating on where he was going, staying close to walls and passing beneath trees. Sometimes a loud carousing wind blew with such ferocity that it took his breath away and he had to turn his face out of its path.

How much further? he wondered. Was he going in the right direction in this dismal city? Now he stopped, took out the crumpled map, examined it again. His flashlight, as jinxed as the car, flickered and went out. Did nothing work on this whole fucking island? He walked until he came to a streetlamp and he stood below it, staring at the map.

Bloody hell—nothing on the map matched his surroundings. According to the route he'd taken he should have reached a small park that was represented on the map by a tiny green square—instead, what faced him was a warren of narrow streets where the houses all looked dilapidated, not at all the kind of neighborhood in which you might imagine the Minister of Finance to live.

Narrow street led to others; old houses mirrored one another. A maze all at once, a territorial riddle, like something you might dream during restless sleep and force yourself abruptly awake into the familiar surroundings of your bedroom.

This was no dream, Frank. No chance of waking up from this.

Sweet Jesus, nothing was familiar here. He flapped the map again, examined it, blinked, remembering that he'd heard once how Communist countries deliberately printed devious maps to throw visitors off balance, to mislead them and prevent them from trespassing in places where they didn't belong or from seeing something 'sensitive'—be it a slum or a military camp or the headquarters of State Security. He also recalled hearing somewhere that street names were frequently being changed as one Party official fell from grace and another rose in prominence. Had Garcia Street, for example, become Munoz Street? Was that the kind of thing that happened? He had an urge to crumple the map and toss it, but even if it was misleading, even if it didn't quite reflect reality, it was still the best shot he had of finding Rosabal.

He walked again. The narrow streets, houses oddly quiet, most of them unlit, threatened him in a way that was more than merely vague. Doorways, darkened and silent, suggested presences that observed him as he walked past. And now he remembered something he'd read once about how each neighborhood in Cuba, each block, had its own organization of snoops who watched from windows, who reported strangers to the authorities. He tried to force confidence into his step. He belonged here. He was a man going home late. That was all. There was nothing odd about his presence. Nobody would look at him twice. He whistled quietly, then became silent. What if you were lost here forever? he wondered. What if you could never find your way out of these streets? Round and round, up and down, never seeing a street name, a number, a familiar face. One bad fucking nightmare. One endless inner scream of panic.

Then, when he'd begun to feel a quiet despair, the streets became wider. The houses were larger now, richer, the foliage more dense. The warrens vanished behind him, the streetlamps became more generous. Across the way he saw it—the small park he'd been looking for before, his landmark. He felt a sense of enormous relief. A tiny darkened park, a scrap of greenery, nothing more, but for Pagan it was a major discovery. He consulted his map again; all he had to do was walk another few blocks north and he would come to Calle Santamaria, which was where Rosabal lived—if the map was even approximately accurate.

For a moment his mood changed. He was elated. He'd come this far without impediment. Even when a car slowed alongside him he didn't let this new frame of mind dissolve immediately. He continued to walk, didn't look at the car, kept his face forward. But when he became conscious of a face perusing him from the window of the vehicle, he understood he was being tracked by a police car, and his sense of confidence slipped quickly.

Calm, Frank. Keep walking. Pay no attention. Pretend you're strolling home after a night on the town— or what there is of it in this place.

The car accelerated, went past him. On the next corner it braked, came to a stop. Pagan kept walking. He saw the door of the car open and a bulky figure emerge just ahead of him. *Can't chat, sorry, got to keep moving.* The cop stood in the center of the sidewalk with his legs spread slightly apart; he clearly meant to halt Pagan. Perhaps some strange law existed about being on the streets after a certain time. Or perhaps

Pagan simply looked suspicious, the late-night straggler whose presence was of universal interest to passing cops.

Shit. There would be questions in Spanish, a request for papers, documents, visas, the whole can of bloody worms. *I am a deaf mute*, Pagan thought. Would that act work?

Pagan didn't slacken his stride. He'd come this far and he wasn't about to be thwarted by any overweight Cuban cop. There was only one way through this, and it wasn't bluff. He stared at the sidewalk as he moved, raising his face only when he was within reach of the policeman, smiling, looking nice, friendly, even innocently puzzled by the cop's presence. He bunched one of his large hands when he was no more than seven or eight inches from the cop, who was already asking him a question in belligerent Spanish.

The punch was gathered from Pagan's depths, coming up from a place level with his hip, up and up, a fine arc that carved through air, creating an uppercut the policeman saw but couldn't avoid. The connection of knuckle on chin was painfully satisfying to Pagan, even though the overweight cop didn't go down immediately. He staggered back and Pagan advanced, connecting with a second punch, this one—viciously unfair, nothing to do with gentlemanly rules—directly into the thickness of flesh round the larynx, a hard sharp blow that caused the cop's eyes to roll in his head. He went over this time, flat on his back with his legs wide.

Pagan hurried away, knuckles aching. He was pleased with the swift accuracy of the performance—he hadn't lost his touch; but what troubled him was the effort it had involved and the way he felt drained as he quickened his stride through drab streets of a city strange to him.

Cabo Gracias a Dios, Honduras

Three hours before first light Tomas Fuentes gave the final orders for the evacuation of the camp; he brought together the squadron leaders and their men. In their neat khaki fatigues they looked smart and trim, fighting men. Fuentes, who had a very big pistol holstered on his left hip, spoke through a PA system. He wished his men well in events that lay just ahead.

Five hundred of them would be going on board two battleships that were presently anchored off the Cape. Six hundred more would be taking to the sea in frigates and transport ships. There would be extensive air cover from Skyhawks, Harriers and F-16s providing protection for amphibious landing-craft. The landing beaches would be unprotected; military maneuvers had ensured the absence of Cuban troops, who were on the other side of the island. Bombing and strafing from the air would knock out any small pockets of Cuban air defenses that were still manned; munitions stores and lines of communication would be destroyed quickly. Tanks and field-guns, unloaded from the ships, would be deployed on the road to Havana; beyond Santiago de Cuba there might be extensive fighting with the *fidelistas*. It was not expected to result in anything but victory for the forces of freedom, Fuentes declared. Besides—and here Tomas paused for effect—it was now known that Fidel was incapacitated and couldn't lead his troops, which was certain to be a blow to Communist morale. This brought cheers from the assembly.

This invasion, Fuentes said, was different from before in every respect. This time they were prepared. This time they had amazing support from their freedom-loving brothers in the Cuban armed forces. This time there would be a popular revolt inside Cuba. This time Castro was hated. In 1961 he'd been revered—well, by God, all that was changed. Cuba was miserable and downtrodden and the people sick to death.

Fuentes looked at his watch. Within four hours, the missile would be in place in Cuba, where it would be made ready to fly upon Miami. Shortly thereafter landing parties would arrive on the beaches and the first air strikes would occur against Communist bases and airfields. As soon as the freedom forces had established their control of Santiago and launched their initial advance along the Central Highway—joined by anti-Castro Cuban troops and the counterrevolutionary resistance—satellite photographs of the offensive missile would be released to every newspaper in the Western world. Fuentes imagined the headlines. *Castro Planned Missile Strike on USA. Aborted by Invasion Force and Popular Cuban Uprising.* Later, there would be pictures of technicians destroying the missile. Fuentes, who had a natural hunger for publicity, would make sure he got into these shots somewhere.

More than thirty years, Tomas said. It was too long a time. More than thirty dry years of wishing and wanting and longing and hating.

Libertad! he shouted. *Viva Cuba Libre!* His amplified voice tumbled away in the breeze.

He saluted his men, who broke ranks and headed in an orderly manner toward the beaches.

Tomas Fuentes, who would fly to Cuba on one of the F-16s, and land as soon as the fighter-planes had done their demolition work, went inside his tent for the last time. After today, the whole camp would be a mere memory. Bosanquet followed him. Both men sat for a few minutes in silence. This quiet was broken by the noise of bulldozers churning over the pathways between tents, obliterating all traces of this small temporary city; soon the jungle would have ascendance again, the landscape would take back that which had been borrowed from it.

"I hate this goddam place, but I'll miss it," Fuentes said with the snarl in his voice of a man who considers sentimentality a weakness.

Bosanquet concurred. In a moment he'd rise and go to his own tent and there dismantle the radio. He wanted to wait until the very last moment to do so, because he had been expecting a message from Harry Hurt—a rousing speech, some fine words of encouragement—but the radio had been silent for many hours now.

Perhaps Harry maintained his silence for reasons of security.

Yes, Bosanquet thought. That had to be it.

Harry believed in security.

Havana

The woman who answered the door was the one Magdalena had seen in Duran's photographs. She was pretty if you liked a certain fine-boned Castilian look. Her hair, which normally she would have worn pulled back like a skullcap and tied, was loose and lustrous and hung over her white shoulders; her deep brown eyes, the color of bittersweet chocolate, were her best features. Her mouth was ample and she had a fine straight nose with expressive nostrils.

"Yes?"

Magdalena, who very lightly touched the gun concealed in her pocket, said nothing for a moment. She realized that she'd been floating along on the possibility that Duran's photographs were fakes prepared by him for some vindictive reason of his own. She hadn't wanted to believe in the existence of this woman, this Estela. Now, faced with the reality, she felt as if her blood had begun to run backward. Her voice was unsteady. "I want to see Rafael."

The woman stared at Magdalena as if she'd been expecting her. "He's out," she said. "He should be back soon."

"I'll wait if you don't mind." Magdalena stepped into the apartment, which smelled of something very sweet, like lavender water. She hadn't expected Rafael to be absent. She made absolutely sure the woman was telling the truth by strolling uninvited through the apartment. Estela, protesting, followed her. Artwork, reminiscent of old-fashioned cubism, hung on the walls. The entire place was lit by dull table lamps which cast an odd yellow light through their shades. Magdalena went into the bathroom, then the kitchen. They were empty.

"What are you looking for?" Estela asked. "I didn't ask you to come in. What do you want here?"

Inside the bedroom Magdalena saw crushed white sheets, a jar of skin lotion on the bedside table, a silk robe she recognized as Rafe's laid across the bed. There was an intimacy here she couldn't take. Rafael and his wife in this bed, bodies locked together: this dreadful picture reared up in her mind. Did he experience the passion with his wife that he did with her? Was it the same? How could it be? Nothing could have that scalding intensity.

Back in the living-room Estela said, "Are you satisfied now? What did you hope to find anyway?"

"Where is he?"

"He had business." Estela sat down again and looked at an electric clock on a shelf. "Why do you want to see him?"

"Do you really want to know?" Magdalena asked.

"I'm not sure." Estela was quiet. The clock made a slight humming noise. "I have a feeling about you. You and Rafael. A feeling. As soon as I saw you on the doorstep. And then the way you just walked through the apartment . . ."

"What kind of feeling?"

"Not a good one."

Magdalena had one of those small vicious urges, experienced so rarely in her lifetime, to smack this young thing across the face, but she let the desire go. Was it Estela's fault that she was the wife of Rafael? Estela probably knew nothing of Magdalena's existence. Besides, there was something pleasant about Senora Rosabal, an unexpected intelligence in the eyes. This was no airhead, no mindless bimbo, to decorate Rafe's arm. There were depths to Estela Capablanca Rosabal. This realization only made Magdalena feel more endangered than before; Rafe could love this woman, and it would be almost understandable. It didn't have to be a political marriage, a match of mere convenience: *he might actually love this woman for her own sake.*

Magdalena said, "We're friends. I've known Rafe a long time."

"No, you're more than friends. I get the impression . . ." Estela didn't complete her sentence.

She made a small gesture with her hand, palm up-turned, as if she despaired of words.

Magdalena was silent. She might have said *Yes, yes, we fuck, we meet in foreign cities and we fuck our brains out,* but she didn't. She had come to confront Rafael, not his young bride.

Estela said a little sadly, "Sometimes I imagined there was another woman in his life. I didn't know who. You're very beautiful. What's your name?"

Magdalena told the woman. Estela repeated the name quietly a couple of times. "It has a nice sound."

Magdalena wandered to the window, drew back the drape, looked down into the street. It was all too civilized, she thought. This meeting, the way Estela purred over her name and looks, the politeness. She wished Rafael would come back and she could get the confrontation over with one way or another. This apartment where Rafe lived with his young wife was making her feel weird, off-center. Her head ached. Rafael doesn't live here, she thought. Not the Rafael you know. It's somebody else. A stranger.

"You love him?" Estela asked.

"Yes." *Despite it all, yes, yes, yes.*

Estela Rosabal hesitated: "Does he love you?"

"He married you, not me."

"He didn't tell you he was married, did he?"

"What Rafael told me or didn't tell me is none of your concern."

"I think it is." Estela laid her hands on her lap. The wedding ring flashed under lamplight. "Anything that involves my husband affects me too. That's the way it is. Tell me why you have to see him."

Magdalena gazed at the street. She could see a small swimming-pool, surrounded by a fence, to her left. A shimmering light burned under the surface of blue-green water.

How reasonable Estela sounded, how collected. What reserves of strength did she have that allowed her to handle her husband's mistress with no displays of hysteria? It wasn't fair, Magdalena thought. She could never have behaved with such dignity and resolve herself. The young woman had grace beyond her years. Magdalena was jealous now, and not just because of the insight she had into the life Rafe shared here with his wife. Something else. The other woman's youth. Her enviable maturity. The quietly reasonable manner that concealed firmness and iron. These were qualities Magdalena realized she had recently lost in herself. In loving Rosabal she had given up more than she'd ever really imagined. *I was going to be independent. My own person. When I married Rafe I was going to be more than just his wife. Married, dear Christ!*

Something cold went through her. She shivered. Below, wind altered the smooth surface of the pool, creating concentric circles of disturbance.

"Tell me why you need to see him," Estela said. She got up from the sofa and stood some feet from Magdalena, her arms folded under her breasts. Perfect breasts, Magdalena thought. Perfect skin. Smooth and unblemished, unworried as yet by time. There would be no anxious scrutiny of that fine, strong, young face in mirrors, no depression when age made another unkind incision. In the future, sure; but when you were as young as Estela age was like death and disease—it never happened to you, always somebody else.

Magdalena was filled with a sudden resentment of Estela so fierce it surprised her. The Senora had youth, she had Rafe, she shared his life, his world, the future in which Magdalena was supposed to figure so prominently. What was left to the rejected mistress? What was she supposed to do with this sense of loss?

A car drew up in the street below. Magdalena moved back from the window. "Does he have a BMW?" she asked.

"Yes."

"Then I think he just arrived."

Magdalena took her gun out, told Estela to sit down and be still.

"Why do you come here with a gun, for God's sake?" Estela asked.

Magdalena went to the door, stood there motionless, listened for the sound of footsteps on the stairs. Instead what she heard was the quiet hum of an elevator rising in a shaft.

"Why the gun?" Estela asked again.

Magdalena didn't answer.

"Are you going to shoot him?"

"Shut up." Magdalena gestured with the gun and Estela, who had begun to rise, sat down again.

"Please. I beg you. Please don't shoot him."

The elevator stopped, a door slid open, closed again, *clang.* Silence. Somebody stood outside the apartment. There was the faint noise of a key-chain. The tumblers of the lock turned, the door opened.

Rafael came into the room wearing a dark blue windjammer and jeans and sneakers; handsome as always, unbearably so. And cool. If the appearance of Magdalena shocked him, he didn't show it. A momentary apprehension perhaps, a quick dark cloud crossing the eyes, but hardly noticeable.

"What a pleasant surprise," he said. His smile filled the room and lit it. He had the gift of illuminating a whole environment with that one white spellbinding smile. The same gift could also charm and distract.

Magdalena resisted an urge to put out her hand and touch his face.

"I assume you can explain," Magdalena said. There was frost in her voice.

"Explain? Ah, you mean my marriage."

"You didn't tell me," Magdalena said.

"Why should I? What claims do you have on me?"

"Several million dollars worth. Let's start with that."

Rosabal poured himself a small glass of sherry from a decanter. His hand was very steady. "I don't like guns pointed at me."

"Too fucking bad," she said. She hadn't meant to sound upset, hadn't wanted anything to show in her behavior or language, she wanted to be as cool as Rafael.

"The money went to a worthy cause, dear."

"Not the one for whom it was intended," she said.

"There are degrees of need," Rosabal said. "I tried very hard to be equitable. A little here, a little there—"

"And a little in your own pocket for a rainy day."

Rosabal shrugged in a rather puzzled way, as if he hadn't understood Magdalena's accusation. He said nothing; he looked silently offended. He sipped his sherry and she thought: *he has a good act, a terrific act. I fell for it time and again.*

From the corner of her eye she was conscious of a troubled expression on Estela Rosabal's face. Secret aspects of her husband's life were being uncovered, she was learning new, unwelcome things about the man she'd married.

"Do you intend to shoot me?" There was a patronizing tone in Rosabal's voice. Magdalena remembered that same voice in other situations, in twisted bedsheets when it became a slyly satisfied whisper, in crowded restaurants when it made outrageous suggestions over the pages of a menu, at heights of passion when it spoke of love in a secret language. *God help me*, she thought, *I still want him*.

"Keep this in mind, Magdalena," he said. "Kill me, you kill the new revolution."

"Oh, yeah, sure, I vaguely remember the new revolution. *Our* revolution. But refresh my memory. I want to hear all about it. I'm sure your wife will be interested as well. And the people you cheated, they'd love to learn about the revolution they paid for."

"You should give up sarcasm, dear. It's beneath you." He paused, stared into her eyes with the same knowing look he always used on her. He said, "Castro will be dead within a few hours."

"Castro dead?" Estela asked, apprehension in her tone of voice. She might have been expressing surprise and dread at the destruction of some ancient icon.

"Dead," Rosabal said, without looking at his wife's frightened face.

"I don't believe you, Rafe," Magdalena said. "You're lying about Castro. You've been lying all along. You've been doing nothing except stealing from people who trusted you."

Rosabal made a small injured sound, as if the notion of somebody doubting him were preposterous. "On the contrary, dear heart. While you stand there and wave your gun in my face, officers of the Cuban armed forces have already taken decisive steps to prepare a successful overthrow of the *fidelistas*. You're looking at the next President of our nation."

Estela said, "The next President? You?" Rosabal silenced her with a swift, commanding gesture of his hand. She shut her eyes, turned her lovely face to one side and looked sad.

Magdalena reflected on the unexpected solemnity

in Rosabal's voice. He'd changed course suddenly, going from alleged felon and confidence trickster to potential President within a matter of moments. It was a fast transformation, and it shouldn't have surprised her as it did. She should have been able to see directly into Rafael's heart by this time, but it remained unpredictable territory to her, by turns swamp and glacier, meadow and quicksand.

"Let's assume for a moment you're telling the truth. What happens to the exiles? What happens to Garrido? The people in Miami and New Jersey and California who gathered money for you—what role do they play?" she asked.

Rosabal sat on the arm of the sofa. He looked comfortable now, as if some minor crisis had just been overcome. "People like Garrido have an important function in my new Cuba. They will not be overlooked. You may remember I gave my word."

My new Cuba. The proprietary way he'd uttered this phrase bothered her, but she let it pass, just as she chose not to question the value of what Rosabal called his *word.* She was like an impoverished woman confronted with money she knows to be counterfeit and yet hopes, in the face of all the evidence, that it might still be real, it might still offer a way out from a lifetime of hardship.

"What about everything else?" she asked. "The new society. Democracy. All the things we ever talked about. The future we planned. What happens to all that? Does that still come into existence?"

Rosabal's smile was tolerant, like that of somebody obliged to explain the simple principles of arithmetic. "In time, my dear. Change can't be hurried. People have to be prepared. You know that as well as I do."

In time, she thought. Yes, he was right, a whole

society couldn't be changed overnight. Then she caught herself: goddam him, she was thinking the way he wanted her to think! She was blindly agreeing with him. Love had petrified her will. Step away from him, she thought, distance yourself, make believe you never loved him, fake the impossible. *Pretend he never asked you to marry him. Pretend there was never any planned future. Pretend the sun rises in the west and the moon comes out at midday.*

"After you throw out Castro's Communism, Rafe—what takes its place?"

Rosabal said, "I'll rule as fairly as I can. But don't expect me to be weak. I won't allow anarchy any more than I'll permit instant democracy. Down the road somewhere, perhaps five years from now, I may hold free elections."

"*Five years? Five years?* I imagined free elections within a few months, six, nine at most."

"Your optimism is touching. But the Cuban people aren't ready to control their own future."

"And in the meantime?"

"In the meantime, we prepare the people for eventual democracy—"

"With you in total control—"

"Naturally."

"And your five years might become ten. Fifteen. Twenty. What happens when you don't step down, Rafe? What happens if you don't want to relinquish power? Then nothing has really changed except the name of the dictator."

Rosabal shook his head. "You're overreacting. Everything changes. No more Communism. No shortages. No more reliance on the Soviets. Cuba will be a free nation again."

Magdalena turned away. It was better if she didn't

have to look at his face. Even now he could be so convincing. A free nation, she thought. Was that what he'd said? But how could Cuba be free without elections? How was freedom to be achieved if Rafael Rosabal alone controlled the country's destiny? Dictators might all start from different points of view, some might begin with benign notions, even with charity, but in the end greed and power rotted all of them and they resorted to the same kind of apparatus that could be found in a score of countries around the world—secret police, political prisons, the disregard of basic human rights, torture.

She faced him again. He was watching her, counting on her to put the gun down and tell him she'd been mistaken, that she'd overreacted but still supported him.

Fuck you, Rafe. All she wanted was to lash out at him.

She looked at Estela and in a voice that was both flat and uncharacteristically spiteful said, "He told me he'd marry me. We used to lie in bed together and plan our wedding. We used to meet in Acapulco. London. Barcelona once or twice. But I don't imagine he mentioned that kind of thing to you."

It was a sleazy little shot intended to cause him discomfort, but he reacted only with a curious laugh, as if he were embarrassed for her. He didn't need to be. She had more than enough embarrassment for herself. Only the way Rosabal had hurt her could have made her sink so goddam low as to proclaim his indiscretions before his innocent young wife. Magdalena suddenly wanted to deny what she'd said. She felt a sense of shame.

Estela started to say something but another gesture from her husband quieted her at once. She hated his habit of silencing her with that bossy, chopping motion of his hand. Did he think he could shut her up any time he liked? Despite her calm appearance she wasn't really any better equipped to deal with this situation than Magdalena, for whom she felt an unexpectedly strong pity. How could she not? Crushed, Magdalena had lost all composure. Only a heart of clay could fail to be touched.

It was obvious he'd lied to this woman who was clearly the mistress Estela had often imagined. And he'd betrayed his own wife. Without apparent shame. Without remorse.

Estela clasped her hands, folded them across her stomach. She was afraid. Afraid of her husband, afraid of what she'd heard in this room. It was more than the personal revelations that scared her, the deceptions of love. After all, she knew these things happened to people every minute of every day, and they brought pain, but life went on because it had to, and people recovered in time if they had resilience, and old scars faded. What scared her on some other level was the understanding that Castro was to be killed and Rafael was to become the new President of Cuba.

This was the secret matter in which Rafael and General Capablanca and that *solteron* Alonzo-Diaz were involved. This was what the late-night meetings amounted to. Politics was the domain of men, and they were welcome to its animosities and hatreds. She wanted no part of that hazy world. But she knew Castro would not die easily. He would fight. He was a survivor. He'd outlived most of his rivals. She had a terrible image of roads filled with tanks and guns, corpses in ditches, fields of sugarcane blazing, neighbor fighting neighbor, small children suffering as they always did in the world of grown-up violence. Cuba would turn into another Salvador, a Nicaragua. How could the ambitions of men like her husband and her father threaten to engulf the island in destruction? What if their revolution failed? What if Castro emerged victorious? Rosabal would be branded a traitor and she would be guilty by association. *And the baby, this nameless infant inside her, what would become of it then?* She felt sadness, then the kind of anger that always grew in her slowly.

"If you don't want to talk about your proposals of marriage, Rafael, why don't we talk about the missile instead? That ought to be an easier topic for you." Magdalena decided to come in at Rosabal from another angle now. Her fist was clenched tightly around the butt of the pistol.

How close was she to firing? she wondered. It scared her that she didn't know. But she no longer had any familiarity with the limits of her own behavior. It was as if an unpredictable stranger lived inside her. She understood that she wanted to keep after Rosabal, haranguing him, paining him if she could, but she also wanted the opposite, to hold and comfort, to love him. *Unhealthy, Magdalena.* How sick am I? "I suppose you're going to lie about that too. I suppose you're going to say you didn't arrange to have Gunther Ruhr steal it."

Rosabal set his empty glass down and ran a fingertip drily round the rim. He looked very calm. "You have some useful sources of information, Magdalena. I'm impressed. I'm not going to deny there's a missile. But it isn't real. It's make-believe. A ruse, a nice ploy to discredit Castro, nothing more. It's merely for show. It's quite harmless."

"For show?"

He began to explain how the missile would be disarmed and Castro overthrown. His voice took on the kind of enthusiasm he'd always used to sweep her along, as if she were no more than an object floating on his energetic tide.

She interrupted him as soon as she understood. "You disable the weapon and the whole world loves you for your heroism. Right?"

"Why not? The world loves heroes. We're in short supply, after all."

You're good, Rafe, she thought. *You lie, you tell the truth, you go back and forth between the two so often that the only outcome is the one you want most: confusion. How much of what he'd said was true, how much false?*

"Okay," she said. "So there's a missile, and it's only for show. Let's take that at face value for the time being and move on. Let's discuss something else. The girl. The hostage. What becomes of her in Ruhr's hands?"

"A girl? What girl?" Estela Rosabal asked. The conversation had gone into baffling areas. Missiles, hostages, things she knew nothing about.

Rosabal gestured for silence again, but this time Estela ignored him and got up from the sofa. She approached Magdalena and asked, "What hostage? What girl? What are you talking about?"

Rosabal was irritated, his facade altered for the first time. His wife's small act of disobedience had undermined his *machismo* in Magdalena's eyes. "Mind your own goddam business," he said.

Once again Estela ignored her husband. She looked at Magdalena and asked, "You're certain Ruhr has a child as a hostage?"

"Yes," Magdalena said.

"What age is she?"

"Thirteen, fourteen."

Estela Rosabal had read in Central American newspapers about Ruhr and the bestial way he was reputed to have attacked young girls in England and elsewhere. There were pictures of his alleged victims. Such sad faces. Such dead eyes. Estela had never been able to tolerate violence, far less the needless kind done to children. It was a crime against innocence, a violation of nature.

She turned quickly to her husband. Her jaw was firm, her eyes fiery. Aggression altered her features, tightening the skin, emphasizing the solid strength of the cheekbones. She reached out, caught the sleeve of Rosabal's shirt. "What do you have to do with this?" she demanded. "What in the name of God do you have to do with the business of this child?"

"Child, what child?" Rosabal pulled his arm free.

"Tell me the truth, Rafael."

Rosabal poured another small sherry. He didn't speak.

Estela asked, "Does my father know? Does the General know about this? I can't imagine him approving of a hostage situation with a child involved."

"The General is in no position to withhold his approval of anything I choose to do," Rosabal said.

"Shall I telephone him? Shall I ask his opinion?"

"Do what you like," Rosabal said, but without conviction. The plain truth was that he needed the General, at least during the next twenty-four hours. And that stiffbacked old-fashioned bastard, who had never approved of Ruhr to begin with and barely acknowledged the man's existence or his part in the plan, who would have preferred to believe that the missile had materialized out of thin air, was sure to become apoplectic at the idea of a hapless child held captive by the Claw. Rosabal couldn't alienate Capablanca at this stage. He couldn't risk losing the support of Capablanca and his officers. Things would fall apart if Estela contacted her father.

Estela reached for the telephone. She was bluffing. She had absolutely no idea of the whereabouts of her father or how to contact him. The General was frequently on the move and for years his staff had been under strict orders to keep his movements secret. He drew a very firm line between his private life and his soldierly one, a definite boundary that could not be crossed, no matter what.

Rosabal placed a hand over hers, preventing her from raising the receiver. "All right," he said. "There's a kid. But I had nothing to do with it. It happened without my approval. Ruhr kidnapped the child—"

"Then you have to arrange for her release."

"For God's sake, what difference does one child make anyway? It's one life, that's all. I'm talking about millions of lives, a new Cuba, new freedoms—"

Magdalena said, "That's not what you're talking about, Rafael. Do you really give a shit about freedoms in Cuba? You already said all the power will lie in your hands indefinitely. If all you intend to do is make some pointless cosmetic changes inside Cuba, the exile community in Florida will fight you the way it fought Castro—"

"You are both being foolish," Rosabal said, suppressing the anger of a man suddenly assailed by two women who had formed a collaboration that baffled him. "You understand only this much," and he held his thumb a quarter inch from the tip of his index finger. So attentive in such matters as kissing the back of a hand, so skilled in the bedroom, he consistently failed to take women seriously.

"Have the child released," Estela said. "Do it now."

"Don't ever tell me what to do and when to do it. I don't even know where the kid is."

Estela reached once more for the telephone. Rosabal was quicker. He grabbed the instrument, ripped it from the wall, tossed it across the room. It struck a door and broke apart in useless little bits and pieces.

Estela was quiet for a moment before she turned to Magdalena and said, "There's a ship called the *Mandadera.* If the child is with Ruhr, then she's on board this ship. Because that's where Ruhr is."

"Don't listen to her," Rosabal said. "She knows nothing!"

"The *Mandadera* is on its way to Santiago," Estela said. "It is expected to arrive there soon. Within two, perhaps three hours. Rafael is supposed to meet the ship when it docks. I listen to everything. My husband thinks I'm asleep when he sits here and conspires with his associates. But I don't sleep. I hear everything. What else am I supposed to do when I'm lonely? I heard about Ruhr, about the ship—"

Enraged, Rosabal struck his wife across the side of her head. Her legs buckled dreadfully and she almost slid to the floor. She clutched the arm of the sofa for support and looked at her husband in astonishment. Magdalena, shocked by the sudden act of violence yet oddly impressed by this show of force, raised the gun and pointed it at him. Shoot him, she thought. *Shoot him now.*

He held his hand out. He was marvelously cool again, smiling as if nothing had happened. He had the ability to change everything with charm. He looked quite incapable of violence now. All the tension in his handsome face had dissolved. "Enough," he said. "Give the gun to me." He took a step toward her.

"Stay away from me, Rafe."

"Magdalena. We aren't enemies, you and I. We've been too close for all this hostility."

"Don't move." She tried to stop the hand that held the gun from trembling. He took another step. He stood about three feet from her, calmly running a fingertip over his forehead. His suntanned skin glistened. His perfect mouth continued to smile, infuriating and seductive at the same time.

"We can still be together," he said. "Our plans don't have to be thrown away."

"Bullshit, Rafe." *She wasn't going to fall for any of it.*

"Be with me. Support me."

"Rafe—"

"We can talk our problems over. We can resolve them, Magdalena. Or else you can shoot me. You can kill me."

"There's nothing to talk about—"

"On the contrary, there's everything." He closed his eyes a moment. Lamplight glowed on his eyelids and his long lashes. He did something strange then. He repeated her name a couple of times to himself, as if it were a sound he'd never uttered before, one he found unexpectedly enchanting.

Estela said *Pay no attention to him* but Magdalena didn't hear, she was concentrating on Rafael, whose voice had become a soft whisper, almost an hypnotic caress. And she remembered how they'd undressed each other in hotel rooms in various cities of the world, the thrillingly indecent haste of their love, she recalled the ritual of the sugar cubes and how once, in a moment of erotic splendor she would savor for the rest of her life, he had slid a cube between the warm lips of her vagina and licked it away, crystal by crystal, *dulzura, dulzura,* drawing it out with the tip of his tongue, then playfully pushing it back inside. She remembered intimacies that terrified her because they exposed her, times when she couldn't dream of her world without Rafael Rosabal. Nor could she contemplate such a world even now. It was a barren place, a planet devoid of life.

"Let us put the gun aside, Magdalena," he said. His tone was firmer now. "We'll go somewhere and talk."

"No—"

He stretched out his hand. "We can work things out, I promise you. But we can't make any progress so long as you hold the pistol," and he shrugged, as if to say further talk was pointless, and he was disappointed by her.

"Rafe," she said quietly. She didn't want to weaken. But he overwhelmed her the way he always did. She saw how deeply she needed him, a fact of nature, incontrovertible.

He ran his strong fingers through his hair, then took one more step toward her.

"Rafe . . ."

She had the curious feeling that her peripheral vision had been destroyed, and she could see nothing but his face in front of her. It dominated the room, throwing everything else into shadow. She was sick from the fever of love, and she knew, with all the certitude of her own addiction, that she could no more shoot this man than she could stop loving him. She'd known it all along, from the moment he'd first entered the apartment. She'd find a way to forgive him for the theft of the money, his marriage, how he'd altered the shape of the new revolution and changed the dream, everything. *Shoot him*, she thought. How could you shoot the thing you loved most? Who was she trying to fool?

She lowered the pistol to her side, a movement she performed as if she had no volition. She was no longer listening to her own warning system; the voice of reason had been struck dumb inside her. Even as Rosabal took the weapon out of her hand and put it in the pocket of his jacket, a part of her knew she should have resisted. And when he spoke she infused his words with a warmth nobody else would have heard.

In a voice that might have persuaded birds to come down from trees, he said, "We'll go someplace quiet now, Magdalena. We'll talk in private."

Yes, yes, she thought. The idea of intimacy excited her. She wanted to be alone with him.

Estela pressed a hand to the side of her head where she'd been hit. "Where are you going?"

Rosabal didn't answer. Estela watched him go out of the apartment. This was not the man who had courted her with such bewitching charm. This was not the beautiful man who had observed all the elaborate etiquette of courtship, who had come with flowers and Swiss chocolates and cosmetics, and such obvious affection in his eyes.

Rosabal ushered Magdalena to the stairway. She took his hand, clasping it tightly. It would work out, it had to, there was no other option.

"This way, my dear," he said to her.

When they went down to the empty lobby, the wind was screaming round the building. The glass doors flapped and palm trees creaked. The night was becoming furious.

She turned to look at him. He smiled, then touched the side of her face with an open hand. The contact was tender. She wanted to make love to him here and now, the place didn't matter. She kissed him, sliding a hand under his jacket. She heard the wind rage at the building and one of the glass doors was blown open, but these were sounds from another world far removed from her. He was hard against her. *He wanted her.* She felt his need and it justified her. Giving up the gun had been the right move.

"Not here," he said. "This is too public."

"I love you," she said, and drew away from him reluctantly.

"And I love you. But we must find a more intimate place."

They went outside where the air was filled with electricity and moisture, like a damp sheet stretched across the city.

"My car," he said. He held her by the elbow as he led her toward the curb.

"Where are we going?" she asked.

"I have a place in mind."

"And after we make love—"

"After we make love, we settle our differences, if we still have any by then," and he laughed in an oddly nervous little way. He opened the passenger door for her.

Something made her hesitate, perhaps his uncharacteristic laugh, perhaps a sudden insight into how witless her feelings had made her, perhaps the lightning that flared with stunning brilliance. She had the unsettling sensation of coming out of a sweet dream into a menacingly real world.

"Get in the car," he said.

She didn't want to go inside. She looked at him. His lips were narrow and uncharitable, his eyes curiously bright, and not with love. Something else, something she couldn't quite read.

"The car," he said again.

She opened her mouth, which was suddenly very dry. He had the pistol in his hand, aimed at her stomach.

"Why are you pointing that at me, Rafe?" She couldn't get this situation into focus. It was slipping away from her, and she felt panicked.

"Get in the car," he said.

"Not until you put the gun away."

He pressed the weapon into her flesh with such ferocity that she gasped. The abrupt chill of understanding she felt horrified her. He was going to kill her, she hadn't seen it coming, she'd been as careless and dumb as any fifteen-year-old girl in love for the first time. "Rafe, for God's sake—"

"Do as I say."

"Dear Christ, Rafe—"

"Let me tell you how it really is, Magdalena. You would be a problem to me. Today, tomorrow, a problem. You know too much about me. You know about my connection with Ruhr. Too much. So now we go to a quiet place. It won't take more than a second. A fraction of a second. Painless."

Painless, she thought. He sounded like a dentist making a promise to a nervous client, but he was talking about murder, her murder. His tone of voice was utterly reasonable. A calm she found even more frightening than the gun. There was a madness in him, and she'd been blind to that the way she'd been blind to everything about him. He didn't want her, didn't need her. She was a problem, therefore she had to be eliminated. He might even have sent the killer after her in Miami.

The notion devastated her. She couldn't breathe, couldn't swallow. Paralyzed, she was only vaguely aware of lightning over the city. The thunder when it came was the kind that clapped and echoed inside her head in a mocking way.

"Get in the car," Rosabal said again. "I am running out of time, Magdalena. Hurry. Hurry."

A small vehicle moved slowly along the street. It took Magdalena a second to recognize it as Alberto Canto's Lada. It began to pick up speed. Rosabal turned his face toward the car, which was coming toward his BMW in such a way that a collision was unavoidable. As he levelled the pistol at the Lada, he experienced a moment of indecision. He was beset by doubts about firing the gun in the street. Neighbors. Police. His ministerial status would almost certainly afford him immunity from a murder investigation if he killed somebody, but these were sensitive hours, and he couldn't take the chance of having to answer questions of any kind. Too much time had been wasted already. He should have been on his way to Santiago by now. The clocks were running.

The Lada mounted the sidewalk and kept coming. On and on, doggedly, it kept rolling. Rosabal finally fired when the small car was about twenty feet from the BMW. The windshield shattered but the Lada wouldn't stop. It struck the side of Rosabal's car and swerved across the sidewalk and the passenger door was thrown open. Magdalena reached for the open door, then threw herself toward it with a gymnast's grace; she managed to grab the edge and hang on as the Lada grazed the wall surrounding the apartment building. She closed her eyes. Air rushed against her. The little car bounced off the sidewalk and back into the street.

Rosabal fired a second time. The sound of the pistol coincided with the roar of more thunder. You couldn't tell one from the other.

Magdalena slumped into the passenger seat. "You're braver than you thought, Canto," she said. *Jesus, the pain. The swift knifelike pain.*

"I saw your predicament. What was I supposed to do?"

Magdalena turned her face, looked back, saw Rafael on the sidewalk surrounded by a few inquisitive neighbors. "He'll call the cops. He's bound to. Can you stick to back streets?"

"I can try," Canto said.

"Take me to the place where you found me," she replied. She was breathing hard. "The airfield."

Canto glanced at her. "You sound terrible. Is something wrong?"

"It's nothing."

He saw it then: blood stained the front of her shirt. She was holding a hand loosely over the place, as if trying to conceal it.

"You've been hit."

"It's nothing. It's not important."

"You're talking to a physician. I decide what's important."

"Take me to the airfield. That's important."

"Not before I've checked your wound."

"What do you want to do? Stop the car right here in the middle of this street? Bandage me? Drive, Canto. You can fix me when we get to the airfield."

She stared through the windshield. Imagine Rosabal's bullet didn't hit you. Your lover's bullet didn't pass through your flesh. Imagine nothing happened. You're well. Everything's fine. You're going back to the airfield. Intact. *It wasn't like that, though.*

She moaned, bent forward, held her hand over the wound. It wasn't clean. It was soft and wet, ragged and appalling.

"I'm going to pull over the first chance I get," Canto said.

"The hell you are."

"I have a stinking bedside manner at the best of times. Don't argue with me."

She tipped her head back, closed her eyes, bit on her lower lip. She had a gloomy sense of futility, an emptiness in her heart. Had she come all the way to Cuba only to lose her life? Was this it? Was this the shitty sum of things?

This miserable exit. What a way to go. She wanted another kind of ending. Now she wanted some justice. She wanted revenge the way Garrido had yearned for it. She realized she still loved Rosabal with all the intensity of a victim's love—a pathetic compulsion, a deficiency of her character. She had no more control over the feeling than she would a virus in her blood. A victim's love was not what she wanted. When you loved like that you could never know any freedom.

There was only one way to be free from it.

She opened her eyes and looked at Canto through her pain. "I'm a fighter, Canto. I always have been."

"Somehow I don't doubt it," Canto remarked, although he didn't remotely like the sound of her erratic breathing.

Rain had begun to fall in huge drops when Frank Pagan reached his destination some forty-five minutes after Magdalena Torrente had gone. The street was quiet and empty by then. A badly dented BMW was parked outside the apartment building. Pagan, damp and not very happy, went into the lobby, passed the desk, headed for the stairs. He reached the top floor, took out his Bernardelli. First things first. Lightly he tried the door handle. Predictably locked.

He knocked. He held the gun pointed at the door.

The woman who came to answer was lovely and pale and indifferent. She held a white lace handkerchief, in which was wrapped an ice-cube, to the side of her head. The sight of Pagan's gun made little impression on her. Pagan walked into the apartment.

"Do you speak English?" he asked.

"A little," and she shrugged. She took the ice-cube from her forehead. There was a marked swelling between ear and eye. "Where is Rosabal?" Pagan asked.

"Gone." Spoken without interest. "*Solito.* Nobody else is here. See for yourself."

Pagan looked inside the other rooms of the flat. They were empty. "Where did he go?"

"What difference does it make to you where my husband goes?"

So this was the wife, this was Magdalena's rival for Rafe's affections. Pagan wondered what had taken place in this apartment that had left her with such a vivid contusion. Was Rafe a wife-beater as well as a philanderer?

"I need to find him," Pagan said. There was a shelf of photographs behind the woman. One, prominently displayed, depicted Rosabal in the company of Fidel. Both men were smiling polite smiles. It was posed, artificial.

"Why?" the woman asked.

"I'm looking for a child. I believe your husband can help me find her. She's with a man called Ruhr."

Estela Rosabal walked to the photograph of her husband and Castro and picked it up. She studied it for a moment, then she dropped the picture to the rug and twisted her heel in the dead center of it. Estela gazed at the slivers, the way Rafael's face appeared imprisoned behind bars of broken glass.

Then she looked at Pagan. "You've come a long way," she said.

"Yes. A long way."

"I will help you find the child."

She told him about the *Mandadera,* about Ruhr on board the vessel, about the destination in Santiago. Sometimes her voice dropped to a whisper and Pagan had to ask her to say things over again.

"How can I get to Santiago?"

"By road is too slow. You must fly there." She told him it was about five hundred miles from Havana to Santiago. She wasn't sure exactly.

"How can I find a plane?" he asked.

Estela Rosabal shut her eyes and did not answer for a long time, so long indeed that Pagan assumed she hadn't heard the question.

"I will help you with that too," she said finally.

19

The Caribbean

The storm that had begun in the Gulf of Mexico carved out a wide path as it rolled in a southerly direction. Around Havana winds measured forty miles an hour; over the Isla de la Juventud and southeast between the shoreline of Cuba and the Caymans they were fiercer, reaching fifty and sixty. Later in the morning, when the storm would move due west of Jamaica, hundred mile winds would rage over the Caribbean.

Had *La Mandadera* sailed from Cabo Gracias a Dios some two hours earlier, it could not have avoided the impenetrable black heart of the storm that would make the sea west of Jamaica a roiling nightmare; as it was, the ship still couldn't escape brutally damaging gales and cold blinding rain squalls that assailed it after it had passed between the Caymans and Jamaica. Captain Luis Sandoval, whose experience of tempests had never lessened his fear of them, estimated the wind at between fifty-five and sixty miles an hour, ten on the Beaufort Scale.

His ship lurched and plunged on huge swells. Leaden clouds darkened the early sun as they raced. Rain, sometimes turning to a hard hail, relentlessly scoured the decks. There was a deranged fusion here of elements and artifacts, weather and steel, cloud and smoke, one became the other in that dire place beyond boundaries. Day turned back to night within a matter of minutes, a weird compression of time, a suspension of natural laws.

Steffie Brough lay on her bunk. The tiny cabin pitched and rolled as if on castors, and the ceiling rose and fell. Waves covered the small porthole. The battered ship creaked. In her imagination Steffie could see bolts and screws come loose and whole metal panels crash into the sea.

She shut her eyes and fought the urge to throw up. She clutched the side of her bunk and held on, thinking that with every pitch of the vessel it would surely capsize and sink to the bottom of the sea.

Once, when she propped herself up on an elbow and tried to rise, she was thrown back against the wall and struck her head, which ached now. She hauled a blanket up over her face and tried to make herself very small—microscopic—as if she might go unnoticed by the vicious weather.

She heard the cabin door open. Gunther Ruhr, soaked, hair plastered across his head, came inside. He was dripping, his feet squelched. She didn't look at him. She kept her face under the blanket. She heard him dry himself with a towel, then he was so curiously silent for a long time that she sneaked a look.

He was standing at the small sink, the mirror—sharpening something—swish swish swish, the sound of an old-fashioned razor on a leather strap—swish-swishswish—she saw it was no razor, but his knife—and he was whistling under his breath, a whistle that was practically a throaty whisper, spooky and tuneless—

The cabin shifted, spun round. *She was back home, she was riding her mare across wintry fields, and she'd never gone near the old Yardley farm, it was just too dull and drab, it didn't attract her, so instead she rode over Crossfields Hollow and into the village where she stopped by the ice-cream shop and had a chocolate cone and then and then and then . . .*

She felt Ruhr pull back the blanket. She turned her face away from him. He held his knife in one hand. Steffie drew herself back as far as she could until her spine was pressed to the wall. Ruhr looked the length of her leg to the place where his fingerprints had left bruises from before. She snatched the blanket, covered herself.

He sat down, placed the knife upon his thigh.

He listened to the way the storm blasted the ship. If there were different kinds of weather to suit different personalities, storms were what most pleased Gunther Ruhr. They created chaos, they broke down peace and order. They raged for hours and drove the sea and the sky together in one cauldron of turmoil. They sank ships. They excited him; liberated him.

Waves rose across the deck; up and down, down and up, the sea tossed the *Mandadera* as though it were a craft made from matchsticks.

Ruhr laid a finger against the scar the girl had inflicted around his eye with her nail. Then he picked up his knife from his thigh and drew the blanket back from Steffie Brough's body; she held the edge of the blanket tightly, resisted, refused to yield even when he slid the point of the blade gently across her cheek and drew to the surface of her skin a thread of blood. She would hold on forever if she had to, she'd struggle no matter what it took—

Without any trouble, Ruhr hauled the blanket back and laughed. He cuffed the child and she cowered, huddling in the corner, staring at Ruhr with hatred and fear and hopelessness.

The knife flashed just as there was a loud knock on the cabin door.

In the dark hold one of the lashes that bound the missile had come undone. The cylinder, with its armed nose-cone, tipped forward at an angle of twenty degrees. A report had reached Luis Sandoval on the bridge that the weapon was listing in an alarming way. A simple man, he did not know that the missile would not explode accidentally. He believed there was every chance of a holocaust and so he sent an agile seaman, harnessed for his own safety, with an order for Gunther Ruhr to descend inside the hold and secure the *proyectil*.

Santiago de Cuba Province

The outer reaches of the storm spread inland toward the province of Holguin, where General Capablanca was forced to postpone his diversionary maneuvers; tanks were stuck on beaches, sodden soldiers sheltered beneath trees, airplanes were grounded, ships anchored unsteadily three miles out in the Atlantic.

The ill-tempered gale blew over Bayamo and into the Sierra Maestra, where several hundred anti-Castro rebels sheltered in damp caves with their rifles. Then it slashed across Santiago itself, whipping the Bay, blowing down telephone lines, taking off the roof of the Leningrado Restaurant on San Juan Hill, flattening cabins at the Daiquiri Motel on Baconao Park Road, sinking a fishing-boat two miles out of Siboney Beach.

From the rainwashed helicopter in which Frank Pagan uneasily sat, nothing could be seen of the ground below nor the sky above. The chopper, rocking in wild currents of air, was piloted by a blunt torpedo of a man Estela Rosabal had summoned—former Lieutenant Alejandro Bengochea, a sixty-three-year-old flyer retired from the Cuban Air Force.

It was the worst ride in Pagan's experience. He expected the flying machine to plummet down at any moment through rainy turbulence and explode on the landscape, but Bengochea, as if he had a special contract with gravity and air currents, kept the machine magically airborne. Bengochea, who wore an old revolver on his hip, spoke no English, nor did he appear to question his flying mission—it had come to him from none other than General Capablanca's esteemed daughter, and that was good enough for him. Had Estela asked him to fly through a ring of fire or aim directly for the moon he would have done so.

For most of his adult life, Bengochea had built his world around the Capablanca family. He was a courtier, Estela his princess. He had known her since she was a small child. He even had home movies, which he sometimes watched all these years later in his small empty apartment in Marianao. They depicted him with the princess riding on his shoulders at the age of seven or building sand-castles with her on the beach at Varadero. The Capablancas had been his only family in a life of unbroken solitude imposed upon him by a military career of complete dedication.

Nothing scared Alejandro Bengochea. Notions of immortality were for the very young. He'd fought against the Yanquis at the Bay of Pigs, flown helicopter missions in Angola ten years ago, been imprisoned and tortured in the time of the Batista regime, he had even fallen out of favor with Castro's government in the early 1970s (he was 'a reactionary', they said), only to be spared imprisonment by the intervention of General Capablanca. What was there to be afraid of? His body was scarred everywhere, one eye had been partially blinded under the ministrations of Batista's thugs. Now he wore black glasses as if they were fixtures never to be removed, not even in sleep. He was a human being living beyond his span. Lucky Alejandro he was called. But he knew how to fly this helicopter with amazing skill, how to keep it aloft in gales.

Here and there, between squalls when the wind withdrew, the beaten landscape could be seen—beaches, a shoreline, sand dunes, visible only for seconds then swallowed again. Pagan shut his eyes. The roar of the helicopter was stunning, thudding inside his head. What he'd seen of the ocean appalled him. White, frenzied, it seethed and foamed furiously over beaches and sea-walls. He would not have been surprised to see it reach up and drag the helicopter down into its demanding depths.

The storm caught the chopper, raised it in the sky like a leaf. Alejandro Bengochea enjoyed it. The weather challenged, even amused him, as if this were a personal test between himself and the vicissitudes of the planet. He took the chopper up and up, forcing it beyond the reaches of pandemonium into a momentary calm, an oasis in the sky.

Through another brief window in the ragged rain squall Pagan saw that the helicopter was directly over water now. Land was no longer visible. Fall from this place and you were a dead man; in that frightening, tumultuous sea your body might never be found.

He constantly scanned the waters. How was it possible to spot anything down there in that fury? And if you stared long enough and hard, you could even begin to hallucinate the appearance of small islands, or whales, or sea-troubled freighters—grays imposed on grays, and nothing distinguishable. Pagan, whose usual determination was weakening, felt the search was hopeless. But Bengochea loved this sea-hunt with all the devotion of a bird-watcher on the trail of a rare species. He wouldn't give up and go back to the shore.

The chopper rocked, lost height, Bengochea laughed; he had a relationship with destiny quite alien to Pagan, whose personal preference was to avoid a confrontation with his own demise. Down and down the helicopter went, until it seemed inevitable it would plunge into the water.

"There!" Pagan pointed downward.

A freighter, camouflaged by the sea, pitched. Waves frothed over the deck. The ship looked appallingly insubstantial on the swell, something that might have been set on a pointless journey by a child's hand.

Blinding rain and spray rose up. There was nothing to see, no world beyond violent water, no sky, no ship, nothing.

The freighter seemed to have vanished entirely, leaving Pagan to wonder if, after all, he'd seen anything.

The intensity of the storm overwhelmed Captain Luis Sandoval. His radio had ceased to function, his navigational equipment was useless. Locked in his sightless, airless bridge, a glass prison, he guessed he was some fifteen miles from Santiago. His first mate was an experienced old seaman named Zaldivar, but even this seasoned mariner had no idea of the exact location of the freighter. The storm reduced perceptions, destroyed instincts, threw men back on guesswork.

Luis Sandoval cursed this weather, this *tormenta*. When he looked up he prayed for a break, a sign of sunlight—but the rains kept coming and the decks were submerged. From the engine room had come an ominous report that about nine inches of water had collected below and that the pumps were laboring. This goddam bitch of a boat! Sandoval thought. This *puta!*

Zaldivar, his white beard grizzly, his face etched by the acid of too many suns, was a superstitious man who blamed the presence of Ruhr and *el proyectil malvado* for the freighter's predicament. Without the crippled *aleman*, none of this would have happened. Hadn't the day begun quietly? Hadn't there been a clear sky and a quiet sea? *Aiee,* it was the fault of the freak with the vile hand. There could be no disputing Zaldivar's nautical logic, grounded as it was in a system that transcended the empirical. The sea operated under the laws of its own gods, who were furious beyond all reason.

Sandoval ceased to listen to the old man's babblings. He peered from the bridge. Along the deck he saw, as if it were a figure from an hallucination, Gunther Ruhr moving toward the hold. A rope was tied round his waist and snaked behind him to some safe point. He was going to secure the missile. Zaldivar rubbed his beard and shook his head as Ruhr opened the hold and vanished into darkness.

"*El Diablo,*" the old sailor remarked quietly.

Sandoval looked upward. Out there in the dense structure of the squall he saw a flying ghost, a bizarre outline that was gone before he was certain he'd even registered it.

Ruhr could barely catch his breath in the storm. Only when he reached the hold and lowered himself into the darkness were his lungs able to function again. Exhausted by the struggle along the deck, he sat on the floor, breathing fast and hard until his energies returned. He turned on a flashlight and saw how the cruise missile, having slipped one of the mooring cables, lay out of balance. It was no great matter to secure it again. He followed the line of loose cable to a metal hook on the wall and there he anchored it, making certain it was tight. His hands were cold, his fingers stiff.

The freighter rose in the swell, dropped again. The storm was magnificent still. He hauled himself out of the hold, clutching the rough fibers of the damp rope knotted round his waist. The other end of the rope was tethered to the handrail about thirty feet along the deck. He loved the idea of his life hanging by such a feeble lifeline.

He reached the deck.

Seventy feet above him, a gray helicopter swayed in the gale.

Alejandro Bengochea took the chopper down toward the deck of the ship, but it was hard to hold the machine steady against the energetic frenzy of the wind. At sixty feet he was driven back; the chopper swung in a great circle, then returned to roughly the same point. Bengochea, sometimes bellowing with a sportsman's laughter, sometimes quietly coaxing his craft, fought to hold the machine steady. Both chopper and freighter seemed tied together now as if bound by strands of the same rainy web.

Pagan saw the deck briefly, then it was gone under water; up again, wet timbers, an upturned lifeboat, tar-black smoke zipping away from the funnel. The figure who appeared on the deck seemed to have come out of nowhere; he was roped and threading his way astern like a man following a string through a maze.

Pagan, whose stomach came into his throat, felt the helicopter turn at an awful angle, tilting back down toward the ship before righting itself and hovering one more time, like a demented albatross, over the deck. There was the figure again, looking up this time at the chopper.

Pagan recognized the man. As soon as he did so, he took the rope-ladder from behind his seat and pulled it out. "I'm going down," he said.

Bengochea smiled with approval and gave a thumbs-up sign. Pagan, despite the obstacle of being born English, was a man after his own heart.

The chopper dropped another few feet. The daring Bengochea, the crazy Bengochea, would have landed the machine directly on the deck of the *Mandadera* if he'd had the maneuverability. Now the helicopter hung some fifty feet over the deck, dangerously close to the masts of the freighter. The ship, rising and falling twenty-five feet on the vicious swell, threatened at times to crest high enough for its masts to crash into the underside of the chopper or to snag the rotor blades. To avoid this calamity required a very fine judgment on Bengochea's part, an instinct for prediction in unpredictable circumstances—two feet higher, then three, four, whatever it took to keep the chopper just beyond the reach of the masts.

Pagan opened his door, was almost sucked out into

the skies. It was madness, and he knew it. He also knew there were certain kinds of lunacy you could transcend briefly because the fear of the moment carried you over the hurdle of craziness, imposing upon you an illusion of indestructibility. The notion of throwing down a rope-ladder from a helicopter perched precariously above a freighter sailing in a violent sea seemed almost logical to him just then; and he himself the kind of man who, because he was on the side of the angels, the elements would not destroy.

Sweet Jesus! how frail the rope-ladder looked as it unfolded on its way to the deck.

Alejandro Bengochea dropped as low as he could but the wind bedeviled his machine and he had to rise again another twenty feet, and now the deck seemed a long way down and the rope-ladder too flimsy altogether. It blew violently back and forth beneath the chopper, more a means of transportation for a trapeze artist than for a London policeman with a wound in his chest and no great fondness of heights.

Pagan took a breath, stepped out into nothing.

Rain swirled in cold halos about his head. His hands, gripping the fibrous rope, were red and numb. He hung in the air, defying physics and sanity. He imagined the storm picking him off the ladder and spitting him out into the maelstrom of the sea.

He held on tightly; with the determination of a man who has no desire to look death in its seductive eye, he lowered himself. The storm threatened to suffocate him. He could barely get air into his lungs. Turning his face out of the direct roar of the wind, he gasped.

Gunther Ruhr clutched the sixty-foot rope that would lead him back toward the cabin. His balance on the watery deck was poor and sometimes he slipped, tumbled, but always managed to rise again. Once, seeking a moment's shelter in a doorway, he wiped water from his eyes and observed the man who hung from the rope-ladder. The ladder twisted round and was knocked by the sea-wind back and forth, but the man— the man was unmistakable. And Gunther Ruhr smiled.

It was a fine effort on Pagan's behalf. Ruhr, who realized he had underestimated his adversary, grudgingly admired the sight of the Englishman clinging to the ladder and descending rung by miserable rung toward the deck. Ruhr stepped out of the doorway, removing his gun from his belt and firing once, more a form of greeting than anything meant to hurt Pagan, who ducked his head and almost slipped from the middle of the ladder to fall the final twenty feet to the deck.

Ruhr continued along the deck, holding hard to the rope. He had thirty, perhaps thirty-five feet to go before he reached the tiny room and the girl. Turning, he looked up again at the acrobat Pagan.

Once, during an August Bank Holiday in Margate when he must have been about nine or ten years old, Pagan had thrown up during a ride on a roller-coaster. He remembered the screaming wind in his face, the shrieks of girls, and the way the thin trail of his vomit had caught the breeze and flown away and how his Aunt Henrietta had shoved a handkerchief into his face with a sigh and a tut-tut and *I should've known you wouldn't have the constitution for this, Frankie. Silly silly boy, oh dear oh dear . . .*

Where was Auntie Henrietta now when he really needed her? Pagan wondered. What the fuck. He needed something more than her big white handkerchief that smelled of mothballs, he needed a bloody weatherproof parachute. The rope-ladder was tossed first to the left, then to the right, and Pagan held on, watching Gunther Ruhr move along the deck, waiting for the German to fire the gun again. Ten feet, fifteen, Pagan wasn't sure how far he'd have to drop to hit the deck, but he didn't like his chances anyway. Overhead, the chopper roared and the big blades churned the air; the tumult thrust at Pagan, threatening to blow him back up far enough so that he'd collide with the blades. Hamburger meat. Mince. Razored neatly out of existence.

Oil drums slithered and clattered across the deck, then bounced overboard; a Cuban flag, looking like a used designer kleenex, was sucked away, as if it had imploded. On the bridge, Luis Sandoval shook his head in disbelief. The man who was coming down the ropeladder was clearly *loco,* and so was the pilot of the helicopter. Who these men were, and what their purposes might have been, were matters of no importance to Sandoval. They were intruders. They were no part of any plan. He unlocked the rifle cabinet. He handed a weapon to Zaldivar, and kept one for himself. Both men loaded the weapons then continued to watch the maniac descend from the chopper which, at any moment, was certain to collide with the freighter's masts —*kaboom!*

"He'll never make it to the deck," Zaldivar said.

Sandoval shrugged. "He might. He's crazy enough."

"I'm not going out there," Zaldivar said. "Let the storm take him. Let the storm take the German and his goddam missile as well."

Inside her cabin Steffie Brough felt the ship tilt, then correct itself again. Water covered the porthole, darkening the cabin. She felt claustrophobic. Even though she knew the deck would be exposed and un-safe, she needed to get out of this wretched coffin. She couldn't breathe. She'd been in this stale little room for too long. She wanted air, rain in her face. Mainly she didn't want to be here when Ruhr came back with his knife. Especially that. It was better to get out and take her chances with the weather than to wait in this place for his return.

She tried the door, but it was locked. She yanked on the handle—nothing. The ship listed again, and she was thrown back across the bunk. She got up, hammered on the door, but of course nobody came to answer because nobody heard her voice.

The only voice in the world was that of the wind.

Was the storm faltering? Losing some fraction of its power? It was hard to tell because it was a deceptive thing, a prankster, dying for thirty calm seconds then flaring up again just as you imagined it was fading. In one such lull Frank Pagan hit the deck, bent his knees, curled his body forward to spare himself the jarring effect of contact between skeleton and wood. He lost his balance at once, slid on his back and skidded toward the side of the freighter, seized a rail, held on, his mouth and eyes flooded with salt water. He blinked, saw Gunther Ruhr some yards ahead.

Staying upright was impossible. Pagan fell again, tumbled forward, came to a halt on his ass. Ruhr looked back, fired his gun. Pagan pulled his head involuntarily to one side but the shot was wide anyway. He stood again and aquaplaned a few feet as the freighter creaked then listed to the starboard side. The ocean swept the deck and Pagan, with as much strength as he could still muster, clenched the rainslicked handrail.

Staggering, he followed Ruhr. He almost missed

the hold because its hatch was closed save for a narrow space at one side where it had either been carelessly placed or budged by the storm. He almost missed seeing the section of covered missile below him in the dim light. For the moment he passed it by, rather as a man might hurry past a glass case in a museum that contains artifacts of no fascination for him.

He tried to keep Ruhr in sight. Catching up with him was impossible. His principal objective was not to be washed overboard. Ruhr clutched his rope, his life-line, hurried, hurried, slid, hurried. Pagan, his breath knocked out of him by the storm, kept following. He took his pistol out and fired, but you couldn't hit anything on board a ship that bucked like a mad horse. Water streamed across his face and eyes and into his mouth. He thought it was possible to drown without having to sink underwater to do it.

Ruhr glanced back once, then kept moving, holding still to his safety rope. Pagan fired his gun again—useless, useless; and then the wind blew him back and the Bernardelli was jerked out of his hand and carried overboard and he saw it vanish into the heart of the foam. Christ! Unarmed, how was he supposed to catch this bastard Ruhr now? And where in God's name was the kid?

Ruhr kept moving with the assistance of the rope. Pagan, scudded by water, cuffed, landed on hands and knees. He crawled, rose, glanced up at the helicopter: it looked fragile and exposed and altogether unnatural where it hung. How much longer could Alejandro keep it hovering there? Pagan had to find the kid, get her into the chopper, and get the hell off this ship.

Drenched, blinded, he kept going.

Gunther Ruhr, about twelve feet from the door of the cabin, looked back at Pagan. It was amusing to see the Englishman struggle to stay upright—but then the whole day was one of imbalances and upsets, of symmetry broken down, composure destroyed. Ruhr wiped his eyes with his knuckles, saw the place where he'd tied the rope, saw the cabin door.

He turned to look back one more time at Pagan.

Frank Pagan thought he saw Gunther Ruhr toss back his face and laugh. It was something of which he'd never be certain.

Steffie Brough hammered and hammered on the door until her fists ached. Useless. Then she tugged again and again on the handle.

—why hadn't Ruhr come back?

—she caught the handle, twisted, cursed, strained.

—the bloody thing wouldn't turn, wouldn't, just wouldn't.

She closed her eyes; small tears slithered out from under her eyelids. There has to be something, she thought. There has to be some kind of way out. She kicked the door panel; nothing yielded.

She took a deep breath, bit her lower lip in sheer determination, puffed out her cheeks, pulled together every fragment of strength she could find. She hauled on the handle, and felt a screw pop out from damp wood, a small, warped screw, and the handle itself was loose and a second screw fell away and the door, warped by seasons and sea-changes, split slightly. In the core of the wood were tiny worm-holes, small tunnels that released very fine sawdust. Now the entire handle came away in her fist and she opened the door and the sea blast winded her.

She saw Gunther Ruhr coming along the deck.

He was attached to a rail by a length of rope. It was knotted only twelve inches from the open door of the cabin. She was conscious of a second man hanging on to the rail, trailing Ruhr from behind.

She stepped forward. The idea that came to her was both inevitable and compelling. She had to do it.

With frantic fingers she took the loose end of the knot, the kind known to sailors as a double timber-hitch, and passed it through two loops of rope, which undid the knot swiftly. She dropped the rope. She heard Ruhr shout at her in alarm. Released from his anchor of safety he slipped. She saw him fall flat on his back. The rope curled about his ankle and he slithered toward the side, toward the dreadful sea, even as the other man hurried to prevent him sliding out into the waves.

Fingers clamped on Ruhr's wrist, but he kept slipping away.

"I cannot hold," he shouted. "I cannot hold, Pagan—"

"You have to fucking hold, you bastard!"

Pagan groaned, clenched his jaw, caught Ruhr's shirt under the neck and pulled with all his strength, dragging Ruhr back from the edge. He couldn't let Gunther go, not now, not after all this distance had been travelled. If he released Gunther, then what had been the point of everything? He owed it to the dead men in Shepherd's Bush to take Ruhr back to London. He owed it to the soldiers murdered during the hijack of the missile in Norfolk. And he owed it to Steffie Brough, to her parents, to all the people Gunther Ruhr had hurt.

He couldn't let Ruhr slide into the sea. Couldn't lose him.

The German wasn't heavy, but the effort of rescuing him drained Pagan. He hauled him away from the rail, then released him; Ruhr lay flat and drenched and breathing badly near the cabin door. Landed, Pagan thought. Like a bloody great fish. Harpooned at last.

Pagan's sense of achievement lasted a second before he felt his heart frost over.

In his good hand Gunther Ruhr held his pistol. He pointed it directly at Pagan. "You overlooked this, Frank. Stupid of you."

Pagan stepped back, alarmed. Why had he forgotten Ruhr's gun? Why the hell hadn't he let Ruhr slide into the bloody sea? Too damned anxious, Frank. Too damned keen to play Mr. Justice, to take Ruhr back to London and the law. He didn't deserve due process, did he? He was a killer, a terrorist. He had no sense of right and wrong, no charity, no humanity. He didn't deserve his moment in a court of law, for Christ's sake. Pagan glanced at the girl, who was clinging to the cabin door as if her life depended on it.

Ruhr said, "Wonderful effort, Pagan. But futile—"

The ship bucked suddenly again. The swell, surging under the hull with great might, momentarily forced the bow out of water. The deck tilted up. Gunther Ruhr, slick and wet, slid seven or eight yards on his back away from Pagan, flailing his arms like a man tumbling down a slippery chute.

It was an opportunity, and Pagan had to seize it before the ship righted itself. There might never be another. Fighting to keep his own balance, he caught the girl by the hand and they ran skidding together toward the rope-ladder which shimmied and flapped as if possessed by a life force of its own, and was difficult to grasp. Pagan finally gripped it, brought it under control, helped the girl on to the first sodden rung. The climb was strenuous. The ladder blew sideways, the helicopter swayed, all the balances were so delicate that everything seemed destined to fall at any moment from the sky. The girl climbed a couple of rungs, and Pagan came behind. There was a lull then, a few wonderful seconds in which the storm abated a little and the rain lessened and the sea pounded with diminished vigor at the *Mandadera*. Pagan and the girl were able to advance about one third of the way up, which was when Steffie Brough stopped climbing.

"Keep going, for Christ's sake." Pagan looked down—always a mistake. He saw Gunther Ruhr, upright now, trying to steady himself on the deck for a shot.

"Can't," the girl said.

"Yes you can."

"My legs won't work. They won't work. I can't make them work."

"Bloody hell." Pagan heard the sound of gunfire; overpowered by a revitalized wind, it was strangely unthreatening. But it came close, and he knew it. So did Alejandro Bengochea, who had been watching Ruhr from the cabin. He turned the helicopter away from the *Mandadera* and out over the water beyond the range of Gunther Ruhr's gun.

Pagan reached up with one hand, placed it against Steffie's spine, pushed gently, tried to ease her further up the ladder. She moved then, one slow rung at a time, panting, terrified of falling. He supported her even when the ladder swung to positions that made climbing impossible.

Once, unable to resist the impulse, he glanced at the sea again. *An evil dream of endlessly falling.*

The chopper keep moving back toward land as Pagan and the girl made their way slowly upward to the cabin. The rain was falling hard, but the closer the aircraft came to the shore the more the wind dropped and the sea quieted because the storm was pulling back and rolling out, to renew itself with a vengeance, across the Caribbean. It wasn't completely dead yet. It gusted, still creating havoc as Pagan and the girl pulled themselves up, exhausted, gasping, inside the cabin.

Pagan slumped in the narrow seat, squashed alongside the child. His eyes stung from salt, his hair was plastered to his skull, his clothing and skin so completely soaked he had no idea where fabric ended and flesh began; the storm had welded him to his clothes. His skin was numb.

"We've got to keep the ship in view," he said to Bengochea.

Bengochea appeared not to have understood. Pagan grabbed his arm, pointed down toward the sea. "The *Mandadera*. We've got to follow the bloody ship to Santiago. Understand?"

Bengochea shook his head and pointed to the dials in front of him. "*Necesito gasolina. Comprendo?*"

"*Gasolina?*"

Bengochea rapped a dial in front of him with his fingertips. "See? *Vacante. Comprendo?*"

The chopper lurched suddenly; the fading storm, as if made petulant by its failure to down the craft, seized the machine and gave it one final, terrible shake. The girl, stricken by panic, pressed her face into Pagan's shoulder. The helicopter dropped rapidly, but then the storm, like a fist at last unlocking, released it; now there was only rain and a slight wind and a green rainswept landscape just beyond the shoreline ahead.

Pagan stroked the girl's wet hair. She was uncertain about his touch, but she tolerated it the way a suspicious animal might put up with a stranger's caress.

Bengochea flew directly toward the coastal road that linked Manzanillo with Santiago. On an airstrip outside Palma Soriano, forty miles from Santiago, he brought the craft down. He got out. Pagan watched him walk toward a one-story building where he went inside. The girl, her face still pressed against Pagan's shoulder, stared vacantly across the tarmac. She shivered, said nothing. Pagan looked out at the gray sky and listened to the way rain fell sharply on the roof of the cabin. He was bitterly cold, sneezed once or twice, longed for a good fire, warm clothes, dry shoes.

Soon the *Mandadera* would reach Santiago. Presumably Ruhr and the missile would go ashore there. In her rather glassy, dazed manner, Estela Rosabal had said that the missile—according to her husband—was intended to do nothing more than discredit Castro.

Pagan mulled this over while he waited for Bengochea to return. A missile to discredit Castro, to make him look like a warmonger. To justify his overthrow. To justify the coup Magdalena had talked about. *Fidel has a missile! Look! He intends to use it! He intends to blow up some part of the world! Crazy bastard!* But Rosabal overthrows the old dictator in an heroic coup; nuclear holocaust averted by dashing new President of Cuba. Wasn't that what Estela had whispered? *Rafael believes he will be the next President.*

Question: What nation would be most threatened by a missile on Cuba?

That was obvious. Ergo: by overthrowing Fidel and destroying the missile, Rosabal would be nothing less than a saint in American eyes. American aid would flood the island. American trade would bring riches. Rich tourists. The old guard would flock back to Havana: gamblers, call-girls, pimps, the drug-dealers, gunmen, lowlifers, outlaws, the dubious bankers and lawyers.

Pagan sneezed again and lost his chugging train of

thought. His chest throbbed. His eyes watered. His mind was a cold, numb place. What he wanted was dryness, and food, then sleep.

Bengochea came out of the building and walked back toward the helicopter. He was smiling. He had clearly found a source of fuel. He looked up at Pagan and made a thumbs-up sign.

"*Abundancia,*" he said cheerfully. "*Immediatamente.*"

Rafael Rosabal had flown by jet through the edge of the storm from Havana to Santiago. There he'd been met by a half dozen of Capablanca's officers—two of whom carried expensive cameras to photograph the missile in the launch position.

Followed by a truck containing a score of armed soldiers, Rosabal was driven by jeep out of the storm-swept city and along the coastal road toward Siboney. The nice irony did not escape him. It was from a farmhouse at Siboney that Castro had planned his first assault on the Batista regime in 1953, six years before his ultimate triumph. From this place Castro's revolutionaries had carried out a failed attack, a comedy of errors and confused timing, on the garrison at Moncada. Now monuments to the dead rebels lined the roadside and the farm had become a shrine to deify El Viejo. It was one of Communism's many hypocrisies: God was an unofficial entity, forbidden, but men like Castro could ascend to the vacant summits formerly occupied by the deity.

The jeep took Rosabal to a site about two miles from Siboney, a secluded meadow, ringed by trees and sheltered somewhat from the wind, where the missile would be placed. A house—in the possession of a farmer sympathetic to the new revolution—had been placed at Rosabal's disposal. Rosabal sat silently with Capablanca's officers on the screened porch and listened to what was left of the storm and waited.

He would have preferred better weather, but the storm was gradually diminishing; the *Mandadera* would surely reach its destination. The missile would get here. Delayed, but it would still get here.

Rosabal looked at his watch every so often. Now and again he rose and walked up and down the porch and stared out across the rainy meadow, watching rain sweep through the trees. He was tense. The moment he'd worked for was almost here. The time he'd dreamed about for so long was almost upon him. How could he remain perfectly cool?

He thought about Magdalena Torrente.

He was positive he'd hit her with his second shot. He'd seen a look of pain go across her face before she vanished inside the unexpected Lada. When she'd disappeared, he had telephoned influential friends at the Ministry of the Interior, who immediately set in motion an intensive search of Havana for the Lada and its occupants. At Rosabal's insistence, the search, though widespread, was being conducted with a certain discretion. Delicate matters of state, Rosabal had explained, were involved. Make no noise. Break down no doors needlessly. Do not arrest people carelessly. When the occupants of the Lada were discovered, the female passenger was to be shot on sight.

Magdalena Torrente meant nothing to him anyway. Nor had she ever. She was somebody he fucked, somebody who brought him bundles of cash contributed by the misguided. It was almost as if he were being paid exorbitant sums of money for servicing her.

Rosabal sat down. Suddenly he could feel building inside him the kind of doubts he so rarely entertained these days. What if everything went wrong? What if Magdalena Torrente survived and informed the *fidelista* authorities about Rosabal's revolution? What if this, what if that? He had to keep cool, serene, maintain a calm center. The poor boy, the canecutter's son from Guantanamo, still lived somewhere inside him, that undernourished child who felt he did not deserve any kind of success. He was angry all at once with the ghost of his upbringing. A familiar darkness clouded his vision. It was not the time to be insecure. It was time for resolve, for confidence. It was time to assassinate the past.

Rain pelted the windows, but the heavy skies were less ominous now. The officers smoked cigarettes, studied the rain, said nothing. They too were tense. Now and then a vehicle passed on the road nearby, at which times Rosabal always stared at the meadow expectantly. But the truck carrying the missile did not appear.

When the telephone rang Rosabal's first reaction was one of unease: bad news, he was sure of it. Perhaps the scheme had been discovered and already those forces aligned against Castro had been routed and arrested, and the names of the conspirators given to Castro loyalists.

An officer picked up the phone. The caller wanted the Minister. Rosabal took the receiver and heard the voice of a certain Captain Sanchez of the political police in Havana. The connection was terrible. Sanchez's voice echoed.

"We found the car in San Jose de las Lajas driven by a certain Alberto Canto. A physician, Minister."

"And?"

"He was taken for questioning."

"Has he spoken? Did he mention the woman?"

"He said she was badly wounded. He claims she

was going to make her way to Matanzas. It seems she intended to arrange some kind of black-market transportation back to the United States. He didn't think she could possibly survive. The wound is deep."

"Shoot the physician. Concentrate on the woman. It can't be impossible to find a wounded woman in the fifty miles between San Jose and Matanzas."

"We're looking, Minister."

"Look harder. Report to me the moment you have killed her."

Rosabal put the receiver down. So she was wounded, badly so. Poor ambitious Magdalena, who thought she had it all. He shook his head. Ambition could sometimes be a court jester, a fine deceiver. Rosabal smiled to himself, then turned to look across the meadow.

There it was. At last. There it was.

The big truck carrying the tarpaulined missile and the control module came slowly across the muddy path that traversed the meadow. It was followed by a van in which sat a group of technicians who were here to disarm the missile. Gunther Ruhr was visible behind the windshield of the large truck. Next to him was a driver provided by the General.

Rosabal stepped from the porch. Magnetized by the missile, unmindful of the rain—softer now—that fell upon his eyelids, he hurried across the glistening grass to the place where the truck had come to a halt.

20

Santiago de Cuba

Alejandro Bengochea's optimism about refueling quickly was unfounded. It took almost an hour for a fuel truck to show up and another fifteen minutes during which he haggled with the driver and a bribe was eventually negotiated. Pagan, an impatient man at the best of times, was sorely tested by the length of the transaction. He had images of Gunther Ruhr and the missile disappearing from the face of the earth.

Then, at the conclusion of the deal, the chopper would not start. Plugs and cables in the engine were damp, electrical connections failed to make contact. It took Bengochea another hour of patient labor to bring the machine back to life and fly the forty miles from Palma Soriano to the city of Santiago. He cursed for a while, muttering about low-grade plugs and cables without waterproofing, thieves and cheats and black-marketeers who profited from the re-sale of state gasoline.

In the gray morning light the storm's path was evidenced by fallen trees and upturned huts and cars that had been tossed on their sides. Inside the city itself were houses without roofs and statues that had been blown ingloriously down and small parks where everything had been flattened—plants, trees, fences. Rain thudded against the skin of the helicopter, but the wind had died to fifteen, twenty miles an hour.

Pagan saw the docks come in view below the railway station. A score of ships were anchored there. They flew a variety of flags—South American, East European, Scandinavian, Panamian. Alejandro Bengochea directed the chopper up and over the harbor, while Pagan, conscious of the silent child who sat directly behind him breathing in a shallow, monotonous way, scanned the vessels below. Rain blew over unloaded cargo; discolored crates littered the docks, unpacked agricultural machinery lay exposed; brand new trucks, recently unloaded, filled up with rainwater.

The *Mandadera* was docked between a Norwegian freighter and a Venezuelan tanker. Bengochea steered the chopper over her deck. There was no sign of life. Ruhr and the missile had already gone.

Bengochea was undismayed by the ship's emptiness. He flew back over the city, surveying the streets, eyes narrowed; how could a missile be hidden from view? Since the ship could only recently have docked, the missile couldn't have gone far. It wasn't the kind of cargo a truck could transport quickly and easily. Bengochea took the chopper up higher, following the line of the coast that led out of Santiago in an easterly direction.

Pagan had the nagging feeling that he should cut his losses and somehow get the girl back home and forget Ruhr and the nuclear hardware. But how could he simply take Steffie Brough back to London and leave Ruhr and the weapon behind? No: he couldn't go back, not now, not after all this; besides, he had the belief, common to men who are more optimist than cynic, that the deeper the shit one had to go through to get to it, the happier the ending had to be.

Hold the thought, Frank.

Bengochea flew out of the city in a northerly direction. He passed over a rum factory and a flour mill and an oil refinery. There was no sign of a truck carrying a missile through the streets. He turned the helicopter around and flew southwest, back in the direction of the sea. *Donde?* he kept asking. *Donde?* Shaking his head in frustration, he flew the chopper low along the shoreline. Then he swung away from the water's edge and back through the rainy haze. The Sierra Maestra mountains, forlorn and unwelcoming, could be seen in the distance.

"It's got to be some bloody place," Pagan said. The nuclear needle in the haystack.

Bengochea may not have understood the words, but he recognized Pagan's tone. He shrugged sympathetically, then lowered the chopper so that it barely skimmed the tops of trees.

Bengochea turned the aircraft round again. He flew directly over Puerto Siboney, then swung inland away from the beaches, over farmlands and a coffee plantation.

And then the missile was suddenly visible in a meadow surrounded by tall trees. It sat on the back of a long truck and looked incongruous in this rainy pastoral setting. Pagan saw it too. He wanted Bengochea to bring the chopper down into the field, his first quick impulse, but there were too many people on the ground. From a height of fifteen hundred feet Pagan could see men work around the missile, which was being raised by hydraulic jacks into a launch position on the back of a long truck. Uniformed soldiers, armed and ready, stood guard in the grassy field.

As a ruse to discredit Castro, Pagan thought, it was elaborate and convincing, right down to the detail of the missile being cranked into a firing position. Somebody down there would have the responsibility of taking pictures, of course. Photographers, not scribes, were the true recorders of history. Nothing in this world was so persuasive as a striking image, one the masses might digest easily: here was Castro's dangerous missile in true living color, proof of his nuclear calumny. Universal recognition—you didn't even have to be able to read to grasp the horrifying potential of it. And Rosabal would have himself snapped with the missile in the background, naturally. The hero. The savior. The man who rid the world of crazy old Fidel.

Pagan gestured for Bengochea to circle the meadow again. Looking down, he saw two figures approach the missile-truck. One was Gunther Ruhr. The other might have been Rosabal. Bengochea flew round a couple of times, dropping as low as he thought prudent.

But now there was gunfire from the soldiers in the field. It came uncomfortably close to the cabin. Bengochea pulled the chopper up deftly, but he wasn't swift enough to avoid several shots slamming into the fuselage. Steffie Brough, silent for the last hour, whimpered when she realized the helicopter was being fired upon. Pagan tried to comfort her with some soothing words, but he'd never been very good with kids, never had that saintly mixture of patience and assurance. He thought he would have made a rotten father.

Bengochea went higher as a spray of bullets pierced the window of the cabin and continued past his skull and exited through the roof. Then he took the chopper up beyond the range of gunfire.

Looking down, Pagan saw Rosabal and Ruhr move toward the control module. Was Ruhr about to show Rosabal what the machine was made of? A sightseeing tour? Pagan shuddered at the notion of those two fine upstanding characters controlling a missile. He wished for a grenade, something that would wipe out both Ruhr and Rosabal and render the missile utterly useless at the same time.

He gazed down from a height of three thousand feet into the trees. Think. There must be some course of action to take. He concentrated, but couldn't come up with anything. He understood only that he couldn't ask Bengochea to fly back in again, because he couldn't risk Steffie Brough's life a second time. In the rain, Gunther Ruhr and Rosabal watched the chopper retreat above the trees, then hover for a time at a safe distance.

"Who is in that goddam helicopter?" Rosabal asked.

Gunther Ruhr said, "A man called Frank Pagan."

"Pagan?"

"An English cop. You know him?"

"By reputation. We can take care of him," Rosabal said.

"Don't underestimate him."

Rosabal made a dismissive gesture. Pagan was a dogged bastard. How in God's name had he managed to come all the way here? But what did it matter now? Pagan didn't worry him. Automatic rifle fire would either bring the chopper down or drive it away if it returned. Rosabal had no time to be bothered by anything so trivial as an English policeman in a helicopter. He absent-mindedly watched one of the cameramen take photographs of the weapon.

Gunther Ruhr looked at the missile. It was beautiful in the rain. "It's time for me to leave. The missile is delivered and armed. That's what my contract called for."

Rosabal raised his face, looked at the sky. The chopper was hovering beyond the trees about a mile away. Then he turned to Ruhr, whose colorless face and lips offended him; for a second his attention was drawn down to the ugly hand, which hung at the German's side.

"Don't rush away, Gunther," he said.

"Why should I wait? Is there some problem? I was promised air passage to Haiti after delivery. I was also promised a considerable sum of money when I reach Port-au-Prince. I hope you are not thinking of doublecrossing me. If anything happens to me, I can guarantee you the kind of exposure that will bring your little world down around your ears."

Rosabal smiled. "Nobody is going to doublecross you, my friend. Relax."

"So why are you asking me to stay?"

"Because this intrigues me. Because I want to know more. Because you're obviously a splendid teacher." Rafael Rosabal, adept at flattering men whose lives had inspired very little approbation, smiled a warm smile. *We're friends, Gunther, we are in this together*, the smile said.

Rosabal indicated the rectangular control module, from which the wet tarpaulin had been removed. Both men climbed up on to the truck. The door of the module was opened; they squeezed inside.

It was a small chamber some eight feet by seven. There was barely enough room for two men to sit in cramped positions in front of computer screens, directional equipment and the firing mechanism. From the control center to the missile, which was raised to an angle of some forty-five degrees at the front of the truck, ran sets of cables that relayed commands to the missile's navigational system.

"I am interested in the controls," Rosabal said. "Show me."

Ruhr turned on switches. The screens flickered.

"You enter data here and the missile goes wherever you want to send it," Ruhr said. "Within its range, of course."

"Fascinating."

Ruhr touched the instrument panel. He loved it. The design was economical, splendidly functional. He ran the tips of his fingers lightly over the console. He demonstrated how one plotted a course for the missile. There was fervor in the way Ruhr talked; it was the attitude of a man bewitched by his subject. Rosabal was more interested in Ruhr's nuclear fascination, his obsession with destruction, than in the technical details with which the German was bombarding him. Technical matters always made Rosabal's eyes and mind glaze over. He really didn't care how a thing worked, only that it did.

"It would be interesting . . . to fly the missile," Rosabal said.

Gunther Ruhr said nothing. He thought how exhilarating it would be to see the missile riding the skies through the rain, unerring, a twenty-foot steel arrow piercing the heart of its target.

Rosabal pressed the tips of his fingers together, placed them against his lips in an attitude of deliberation; an uninformed observer might have thought he was praying. But Rosabal was imagining Miami, a city he'd never visited, one he'd seen only in books and movies. He was imagining the hotels of the Art Deco district, old men and women sitting on the porches of pink and turquoise hotels, frowning at the hazy sea; he was imagining the exclusive little shops of Coral Gables and the huge hotels on Collins Avenue and the Cuban cafes along Calle Ocho where the troublemakers gathered to squabble about politics in Havana. And then he remembered his sick father who had gone to Guantanamo, to the American Naval Station, and asked for asylum in the United States, how he'd been laughingly turned away, and then made to disappear by Castro's political police afterward.

Yes, it was right, everything he had planned all along was correct and just. He had absolutely no doubt.

He looked at Gunther Ruhr and he asked, "Can you make it fly?"

"Of course," Ruhr replied. He could hardly breathe: *was he being asked to do the very thing he'd dreamed of doing?*

"Then why don't you?" Rosabal asked.

Ruhr felt a shiver of anticipation; the hairs on the backs of his hands bristled. "What target would please you?"

Some hours before the capture that would result in his execution, several hours before he lied to his interrogators about Magdalena Torrente's whereabouts, Albert Canto had driven his car to a secluded place and bandaged her side. He'd applied antibiotic cream over the wound, then gauze. The ointment came from Russia, he apologized, and its potency was suspect, but it was all he had in his possession. He wished he had an x-ray machine to assess the damage and fix the position of the slug in her body. The repair he made was a temporary measure, and a poor one at best; she'd need treatment within a few of hours at a good hospital. Her breathing was unsteady, her temperature certain to rise. Either she would have to return to the United States or run the risk of a hospital in Havana, where her illegal status might be discovered, and the consequences dire.

She announced she'd fly herself to Florida if a plane could be found. Astonished by her confidence, Canto argued she was certainly in no condition to fly an aircraft despite the painkiller he'd injected into her. Consider the turbulent weather, Canto had said. The darkness. Consider the seriousness of your wound. Your condition is terrible.

Canto had strongly recommended trying to find a pilot to take her. If she had to fly home, she shouldn't be at the controls herself. But she defied him. She could do it alone. She stubbornly insisted. He argued from the medical point of view but Magdalena Torrente, unmoved, had reservoirs of determination that Canto could not even begin to fathom.

At the airstrip outside San Jose de Las Lajas she stole without difficulty a small plane, a single-engine Beechcraft Bonanza, made in the United States and imported circuitously into Cuba, that belonged to some official in the Ministry of Construction. She'd learned how to steal planes from the old flyers at the exile training camps in the Everglades. Canto still tried to prevent her. There on the rainy field, barely able to hear each other over the scream of the wind, they had argued passionately. It was madness, Canto had shouted. She couldn't fly a plane in her state. If she didn't get to a hospital quickly she might hemorrhage, perhaps bleed to death. But in the end Magdalena's determination overcame the physician's compassionate caution.

She wasn't troubled about flying, despite the weather and her condition. Canto's painkiller kicked in quickly; besides, the storm had begun to diminish by the time she was ready to fly out of San Jose de Las Lajas. She embraced the physician, expressed her gratitude, kissed him, and left a smear of her own blood on his shirt.

There were maps in the cockpit. The instrumentation was simple. She took off into the driving rain, looking down once for a sight of the physician, but Canto had gone.

She had lied to him. She had absolutely no intention of flying this plane to Florida.

Inside the cramped control module Rafael Rosabal pretended to deliberate a moment before he answered Gunther Ruhr's question about a target.

"I think Miami," he said.

Alejandro Bengochea landed the chopper in a field a mile from the missile. He got out, checked the body of the craft, which had been struck on the fuselage by rifle fire but the fuel line was intact.

Pagan stepped down from the chopper and gazed thoughtfully into the rain. What was he supposed to do next? His head ached, his mind was an empty room. Armed with an ancient revolver he had borrowed from Bengochea, a gun that should have been retired years ago, how could he possibly slip past soldiers with automatic weapons and get to Ruhr? Even if he did, how could he disable that bloody missile?

He was aware of Steffie Brough watching him. He looked up, half-smiled, tried to appear encouraging, the friendly, reliable London cop who knew which bus to take to Battersea Park or the quickest way to Buckingham Palace. There was some element of accusation in her trance-like expression, as if she couldn't understand why she wasn't going home. She breathed upon the glass and, like a small child fascinated by condensation, drew a shapeless pattern with a fingertip. Then she turned her face away from Pagan, her profile sullen.

Pagan looked across the field. He was wet, but wetness and misery had quickly become conditions of his life, and almost acceptable. He turned Bengochea's revolver over in his hand, and stared once more across the meadow. He shrugged. It wasn't the best idea he'd ever had, but it was the only thing that occurred to him.

"I'm going back there," he said to Bengochea.

"*Que?*"

"On foot. Alone. Solo."

Bengochea looked puzzled.

Pagan said, "You stay here. Keep an eye on the girl. If I don't come back, you take her to the British Embassy in Havana. Understand?"

Pagan turned, walked away from the helicopter, looking back once. Steffie Brough wasn't watching him, but Alejandro Bengochea was still shaking his head. He hadn't entirely understood Pagan's words although he was convinced that the Englishman, even if a little *estupido*, was nevertheless a brave man.

Magdalena had flown for three hours at seven thousand feet, trying to keep the Bonanza above the turbulence, but the erratic wind shook the plane. When she climbed higher, clouds obscured the Central Highway she was trying to follow. She didn't want to fly without some kind of direct visual guide. She came down again to about three thousand feet.

When she'd been flying for just over three hours the painkiller began to wear off. It was hard to find a comfortable position. Maybe there wasn't one. She swallowed two of the codeine Canto had given her, but they didn't quell the fire in her side.

Rain pummelled the plane. Mist and cloud created mysterious shapes around the cockpit. She lightly touched the place Canto had bandaged. Painful. It was a weird thought to realize you had a bullet in your body, a foreign piece of metal in your system. What had it shattered? What had it punctured? Was some vital organ threatened?

But was it any more weird to have a foreign object in your body than to have a broken heart?

Sweat formed on her brow, ran down into her eyes. And yet she was cold, cold inside.

She gazed down at the highway. At some point she would have to fly southwest to Bayamo.

And then Bayamo to Santiago. About a hundred miles. Less than an hour's flying time.

If she could make it.

When she'd flown three hundred miles the sky had turned to a fuzzy kind of gray. There was light but no sun. The harsh unremitting rain created a bizarre tattoo on the cockpit. She wiped sweat out of her eyes, concentrated on the skies ahead, the highway below.

Why was she so damned cold? Then so warm?

She looked down at her bandage. Redness seeped through the material.

I lost more than blood, she thought. I lost myself.

She touched the bandage, brought her hand up; her fingertips were red.

Think good things. But she couldn't keep her head from filling with images of Rafael. His lovely deceptive face kept rising in her mind.

If he materialized here right now, if he appeared beside her in this cabin and asked for forgiveness, what would she say?

Yes.

Yes I forgive you again.

You'd do that, wouldn't you? You'd do it all over again. You never learned a thing. Where Rafael was concerned, her heart always flew ahead of her reasoning like a canary sent by coalminers into the deep, unmapped caverns of underground shafts to check for poisoned air.

Her love was more than a sickness. She breathed her love for Rafael. It was as necessary to her existence as oxygen. It was inside her the way her bloodstream was. And yet it was poisoned.

She loved him. And she wanted him dead.

She looked down at the gray-green landscape; she could see the ocean flooding over beaches, great clouds of spray.

She flew over Bayamo at one hundred and thirty miles an hour. The pain burned all the way through her. She shut her eyes because it was so goddam fierce. She hadn't ever known anything so intense. Once, years ago, she'd had an abortion, the consequence of a dalliance with a young boy at a military camp in the Everglades, and the physician had done something wrong and her womb had become infected, and she remembered the way pain seemed to scream inside her, but even that agony, which had been like a hat-pin pressed into the walls of her womb, was nothing to what she felt now.

She dropped her hands from the controls. She was cold, so damned cold, and even though she had no mirror she knew she was pale and the skin under her eyes black. There was sweat on her upper lip and her hands shook and something made from steel, some kind of pincer, clutched her intestines. She cried aloud. She felt herself slip toward blackout; around the periphery of her vision was darkness. She opened a window, let the cold wet air blow at her and keep her awake.

She placed her hands on the controls again and steadied the plane, but her grip was loose and weak and the tips of her fingers numb in a way that filled her with dread. She thought she could hear a specter whisper, a nearby voice, a hint of a song she'd never heard in her life before now—seductive, distant, bittersweet.

She didn't want to hear that song. She knew what it meant and it scared her, but the fear lasted only a moment before she moved beyond it to some other level of understanding, that place where all outcomes are neither sad nor joyful, good nor bad, but simply inevitable.

Pagan sneaked between the trees that surrounded the field. There was perhaps a score of men, many of them armed, clustered around the missile. Was he mistaken or had the angle of the missile changed since he'd last seen it? It seemed to have been raised to a higher elevation. It pointed toward the sky with a certain dark purpose, angled at approximately seventy-five degrees. Through the rain he could see the open door of the module. Although his angle of vision prevented him from seeing anything more than shadows, he was certain that Ruhr and Rosabal were inside.

Pagan crouched, tried to make himself invisible. If he stepped out of the trees he'd be seen and shot. How was he meant to reach the module? The only possibility that suggested itself—tucking his head well down and running hard at the module—was ludicrous, and utterly suicidal, and he wasn't in much of a mood to slit his own throat. Not yet.

There had to be a better way.

He considered circling the meadow, making an approach from another direction, but the obstacles were exactly the same. Uniformed men carefully watched both landscape and sky in all directions.

It was useless. There was nothing he could do. He could crouch here in the trees five hundred feet away and fire the old revolver toward the missile-truck and perhaps puncture a tire if he got really lucky. Terrific. But as soon as he fired he'd be shot at: end of Frank Pagan.

He stared at the missile.

It moved noticeably by perhaps a foot, then it stopped. Pagan held his breath. They were playing with the thing from inside the module. Perhaps Ruhr was simply demonstrating it.

Perhaps not. But Pagan didn't like the suspicion that formed in his mind just then. He wanted to discard it.

No, no. They couldn't be planning to fire the bloody thing. Not in a hundred years. Ruhr was just showing Rosabal how it worked, that was all, then it would be dismantled, and defused, and destroyed. Wasn't that the plan? Yes, yes, of course that was the bloody plan, what else could it be?

Pagan felt an extraordinary sense of futility. If the men inside the module intended to fly the bird, he couldn't do anything to stop them—except take a pot-shot at the control module with Alejandro's stupid revolver. What else was there to do?

He aimed the revolver at the control chamber on the back of the big truck; he was very careful, lining up the module in his sight with a kind of concentration that made his head ache. If he struck the module with a shot—perhaps he might hit something important, the wiring, the connecting cables, perhaps his bullet might penetrate the shell of the control center and rupture some essential component inside. You couldn't bank on perhapses, you couldn't pay bills with them.

His hand trembled.

He squeezed his finger upon the trigger.

He fired.

His shot passed through the space between missile and module, harmless, feeble, desperate. The fire was returned, the air split by the vicious spray of automatic weapons. He threw himself flat and crawled toward a clump of shrubbery as he listened to the air whine around his skull.

But there was another sound now, and it came from the sky.

He looked up.

Magdalena had flown three times over the city of Santiago de Cuba before she found what she was looking for. Dimly, she registered the meadow, the ring of trees, the missile-truck fifteen hundred feet below her. It was tiny and it wouldn't stay still in her vision, and spots the shape of amoebae kept prancing in front of her eyes. But it was the chill that bothered her more than anything else, the voracious cold that consumed her. She'd never known such a sensation before.

The death cold, she thought.

The cold of the coffin. Frozen earth.

She passed across the field, wheeled the small plane, made a second sweep; the craft lost height, dropping two, three hundred feet. Then she must have blacked out briefly because she couldn't remember bringing the plane even lower, bringing it down to a height that was only five hundred feet over the missile truck. She clutched her side, drew her hand away, saw how her palm and fingers were covered with blood that had seeped through Canto's bandage. But the bloodied hand was no longer her own, it was some spectral thing, an appendage without substance. And it seemed to her that the blood froze on her flesh, and changed to crystals, pale pink crystals that were swept from her skin by the draught that rushed through the open window.

Dying, she thought. Dying, dying.

She made another pass over the field.

She was so low now she could see the faces of the men who fired guns at her. Their bullets slammed against the fuselage. She watched the marksmen rush out of her path as she flew no more than fifteen feet over the surface of the meadow.

Dying, she thought again.

It had its own kind of perfect madness.

The truck loomed up in front of her. The missile, angrily poised for flight, the open door of the control module—she saw these things rush toward her, and then it was as if everything in the world were being sucked in by her propellers, leaves, blades of grass, men, guns, clouds, everything was disappearing inside the slipstream of her rushing aircraft, crowding her vision, her brain, stifling her ability to take air into her lungs. Inside the module Gunther Ruhr set the course of the missile. He calculated it would strike directly into the heart of Miami. But accuracy wasn't very important when you were talking about the total devastation of a city; a mile or two either way hardly mattered.

"How much damage will it do?" Rosabal asked. "How many will die?"

"Consider Hiroshima," Ruhr answered.

Hiroshima. Two hundred thousand people had died there, many thousands more had become sick from radiation. The city had been totally destroyed. Rosabal said nothing. He heard gunfire outside, ignored it. He merely imagined the chopper was circling the field again. Sooner or later it would be shot out of the sky. Nothing in the external world was important; only this small chamber mattered.

"This will be worse," Ruhr said cheerfully. "Much worse. Ten times as many people will perish. Perhaps more."

"Do it," Rosabal said.

Ruhr leaned forward over the console. Like a card-shark about to shuffle a deck, a conjurer ready to perform an illusion, he rubbed his hands together a few times as if to stimulate his circulation, then he held both hands over the console. He might have been born for just this moment, his trick of all tricks.

"Do it! Goddamit, do it now!" Rosabal snapped.

Gunther Ruhr smiled; it was perhaps the singular most blissful expression that had ever appeared on his face. His hands dropped toward the console.

In a fraction of time too small for even the finest chronometers to measure, too short for the senses to organize detail from chaos, Magdalena saw Rafael Rosabal in the open door of the module. His face was turned slightly away from her, but his profile was visible, unmistakable. She felt her chilled blood rush to her head and through the window of her small failing plane could smell wet grass and black mud—and then everything came together in that one chaotic reduction of time, module and airplane, sky and mud, Magdalena and the man she loved, the man with whom she might now spend eternity if there happened to be one, it all fused, melded, and even as it came together it also exploded and blew apart, white flame conjoining the aircraft and the missile-truck, searing the fuselage, disintegrating the module and the men inside it, setting aflame the cables that married the missile to its control center, then finally toppling in fire the missile itself, which rolled from the truck and slithered from its erector and slumped, fuses melted and shot, navigational system destroyed, its function rendered harmless, into the soft mud.

Frank Pagan saw Magdalena for only a second as the plane savagely struck the module, and then he closed his eyes against the intense heat he could feel roll across the meadow toward the trees where he stood. When he opened his eyes he looked at how tall flames rose in a great white dance from the truck, a noisy dance set to the strange crackling music of fire. There was a quality of illusion to his perceptions: had he really seen her in the tiny cockpit of that doomed plane? Had he imagined it?

He stepped back under the cover of the trees. The soldiers who had been shooting at him only minutes before were running from the fiery ruin of the truck as fast and as far as they could, some with their uniforms on fire. He saw one wing of the plane collapse like burning paper, but after that there was very little distinction between objects trapped in the furnace. They all glowed with the same hallucinatory intensity.

He turned and ran as quickly as he could to the place where Bengochea and the child waited in the helicopter.

Cabo Gracias a Dios

The storm uprooted the tent of Tomas Fuentes and blew it across the airstrip toward the ocean, where anchored boats precariously rode the swell. A freighter that had set sail some thirty minutes before had already turned back, and another small ship was reported capsized. On the airstrip fighter planes were chained to stone chocks lest they drift and roll in the wind. Tomas watched his tent go flying off like a great bird with drab olive plumage and the grace of an ostrich, and then it was lost from sight. Bosanquet's tent went the same way, flapping like loose laundry, dragging its guy ropes behind it.

Fuentes studied the roiling sea just as the wind ripped the panama hat from his head and launched it up into the tall branches of trees where it was blown from left to right, up and down, then out of sight, a symbol—if Fuentes wanted to see it this way—of a lost cause.

He preferred to think of it as a cause postponed. There would be other days, and they would be stormless, and the sea clear all the way to Cuba and that *hijo de puta,* Fidel Castro.

21

Frank Pagan looked from the window of the Boeing 727 as the electric coastline of Florida faded and the darkness of the ocean replaced land. Then there were clouds, becalmed in the storm's aftermath. He pretended to read the in-flight magazine but his attention was drawn time and again to Steffie Brough in the seat beside him.

She was lost in a glossy magazine of her own, a world of models, a synthetic reality, clearly preferable to the one she'd just experienced. She was oddly quiet most of the trip, unwilling to answer even the most innocuous of Pagan's questions. He realized that sooner or later this little girl was going to need expert help, a counsellor, a therapist. Ruhr had left his mark on her—the question was how much damage had been done?

Pagan, who had no great mastery of small talk, made idle comments, and Steffie Brough responded, if at all, in a dull way. Strangers with nothing to share, Pagan thought, which in one sense was true—he a London cop, she a horse-breeder's daughter from farmlands, what could they have in common? The girl, though, had a certain dead look in her eyes, as if curiosity were a capacity she didn't have; no questions about Pagan's investigation, no gratitude. Although Pagan sought none, he nevertheless would have thought it natural in the circumstances. She flipped magazine pages, picked at her airline food—chicken pellets with almonds, a glutinous matter masquerading as rice. She was quite lost to Pagan's efforts to reach her, beyond any kindness he showed, any concern he demonstrated. And he tried; despite what he considered a lack of any natural affinity for kids—here he underestimated himself—he made a good effort. Her retreat defeated him.

It was after five AM when the flight reached London, a gray English dawn with a spiteful, jaundiced sun. Heathrow was out of the question—too many journalists and photographers waiting for snapshots of that most beloved of human occurrences, the tearful reunion. Consequently, the plane was diverted to Gatwick, and Stephanie Brough's parents were taken there in an unmarked car.

Pagan disembarked with the girl. Outside, in a lounge set aside for the child's return, a small crowd had come to meet her—her parents, a grandmother, a brother (a gangling youth of unsurpassed awkwardness who had somehow contrived to break the stems of roses he brought to his sister), a dozen or so uniformed policemen, half of them women, detectives in plain clothes, Billy Ewing from Golden Square, and Martin Burr, who clapped Pagan's shoulder as if to say it was a job well done. And so it was, but Burr was never expansive in his appreciations. A professional did what was expected of him: a professional needed no special thanks. Later, there would be reports and interviews, but not for the moment.

Pagan, tired, trying not to yawn, was thanked by the gushing parents and the grandmother who planted a perfumed kiss on his lips. All he wanted was to drift away, go back to his flat, sleep for days. It was a lonely prospect and he was apprehensive about the possibility of bad dreams, a missile rising into the launch position, the sight of a small airplane burning in a Cuban field—but it was time to slow down his private clock.

He watched the happy crowd inside the lounge, the smilingly tearful family, Steffie's mother with her white insomniac face lit like a bright lightbulb, Mr. Brough in a three-piece check suit with a camel hair waistcoat, Steffie herself clinging quietly to her mother.

And yet Pagan felt weird. Displaced. Out of sorts. A feeling that had nothing to do with his fatigue. There was something not quite right about this whole gathering.

He walked to a soda machine, pressed in a coin, heard a can of Coca-Cola come hurtling down the chute. He popped it, sipped the stuff, longed for a dram of the Auchentoshan to spike it up, and wondered what it was that left him so chilled, that sense of missing something. And then he knew what it was even before Billy Ewing—hushed, confidential, looking like a bookie's clerk—grabbed him by the elbow and took him aside. They stepped out of the lounge and into the grubby dawn, where Billy blew his nose with distinctive flair, a trombonist of the sinuses.

"It's Foxie," Billy Ewing said.

Of course, Pagan thought. That was it. Foxie wasn't here. Good old Foxie hadn't shown up. He gazed at Billy Ewing and waited for more, but the Scotsman hadn't much to add.

"He hasn't come back yet, Frank. Off he went to Glasgow, called in with one message, and that was the last we heard from him."

"You've tried to contact him?"

"Oh, aye, last night I talked with Glasgow Central myself."

"And?"

Billy Ewing shrugged. "And nothing. No trace. He borrowed a car belonging to Glasgow CID—and it hasn't been returned."

"Do you have a copy of his last message?" Pagan asked.

"Back at the office."

"We'll go in your car, Billy," Pagan said.

"Whatever you say."

They went in Ewing's Ford through central London, through streets springing to daily, prosaic life, and by the time they reached Golden Square Frank Pagan's sleepiness had evaporated, replaced by a general sense of uneasiness.

The message was already two days old and as Pagan fingered the flimsy piece of paper he had the unsettling feeling, given perhaps only to mediums and soothsayers, that Foxie's silence indicated a serious condition.

"Mibbe he's following up on something," Ewing suggested. "Mibbe he's on to something hot."

"And he couldn't find change for a telephone call, Billy?"

Ewing, baffled, shrugged. He knew as well as Pagan that Foxworth was a diligent man who paid conscientious attention to detail. Pagan went inside his office and sat for a time on the sofa. He shut his eyes, rubbed them, worried about Foxie.

He looked up at Billy Ewing. "Get me on the next available flight to Glasgow, Billy. And get me a gun."

"Do you want some company, Frank? I know the territory, after all."

Pagan shook his head, stood up, felt an immense pressure in his chest. He didn't want company, talkative or otherwise. He would follow Foxworth's trail alone. He borrowed Ewing's pistol, a Smith and Wesson, and Billy drove him from Golden Square out along the motorway to Heathrow.

On the way Billy Ewing mentioned the result of his inquiries into Harry Hurt and Sheridan Perry. Pagan could barely recall having made the request; it seemed such a long time ago. Rich pair of buggers, Frank, was how Billy Ewing phrased it. "But wealth, as my old Grannie used to phrase it, is no guarantee of immortality."

"Meaning?"

"Harry Hurt was assassinated in Washington, and Sheridan Perry has disappeared."

"Somehow I'm not surprised," Pagan said.

Billy Ewing sighed. "There's a lot of dying going on, Frank."

Scotland

The flight to Glasgow was uneventful. It was just after eight AM when Pagan arrived and took a taxicab to the city center. Morning sunlight in the city, an unexpected state of affairs, and lovely, the breeze off the River Clyde bracing, the clouds rushing across a clear blue sky. In the heart of Glasgow Pagan went at once to the offices of the Executive Motor Car Company in West Nile Street. This was the new Glasgow—gone was a certain tired, washed-out drabness, a weariness of the soul that had given the city the appearance of a place down at the heel, like some Baltic capital. Uplifted, scrubbed, renewed, it was as if the city had overcome an inferiority complex after many years of arduous, expensive therapy.

Pagan found the Executive Motor Car Company located over a philately shop. He climbed the stairs. Halfway up, winded, he paused. A telephone rang somewhere above him, a kettle whistled. This was the way Foxworth had come, these were the stairs he must have climbed. Pagan reached the landing where a lovely young woman stood in a doorway, holding in one hand a mug of hot tea.

"You don't look terrific," she said. "Are you feeling sick? Can I get you anything?"

Pagan smiled, shook his head, showed his ID, asked about Foxie. The woman said her name was Miss Wilkie and, yes, she remembered Foxworth, he had been very charming, very much a gentleman of the kind one rarely saw these days—and she blushed, Pagan noticed.

Miss Wilkie frowned, as if she had become suddenly concerned about Foxworth's fate. "Has something happened to him?"

"I'm not sure," Pagan replied. "Where was he going when he left here?"

"I gave him very specific directions, Mr. Pagan, to a house in Ayrshire. In fact, I kept a copy of the map our driver made for him. It's a bit rough, but easy to follow." She paused. She had small, trim hands that gleamed because they had recently been rubbed with skin lotion. "He hasn't come back yet, is that it?"

Pagan nodded. "That's it exactly."

"He asked about some men—let me think a minute. They had names that began with the letter C. One was called Chap, Chap something or other."

"Chapotin?"

"I believe you're right," said Miss Wilkie. "The other man was named Caporelli. Both these men used our limousines to visit the country house in which Mr. Foxworth showed such interest."

Pagan felt a very small pulse in his dry throat. He tried to imagine Foxie's excitement when he uncovered the information that both Chapotin and Enrico Caporelli had visited the same house. That link, that complex knot tying together Caporelli and Chapotin, the same knot that brought both Rosabal and Gunther Ruhr into its ornate folds and twists.

"He might have been in an accident," Miss Wilkie said in a kindly, hesitant way. "Some of the roads are bad. Then there are cliffs . . ." She left this line of thought alone, and smiled, and there was bravery in the expression. "You'll find him, you'll see. People always turn up."

But in what condition? Pagan wondered. He took the copy of the map, studied it, felt dizzy. He asked about renting a car and Miss Wilkie said she could oblige very easily. A few forms to complete, that was all. Pagan filled in the requisite paperwork, thanked Miss Wilkie, shook her hand, went down into the West Nile Street. The city seemed unduly loud to him suddenly, the clatter of buses, clogged streets. He found a small coffee shop near Royal Exchange Square and went inside, drank two cups of strong Kenyan quickly, then returned to Executive Motor Cars Limited to pick up his hired car, a Fiat Uno.

Out of the city and on his way south; easy enough on paper, but his sense of direction was skewed and he went in circles for an hour before finding the route that would take him into Ayrshire, presumably the same route Foxworth had taken before. Pagan drove carefully; sleep kept coming in now, dark wave after dark wave. He studied Miss Wilkie's map now and then, noticing the sparkling greenery of the countryside through which he drove—wishing he were a tourist and this some casual jaunt directly into the heart of beauty.

He stopped in Ayr, stretched his legs near the harbor, breathed the sea air into his lungs, watched gulls squabble like spectators in search of a sport. Perhaps Foxie had come this way too; pursuing a ghost, Pagan thought. He half-expected to see Foxie by the side of the road, his automobile broken down and young Foxie resting indolently upon a grassy bank while awaiting the arrival of a mechanic. But Pagan saw no Foxworths and no broken-down cars. He drove south out of Ayr and almost at once the countryside became forlorn—lovely, yes, but in a different way, more starkly melancholic, and ancient, whitewashed stone cottages and old farmhouses erected in quiet isolation, here and there a TV antenna to bring another world, an incongruous one, into old parlors. Pagan continued to drive south.

He parked in a place overlooking the sea, examined the map again. Why did his hand shake as he held the piece of paper? He saw Ballantrae on his rough map, and out of that village led a narrow track, and there—an inked rectangle, underlined—was presumably the house. It was unnamed, a simple inky square on copy paper. Had Foxworth gone there? Had he found it? If so, why the fuck hadn't he called Golden Square to say so?

Pagan's head throbbed as much from anxiety as pain; dread created a stress all its own. He drove again, thinking that Foxie could take care of himself, he was a grown man, a good cop, he knew how to handle situations: *so why all this damned worry?*

The town of Girvan, sunlight on deep gray water, seabirds, a miniature fairground, tarpaulined for the dead season, near the sea. Pagan was blinded by bright sun rippling on the tide. And then Girvan was behind him and he was headed for the village of Ballantrae, remembering that Robert Louis Stevenson had once written a novel entitled *The Master of Ballantrae*, but Pagan had never read it, never read a word of Stevenson; how remiss of him, he thought now. Foxie, who had gone to an expensive school, had probably read the bloody book.

The track outside Ballantrae was narrow. Birds flew from hedgerows—bright starlings, thrushes, plain little sparrows, and once a plump plover that flew toward Pagan's windshield as if intent on bringing to a swift conclusion some avian depression. Frank Pagan continued to drive the uneven track. The hedges that rose on either side prevented any kind of view of what lay beyond, and he wondered if Foxie had come this way and felt the same sensation of isolation, almost an eeriness that the forceful sun could not dispel.

Foxie: where the hell are you?

What did you find in this place?

The track grew worse; the hedgerows eclipsed the low morning sun. Pagan felt the Fiat bump and shudder, but it was nothing compared to the ride in Bengochea's chopper. He slowed where the hedges thinned, seeing flat meadowlands vanish toward stands of trees, an empty landscape with neither animals nor people. Only a solitary hawk, casting a squat shadow, suggested motion. He continued to drive, the track became worse, the hedges thicker again. He examined the map, which seemed to bear very little resemblance to the reality of the terrain. He ought to have reached the house some time ago, but then he understood that this roughly-drawn map bore no resemblance to actual scale.

When he finally saw the house it surprised him. It rose in sunlight and shadow as though it were a deformed sandstone dream, grand circular towers and narrow windows, a pretension here in a landscape without airs of grandeur. He stopped the Fiat, got out, peered through the hedgerow at the edifice, then pushed his way through—branches springing at him with unexpected harshness—and stepped into a swampy meadow littered with yellow wildflowers.

The house glowed red in morning sunlight. In crannies, in abysses of brickwork, between turrets, shadows were wine-colored and warm. Pagan walked across the spongelike grass toward the mansion, then paused when he reached a copse of trees. Somebody had been working there—a wheelbarrow was propped alongside a tree, a spade stuck in the soil, there was the soft scent of good earth newly turned over. A sizeable trench had been dug in the ground. Pagan stepped between the trees, paused, looked off in the direction of the house, which was a half mile away.

A car was parked in the driveway, a Jaguar, he thought, but sunlight obscured the lines of the vehicle; there was also a jeep just behind it. Nobody moved, though; the house showed no sign of life. Had it not been for the presence of spade and wheelbarrow and the clammy black perfume of newly-shovelled earth, he might have thought the estate abandoned. He took a few steps forward between the overhanging branches of the trees and loose leaves, disturbed by his passage, drifted to the ground around him. Earth made soft by recent rains sucked at his shoes.

Bloody hell, he was tired. He leaned against a trunk, listened to the lazy buzz of a bee nearby, a lark impossibly high in the sky. There was a narcotic conspiracy here, something to lull a man toward sleep.

The sound of a footfall made him open his eyes and turn around. The twin-barrelled shotgun, large and vicious, was held by a short man with center-parted hair and the relic of a hare-lip that had been removed surgically years before but had left behind a tiny scar that distended the upper lip, where a thin moustache had been grown as a feeble disguise.

Pagan reached inside his pocket for his identification, but the man gestured with the shotgun. Frank Pagan stood very still. The man, whose voice had a nasal edge, poked the barrel closer to Pagan and said, "Another bloody snoop."

Pagan finally fished out his wallet, but the man was unimpressed and didn't even look. *Another bloody snoop:* had Foxie been the first one?

"I'm looking for somebody," Pagan said.

"Are you indeed?" the man said.

"A colleague of mine."

"A colleague, is it?" The man raised one thin eyebrow. For some reason he didn't immediately understand, Pagan's attention was drawn to the spade propped against the tree, the mound of earth inside the wheelbarrow. These simple perceptions, rustic and yet sinister, shook him and he didn't know why; but now the sunlit day seemed bleached, as if color had drained out of it.

"The man's name was Foxworth. Detective Foxworth."

"Is that a fact?" asked the short man.

"From Scotland Yard."

The man was still unimpressed.

"Could you lower your gun?" Pagan asked. "You make me nervous."

The shotgun stayed where it was, level with Pagan's heart. The man glanced through the trees toward the house. Pagan turned, saw three figures coming across the landscape, perhaps a half-mile distant and small. There was an instant familiarity about two of them; after a moment Pagan recognized the man who walked in front as Foxworth. The red hair, made almost blood-colored by sun, was unmistakable.

Pagan's relief at the sight of Foxworth alive and breathing was immense but brief; immediately behind Foxie was a man who carried a shotgun trained on his spine.

At the rear, moving with brisk steps, hands clasped behind his back in the manner of a laird walking his terrain, was the third man. Pagan had one of those odd moments in which inversions take place—the sky tilts, the sun darkens, the heart is suddenly stilled, and perceptions are tunnelled as if through reversed binoculars.

A mistake, Pagan thought.

It had to be.

A resemblance, nothing more.

But as the three figures came closer Pagan saw Freddie Kinnaird sweep a lock of hair from his forehead in that characteristic gesture he had. There was a smile on the famous face, but cold, very cold.

No mistake.

Pagan couldn't swallow. Astonishment and a brutal, burning anger denied him that simple reflex. He thought of all the information to which Kinnaird had been privy. Everything that passed across Martin Burr's desk eventually reached Freddie. He thought of how Freddie Kinnaird had known of Gunther Ruhr's route through Shepherd's Bush, of how Freddie must have passed that juicy item along the line to Rosabal, who had arranged the drastic rescue of Gunther and rented the country hideout. At every turn, every angle, nothing of substance had been withheld from Sir Frederick Kinnaird. And he must have shared everything with his associates who had come to this house in the secret depths of the Scottish countryside—Chapotin and Caporelli, perhaps the late Herr Kluger and the two Americans as well, a tight little gang of old pals.

Pagan raised his face to the sun. He was hot in his raincoat. Freddie Kinnaird approached, stopped some yards away. Pagan glanced at Foxie, who had the slightly red-eyed look of a man who has been held captive for days in a dark room and now sunlight astounds him.

"Well, well, well," Kinnaird said with a certain cheerfulness. "Frank Pagan himself."

Pagan said nothing. He had the unbearable urge to reach for Kinnaird and grab him and crush that smug face until nothing recognizable was left of it. But how could he move with a shotgun shoved into his back?

"We had that whole damned island sewn up," Kinnaird said and grabbed air in his hand and made a fist, as if what he held there were locks of invisible hair. "We had it all. Why did you have to stick your nose in?"

Pagan gazed upward again. The lark he'd seen before was imposed against the sun, like an inscrutable punctuation mark in the sky. "It's my job to stick my nose in, Freddie. You know that." There was an ugly note in Pagan's voice, which came close to breaking. Control yourself, Frank. It wasn't easy. The depths of his own loathing astonished him.

Kinnaird appeared to be elsewhere, concentrating on some inner lyric of his own. He had in his eye a very small, sharp light that suggested some quiet, well-bred form of craziness. "You helped bollix the whole damned thing."

"I think you overestimate me, Fred. I'd dearly love to take the credit for fucking your scheme up, but it wouldn't be fair. All I did was get a young girl out of Cuba. That was my job. I wanted to bring Ruhr back to stand trial, also part of my job. I lost that one. I did the best I could with what I had. But I'm not personally responsible for screwing up your plans for Cuba, Fred. I didn't kill Rosabal. Blame Magdalena Torrente. Blame Rosabal himself for choosing the wrong woman to fuck over. Blame any damn thing you like. All I did was my job."

"I rather think you're hiding your light under a bushel, Pagan. After all, you managed to save Magdalena Torrente's life in Miami."

Pagan shouldn't have been surprised by Kinnaird's knowledge of the murder attempt, because it was plain that very little had escaped Freddie. He'd obviously learned from the Commissioner that Pagan was going to be in Miami with Magdalena Torrente. That simple. But somehow Pagan was surprised anyway, although he wasn't going to give Freddie the satisfaction of showing it.

Kinnaird, who looked all at once like a large, sulking boy, said, "If you hadn't saved her, she'd never have gone to Cuba. And if she hadn't gone there—"

"If she hadn't gone there, Rosabal might have fired his missile."

"Nonsense. There was never any question of firing it."

"That's not the way I saw it."

"Then your observations are very wrong," Kinnaird said impatiently. "Rafael wouldn't have fired the bloody thing. It was a prop, a piece of scenery. What the devil does it matter now anyhow? Castro is still in charge of Cuba—did you see that as part of your job, Pagan? To help keep him in power?"

"I didn't help keep anybody in power. I don't give a shit who runs Cuba, Freddie. Castro or some other old geezer—it doesn't make any bloody difference to me in the long run. They're all the same when you get right down to it."

"What a dreadfully narrow view of the world stage," Kinnaird said. His expression was that of a man who finds some foul morsel of very old food between his teeth.

Pagan shrugged. Of course it was a narrow view; he'd never found a broad perspective conducive to his sense of right and wrong. If your view was too wide you encountered too many ambiguities. If you sat around pondering all the issues, and trying to understand all the sides, you froze eventually into inactivity. So he always tried to keep it simple, tightly-focussed. He didn't know how to do his job any other way.

Kinnaird looked down into the hole in the ground, nudged a pebble with his foot, watched it drop inside the trench.

A grave, Pagan thought. Of course. Foxie's grave. Make it a double. A chill went through him.

He said, "Here's what I wonder, Fred. How is it that your friends and associates keep getting themselves killed off? How does that come about? If I was a cynical kind of fellow—and I'm not, as anybody will tell you—I'd say you developed some pretty bloody selfish ideas. I'd say you did a hatchet job on your chums. What was it? Afraid there wasn't going to be enough Cuban pie to go around? Needed more than your share, Fred?''

"We all need a little more than our share at times," Kinnaird said. He folded his arms across his chest. He reminded Pagan of a squire in a magazine ad, a handsome tweedy figure advocating the merits of a certain Scotch, a malt liquor, something expensive.

"But now there's no pie, Fred," Pagan said. "The cupboard is bare and there's no fucking pie at all! Pardon this malicious smirk you see on my features, but I find that hilarious.''

Foxie laughed at Pagan's remark. It was a nervous little sound, but Pagan welcomed it; it established an audience, it gave him a sense of support. He stared at Kinnaird—Sir Freddie, darling of his party, beloved by the electorate, man with a Great Future, tomorrow's England, tomorrow's Europe, Freddie, slavishly devoted to wealth and position and seemingly equipped with a vampire's appetite for blood. Dear Freddie.

Pagan went on, "I'm not saying you did the hatchet job on your own, Fred. I'm not saying you personally pulled any triggers. You don't have the guts for that. You had some help along the way. Maybe you had other associates, maybe you saw a way of slicing the pie up in thicker pieces. I don't suppose I'll ever get an answer to how it was all supposed to work."

"Certainly not from me, Pagan. I owe you absolutely nothing. No explanations. No details. Nothing."

Pagan looked down at the hole in the ground. "You think you can fit us both in there, Fred?"

"I don't see why not."

"Bit tight," Foxie remarked. A brave little comment, a flippancy that almost worked, but Foxie's anxious eyes revealed his fear.

"I really don't think it's going to cause either of you any discomfort," Kinnaird said. "Actually, it's all rather convenient for me. Two for the price of one."

Pagan sniffed the air deeply, like a man doing something he enjoys for the very last time. The smell of earth in his nostrils was the stench of death; simple, unaffected, plain old death. He glanced at the man who held the shotgun at Foxie's back. He was a bulky character with thin white hair flattened across his large skull. The other gunman, the one with the moustache that covered the scar, stood about three feet behind Pagan. It was one of those situations in which there could only be one outcome. You could try to stammer and stall, you could put up this objection and that, and play for time, but finally the result would be the same—a double-decker grave.

Pagan moved his feet very slightly; he was practically standing on the lip of the trench. Less distance to fall when the time came, he thought. He looked down inside the grave, saw a black stag beetle pick its way laboriously through its ruined territory, then he raised his face back to Kinnaird.

Stall. Kill time.

Pagan put one hand to his chest, which had begun during the last few minutes to ache. Ghose's stitches were perhaps coming undone again. What did that matter? He was about to be administered the ultimate painkiller anyway. He stared across the grave at Foxie, whose expression was one of discouragement, as if he'd just frantically searched through his own box of tricks and found no way of pulling a rabbit, at the last possible moment, out of a hat.

Stall.

"As a matter of curiosity, Fred, how do you propose to get away with our murders?" Pagan asked. A desperate little question, a last bleat.

Kinnaird clasped his hands behind his back in a pontifical manner that Pagan despised because it suggested superiority and power; Freddie Kinnaird must have thought he was invincible. "You forget I'm the Home Secretary, old chap. I'll take an active interest in your disappearance. I'll stage-manage the investigation, if I need to."

"Martin Burr's going to go after this one very hard. He's a tenacious bastard. He'll find his way here. After all, Foxie did. And so did I. It's not exactly a cold trail, *old chap.*"

"But you never came here, Pagan. Nor did your young friend. Nobody saw you. Your car will be found on some side street in Glasgow. You and your associate will simply become mysteries that start on page one and then find their way to page five, and after that oblivion and amnesia and God rest your souls, etcetera."

"Burr can be persistent," Pagan said.

"Then I'll fire him," Kinnaird remarked.

"You've really got it covered, Freddie." There was that anger inside him again, rising in his throat with the persistence of a gas. What wouldn't he have given to have Kinnaird alone in a locked room for sixty seconds? It was useless to feel such a sense of violence when there was nothing you could do to vent it. But it wouldn't leave him.

"Farewell." Kinnaird turned away, then stopped, looked round again. "I'd stay for the finale, but some things simply do not attract me on an aesthetic level."

"One last question, Freddie. How do you sleep? How the fuck do you manage to sleep?"

Kinnaird said nothing. He moved between the trees.

Pagan called out, "You ever have bad dreams, Kinnaird? Do you have bad dreams about Shepherd's Bush? Does that ever cross your fucking mind?"

Kinnaird stopped, looked round. "I never dream."

Then Kinnaird kept going. Pagan, who heard the faraway song of the lark again, felt the shotgun against his spine. He clenched his hands at his side in useless anger. The sun, unseasonably hot, beat at his face; he raised a hand, wiped sweat from his eyelids, blinked across the trench at Foxworth, who looked haggard and resigned.

"This isn't how I imagined an ending," Pagan said. He felt the pressure of the shotgun and heard the gunman say *Move your arse, jack,* in his harsh nasal way. He was being forced back to the edge of the grave.

"Nor me," Foxworth said. "In my pajamas. Middle of the night. Heart attack in the arms of some gorgeous thing. I always thought that was the way to go. Bit of bliss for the big ending."

"I don't think I expected to die in Scotland either," Pagan said.

"Do you think it's unhallowed ground, Frank?"

Banter on the steps of the guillotine. A quip or two for the executioners. Gallows humor.

The man with the white hair pushed Foxie toward the trench too. Pagan and Foxie faced one another across the hole. There was a moment of intense silence suddenly, as if nothing flapped or flew, sung or buzzed. Pagan saw Freddie Kinnaird still walking between the trees, perhaps now three or four hundred feet from the killing place and stepping briskly, hurrying away from the distasteful scene he had himself arranged. Strangely Kinnaird made no sound either, no crackle of leaves underfoot, no whisper of clothing against tree trunks or low branches. The whole world had become mute.

Pagan stood at the very edge of the trench. He held his breath, thought about the gun in his coat pocket, imagined trying to turn, trying to wrestle the shotgun from the man who held it, but he had nothing going for him, no advantage, no chance to surprise, because the shotgun was pressed to his spine and if he made even one aggressive gesture it would go off immediately.

Out of time, Frank.

He looked down into the bleak cavity, then raised his face in the direction of Freddie Kinnaird.

The man in the black raincoat who stepped unexpectedly from the trees shot Freddie Kinnaird through the skull with a pistol.

It was done swiftly, with professional economy, one bullet that shattered Kinnaird's head and demolished half of his face. Freddie Kinnaird went down on his knees, then pitched forward, and the gunman—the same killer Frank Pagan had last seen shooting Caporelli in his Paris apartment, and who clearly had no interest in anything other than the task he'd just accomplished with such ease—disappeared through the trees like a man accustomed to sudden vanishing acts.

It was a diversion, shocking in its abruptness, and Pagan seized the unattended moment with all the passion of a survivor; he brought one clenched hand up and back, swinging the fist in a tight, powerful arc that ended when his knuckles made noisy thudding contact with the forehead of the hare-lipped man, who gasped and moaned and lowered his shotgun involuntarily. Something was broken in the man's face—the upper part of the nose, the ridge of bone above the eyes. Pagan, whose hand felt weirdly numb, wasn't sure what. The man bled profusely through the nostrils and made a choking sound. Pagan raised a foot, kicked at the shotgun, struck the barrel, but didn't force the gun out of the man's hands. The man stepped back, the contours of his face filled with flowing blood, his flop of a moustache turned scarlet. Pagan whipped the Smith and Wesson out of his pocket and fired it directly into the man's chest even as the other gunman, who had been standing behind Foxie, pulled the trigger of his shotgun despite the fact that Foxworth, alert as only a frightened man can be, had brought his shoulder into contact with his guard, knocking him just slightly off-balance.

The sound of the shotgun was so deafeningly loud that it rolled through Pagan's head like a thunderstorm. He fired his gun once at the white-haired man who took the bullet in the eye—but then Pagan was slipping, tumbling, earth crumbling under the soles of his shoes, and he was going down inside the very grave he'd tried to avoid, a weird view of the world, all sky and branch seen through eyes made half-blind by pellets of damp soil. He spat earth from his mouth, wiped it from his eyes, rose, clawed the sides of the trench, hauled himself up to a standing position.

Foxworth was looking down at him. He extended a hand toward Pagan, who grabbed it, and pulled himself out of the hole. Breathing heavily, badly, he shook clinging earth from his overcoat and hair, but it was everywhere—in his ears, his mouth, his shoes, fragments of the grave.

For a time Pagan said nothing. He surveyed the trees, the quiet landscape, the house in the distance. He looked at the two men who, only seconds before, had been potential executioners. The white-haired one was dead and had fallen under a spray of dark green fern so that his face, thankfully, was concealed from view. The other sat slumped against the trunk of a tree, holding both hands over his chest and groaning in pain.

"He'll need an ambulance," Pagan said. "We can call from the house."

Pagan, followed by Foxworth, walked to the place where Kinnaird lay. Ants, having scouted an abundant source of unexpected protein, were already filing in an unruly manner over the ruined side of Freddie's face. A fat horsefly crawled across Freddie's hair. Pagan spat a crumb of black earth out from between his teeth; it had the taste of death about it.

Foxie said, "I was never more glad to see you, Frank. I'd been stuck in the cellar of that bloody house for God knows how long. Our guards here were waiting for Kinnaird to turn up and make some kind of decision pertaining to my fate. When he finally showed up he didn't waste time deciding what to do with me. I'll say that for Freddie. He wasn't the vacillating sort."

Pagan smiled by way of acknowledging Foxie's remarks, but it wasn't much of an expression. He had no energy left to him. It seemed to him that he stood outside of himself, that he had left his own body and was floating like some weird wind-lifted speck toward the sun, a strange sensation. But the pain in his chest anchored him, brought him back to earth.

"New tenants are already moving in, I see." Foxworth nodded down at the armies of ants. "I only hope they find Freddie edible. Who killed him anyway?"

"It's a story. We'll talk about it later." Pagan's voice was dry, cracked, almost gone. He walked away from the corpse of Kinnaird. Followed by Foxie, he went down through the meadow toward the big red house. He paused once, looked up at the sun; in the distance, the smallest flash of silver, was a tiny aircraft that could be heard droning, then it was gone and the sky, too blue for this season and this country, was empty again. Inevitably he thought of Magdalena, but it was one of those thoughts that opened and closed like a certain kind of ghostly flower.

Epilogue

Several days after the death of Frederick Kinnaird, the
Lider Maximo spoke in the Plaza de la Revolucion in
Havana. His speech started at two in the afternoon. If
the past was any guide, he would not finish until six,
perhaps six-thirty, and his audience would by then be
numbed and hungry. The day was breezy and warm;
flags busily flapped around the Plaza.

The crowd was estimated at three hundred thousand people, many of them bussed in from rural areas.
Usually there were some who surreptitiously listened
to tiny transistor radios relaying football games or pop
music from the USA. But not today. Today there was
an atmosphere of tension and uncertainty. Throughout
the crowd plainclothes members of security forces min-
gled, took notes, eavesdropped, dragged away for interrogation anyone who struck them as odd. Security was
tighter than anybody could remember—even veterans
of these affairs, some of whom had listened to the Lider
Maximo for thirty years and knew all the man's nu-
ances and could tell from experience when he was lying

or when—the less frequent occurrence—he was telling the truth. There were metal detectors around the Plaza, and certain people were being searched, and scores were being herded inside police vehicles.

Nothing was normal now. Nothing predictable. During the last seven days there had been arrests on an unprecedented scale throughout Cuba. There had been 'disappearances'. The Armed Forces had been purged by Raul Castro himself, who had hurried back from Angola with the indecent speed of an executioner anxious to use his newly-sharpened ax. Everybody had at least one story to tell about a neighbor taken away, a son missing, or a daughter, a nephew, a cousin.

Estela Capablanca, who pushed her way through the warm crowd toward the platform because she needed to be as close to the Lider Maximo as possible, had more stories to tell than most. At first she'd been advised that Rafael had been taken prisoner; then two days later that he'd committed suicide. The next day she received a phonecall from the Ministry of the Interior telling her that he was alive and well after all and she would be taken to see him. An hour or so later, when she was beginning to allow herself some limited optimism, the coffin was delivered to her apartment by men who said nothing and who wouldn't look at her. They simply dragged it inside the living-room and left it there, lidded, loosely bolted, a long cheap pine box she couldn't bring herself to open.

She had experienced nothing so cruel in her life as that. *He's dead, he's alive, he's dead again.* They had known all along. They had played a malicious game with her because she was the traitor's wife. Then they had interrogated her in a hot windowless room for almost twenty hours about her role in her husband's treachery. Seemingly convinced she was innocent, they had released her. But she wasn't fooled. They would come for her again. They would find 'evidence'. They always did.

Now she pushed herself between a pair of young lovers who stood hip to hip, then past an old man with thick eyeglasses and one sleeve of his jacket hanging empty, then a bunch of fat women who smelled of fried food and beer.

The Lider Maximo rose on the platform to speak. His voice, carried by a sophisticated sound system, floated out beyond the Plaza itself and into adjoining streets. Television cameras relayed the event through the whole of Cuba, despite power failures, officially attributed to recent rebel activity, in the provinces of Holguin and Santiago.

The speech began quietly. The Lider Maximo's face was bloated behind the graying beard. His gaberdine fatigues were brand new and stiff; he wasn't altogether comfortable in them. Observers noticed that his movements were somewhat erratic, as if his coordination had been affected by something. Age, many people thought in their secret hearts; he was too old, too rigid, too inflexible, he had to step aside. But who was going to say so to his face?

He gazed across the crowd and the fluttering flags. Chopping the air with one hand for emphasis, he spoke of an evil plot instigated by the imperialist government of the United States to overthrow him and replace him with a puppet regime, at whose head was to be the late Minister of Finance, Rafael Rosabal, assisted by General Capablanca, now arrested (actually dead in a cell even as Castro spoke, hung by bedsheets from a ceiling beam, an official suicide), and a number of misguided officers in the Armed Forces. These men would have a fair trial because that was the Cuban way, the socialist way.

Agents of the Defense of the Revolution moved through the crowd and acted as cheerleaders, whipping up enthusiasm with their menacing manners. Estela Capablanca had come to a stop where the crowd was jammed together so tightly it created a solid wall of flesh and bone. She couldn't get through. The Lider Maximo's voice boomed in the air all around her, but she wasn't paying any attention. She heard both her husband and father mentioned in a hateful way, but it was background noise, no more. Her father's fate was probably the same as Rafael's anyhow, and how much more grief did she have? Frustrated by the mass of people, she moved in another direction, where eventually she found a way forward between a group of slick young men in fresh white guayaberas and blue jeans. They made appreciative noises as she pushed among them, and one laid a hand on her thigh, but she slipped away without looking back. She was lost again in the density of the crowd, surrounded by strangers, and all the while the voice went on and on, now droning, now rising to an hysterical pitch.

Up on the platform the Lider Maximo, his head filled with the approving roar of the audience, closed his eyes a moment; sweat slid from his brow into his eyelids and he wiped it aside. He drifted away, remembering other times, other speeches, when he had stood in this very spot and addressed his people, when La Revolucion had been young and glamorous, when he had been filled with vigor and the kind of self-confidence that belongs only to youthful believers.

He spoke of how he had been poisoned by his trusted physician, Zayas, whose task it was to weaken the Lider Maximo, to confuse him with tranquilizers and tiny doses of a slow-acting poison. That way he could be manipulated and made to believe anything he was told.

There were gasps from the crowd.

But the Lider Maximo was strong the way the Revolution was strong! The Lider Maximo survived the way the Revolution survived!

The crowd cheered again and again.

The Lider Maximo pointed to his bloated face as if by way of proof. His very appearance was the result of Zayas's infamous medications!

Now he condemned treacherous civilians, those who would see the Revolution dismantled, who would see the course of Cuban history altered. Nothing can stop the course of history, he said. Nothing could prevent the destiny of the Cuban people, which was socialism and freedom.

A drunk in the crowd whispered to Estela Capablanca: *Sure, but will we have the freedom to leave socialism?* And he winked at her, but she hardly noticed, because she was still trying to get closer to the platform, pushing, pushing, squeezing between two crones who looked half-dead, wrinkled, their flaccid breasts hanging loose behind cheap floral print dresses. She thought of Rafael's child in her womb. The baby should have been her priority, but somehow it wasn't, not any longer. It lay inside her, a tiny, unformed stranger whose meaning was lost to her. So many things had become lost to her lately.

The Lider Maximo continued to use his hand as a cleaver, a gesture of emphasis. He stared upward into the mid-afternoon sun which was pleasantly warm against his face. He wished he could sit down, and not stand the way he always did, but to sit was a weakness. He had to remain upright; he had to look down from the platform across the multitudes. It was important to maintain the image of standing in a high place.

He spoke about ungrateful civilians who worked against the Revolution. They were scum, murderous scum, with their secret printing-presses, and their illegal radios, and their hidden caches of American rifles. But they would be rooted out and destroyed. *And here his mind strayed again and he remembered how Batista had made similar speeches about La Revolucion more than thirty years ago, and how the dictator had sent his armies into the Sierra Maestra to kill the rebels. There was a world of difference, of course, between himself and the evil Batista, who had been an American mannequin, immoral, indecent, corrupt.*

He praised the bravery of loyal Cuban troops who had rounded up treacherous officers and their men swiftly. He praised the officers and men of the reservists who had brought a dangerous situation under control and had captured illegal weapons in the hands of those who misguidedly called themselves rebels and freedom-fighters.

Estela Capablanca didn't think she could get any closer. Strained, sweating, she had come within a hundred and fifty feet of the platform. Behind ropes stood armed guards and security agents with black glasses and all kinds of uniformed men. She fanned the listless air with her hand. She could hardly breathe; the weight of the crowd pressed down on her ribs. Her eyes watered. A streak of eyelash makeup slithered down one cheek.

She thought about the coffin again even though she had resolved never to do so. She remembered sitting in her living-room and looking at the thing hour after hour, remembered the sun rising and falling and the shadows thickening, remembered her hands clasped upon her stomach—and the smell that had begun to emerge from the coffin and fill the room, something she couldn't name, didn't want to identify, that awful charred smell like nothing in her experience. And she had thought about the barbarism in the world, a cruelty beyond her understanding, and how it numbed her.

She fumbled with her purse, which was jammed against her side because of the pressure of people around her. How was she ever going to open it? She suddenly wanted to scream in sheer frustration. What could she accomplish here? Nothing. Nothing. She should go back. Go home. She had been so scared avoiding the metal detectors and now her nerve was going to collapse entirely.

She wouldn't let it. She would be strong.

The Lider Maximo had become quiet, surveying the crowd; the shadow of the tall obelisk known as the Jose Marti monument fell across the Plaza. It rose some four hundred feet in the air, a monument to a famous independence fighter, the Lider Maximo's hero. Its shape was faintly reminiscent of a rocket. The Lider Maximo gripped the edge of his lectern with both hands. He was assailed by a dizzy sensation. He was thinking of the nuclear weapon destroyed outside Santiago.

Something about the notion of a missile on the island had created pleasing echoes inside him . . .

He coughed into his hand. He talked quietly now, and his hands were still. He talked about the weapon that had been brought to Cuba by imperialists and traitors, and assembled in a field outside Santiago, and made ready to fly. To discredit the Revolution! he roared. To make us appear like warmongers! But it was destroyed by the quick actions of the Cuban Air Force. He was allowed to bend the facts and shape them as he saw fit because nobody contradicted his view of reality, they merely adapted to it.

The Lider Maximo's mind wandered back to the missile again because it reminded him of those glorious days when Cuba stood at the center of the world, when Kennedy and Khrushchev almost went to war, when the Lider Maximo commanded international respect, when he was a hero and did not have to curry favor with anyone or beg . . .

He struggled to focus his attention on the crowds again. Why did he keep drifting? Why was it so hard to concentrate during his speeches these days? Now he leaned forward, speaking rapidly, spitting as he spoke in denunciation of those enemies of peace who had brought such a monstrous device to Cuba. The crowd, aroused, prodded like animals in a vast holding-pen, cheered louder than ever.

Estela Capablanca felt she was trapped inside the noise, like an atom surrounded by other reverberating atoms. She was overpowered by the sounds of so many people. The well-dressed man alongside her, eyes glazed from alcohol, had a tiny flag he waved now and again. She stared at him, looked away, glanced up toward the platform at the face of the Lider Maximo, that face with which she'd been familiar from the very day of her birth—posters, photographs, history textbooks, newspapers. He was everywhere always. He was the great endless noise that surrounded and overwhelmed her. He was the noise of Cuba.

He was a monster. But he wasn't immortal.

The Lider Maximo thought: *he hadn't had so much attention in years, every journalist in the world wanted to talk to him about the nuclear weapon, he had almost forgotten how good such power felt . . . and all because of one stolen missile.*

He raised his hands, shaking both fists at the sky. This was his response to the cheers of the crowd and suddenly it was almost like the old days, a dialogue between the Lider Maximo and the people who loved him, back and forth, give and take. He didn't see the agents milling through the swarms, didn't see the prompters and persuaders and those who coaxed and menaced the appropriate responses from people who had lived for a whole generation on promises, promises, promises.

How hard would it be to steal a missile? he wondered. *How much planning had gone into it? How long had it taken the conspirators to grab the weapon? It was an idle line of harmless speculation, of course. But interesting just the same . . .*

The Lider Maximo swayed very slightly. The breeze grew in strength, the flags shook, plastic bunting creaked. Somebody set off a firecracker and was immediately dragged away by security agents. The Lider Maximo hadn't heard the noise, didn't see the scuffle in the crowd.

If there was a nuclear missile on Cuba what would the consequences be? Respect? Prestige? Would Cuba then have a strong voice to which others in the hemisphere would be obliged to listen? And how would the Yanquis react? Would they risk invasion? Would they retaliate with force? Not if the missile was pointed, for the sake of argument, at Miami Beach . . . No, they would talk and bargain, they would want to sit down and negotiate the removal of such a missile, because that was their way, all capitalist politicians loved to deal, and something very favorable could come out of it all—say, the removal of the missile in exchange for the return to the Cuban people of the

Guantanamo U.S. naval base, which was Cuban soil after all . . .

The Lider Maximo thumped the lectern with the flat of his hand. Cuba, he told the masses, will not be a pawn in anybody's game. He spoke of courage and bravery and loyalty with all the confidence of a man comfortable in a world of abstract nouns. The sun set over the Plaza and the Marti monument and the breeze died and the flags no longer stirred.

Estela Capablanca managed to get her purse open. She found what she wanted inside, exactly where she'd placed it under a packet of tissues. How ordinary the gun seemed to her, surrounded as it was by lipsticks and a makeup compact and a bottle of eyeliner and coins. Everything was ordinary now, and yet oddly heightened, as if the commonplace contained more secrets than she'd ever realized. The smoothness of a lipstick tube, the fiber of the suit worn by the man standing beside her, the colors of his small flag—everything was sharp suddenly, and richly textured.

She managed to get her fist round the gun.

She looked up at the Lider Maximo, who was silent again.

He was thinking.

He was thinking he knew a wonderful site for such a weapon. A site whose irony amused him. The missile would be placed east of the Peninsula de Zapata, and Playa Giron, where on April 17th, 1961, the last invasion force to make an effort to land on Cuba had provoked the great Cuban victory the Yanquis called The Bay of Pigs—it was the perfect place, and fitting, and comical in its own bleak way . . .

An old flame burned in him, an old taste, barely familiar but delectable still, filled his mouth. He stared out across the crowd, which was quieter now, but he didn't see it as a group of individuals. In the shadows each person had receded, diminished, shedding his or her particular characteristics: one great amorphous mass, controllable, manageable.

Such a weapon would never be fired, of course. It would be a useful negotiating strategy, a device to back up firm diplomacy, and it would give Cuba entry into the nuclear club, where by rights it belonged . . .

Then he wondered where could he acquire such a weapon and who could he get to steal one, if he made such a radical decision. And from where would it be stolen? Fascinating questions.

But pure speculation.

He turned his face in the general direction of Havana Bay, and considered that stretch of water separating Cuba from its natural enemy. Over there, he thought. Over there was a whole arsenal of missiles, each doomed to be scrapped under the terms of a misconceived treaty between the Yanquis and the Soviets.

Perhaps.

Then he faced the crowd again. He didn't see the lovely black-haired woman who stood beyond the barrier where the guards were massed.

Estela Capablanca took the gun from her purse. She drew it up slowly from her hip, her arm jammed against that of the man with the tiny flag. And then she could bring the hand up no further unless the man moved. The pressure was intolerable. She tried to make herself smaller, slimmer, tried to create space for the pistol.

She breathed deeply, drew her ribcage in, released the pinned arm. The man, who suddenly realized what the stranger beside him held in her hand, called out in alarm. Estela pointed the pistol at the platform, directly at the head of the Lider Maximo. The guards, who had been trained to that level of readiness which is almost paranoid, reacted at once. They rushed at her fiercely. She saw their massive shadows eclipse the sky as she was knocked over. And then she was being punched in the face and kicked in the stomach and the gun fell from her hand. It was funny how little she felt, how little pain from the boots and the nightsticks, as if she no longer had the capacity for it. Brutality could no longer touch or surprise her. She was dragged roughly along concrete. She saw through eyes swollen half-shut the TV cameramen and press photographers who ignored her. She saw the receding face of the Lider Maximo, so lost in his own speculations that he paid no attention to the skirmish, handled so efficiently that it would never be mentioned in any newspaper, never seen on any TV screen.

Another firework was lit, a rocket this time, which flew from the rooftop of a nearby building in a burst of orange smoke and went sailing past the Marti monument as it died. Estela, thrown inside a van without windows, noticed how the firework's rich plumage exploded almost cheerfully in the sky before the door slammed shut and everything became black and smelled of sweat and urine and fear.

The Lider Maximo, who in recent years had come to look for signs and omens as deliriously thirsty men seek oases, saw the firework too, and he smiled for the first time that day.

A rocket, he thought. *How appropriate.*

In the eight or nine days since Sir Frederick Kinnaird's cremation and quiet funeral service, after the newspapermen and columnists and stringers had cobbled together a story out of alleged facts that were frequently no more than the kind of half-truths various

Government agencies in the United Kingdom and the United States saw fit to provide; days after Frank Pagan, weary of meetings with the Commissioner and interviews with surly men from security agencies he'd never before heard of, took a dreary train down to rainy Brighton for a few quiet nights at an off-season hotel; days after Castro had spoken to the people of Cuba about a capitalist plot against him; after Steffie Brough and her family, harried by newshounds, had gone into seclusion, and Allen Falk had entered hospital for the treatment of a hitherto inactive ulcer, a tiny bespectacled lawyer from Hamburg, Wilhelm Schiller, surfaced in the offices of a German tabloid in Frankfurt with an offer to sell the diaries and papers of his late client, Gunther Ruhr.

Schiller, an unassuming man with a gentle manner, had been advised years before by his client to make certain matters public in the event of the client's untimely death. And since such a circumstance had come alas to pass, Schiller was simply following Ruhr's instructions. The sensitive material, which filled eight stout cardboard boxes and covered many years of Ruhr's life and business dealings, would certainly have ruined various influential figures around the world who had used Ruhr's services.

But it never arrived at the editorial offices of the newspaper with whom Schiller had negotiated. Instead it vanished from the safe-deposit box in the Zurich bank where the lawyer had himself placed it.

Horrified bank officials denied any kind of wrongdoing; they were discreet men whose business thrived on privacy and security. The disappearance of Ruhr's papers scandalized them—officially at least. In reality, they had been obliged to turn the documents over to the Swiss government, which had been intensely pressured by its German counterpart. Two officials were dismissed by the bank for malfeasance, a scapegoat gesture. They were later quietly reinstated in different locations.

Herr Schiller, outraged by the loss, promised to give an interview on German television in the course of which he would reveal at least some of the contents of Ruhr's papers. That way, he would discharge a portion of his obligation to his late client; at the same time he intended to raise certain suspicions concerning the fate of the documents. He had guessed that no ordinary thief was behind their disappearance. Only Governments—with instruments of legal blackmail at their disposal—had the power to force Swiss bankers to open safe-deposit boxes.

But the interview did not take place; some hours before it was scheduled Herr Schiller was found dead in his room at the Frankfurterhof, an apparent victim of a heart attack. The death certificate was signed by two physicians, both of whom, as coincidence would have it, had begun vacations in remote places beyond the reach of telephones.

The day after Schiller's death, a group of men and women gathered in the private conference room of an expensive hotel in St. Helier on the Channel Islands. These people, accompanied by aides and lawyers, represented the British Prime Minister, the President of the United States, the West German Chancellor, the President of France, the Prime Ministers of Italy and Japan, and assorted princes and potentates from the countries of the Middle East.

The subject of their meeting was the disposal of Gunther Ruhr's purloined records. An early perusal of the documents, undertaken with haste by an international panel of six lawyers, indicated that Ruhr had set down, in encyclopedic detail, the dates and places of his terrorist acts, the sums of money that had exchanged hands in return for his services, and the names of those who had employed him. It was the kind of record guaranteed to bring Ruhr a form of immortality, although that hadn't been its principal purpose.

Ruhr, scrupulous and smart, had kept his records diligently. It soon became clear to his readers, his team of auditors, that the late terrorist often knew more about his employers than they could ever have supposed. He investigated the men who hired him. He made careful inquiries. He was no casual extremist. He took extraordinary care. Sometimes he succeeded in penetrating the secrecy surrounding those who bought his services: sometimes he managed to go beyond the names of the lesser figures to the larger ones. Intermediaries gave way to principals, minor players to major ones. Men of high positions in government and financial circles who thought they had hired Gunther Ruhr from a safe distance, who believed themselves anonymous, had their names inscribed in his records.

There were photostats of bank drafts, copies of money orders, numbers of bank accounts on small Caribbean islands; Ruhr's manic eye for detail was evident at every turn. Nothing much had escaped him.

It was an enormously damaging set of documents, in some instances shocking in its revelations. In what became known unofficially as the St. Helier Accord, it was decided, within a matter of hours and hardly any debate, that the documents, to be kept from the press at all costs, would be divided among the parties with direct interests—the record of Ruhr's involvement with Basque separatists, for example, would go directly to the Spanish government to deal with as it saw fit; the names of his employers in Japan who had him destroy a resort hotel would be handed immediately to Japanese officials. And so on.

Six hours after it assembled the conference ended.

Two days later, Martin Burr travelled down to Brighton and walked with Frank Pagan along the promenade on a rainy night. They passed the disheartening ruin of the West Pier, which had the appearance in the English Channel mist of a ghost ship. In another age it had been graceful, an elegant edifice that had stubbornly withstood the demands of the sea. Neglected now, it was nothing more than a reminder to Martin Burr of a world that had become bored by the graceful—one that responded only to the quick and the crass. It was a world in which you could find crumpets inside frozen-food compartments and exquisite teas in mass-produced tea-bags.

"You're looking more like your usual self," Burr said. "I'm glad to see that."

Frank Pagan didn't mention the new course of antibiotics he'd just begun, or the ugly infection Ghose had discovered in the chest wound. These things were tedious inconveniences; they could be kept to oneself. He looked out at the Channel. The mist was magnificently damp and mysterious, crawling up over the pebbled beach. He put a hand in the pocket of his overcoat and fingered the bottle of painkillers there; the wound in his chest, agitated by infection, pierced him sharply. He tried to ignore it.

Burr tapped the promenade rail with his cane and listened a moment to the quiet drumming sound he'd set up. "I have teams of people going through Kinnaird's records—which are copious and complicated as befitted a man with a great deal to conceal."

"I imagine," Pagan said. He was genuinely interested on one level, that of policeman; but the recuperating tourist in him felt removed from Burr's world. He'd go back into that world eventually, and he'd become immersed in it as he always did, but for the present he wanted to be nothing more than a man casually watching the secretive mist on a moist night in Brighton.

Burr said, "Kinnaird's phonecalls are rather intriguing. Several were placed to an apartment in Acapulco, which turns out to have been the property of Rafael Rosabal. Kinnaird and Rosabal. Fine bedfellows."

Pagan saw a light out there in the folds of the Channel, a small passing ship perhaps. Then it was gone. He turned to look at Martin Burr. Dampness adhered to the Commissioner's eyepatch, reflecting the lamps along the promenade.

Burr stopped tapping his cane. "Freddie made phonecalls to all the members of his little group. Caporelli, the others. Cocky sod, though. Didn't even bother to take the trouble to make these calls from some public phone. He made them either from his house in Scotland or his apartment in The Albany. I daresay he thought he was above the law. Can't get over the gall of the fellow." Burr shook his head for a while; from his point of view the nefarious activities of Kinnaird and his associates were beyond any reasonable man's comprehension, as was Kinnaird's sense of impunity.

Pagan turned away from the misty sea. He thought how Freddie and Rosabal must have decided to eliminate the others. Then Rosabal, who elevated avarice to chilly new heights, had taken it one step further and ordered the elimination of Freddie. They were charmers. Real princes.

Burr drew his cashmere scarf up around his neck

and shivered slightly. "What a bloody mosaic," he said. "And it doesn't end with Freddie's unprincipled dealings either. I've just seen some of Gunther Ruhr's papers."

Pagan, intrigued now, had heard about these notorious papers and the waves of utter terror they had set in motion through government circles in various countries.

Burr said, "In his documents Ruhr claims he was first approached by Rosabal more than three years ago. Then about twelve months ago in Mexico City he was given the green light. Steal the missile, he was told. Deliver it to Honduras, where an invasion force was waiting with tanks and fighter-planes. Amazing assortment of equipment from all over the place."

Steal the missile, Pagan thought. Just like that. He looked back out into the Channel, which smelled of winter, dead things. The night was as melancholic as his mood, which he hadn't been able to shake for days. He reflected on the coup Magdalena had talked about, the democratic underground in which she'd had such faith, the uprising, but she'd never mentioned an invasion force. Maybe that was something else Rosabal had concealed from her. There were so many unanswerable questions. What had Burr called it? *A bloody mosaic.* Ambitions, lies, rapacity, warped patriotism, all the grubby little ingredients of the big picture, which was elusive still, and would perhaps remain so for a long time.

Burr lowered his voice, as if the dark might be filled with eavesdroppers. "One hears the most appalling rumors of mass arrests, tortures, executions all over Cuba."

Pagan shivered. Cold air rose up from the Channel. He wondered about Estela Rosabal and what had become of her as a consequence of her husband's ambitions. *Executions,* Burr had said. Was that her fate? Had she been propped before a firing-squad and gunned down? He recalled, with a clarity that saddened him, the way she'd looked when he'd seen her in Havana; the ruined innocence of beauty. Had Rosabal in all his life ever touched anything without bringing it to ruin?

Pagan was quiet a moment. He heard the tide whisper coldly over stones. Then, as if to himself, he said, "I keep seeing that bloody missile. And I keep wondering if Rosabal intended to fire it. I can't get the damned thing out of my mind."

Martin Burr shrugged. "If he did, what was his target?"

Pagan had no answer. He looked back into the mist, which seemed to him just then as inscrutable as Rosabal's intention. He imagined the missile on the truck, the way it changed angle, the eerie sense of disaster he'd experienced. And then he remembered Magdalena's doomed little plane and he wasn't sure if the missile had ever moved at all, or if it was something he'd created out of his own awful tiredness, an hallucination, a fanciful perception.

Burr said, "I rather thought Castro's speech might have shed some light on that question."

"People like Castro aren't in the business of shedding light. They prefer darkness."

"Perhaps," said Burr.

Frank Pagan heard the mournful sound of a ship's fog horn, like the cry of something lost in the night. He turned from the Channel, glanced at the forlorn relic of the West Pier. *Magdalena's doomed little plane,* he thought. Lately he'd had the most unbearable dreams of her. There was always the small plane burning—not quickly, as it had happened in reality, but in a very slow way. Then the dream made that awful upward shift into nightmare when her face appeared in the yellow-red pyre of the cockpit and turned very slightly, sightlessly, mouth twisted open and lifeless, toward the trees under which he stood, and he saw an agonizing look in her dark eyes before she was consumed. A horror, repeating itself three or four times during the last ten days.

He always woke with a sense of deep sorrow and depressing loss, as if there were an important word he couldn't quite remember, or a disturbed sensation he couldn't name. Whatever it was, it felt like something burrowing far inside him, something it would take time to destroy.

The fire that coursed suddenly through his chest made him double over against the promenade rail.

"Are you all right, Frank?" Burr asked.

Pagan took out the bottle of painkillers, uncapped it. He tipped one into the palm of his shaking hand. He stared at the pill. Did he need this? Would it really reach the place where the pain hurt most and kill it? He let the pill slip from his hand, then tossed the bottle through the air and watched the capsules vanish in the direction of the darkened beach below. They would fall among the pebbles where they'd lie concealed until the tide drew them back into the Channel and they disintegrated in brine.

"I'm fine, Commissioner," was all he said.